THE TALE OF THE TWO VIRGINS

THE TALE OF THE TWO VIRGINS

Jenny Francis

Matador
9 Priory Business Park,
Wistow Road, Kibworth Beauchamp,
Leicestershire. LE8 0RX
Tel: (+44) 116 279 2299
Fax: (+44) 116 279 2277
Email: books@troubador.co.uk
Web: www.troubador.co.uk/matador

ISBN 978 1783064 113

British Library Cataloguing in Publication Data.
A catalogue record for this book is available from the British Library.

Typeset by Troubador Publishing Ltd, Leicester, UK
Printed and bound in the UK by TJ International, Padstow, Cornwall

Matador is an imprint of Troubador Publishing Ltd

This book is dedicated to fond memories of Barcelona and the happy times spent living there in the early 70s.

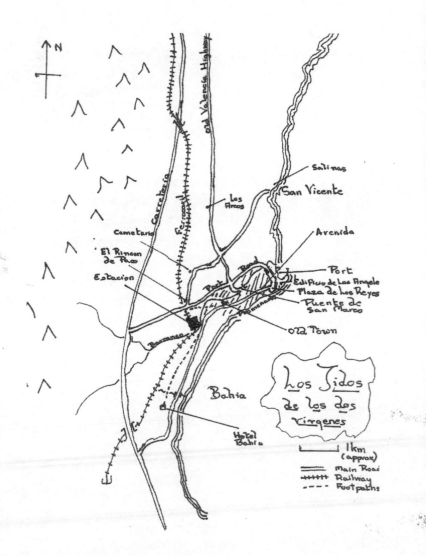

The Spanish Civil War 1936–1939

Sometimes referred to as the forgotten war because of the great struggle between nations that followed, the Spanish Civil War was a bitterly fought-out foretaste of what was soon to come for much of the rest of the world. On one side was the Republic, the democratically elected government of Spain at times on the brink of descending into chaos and deeply divided within itself. On the other was Generalisimo Francisco Franco's Nationalists, a reactionary movement born out of a rising led by right wing army officers and backed by Hitler and Mussolini who sent the soldiers, aircraft and modern weaponry that eventually tilted the balance of power in the Nationalists' favour. The Republic had its support too in the shape of aid from the Soviet Union but countries like France, Britain and the United States stood back behind a policy of non-intervention.

Though atrocities occurred on both sides, at the final reckoning there was more blood on the hands of the Nationalists than their opponents. As well as seasoned regulars Franco's forces had in their ranks mercenaries recruited from the tribes of North Africa who set about their work of 'mopping up' after battles with the rape and butchery of countless innocents. In contrast the Republican army was for the large part made up of workers' militias plus a steady stream of ordinary men from all over the world who came to Spain to fight in the famous International Brigades. In the end though they were no match for German and Italian guns and bombers.

Pushed back on all fronts and only after the heroic defence of the city of Madrid and defeat in the battles of Teruel and the Ebro, the Republic finally surrendered in 1939. As the war came to an end thousands of refugees streamed across the frontier into southern France where they were herded into concentration camps and where many of them died from cold, disease and starvation. Franco meanwhile set about imposing his iron fist on a war torn and battered nation. Few objected because they knew the price they would pay but one by one the freedoms they had enjoyed under the Republic were taken away. Spain became a land where only brave men and fools spoke out against the regime and the prisons and torture chambers were filled with those that did.

Franco, known as the Caudillo to his supporters, went on to rule Spain until his death in 1975. To some he will be remembered as the saviour of the nation who stood for the values of the Catholic Church and stopped Spain becoming a Marxist state whereas to others even today he is a figure of deep and enduring hate.

It is in the time of Franco that this story is set.

CHAPTER ONE

The Aubergine and the Beanstick

T he events in this story took place many years before
the town of Los Tidos de Los Dos Virgenes (or Los
Tidos as people always call it for short) became
known throughout Europe as a popular destination for
package holidays. In 1963 it was still a seldom visited place
tucked away in a quiet out of the way corner of south eastern
Spain. The sky-scraper hotels, the discos and the burger stalls
all came later. For now Los Tidos thrived, as it had done for
centuries, on the fish caught in the sea off its shores and the
trade that passed through its busy port. Some foreign tourists
came, true, but for the most part these were well-heeled types
who arrived in their large yachts and confined themselves to
the area of boutiques, bars and restaurants that had grown up
lately on the waterfront around the new marina. Few of their
number ever ventured up the steeply stepped streets of the
Old Town with its over-hanging, bougainvillea-clad wrought
iron balconies. Here, life went on as it had always gone on and
little ever changed.

The month of November is always a pleasant time of year
in this part of Spain – a time when the stifling heat of the
summer has passed; a time when the oranges and lemons are
ripening on the trees; a time when it is still warm enough to

1

walk outdoors without a cardigan. And it was on one such pleasant balmy November afternoon that two characters well-known in the town were to be seen taking a stroll along the Promenade. One of these characters was noticeably short and stout whereas the other was tall and thin explaining right away why the two of them when seen together, were always referred to as the Aubergine and the Beanstick (though not necessarily to their faces). The short stout one, Pepe Gomez, was the proprietor of a working man's bar in the port quarter of Los Tidos while his companion, the tall thin one, was the local jobbing carpenter: a young man named Jaime Campello.

The promenade along which the two of them strolled was a new construction and, like most things new in Los Tidos, it was slowly falling apart. Successive alcáldes or town mayors had seen to it that they lined their own pockets when awarding municipal contracts and recipients of these contracts, not wanting to see their profits eaten away by the alcálde's back handers, made ends meet by cutting corners and using poor materials. In the case of the Promenade, the result was that after eighteen months, its surface was pitted with holes and, at one point, the sea had made a more serious encroachment, undermining a whole section of the side walk and causing it to cave in leaving behind a jumbled mass of broken concrete and reinforcing iron cascading onto the beach and defying all but the most intrepid pedestrians to go any further.

Since neither Pepe Gomez nor Jaime Campello qualified by any definition of the word as intrepid it was at this point on their walk that they routinely turned round and went back. A brief look out to sea, where the first of the returning fishing boats could be seen out towards the horizon, then they retraced their steps for the few hundred metres back to the

Plaza de los Reyes where the promenade began and the steep Avenida, the road from the town to the seafront, ended.

Any observer of these two as they walked along would have seen that it was Gomez (the Aubergine) who did most of the talking and that Campello (the Beanstick) said little. Also Gomez made great use of his arms to give force and expression to whatever it was he was saying whereas Campello seldom took his hands from behind his back and then only briefly to push back a strand of his curly hair that had fallen forward onto his forehead or scratch his chin. At first they seemed an unlikely pair – Campello in his late twenties, Gomez older by at least fifteen years – and people often wondered why they should be drawn into one another's company. Yet they had and much of what was soon to descend on the town of Los Tidos was to blame on this fact.

After crossing the Plaza de Los Reyes, busy with late afternoon traffic, Gomez and Campello made their way as they always did up the Avenida with its magnificent palm trees, past the little park and its fountain and then the banks and offices of notarios and other professional people before turning off into the maze of dusty unmade back streets and ugly concrete buildings that made up the part of town in which fishermen and those who worked in the port traditionally lived. Finally they came to the Calle de Dos Ojos, the Street of Two Eyes, where the bar owned by Gomez, the Bar Madrid, was situated.

The first two eyes, to fall on Gomez and Campello as they came round the corner that fateful afternoon belonged to a man named Zamora. Zamora was the owner of the bar next door to the Bar Madrid and someone who was not well liked in Los Tidos for reasons that will soon be made apparent. An outsider, from the province of the Asturias, Zamora had arrived three years before with his pockets lined with money he won on the lottery (or so it was rumoured) and which he used to snap up the run-down premises next to Gomez's establishment and spend lavishly on its refurbishment. A pretentious man and clearly a poor judge of neighbourhoods, the intention always for Zamora had been for his place to become a stopping-off point for the rich and famous; a backdrop for photographs in stylish magazines; the haunt of film stars and presidents, and the name, Zamora's, to be on the lips of celebrities across all five continents. So to this end, he discouraged local trade by keeping his prices high; and this explained not only his unpopularity but also why the Bar Zamora was usually empty – together with the fact that no film stars or presidents or anyone else with money to throw round had ever set foot in the Street of Two Eyes.

Yet another of Zamora's traits that didn't endear him particularly to the men folk of Los Tidos was his obsession with tidiness, largely because it was an obsession most of them did not share. So while he waited for the rich and famous to cross his doorstep, it was usual to find Zamora, not with his feet up as any other self-respecting barkeeper in Los Tidos would have done, but in an apron and shirt sleeves polishing his tables and chairs, removing every speck of dust that settled on his blinds and shelves or sweeping the floor.

Sweeping the floor was in fact what Zamora was doing when he caught sight of Gomez and his young friend sloping up the street on the other side. Zamora wrinkled his bulbous nose. Zamora had been wanting a word with Señor Gomez for some time but he had got the impression of late that Señor Gomez was trying to avoid him. The subject was an old bone

4

of contention – the invisible line that divided the pavement in front of the Bar Madrid from the pavement in front of the Bar Zamora and here a few words of explanation are required.

Both the Bar Madrid and the Bar Zamora had tables and chairs outside on the pavement where customers could sit in the fresh air if they preferred. But the problem for Zamora was the customers of the Bar Madrid, being artisans in the main, were a rowdy and intemperate lot and had little regard for the invisible line. So it was that Gomez's tables and chairs frequently became scattered and time and time again Zamora found his territory invaded by dock workers and men from the fish market who shouted at each other in loud voices and dropped cigarette ends on the floor. What if royalty should happen to pass by at such a moment, or Ava Gardner or Brigitte Bardot should decide to drop in? Zamora shuddered at the thought. He had spoken to Gomez several times about keeping his customers in order but he suspected Gomez had done nothing about it for the problem still remained. On this occasion, he decided, he would have to be firmer with Señor Gomez and let him see that the matter needed to be taken seriously.

Pepe Gomez groaned as he spotted Zamora, broom in hand, making to intercept them as he and Campello crossed over the road. He groaned because he knew what was coming. He couldn't walk down the street any more without Zamora accosting him with some complaint or other. If it wasn't the smell from the Bar Madrid's leaky septic tank it was something else.

'Good afternoon, Señor Gomez.' Zamora was always like this, formal and polite to start. It was the way with Northerners, Gomez decided: they used their best manners at you first then the charm quickly melted away.

'Good afternoon, Señor Zamora.' Pepe Gomez had some best manners too. He wasn't some small town nobody like Zamora seemed to think. Zamora then nodded briefly to Campello and Campello nodded briefly back. At this point in time Zamora and Campello were on nodding terms. It was not till later that the relationship between the two of them became inflamed.

'The tables and chairs,' said Zamora by way of an introduction to the subject he wished to discuss, at the same time flicking absently with his broom at the part of the pavement where Gomez and Campello had just walked. 'I am sorry to say the problem still appears to be with us.'

'Problem?' Gomez gazed back at him blankly and wide-eyed. Feigning total incomprehension, he had found in the past, to be a good tactic to use with Zamora. Then, when Zamora reminded him what it was all about he would say the matter had completely slipped his mind, promise to see to it straight away and wish him good day. However, on this occasion, the conversation went no further for Fate intervened in the shape of the person who, next to Zamora, Pepe Gomez least wished to see.

It was Campello who first noticed Conchita. Conchita, the wife of Pepe Gomez, the mother of his twelve children and the bane of his life was standing at the entrance to the Bar Madrid with her arms folded tightly across her bosom and a scowl on her face. How long Conchita had been there Campello had no idea but the look in her eyes reminded him of the mythical Gorgon he'd read about in stories whose stare was enough to turn a man to stone. Just a few seconds later Pepe Gomez noticed her too and immediately his whole aspect changed. Gone was the bravado he was putting on for Zamora.

An uneasy nervous fidgeting took its place as his eyes flicked from one direction to another looking in vain for a way of escape.

'So,' Conchita began taking a few steps forward and completely ignoring Zamora, 'My husband has deigned to come back, has he? He has returned from his afternoon of leisure, swilling coñac and looking at the pretty girls on the beach and now he is here to grace us with his presence.' A feeling of indignation briefly stirred somewhere inside Pepe Gomez. Yes, he may have had the odd glass of coñac but as to looking at pretty girls on the beach, he had been doing no such thing. Yet the look on Conchita's face, warned him to stay silent. Zamora, for his part, was withdrawing slowly – a process he undertook by going backwards one step at a time with his head bowed down and flicking at imaginary pieces of litter with his broom. Zamora had had a number of run-ins with Conchita, run-ins that had taught him not to tangle with the woman and to pick on her fat idle feckless husband instead.

'You have something to say for yourself husband?' Conchita was now standing over Gomez hissing in his face. 'You are now going to tell me now that there was some reason on which your precious life hung for leaving your poor wife and children to serve the tapas and wash the plates and glasses and fetch the barrels and bottles from the backyard all by themselves?'

Gomez shifted uneasily and Campello noticed a thin line of sweat had broken out on the little man's upper lip. He had noticed too how, inside the Bar Madrid, Lopez and the others the usual group of idlers with time on their hands had stopped playing cards and were standing at the window watching what was going on with smirks on their faces. Zamora had now retreated safely into his own domain but his bulbous nose could still be seen poking through the beaded curtain that hung across the doorway.

'It seems my husband has lost his tongue,' Conchita cried triumphantly with a flourish of her hand, that caused Pepe Gomez to flinch. 'See,' she called out to the crowd of onlookers who had stopped to stare from the safe distance of the other side of the street, 'See what a man I married. Just look at him and see how pitiful he is. He is no man. He is a fat idle coñac-swilling pig.'

At this some cheered, some laughed, some clapped their hands and some didn't know quite what to do while Lopez and the others made wagers on what the outcome might be.

'Inside!' Conchita yelled. 'There is a pile of dirty glasses in the sink and crates to be fetched from the back yard. Isn't it time you surprised us all and did some work for a change?'

Gomez exchanged glances with Campello as he shuffled off with drooping shoulders in the direction indicated by Conchita's pointing finger. It was then that she turned to the young carpenter who, up to this point, had been doing his best to merge into the background.

'I hear your Uncle Pablo has fallen down the barranco again,' she said acidly. 'Instead of standing there perhaps you had better go and see to him.'

Campello need no second bidding. He mumbled a few words then took to his heels. It was not until he reached the corner of the Street of Two Eyes that he turned to look back and saw that the little crowd that had gathered to watch the humiliation of Pepe Gomez had now disappeared. The only figure in sight was that of Zamora, outside and sweeping the pavement again.

The barranco to which Conchita had referred was a deep cleft like valley on which the Old Town of Los Tidos was built. Water being a precious commodity in these parts of Spain, the stream had been dammed further up its course to make a reservoir and now, except for the odd stagnant pool here and there, the barranco was dry for the greater part of the year. To the townspeople of Los Tidos it had served for many years as a rubbish dump and down its sides went anything that was worn out, unwanted or no longer worked. Old mattresses, broken chairs, builders' rubble – they were all thrown down the barranco when no one had any further use for them.

Campello quickened his stride. His route from the Street of Two Eyes to the barranco took him through an area of yards and warehouses that lay at the back of the port and as he walked along the dusty back streets, his thoughts were still on his friend Pepe Gomez who he knew by now would be up to his elbows in soap suds with the fearful Conchita standing over him and pouring out further scorn. There were some advantages to not being married, Campello reflected. At least he didn't have to answer for his every movement to a woman like Conchita Gomez. Apart from the demands of his work he could come and go as he pleased.

The point for which Campello was making was the Puente de San Marco, the ancient bridge that spanned the barranco with towers on either side dating from the period when Moorish invaders had laid their claim to the town. It was on the Puente de San Marco, when he reached it, that Campello saw a small crowd gathered who were laughing and jeering and pointing at something in the depths beneath. As if he could not have guessed, the object of their amusement was his Uncle Pablo lying at the bottom of the barranco half-in and half-out of one of the stagnant pools where he was singing at the top of his voice and clutching a bottle of absenta in his hand. Campello sighed to himself wearily. It was obvious to all that Uncle Pablo was very drunk indeed, a state in which sadly the elder Campello found himself often. The ribald song he was singing was one of his own compositions and concerned a certain young lady of the port who bestowed her favours on sailors in an interesting and acrobatic variety of ways. Fortunately for the sailors perhaps, the young lady was entirely a figment of Uncle Pablo's over-worked imagination but verse after verse of her exploits served to keep the crowd up on the bridge entertained – the proof of which lay in the fact they kept calling for encores though Campello saw straight away that not everyone approved. Among the passers-by were the Señoras Crespo who come into the story again later on. The Señoras Crespo were shaking their heads and tut-tutting. Soon the exploits of Uncle Pablo would be a talking point in the drawing rooms of the more conservative and respectable elements of Los Tidos society.

The scramble down into the barranco was by no means easy. Apart from the slope itself and the aforementioned piles of rubbish, a dense scrub of oleander and thorn bushes grew up the sides and made it hard for young Campello to force his way through. There was a path of sorts but it had been made by flocks of sheep and goats not human beings. Finally when he reached Uncle Pablo, his face and hands were covered in scuffs and scratches and the wool of his best pullover was pulled to pieces.

Mercifully perhaps Uncle Pablo had now fallen silent and his eyes were closed. To all appearances he looked like he was in a deep sleep with the lower half of his body, still half submerged in the stagnant pool and Campello noticed that a large bullfrog was sitting on his toe.

The first thought to cross the young carpenter's mind was to call for assistance and he looked up at the line of faces peering down from the parapets of the Puente de San Marco. 'Can anyone help me?' he called out and, with the usual spirit of togetherness the people of Los Tidos show at such times, the faces that had had such amusement at Uncle Pablo's expense promptly disappeared. At that moment, however, there came the sound of someone else descending into the barranco and a glimpse of dark clothing through the oleander bushes. Next, Father Miguel, the town priest, was standing at his side.

At once Father Miguel put to rest the fear uppermost in young Campello's mind – that Uncle Pablo had fallen from the Puente de San Marco in his drunken state and done serious harm to himself. Father Miguel said he had learned from an eye-witness that the old man had simply staggered up the barranco from the point where it emerged into the sea in a series of slimy lagoons. The fact that his legs had finally buckled under him as he passed beneath the Puente was no more than coincidence.

After conferring for a while on what best to do, Campello and Father Miguel managed to get Uncle Pablo onto his feet. As they did, the old man's eyes briefly opened, rolled round a few times then, seeming not to like the way the world looked from the vertical plane, closed again.

Years of dissipation and swilling the potent local absenta had exacted its toll on Uncle Pablo's frame to the extent that these days he was an emaciated figure with little weight to speak of. Between them, therefore, Campello and the priest

11

had little difficulty in supporting him. Before setting off Campello rescued Uncle Pablo's beret from a nearby oleander bush and put it back on his head so all that was left by the stagnant pool when they had gone was a half-empty bottle of absenta and a disconsolate looking bull frog that had rather got used to the idea of sitting on Uncle Pablo's toe.

At various points the barranco was crossed by sheep paths and it was up one of these steep winding tracks that Campello and Father Miguel now pushed and pulled Uncle Pablo till finally they reached the top. The two Campellos, Jaime and his uncle, lived in a small house in the Old Town named the Villa Verde after its green wooden shutters. The house had once belonged to Campello's Father and Mother and it was where almost thirty years earlier Campello himself had been born. Because of the time of year the days were getting shorter and the light was already starting to fade as the carpenter and the priest with an arm each round Uncle Pablo came to a halt outside the big heavy front door. Campello found the key from his trouser pocket and, with Father Miguel's help and Uncle Pablo still unable to stand up on his own, they got the old man inside, laid him on his bed and removed his wet clothes.

Campello made Father Miguel a cup of coffee and for a while the young man and the priest sat and talked.

'You have been good to your father's brother,' Father Miguel said as he made to go. 'Few would have put up with his ways and most would have turned him out on the street a long time ago. Yet you mustn't allow your kindness and decency to come in the way of your own happiness, my son. The years are passing you by and it is surprising how quickly they go. Perhaps your thoughts should be turning to taking a wife and having children. If these things are to be done, they are best done before it is too late.'

Campello's eyes followed Father Miguel as he made his way off down the steeply stepped street. Soon his long cloak and his closely-cropped iron grey hair vanished into the gathering darkness.

Back in the kitchen Campello washed up the coffee cups and looked in the refrigerator to see what there was to eat. His mind flitted back over the events of the afternoon: first, Conchita Gomez and the chastising she had given poor Pepe in front of everybody; a chastising he no doubt deserved but Campello felt sorry for the little man all the same. Then, second, Uncle Pablo bringing the family name into disrepute once more and, now, Father Miguel's strange words that Campello reflected on as he sat down in front of the television with a bocadillo in one hand and a glass of wine in the other. But the day had not quite finished with Jaime Campello as he was soon to find out.

★ ★ ★

Just after dusk, when the bats began to come out, the third inhabitant of the Villa Verde made an appearance.

Waldorf was, strictly speaking, Uncle Pablo's dog or at least it was Uncle Pablo to whom Waldorf had attached himself further back in the past than either of them could remember. Waldorf was a familiar figure in the Old Town where he spent much of his time upending garbage bins and making off with anything edible he found inside. But, as darkness descended, he always headed back to the Villa Verde where he knew a meal of leftovers and plate scrapings would be put down for him. Emerging from an alleyway opposite he paused for a few moments to raise a hind leg and spray the wall on the corner to serve as a warning to any other dogs passing that way that they were entering the territory of Waldorf and to beware because soon they would be feeling the bite of his teeth in their hind quarters or a piece ripped from one of their ears. A reassuring sniff to check that the stain on the wall had the right strength and consistency to do the job it was meant to do then he made his way towards the door that Campello had left open after the departure of the priest a little while earlier.

What caused Waldorf to deviate from his normal track into the kitchen and go into Uncle Pablo's room instead was a mystery. Yet it was there in Uncle Pablo's room that he caught sight of the old man laid out corpse-like on his bed. Though what followed was regrettable it had to be said in Waldorf's defence that it was the way with all scavenging creatures in the Old Town that nothing dead or dying was ever left to go to waste. So it was that in one leap Waldorf was up on the bed and sinking his teeth into the fleshy part of Uncle Pablo's thigh.

The howl of pain from Uncle Pablo's room caused Campello to jump to his feet, drop the bocadillo on the floor and spill the wine all at the same time. He dashed across the hallway and crossed paths with Waldorf who, having no interest in food that fought back, shot between Campello's legs then, sensing retribution might be about to descend, took his mange-ridden form off into the night – pausing only briefly on the way out and without Campello's knowledge to snap up the bocadillo in his jaws.

Back in Uncle Pablo's room Campello could find no explanation for the old man's sudden cry. He did notice, however, the strange row of red indentations in his leg, which he couldn't recall being there before but he failed to make the connection with Waldorf. In any case Uncle Pablo had gone back to sleep again so, after switching off the light, Campello went back to watching television making a mental note to call Doctor Pascal if any further symptoms should develop, Waldorf had vanished, he noticed, and this puzzled him. As did the disappearance of his bocadillo.

★ ★ ★

The weather in Spain's capital city Madrid was far from pleasant on that same November afternoon. A cold wind blew from the north and with the cold wind came rain.

Suarez looked out of the window of his office across the rooftops to where he could just catch a glimpse of the gardens in the Plaza de Espana between the high walls of the buildings. Suarez shivered. He had never liked Madrid at the best of times but most of all he hated the city in the winter when the wind changed direction without warning and brought a chill like today that ate into his bones. More and more he longed for his retirement and the little finca in La Mancha on which he and Carlita had already paid a deposit. A few more months that was all he had to do, a few months to when he could pick up his pension and turn his back on Madrid and his draughty office for ever.

But now clouds other than those that brought the cold wind were gathering on Suarez's horizons. The Caudillo, Franco himself had made it known to those in his inner circle that he wished to take a short break from affairs of state and what better way to do it than go off somewhere quiet where no-one would trouble him? He would travel incognito, or so he informed everyone, and in this way dispense with the tight ring of security that usually went everywhere with him. He would be going as the guest of an aristocratic family who had long been supporters of the Nationalist regime and who could be relied on to be discreet. What was more the aristocratic family owned a hotel set in its own grounds not far from the coast so the Caudillo, a keen fisherman, could spend his days out on the sea aboard the marquis's fine yacht.

Suarez blanched when he first heard about the Caudillo's plans. Twice he'd gone so far as to urge the Caudillo to think again but twice the answer came back the Caudillo was adamant he would not be put off by rumours of dangers that had no substance. Rumours! Suarez almost spat out the word. Had he not spent the last twenty years working tirelessly to protect the Caudillo from men who would gladly give their right arms for the chance to put a bullet in his head? Wasn't it thanks to Suarez and his network of informers that the Caudillo had not fallen victim to an assassin's rifle a long time ago? But now it seemed the Caudillo knew better. Or was it the new breed of men who surrounded the Caudillo these days, yes men who, to Suarez's way of thinking, were only there to feather their own nests? Then at the last time of asking the Caudillo to reconsider someone had had the audacity to suggest that he, Suarez, had cried wolf too many times in the past. As if the plots against the Caudillo were figments of his imagination, tales Suarez had made up for his own entertainment!

Suarez grimaced. Now there were just a few days left before the Caudillo set out on his journey and there was no way of telling what the outcome might be. Yet Suarez knew better than any man that if any misfortune befell the Caudillo on his travels then he, Suarez, stood among those who would be first in line when it came to apportioning blame. Then what of his retirement and the little finca in La Mancha? Suarez had been around long enough in the world of politics to know he would not escape retribution if it came. No, Suarez told himself, he needed someone who would be his eyes and ears, someone of unquestionable integrity who would shadow the Caudillo on his private visit and without him knowing. Someone who would if necessary step in and save the Caudillo.

There was a knock at the door. 'Enter,' barked Suarez making his way over to the calor gas stove that provided the only source of heat in this wretched place. A man came in; a man Suarez had never seen before; a big man in an ill-fitting suit who had the look of a village policeman on a day's holiday.

'Capitan Luis Garcia,' said the man snapping to attention after taking three steps forward. 'My orders are to report to you in plain clothes.'

Suarez took a cigarette from the silver cigarette case that was a fortieth wedding anniversary present from Carlita. To avoid involving the Army whose generals he did not trust Suarez had asked the Guardia Civil Commander in Cordoba to send him an officer of impeccable character to carry out a discreet and secret mission. This, he reasoned, must be the man the Commander had chosen. Suarez inspected the man more closely. Instinct had played an important part in his life and, though he couldn't put his finger on it yet, something about Capitan Luis Garcia made Suarez feel uneasy. He focused his attention again. The Capitan was still speaking showing off a row of gold teeth as he did.

'Allow me to introduce my assistant to you Señor Suarez.'

It was at this point that Suarez realised that the Capitan from Cordoba was not alone. Another much smaller man was standing behind him, a man almost completely hidden by the Capitan's bulk.

'Ramon Ramon,' said the second man stepping forward, clearly not sure if he should salute because he was out of uniform and finally settling for bowing his head and clicking his heels.

Suarez did not understand. He had asked the Commander in Cordoba to send one man not two so what, he wondered, was the meaning of this? On the other hand he realised the time for quibbling was over. The Caudillo would be setting off on his journey shortly and, whether Suarez liked the idea or not, Capitan Garcia and his assistant would have to do.

★ ★ ★

The same cold wind that brought rain to Madrid also brought a steady downpour to the city of Bilbao in the north of Spain where at least the inhabitants were more used to it. Here, in a back street near a factory, Lola Martinez the girl who had once run barefoot through the ramblas of Barcelona pulled up the sleeve of her sable coat and checked her wristwatch. Five minutes to two: it was time to go. She stepped across the street taking care not to break one of her ten centimetre stiletto heels by going down a crack between the cobblestones. The Bar Atlantico had proved easy to find. It was dingy and scruffy looking with faded posters for Coca Cola and La Aguila peeling from its windows. Inside the place was almost empty. Three men, factory workers by the look of them, stood at the bar drinking beer and they each turned and stared in disbelief, when they saw the fine looking woman in a fur coat and a fur hat walk through the door and take a seat at the table by the window. No woman like that had ever set foot in the Bar Atlantico before and they continued to stare. After a few seconds, the one-eyed barman shuffled across. 'Yes, Señorita,' he said wiping the oilcloth with the rag in his hand and leaving it wet and smeary.

'Café solo,' she replied putting a long American cigarette in the cigarette holder she took from her shoulder bag and lighting it. The men at the bar still watched. One of them, she noticed, talked louder than the others.

Raul was already coming up the street. He was wearing a raincoat over his uniform and a tense nervous expression on his face. The one-eyed barman looked up as he walked in. 'Whisky,' Raul called across 'Bourbon if you have it.'

'Buenos Tardes Raul.'

'Buenos Tardes Lola. I am sorry to ask you to come to a place like this.'

Lola shrugged. The place didn't matter. The fact that it was a rough working man's bar in a rough part of town where whores were the only women who walked the streets alone did not bother her. She had been in much worse places in her time. Besides she knew police informers did not visit bars like the Bar Atlantico because, if they did, they would stick out like sore thumbs.

Raul waited for the barman to bring their drinks before he began. The three men at the bar had gone back to drinking their beer.

'The information was correct,' he said looking into her deep dark brown eyes. 'The call I was waiting for came

19

through this morning. Everything is to go ahead as it was originally planned.'

Lola stubbed out her cigarette in the ash tray and raised the cup of black coffee to her lips.

'When?'

'Next week. My contact is certain of it.'

Lola nodded and put the coffee cup back down on its saucer where the two cubes of sugar still remained untouched in their wrappers.

'You have done well, Raul,' she said. 'I am grateful.'

'Lola.' His hand was resting on hers. 'Can you now tell me what this is all about?'

'In time,' she said. 'For now you must trust me.'

'Then I pray that when this is over we will have some time together.'

'We will see.'

'But there is hope? Tell me there is hope.'

'Yes Raul, there is hope.'

Raul left first. They had decided it would be so.

'Good luck,' he said as he finished his whisky and pulled a note out of his pocket to pay the bill. 'Ring me as soon as my ship gets to Cadiz. Hasta la vista Lola. Let's pray it won't be long.'

'Hasta la vista Raul.'

She watched him as he disappeared up the street with the collar of his raincoat turned up.

'Hey chica.' It was one of the men who had been drinking at the bar, the one who had been talking the loudest and who now stood in her path as she made to leave. 'Now your boyfriend has gone how about if you come with me? I can take you to places where we can go dancing then after, who knows?'

Lola looked at him. There was beer on his moustache and sweat stains in the armpits of his shirt. Men like this had pawed at her when she was fourteen and she felt nothing for them other than hatred and disgust. A quick deft movement of her hand was all it took, then the leer on the man's face was replaced by a look of helplessness and confusion. The next second Lola was past him and on her way out of the door.

'Señor,' she called out over her shoulder, tossing back her long black hair. 'I think you should fasten your trousers. You look stupid with your balls hanging out.'

CHAPTER TWO

The Night of the New Jumilla

Zamora had a tom-cat and the tom-cat's name was Theobald. Theobald was large and round and the colour of marmalade but, unlike most tom-cats in Los Tidos, Theobald didn't spend his nights caterwauling on roof tops, fighting with other tom-cats or chasing rats up dark alleyways. Theobald, on the contrary led a sedate and dignified existence. Zamora, who had no wife or family, doted on the cat and fed him with the tastiest morsels that Vilas the Butcher could provide. As a consequence, Theobald had grown fat and lazy and when he wasn't eating or being fussed over, he spent most of his time curled up on a special cushion put out for him either inside the bar or else on a window sill in the sun. The fact the Bar Zamora had few customers suited Theobald perfectly. He could enjoy the idyllic feline existence he'd grown used to without the threat of disturbance.

Uncle Pablo's dog, Waldorf was, in contrast, greatly given to wandering the streets and, though, strictly speaking, his patch was up in the Old Town, his grey flea-bitten shape could frequently be seen as far afield as the rubbish heaps in the bottom of the barranco or poking round in whatever had been thrown out at the back of the fish market.

All the same, there was no reason why Theobald and

Waldorf could not have gone on living their separate lives without their paths ever crossing and the fact that they did has to be blamed partly on Uncle Pablo and partly on Zamora and the night of the New Jumilla.

First, Uncle Pablo. Since the summer Uncle Pablo had taken to drinking in some of the waterfront bars down by the new yacht marina, places that were frequented chiefly by foreigners. The proprietors of these bars were, for the most part, foreigners themselves who knew nothing of Uncle Pablo or his shortcomings and saw in his presence only the splash of local colour that their establishments so sadly lacked. Thus they made the mistake of encouraging him by plying him with free drinks and he responded to their generosity by bursting into spontaneous renderings of traditional Valencian folk songs, which, needless to say, bore little resemblance to the originals and contained many lewd and suggestive verses that Uncle Pablo had made up himself. Fortunately for Uncle Pablo's enraptured audiences in these places, none of them understood the throaty dialect in which he sang for if they had, they would have thought twice about joining in the choruses. Instead they bought him more free drinks, called for encores and, in the general jollity that surrounded these occasions, Uncle Pablo usually managed to get his bony fingers on parts of foreign female anatomy that would otherwise have been out of bounds to him.

Though strictly speaking Waldorf belonged to Uncle Pablo, the two of them were hardly ever seen in each other's company, so it was strange two nights after the night when Waldorf had mistakenly sunk his teeth in the old man's leg that the dog should take it into his head to follow Uncle Pablo on one of his excursions to the Waterfront. Uncle Pablo all spruced up in his best beret and carrying a walking cane, set off from the Villa Verde at just after eight leaving his nephew Jaime at home watching television. As he walked through the steeply stepped streets and alleyways of the Old Town, Uncle Pablo was completely unaware of the grey emaciated shape plodding along thirty or forty metres behind. Uncle Pablo had his mind on other things: like the free glass of absenta waiting for him in whichever foreigner's bar he chose to visit that night or the feel of the soft white flesh up some fraulein's skirt. In his wilder imaginings Uncle Pablo was even considering how the future career of Pablo El Pescador (the name he had chosen to give himself) might unfold. In having these ambitions, the fact that Uncle Pablo had never set foot on a fishing boat in his life did not seem to trouble him in the least.

There were several ways that Uncle Pablo could have taken from the Villa Verde to the bright lights of the new marina but the one he chose that fateful night took him along the Calle de Dos Ojos where the Bar Madrid and, next door to it, the Bar Zamora stood. As he passed the Bar Zamora Uncle Pablo noticed how it seemed to be the centre of great festivities and that a number of large cars were parked outside. He did not know Zamora, but he had heard about his prices so with no further interest in what was going on Uncle Pablo continued on his way.

Zamora, as it has been related already, cherished ambitions for his place in the Calle de Dos Ojos to become a stopping off place for kings and presidents though, thus far, he had failed in all his endeavours to attract the high society clientele he craved. The wall in the Bar Zamora that he had reserved for photographs of himself in the company of celebrities remained as bare as the day on which he had first opened and even the yachting crowd never set foot inside the door except for those who accidentally got lost in the maze of back streets off the Avenida and came on it by mistake.

Determined to do something about this state of affairs that was slowly eating away at his finances, Zamora set about looking for ideas. What was it that might attract the smart set? What appealed to such people? One day Zamora was flicking through a back number of one of the glossy magazines that made up his staple reading diet when he came across an article about the custom in the Beaujolais district of France of drinking the new season's wine no sooner than it had been put into bottles. More interesting still to Zamora's eye, the article was accompanied by photographs of wealthy young men in fast sports cars racing across Europe to be the first with the new wine and the gay parties that followed. Zamora wrinkled his bulbous nose. This was it, he decided, the idea he was looking for – a New Beaujolais party at Zamora's – and the pictures started to form in his mind – the men in their white tuxedos; the women in their strapless evening gowns; the corks popping; the fruity young wine being poured into glasses. But then the reality struck. Beaujolais was a long way from Los Tidos and Zamora didn't own a fast sports car and, even if he did, with several crates of wine in the boot there was bound to be some problem with the customs officers at the frontier.

At this point, not being one to be easily daunted, Zamora hit on the idea of procuring a newly-made wine more close to home. Wine was only wine after all, wherever it came from, and what was wrong with Jumilla, the wine produced not far from Los Tidos? Why go all the way to Beaujolais when there was a perfectly good wine to be had on the doorstep?

So it was that Zamora decided to take a trip to the Jumilla where he talked to a number of people in the trade. For the most part these people were bemused by the idea of anyone wanting to drink their wine when it was just a few weeks old. Yet when they saw the colour of Zamora's money they forgot about their scruples, sold him the wine he wanted and even agreed to stick specially printed 'New Jumilla' labels on the bottles. As far as they were concerned, if the man with the big nose paid the right price he could do what he wanted with their wine – pickle walnuts with it or use it to embalm his mother if he liked.

Two days prior to the night of the New Jumilla, Zamora had gone round the yacht marina giving out handbills advertising the event and sticking posters on lamp posts and walls. Then, on the night itself, resplendent in a red Cubano shirt with frills down the front and frills down the sleeves, Zamora stood at the door waiting and watching as the sun went down. At first in ones and twos then in small groups, then in droves and car loads, the smart set from the yacht marina descended. It was better than Zamora had ever hoped for, even in his wildest dreams: the men in their white tuxedos, the women in their strapless evening gowns: tippling back the fruity young wine, eating Zamora's tapas and remarking on the quality of both. Zamora was delirious with the excitement of it all. He rushed round keeping glasses filled and plates replenished; bowing and scraping when he felt it was necessary to bow and scrape and making polite conversation with those who engaged him in polite conversation. Indeed everyone was happy with the way the night of the New Jumilla was going with one exception and that was Theobald, Zamora's cat.

Theobald was used to spending his evenings curled up on a comfortable cushion inside the Bar Zamora as far away as possible from the loud guffaws and coarse laughter that came from the clientele of the Bar Madrid next door. When the first of the New Jumilla tasters arrived, Theobald had just settled down for a nice nap. As a special treat on that special night Zamora had prepared for him a huge meal of choice chicken breasts and Theobald was feeling more than the usual need for a long period of postprandial repose. But the sound of voices all around him clamouring in a dozen different foreign tongues proved to be dissonance to his ears and soon he decided he could stand no more of it and took himself off to find another more peaceful place to curl up.

Flicking his tail with annoyance, he went outside where the tables and chairs were set out for those who preferred to sit *al fresco*. Being though that the evening was chilly and mosquitoes were about, the New Jumilla tipplers had chosen to stay indoors and the chairs on the pavement with their gaily striped cushions offered what seemed to Theobald a sanctuary from all the racket. What was more the Bar Madrid's outdoor beer drinkers had also been deterred by the cold wind so it was all quiet on the other side of the invisible line also.

Theobald was just dropping off into a pleasant slumber, dreaming about the smell of fish fillets freshly grilled on Zamora's plancha, when he noticed out of one of his half-shut eyes an old man shuffling along the street carrying a cane and wearing a beret. The old man stopped and stared briefly before continuing on his way. Theobald yawned and stretched. He had no interest in old men and the pleasant drowsy feeling and the smell of freshly grilled fish fillets returned.

It was at this point that Waldorf appeared on the scene. Theobald, it has to be said, had no great fear of dogs. The few he had met had been small yapping things that accompanied old ladies and were kept on leads. Certainly in his narrow and cloistered existence Theobald had never encountered a dog like Waldorf before.

Whether it was by sight or by scent, Waldorf became aware of Theobald's presence at about the same time that Theobald became aware of his. Waldorf bristled. A cat that didn't flee immediately struck Waldorf as a cat bent on an act of defiance and that didn't go down too well with him. No creature – no dog, no cock chicken, not even anyone's mule had ever stood up to Waldorf and now here, of all things, was a cat trying to stare him out. In the end, it was too much for Waldorf. He promptly forgot about Uncle Pablo and took off in Theobald's direction with the force of a cannonball.

There are several versions of what happened next though most are agreed on all but the details. Theobald, seeing the danger for himself at the last minute, bolted in the only direction available to him and that was back through the beaded curtain into the Bar Zamora where the New Jumilla drinkers gasped in horror as Theobald chased by the wild-eyed slavering form of Waldorf charged into their midst. To make matters worse, Theobald tried to take refuge among their legs and, for a full minute, the smart set from the yacht marina did their best to extricate Waldorf from between their ankles by kicking at him. Waldorf, who was well used to having kicks aimed in his direction, fought back in spirited fashion and soon there was a melee going on with women screaming and wine glasses smashing on the floor and in the centre of it all, Waldorf's grey emaciated shape and Waldorf's gnashing fangs. The commotion soon brought Zamora running from the kitchen. Seeing Waldorf, Zamora seized his broom and, wielding it in both hands dervish-fashion, he came round the bar with the intention of landing a blow on Waldorf's skull. Unfortunately for Zamora, however his timing wasn't good for a woman in a tight-fitting gold lamé dress chose that precise moment to make a dash for the door and, as the broom handle came round, it scythed her down at the knees and felled her to the floor. Zamora rushed across to proffer his apologies and help her to her feet but by then the situation was well out of control and the man who was with the lady in the tight fitting gold lamé dress mistook his intentions, seized him by the front of his frilly Cubano shirt and head butted him to the ground. And in the confusion that followed Waldorf, the cause of all the trouble, made good his escape. So it was that the Night of the New Jumilla that had started so well for Zamora ended for him with his bar in ruins, his shirt torn from his back and a broken nose.

★ ★ ★

Far away at the Aeropuerto de Bilbao, Lola Martinez rose to her feet with a sigh of relief. Two hours late, they had finally called her plane and she put out her cigarette, put the cigarette holder back in her shoulder bag and made her way to the gate where they were checking in passengers for the Iberia Airlines internal flight to Girona.

For some time though something had been puzzling Lola. All round the departure lounge people were standing in small groups wearing expressions of grief on their faces and some of them were even weeping. One such tearful woman was next to Lola in the queue so she asked her to explain.

'President Kennedy,' she wailed. 'He has been assassinated in Dallas, Texas. Shot by a man with a rifle.'

On the plane Lola sat back and closed her eyes. The flight

to Girona was short but it gave her the time to think through the whirlwind events of the last few weeks.

First there was Raul. She had come across Raul in a fashionable bar in her home city of Barcelona where a contact she was supposed to meet hadn't shown up. Lonely, like she always felt when she was in Barcelona, she said yes when the tall good looking young naval officer came across and offered to buy her a drink. He was on shore leave, he told her, and, as the evening came to an end, she agreed to see him again. They spent two days in each other's company, days in which Raul bought her meals in expensive restaurants and showered her with gifts, then, on their final night, the night before Raul was due back on his ship, they stood together in the square in Montjuich looking at the fountains and Raul told her the strange tale of Franco and Franco's trip.

A moment of indiscretion? Lola wondered. Or was he trying to impress her with his high-up connections? Raul was still talking, telling her how he'd heard Franco was paying a private visit to some place down the coast and trying to keep it a secret so he could go on his own. In Raul's opinion Franco had taken leave of his senses. Some criminal might see the chance to kidnap him. Then what? Five, ten, twenty million US dollars to buy his freedom?

Dangerous words. Lola glanced from side to side. There was the usual crowd of people milling around the fountains. Faces, any one of them an informer; she raised her finger to her lips to signal him to keep his voice down yet the plan was already starting to take shape in her mind. Franco on his own; Franco without his usual army of protectors and, for Lola Martinez, the girl who had once held her hand out for dineros in the street, the ticket to better things?

'In ten minutes we will be landing in Girona.' It was the captain's voice crackling over the intercom and Lola got her powder compact out of her shoulder bag and checked her make up in the mirror. Kidnap Franco and hold him for ransom? Poor Raul who wined her and dined her and sent red roses to her hotel room. Little did he, the son of a rich family, know that Lola Martinez was an orphan from the barrios who knew the true meaning of hunger and poverty and who let no opportunity pass when it came her way.

Then as she looked in the mirror she caught sight again of the small lines around her eyes. A reminder she was getting older, a reminder she only had a few years left to make the fortune she needed to buy her ease, leisure and luxury for the rest of her life a reminder why she was going now to see what help she could get from Franco's enemies.

$$\star \star \star$$

Later that same evening Waldorf returned to the Villa Verde where Jaime Campello was still watching television and where his eye chanced to fall on the grey matted shape as it slunk from room to room looking for something to eat.

The part that Waldorf had played in the wrecking of Zamora's Bar was not to reach Campello's ears for some time but the state of Uncle Pablo's dog had been concerning him for several weeks. Not just the various parasite life forms that had taken up residence in his fleece but also the awful smell, which, though it was to some extent a normal part of Waldorf, had got progressively worse over the hot summer months.

Still flushed with the excitement of putting Theobald to flight and his subsequent battle with the New Jumilla

31

drinkers, Waldorf's hackles rose at the sight of Campello approaching with a bar of soap in his hand. Unfortunately though for Waldorf he was cornered. He snapped, he snarled, he showed the whites of his eyes and bared his yellow fangs right up to the gums – but it was all to no avail: Campello had him by the scruff of the neck and was dragging him along leaving a long trail of claw marks across the tiles.

The fact that Campello had Waldorf's best interests at heart was completely lost on the old dog. Cleanliness had few virtues as far as he was concerned and he stood dejectedly in the old tin bath out in the back yard; up to his hocks in water, growling all the time as Campello scrubbed him and waiting for any chance that came his way to sink his teeth in the young man's wrist.

Dried off with an old towel, the transformation was remarkable. Waldorf's coat was clean and fluffy and the smell, even if it had not gone altogether, was disguised by the even stronger smell of carbolic. One final indignity was awaiting Waldorf, however: a new dog collar, which, even now as he wriggled and writhed and snapped and snarled, Campello was fastening round his scrawny neck.

Finally released from Campello's grip, Waldorf shot off over the back wall with his tail between his legs and into the narrow alleyway that ran behind. That, as it turned out, was to be the last Campello would see of Waldorf for some time.

With Waldorf now off his mind Campello went back to watching television and the news coming through of President Kennedy's assassination. In common with many other people around the world that night he stared in disbelief at the black and white images flickering on the screen and wondered what had brought about such a dreadful thing.

★ ★ ★

Kennedy's shooting was also the reason why Suarez was still at his desk taking telephone calls and why, as he did, it was going through his mind that the killing of the President might at least get the Caudillo to think again about making his trip. Who knew what motive was behind what had happened in Dallas, Texas and, if it was a communist plot, there was still revenge to be had in Spain for the execution of the Communist leader Julian Grimau back in April. So what better target than the Caudillo who had been instrumental in seeing to it Grimau faced the firing squad.

Suarez sighed as he picked up the phone again but this time it was to call Carlita. It had been an hour since he last spoke to her and he knew how she worried when she was left on her own. He realised though that all he would be able to tell her was that he still had calls to make and he did not know what time he would be home.

★ ★ ★

At the same time that Suarez was talking to his wife, in a deserted back street in the Old Town of Los Tidos the grey emaciated shape of a dog could be seen rolling in a heap of fresh mule dung. Satisfied finally that the smell of the soap was almost gone Waldorf next turned his attention to the collar that Campello had just put round his neck. Dogs with collars had no place on the streets and in the alleyways of the Old Town. Dogs with collars were tame house-bound things and Waldorf knew, if he didn't get rid of it, he would become a laughing stock. He scratched with his back leg. He rubbed his scrawny neck along the ground. He succeeded in getting it up round one ear. Then another good scratching session till finally the collar was off and lay on the ground. There Waldorf sniffed at it with his gnarled snout then, as a final mark of defiance, he raised his back leg over it and did what all dogs do when they have scored a victory. With that and with his tail back in the air and an evil truculent gleam in his eye, Waldorf trotted off into the night.

★ ★ ★

Breakfast for Jaime Campello was usually taken at around seven o'clock and consisted of fresh rolls from Penedes' Panaderia – sometimes accompanied by marmalade, sometimes by ham and boiled eggs and always followed by freshly ground coffee. Invariably he ate alone because Uncle Pablo, whose life-style kept him out till all hours, rarely rose before midday.

Anyone who had not seen the inside of the Villa Verde before would have been struck first of all by its drabness. Apart from the television set, the only furnishings were old and there was a lack of any of the kind of prettyfyings that would normally have been put there by a feminine hand. In itself there was no great mystery to this for Jaime Campello's mother had died when he was but a small child and the house had been lived in from then on by Campello and his father joined later by Uncle Pablo and his dog. Campello's father, a heartbroken man, had laboured on for several years to give the boy a decent upbringing but then, six years ago, he himself had succumbed to a bout of pneumonia and an early death. At the end, when all was counted, young Campello's inheritance consisted of the Villa Verde, the business of Campello y Hico, carpenters, into which he had been brought when he left school, a few mil pesetas and his father's wayward older brother, Pablo.

As he was eating his breakfast on this particular morning, Campello noticed a newspaper that had been folded and put on the kitchen dresser, he guessed by Uncle Pablo some time in the early hours. For no reason other than to see if it contained any further news of President Kennedy's assassination, he picked it up and began to look at it it though almost immediately he saw that it was three days' old. He was just on the point of putting it down again when his eye fell on an advertisement at the foot of a page. It consisted of a crude line drawing of a man and woman smiling at one another with the woman wearing a bridal gown. In the air all around this beatific couple were little hearts and Cupids and, beneath, a caption that read 'MAKE HAPPINESS YOURS. PHONE THE DIANE MAITLAND BUREAU OF FRIENDSHIP TODAY. COMPUTER MATCHED INTRODUCTIONS. ABSOLUTE DISCRETION GUARANTEED' and a phone number with an Albacete dialling code.

Campello's eyes drifted back to the beatific couple – the man handsome; the woman pretty beneath her bridal veil – and Father Miguel's words began to come back to him: find a wife before it becomes too late; don't leave it till you are too old. He read the caption again. The name Diane Maitland intrigued him as did the 'computer matched introductions'. The name was English he knew and the English had a reputation for respectability while computers were something he had read about in science journals. Respectability was important and anything done with computers, he knew was foolproof. He hesitated for a few moments then went over to the drawer where the kitchen scissors were kept.

Tidying up the breakfast things and checking, as he always did, that no mishap had befallen Uncle Pablo in the night – which it hadn't because Uncle Pablo was sound asleep in his bed – Campello let himself out of the front door and made his way down the steeply stepped street to where his workshop was situated in an old stable near the bottom of the hill. The walk took him less then ten minutes, the weather was fine, the sky was blue and Campello took care not to walk under the drips that came down from the freshly watered geranium pots up on the balconies. Along the way he passed various people he knew: Old Roberto who had a smallholding on the outskirts of town off to work with his faithful mule Emilia laden with his tools; Doctor Pascal, bag in hand, setting off on his rounds; Father Miguel on some business of the Church. To each of these he called 'Buenos Dias' and greeted them by name. Father Miguel asked about Uncle Pablo and Campello was able to assure him that the old man was none the worse for his experience down the barranco.

The key to Campello's workshop was large and ancient-looking and matched the large and ancient-looking lock. Once inside, in the musty atmosphere that still smelled of mules and harness leather, Campello was able to get out his tools and contemplate the large set of double doors that he had been working on for the last week. The doors were new doors for the Ayuntamiento because the old ones had fallen victim to woodworm.

In craftsmanship it was widely acknowledged that Jaime Campello was the equal of his father and, if there was any criticism of his work, it was that he was too painstaking and slow. The care that he lavished on the shaping of a piece of wood or the fashioning of a moulding had no place in a cut throat world where, if the price was right, it didn't matter if a job was hammered together with cheap nails or a pair of shutters fell off their hinges after two years. As a consequence the business of Campello y Hico had declined in recent times. It still however managed to provide Jaime with a living and to him, a young man with no greater ambitions, that was all that mattered.

★ ★ ★

The experience of being put in a bath tub and scrubbed with soap then the humiliation of having a collar put round his neck decided Waldorf that it would be best to give the Villa Verde a wide berth for a few days. Waldorf, being an enterprising dog, worked out that he could make up for missing the dish of food that Jaime Campello put down for him every evening by stepping up his scavenging in places such as the fish market or round the back of Vilas the Butcher's shop where some discarded lumps of gristle or offal could usually be found: in fact the kind of places where Zamora's cat Theobald would never have set his freshly licked paws. Unlike Theobald, however, Waldorf had no qualms about rooting through rubbish for the scrapings off plates or putting his snout in old cans to get his tongue round whatever was still clinging to the insides. Whether it was edible or not mattered little to Waldorf for anything that found its way down his gullet that later proved indigestible he exhumed by the simple process of turning his stomach over and heaving it out.

Thus Waldorf temporarily opted for a life of vagrancy: a development that was to have a great bearing on events that followed, as we shall see.

CHAPTER THREE

Three Gentlemen in Girona

'Jaime, is that you?'

Campello sighed. He recognised the voice on the phone straight away. It was Pepe Gomez except Pepe Gomez was whispering not speaking in his normal voice leading the carpenter to guess that Conchita wasn't too far out of earshot.

'I tell you my life is hell, Amigo. All I do all day is fetch and carry. She never lets me out of her sight. The only peace I get is when she goes to bed at night. I won't be able to put up with this much longer. Soon something inside my head is going to snap.'

'Pepe...'

'I'm sorry I can't talk now. I can hear her coming back.'

Hearing the receiver go down at the other end Campello took a deep breath. He had been gearing himself up for this moment all morning and the phone call from Pepe Gomez had come at an unfortunate time when he had other more pressing business on his mind. In front of him was the newspaper cutting with its portrayal of the beatific young couple surrounded by hearts and cupids. Taking another deep breath he picked up the phone again and dialled out the number with the Albecete dialling code. He waited. It seemed to take an interminable time for the line to connect followed, even worse, by the sound of the engaged tone beeping out at him. He tried a second time, this time with a cold sweat breaking out on his face – the number rang out, thankfully, and then a lady's voice answered, brisk and business-like, though with no trace of an English accent that he could make out. Was this Miss Maitland herself or one of her staff? As it turned out however the lady was very understanding. She helped him find the words when the words were ones he found hard to say and she filled in with words when words failed him altogether. She asked him a few questions about his age, his height, his occupation, whether he had been married before and what his intentions were. He answered the questions truthfully and the lady seemed satisfied. She explained that it was necessary to vet all candidates carefully because there were some people, usually men of course, who took advantage of services such as hers to procure partners for sexual exploits and with no intention of serious or lasting friendship. She asked Campello if he understood and Campello said he did. He hastened to assure her that nothing of the kind she described could be further from his thoughts. The business-like lady then explained that there were a few formalities, firstly the payment of a non-returnable deposit of one mil pesetas, which Campello thought a bit steep but he felt it best not to say. On payment of the non-returnable deposit, the business-like lady continued, a computer search would be carried out and from this search a shortlist of eligible ladies would be drawn up. On payment of a further fee of five hundred pesetas, also non-returnable, an arrangement would be made for him to meet one of these eligible young ladies. Was this clear to Señor Campello? Señor Campello said it was.

Did Señor Campello wish to ask any questions? Señor Campello said he didn't though fifteen hundred pesetas before he got to meet anyone seemed little short of extortionate.

'Very well,' said the business-like lady. 'The sooner you put your cheque for one mil five hundred pesetas in the post then the sooner we can get on with preparing your path to eternal happiness in the company of a perfectly matched partner. You have much to look forward to, Señor Campello.'

★ ★ ★

As Lola Martinez left the small pension where she had spent the night she told the desk clerk she would be back later and to take any messages while she was out. The desk clerk nodded and went back to her knitting and listening to the news on the radio.

Outside on the street Lola took the short walk along the river then over the old stone bridge into the walled city. She wore little make-up and a plain woollen jumper over a pair of jeans, which made it easier for her to blend in with the groups of tourists. To complete the effect she carried a guidebook in her hand, which she glanced at frequently. She had no reason to think anyone was tailing her but to play safe she took several turns along quiet streets to see who followed. Each time the street behind remained empty so, feeling satisfied, she stopped off at a café in the Ramblas where she spent twenty minutes drinking a cup of coffee and smoking a cigarette. When the time came she made her way to the cathedral and climbed the long flight of steps at the front where she stopped half way up and stood in the place where she'd been told to stand. Five minutes passed then five minutes more. A man approached her, a man with thin wispy hair and wearing an overcoat.

'You are interested in the architecture of the Gothic period?' he said pointing up at the cathedral.

'Yes,' she replied. 'But my taste also includes the Romanesque.'

'Then here you have both,' said the man smiling.

It was the signal to follow which she did at a discreet distance all the time checking to see who was around. He led her into a maze of twisting back alleys into what was the old Jewish Quarter and where under the shadow of the City wall he came to a big iron-studded door and knocked on it four times. The door opened and he went in. Lola followed and, once inside, she saw she was in an open courtyard where the man now stood with two other men – one dressed as a priest, the other much younger with untidy hair and looking like a student.

'So,' said the priest. 'I think we can dispense with the formalities. What news do you bring from your sources? Is the information concerning Franco correct?'

'Yes,' said Lola. ''The information is correct.'

The priest continued. 'What my colleagues and I do not understand is why Franco is taking the risk of making this journey on his own. Surely his advisors will have told him he is placing himself in danger.'

'It is a mystery to my informants also. As for me I am not privy to Franco's thinking.'

'So tell us again why you have come to us.'

'One woman could not carry out an undertaking such as this on her own.'

'I agree,' said the priest. 'But you are only interested in the money you are going to make. We on the other hand fight for our cause.'

'Which is…?'

'To set the people of Catalunya free for all time from the tyranny of Castile.'

Lola smiled. 'That my friend is a tall order.'

'Like us you are a Catalan,' said the man with thin wispy hair who met her on the steps of the cathedral. 'You know what Franco and his followers have done to wipe the identity of our nation off the map.'

'I also know what it is like to beg for money in the street. Ideals like yours my friend are for those who can afford them.'

The student spoke for the first time. 'If we kidnapped Franco we would do it so we could stand him in front of a firing squad. We would not be handing him back in exchange for a ransom.'

'Your way would mean bloodshed. Gentlemen you know in your hearts Franco's death would not go unpunished and any rejoicing would be short-lived.'

The three men looked at one another. Finally it was the priest who spoke again. 'There is one who may agree to help you,' he said. 'But that will be a matter for him. He is linked to our cause but he has scores to settle of his own. Bartering the life of Franco for something he holds dear may interest him.'

'You say one. To take Franco and hold him hostage for what might be many days will take a team of men not one.'

'You need have no fears on that score. The one of whom we speak is better than twenty men put together. He has no equal in all of Spain.'

'How will I find this man?'

'You won't. He will come to you.'

Later that day Lola Martinez was getting on yet another

plane – this time from Girona to Valencia where, because of yet more delays, she touched down just after midnight.

Arrangements for baggage reclamation at the Aeropuerto de Valencia consisted of two handcarts stacked high with suitcases offloaded from the plane's luggage hold and left for passengers to help themselves. Whether this was normal or whether the baggage-handlers had all gone home, Lola never found out but, as she waited for the crush to die down, she noticed, over the smell of aviation fuel the soft seductive scent of late season orange blossom wafting to her across the tarmac. Valencia, the name conjured up dreams of warm nights and the exotic south.

With internal flights there were no green-uniformed jackals to go through her suitcase and ogle at her frillies so she made her way straight over to the Avis desk in the airport's entrance hall where the man in a white shirt sat looking half asleep.

' Señorita,' he said, coming to attention, his pupils turning into pinpoints as his eyes fell on the curvaceous shape of Lola Martinez in her fur coat standing before him.

'I want to hire a car. Something small. Nothing too ostentatious.'

'For how long?'

'For one week.'

The man flicked through some papers attached to a clipboard then slowly started to shake his head. 'I am sorry Señorita it appears there could be a problem.'

'What is the problem?'

'All the cars I have in the pound are earmarked to go out in the next two or three days. There is nothing I could let you have for a week.'

'That is a pity'

'Yes it is a pity.'

'Can you lend me your pen please?

'My pen? Why yes of course.'

Lola took the ballpoint off him and wrote on the corner of one of his sheets the name Rosa and a telephone number, the first five numbers that came into her head. As she handed the pen back to him she smiled and gave him a wink. The man looked suddenly pale and flustered. He swallowed a few times and Lola watched the little lump go up and down in his throat. She imagined the other little lump going up and down inside his trousers.

'I think you are lucky Señorita,' he said going back to his schedules, 'It seems I have a Seat 600 just back in from service that I had overlooked. Does a Seat 600 meet with your approval?'

'A Seat 600 will be fine.'

With the man's assistance, the paperwork was completed in the name of Señora Rosa Ramirez and Lola paid a deposit in cash.

'My name is Enrico,' said the man as they walked over to the car pound with him carrying her suitcase. 'You can call me Henry if you like. My friends call me Henry.'

When they got to the little Seat Henry slid her suitcase onto the backseat then held the door open for her to get in. Lola noticed the little lump go up and down in his throat again as she slipped behind the steering wheel and allowed her skirt to ride up a few extra centimetres.

'You have driven a Seat 600 before Señorita?'

'Yes I have thank you'

'There is some petrol in the tank but only a little. Do you have far to go?'

'No, my apartment is quite close to here.'

'Shall we say "see you soon," then Señora Ramirez?'

'See you soon Henry.'

As Lola drove off she heard Henry shout. Putting the Seat in reverse she went back to see what was wrong.

'What is it?' she said winding the window down.

'I was simply saying ouch, Señorita. You just drove the car over my toe.'

Lola was able to fill up with petrol at an all night gasolinera on the outskirts of town. Here she also bought a road map of the Valencia region. Ten kilometres further on she pulled over on the hard shoulder of a deserted road, turned off the engine then checked the time on the luminous dial of her wristwatch. It was half past two. In the distance behind she could see the bright lights of the city reflected in the sky yet all around was darkness except for a few pin points of light showing here and there: houses, a pueblo perhaps. The road, she saw, was on an embankment and when she wound the window down the smell of stagnant water wafted up to her along with the sounds of insects and frogs. There were rice fields round here, she remembered – miles of them – pools and wetlands stretching for as far as the eye could see. Sitting here, staring into the night, she felt the first wave of tiredness sweep over her. The adrenaline that had kept her going for the last thirty-six hours was starting to run out. Should she stop here and try and grab a few hours sleep? She thought about it for a while but in the end she decided to push on. It would be best to get to the place where she was heading by daybreak and she still had a long way to go.

After an hour's driving she had left the rice fields behind. She was following narrow country lanes, alternately straight and alternately twisting, going through small villages where not a single light showed. For kilometre after kilometre she had gone through orange and lemon groves where she could make out the shapes of the fruit hanging from the trees and the heavy sweet scent of the late blossom came to her again wafting in through the open window of the Seat. This was the night, she reflected, when Franco was supposed to be setting off on his journey. Even now her fortune could be out there somewhere in the darkness, cat-napping in the back seat of a limousine, going the same way as she. She strained her weary eyes, forcing them to concentrate on unfamiliar place names each time a signpost came up in the headlights.

A car! It was the first she had seen for long time. It was stopped at the roadside in front with its brake lights on. A Renault 4, she noticed, with two men sitting inside. Indicating correctly, she steered past, then kept a careful eye on the headlights in the mirror till she was satisfied the Renault made no attempt to follow. Though there was no reason to suspect that the occupants of the car had any interest in her mission, Lola Martinez was a girl who took no chances.

★ ★ ★

Capitan Luis Garcia of the Cordoba section of the Guardia Civil and his assistant Ramon Ramon were studying a road map by the light of a torch as the little Seat 600 went past. They watched its red tail lights disappear into the distance before the Capitan spoke. 'Hombre,' he fumed. 'Don't tell me we are lost.'

Ramon Ramon frowned as he held the map up this way then that. 'No Capitan Garcia, I think if we carry on along this road we should be OK. See on the map – here, here and here.'

'Do not bother me with maps hombre when my mind is focused on the important task we have been given. We have spent too long looking at maps already. Let us be on our way without further delay. Now what is it?'

'The car that has just passed us Capitan Garcia.'

'What about it?'

'Do you not find it strange that someone should be out so late at night in the middle of the countryside?'

'Why should I find it strange? Farmers get up early don't they? Any fool knows they are out of bed at the crack of dawn to milk cows or whatever they do at such times.'

'I was thinking perhaps the car could be linked to our mission. Someone with designs on the Caudillo perhaps.'

'Then you are a fool hombre. Someone with designs on the Caudillo would be skulking in the bushes not driving a car along a road in full view of everyone.'

'Yes Capitan Garcia. Capitan Garcia…'

'Now what?'

'There is a ditch at the side of the road. When you pull away I think you need to be careful not to drive into it.'

★ ★ ★

Away to the south, Los Tidos was slumbering peacefully under the stars. In the town the hours between when the last bar shut and the first light of dawn were seldom disturbed. The odd drunk on his way home might stumble and curse as he made his way up the unlit steeply stepped streets and dark labyrinthine alleyways of the Old Town; two tom-cats might caterwaul at one another on a wall until someone threw a boot at them and sent them off hissing and spitting into the night; but the noises were few and, in the winter months, even the cicadas were quiet. Yet the small hours were the time when the basureros came round and, the basureros were well known for having no reverence for the sleep of others.

The basureros were the grim tallow-faced band of men who manned the municipal garbage cart. They came thrice weekly long after everyone had gone to bed and though it was never claimed to be intentional, did their best to wake them up again. Complaining did no good either. Those who were stupid enough to lean out of their windows and tell the basureros to make less racket ran the risk of finding their garbage bin dumped over a wall next morning – or, as a specially vengeful act, at the bottom of the barranco. For this reason most agreed, it was best to leave the basureros alone and let them get on with their job. They came and they went and that was all there was to it. To get on the wrong side of them was simply inviting trouble.

In the Street of Two Eyes, the passing of the basureros did not disturb Theobald as he slept curled up on his favourite cushion inside the Bar Zamora. The New Jumilla drinkers and the wild-eyed dog that had attacked him without warning were already fading memories. Several meals of lightly grilled fish served by his master had helped him get over the trauma he had suffered and the grilled fish was now digesting pleasantly in Theobald's over-stretched stomach. Upstairs Zamora himself was fast asleep also, snoring loudly with a huge mask of plaster holding his broken nose together. Unlike Theobald, however, the events of the evening were etched indelibly on his mind and he had lain awake for several hours thinking about nothing else except the wretched stray dog and the way the smart set from the marina had complained and walked off without paying. Finally, however, weariness had taken its toll and Zamora had fallen into a fitful sleep in which he twitched and turned and lashed out at unseen assailants.

Sleep, however, was less merciful to Zamora's neighbour Pepe Gomez. Next door in the Bar Madrid a single light burned in the back kitchen far into the night where the fat little man sat slumped in a chair with a bottle of coñac in his clenched fist from which he swigged from time to time. The humiliation that he had suffered in the street at the hands of Conchita still rankled deeply with him and he had noticed now the way Lopez and the others were nudging and winking at one another as he went about his daily chores. He had become an object of fun in Los Tidos. Everywhere he went people were sniggering behind his back and calling him *El Dominado*, the hen-pecked one. He had been reduced to a laughing stock, the butt of a thousand ribald jokes, and Conchita was to blame for it all.

Gomez took another swig of coñac a big one this time. No, he vowed to himself as the hand on the clock moved to quarter to three, he would put up with it no longer. He would see to it people respected him again and he would do it by proving himself a man and paying Conchita back in way that would make people sit up and think.

★ ★ ★

Next morning just as Jaime Campello was clearing away the breakfast things and making ready to go to work, the telephone rang.

'Jaime, is that you?'

49

Again the voice was unmistakable though this time there were street noises in the background telling Campello that Gomez was phoning from a public telephone.

'Can you meet me later?' Gomez hissed, sounding in a hurry and a picture was forming in Campello's mind of the little man standing at the teléfono on the corner of the Street of Two Eyes skulking with his head inside the acoustic hood and keeping out of Conchita's sight. 'Is five o'clock this afternoon alright Amigo? At Paco's Rincon?'

No sooner had Campello agreed to the time and place than Gomez was wishing him 'hasta tarde' and the phone went down. Campello guessed that Gomez had absented himself from his tasks in the kitchen without Conchita's permission. He guessed too that whatever it was that Gomez wanted to speak to him about was not for Conchita's ears.

Checking as usual that no mishap had befallen Uncle Pablo in the night, which it hadn't because Uncle Pablo was sleeping soundly in his bed, Campello left by the front door and made his way down the steeply stepped streets of the Old Town to his workshop. The weather was fine again, fleecy little clouds danced across the sky to show there was a gentle wind and serins, the wild canaries native to this part of Spain, sang up on the telephone wires. He passed Old Roberto, stroked Emilia as she nuzzled up against his arm, wished Doctor Pascal good morning and laughed at the postman's joke about wishing he was paid by the weight of his bag rather than by the hour. As he walked along his mind went back to Pepe Gomez. Paco's Rincon, a strange choice of meeting places: a roadhouse on the outskirts of town and not one of their normal drinking places. He guessed Pepe Gomez was up to some skulduggery but he had no idea what it might be. Then his thoughts turned to the other change of direction of his life: the cheque for one mil five hundred pesetas he had sent off in the post to the Diane Maitland Bureau.

Campello's way to his workshop took him past a vacant lot where over the years people had dumped piles of rubble and where there was a gap between the buildings that opened out onto a vista of the lower parts of the town and the surrounding countryside. Sometimes he stopped at this place for a few seconds to take in the view – which is what he did on this particular morning. He stood among the heaps of broken bricks and tiles and the dried off heads of fennels and camomiles and looked out over the red terracotta rooftops to the terraces of almond trees and the stone walled fields where Old Roberto had his few hectares.

In the furthest distance he saw a little red and cream train on the ferrocarril, the narrow gauge railway that ran along the coast and he heard the noise it made as it rattled over a bridge. The wind was coming from the north, he noticed, and that was what was bringing the sound of the train to him. At this season a wind from the north sooner or later meant rain.

At that moment a movement above caught his eye – three large birds with long legs and long necks flying high in the sky and too far off for him to make out clearly. He watched them till they became specks in the distance. He had no idea what kind of birds they were but he had never seen any like them before.

★ ★ ★

Other eyes had seen the birds too. Out on the Old Valencia Highway in the grounds of a big hacienda hidden from

Campello's sight by a ridge, Nathalie Theroux held her hand up to shade the sun from her eyes and looked up at the sky.

'Flamingos,' she said finally to Christine, her sister, who sat in her wheelchair rocking backwards and forwards with the excitement of it all. Flamingos were an uncommon sight in Los Tidos in those days. Only in later years did they become more plentiful.

The hacienda was one of several out that way, places where the rich people of Los Tidos lived, though the road on which they were situated had grown quiet since the opening of the new carretera. Now apart from the owners of these large properties, only local people used the old highway and cars and trucks were few and far between.

They were getting close to the gates, now, Nathalie noticed, feeling the strain on her arms of pushing Christine along the soft gravel path into which the narrow tyres of the wheelchair sank. Christine was gurgling again, pointing this time to a Sardinian Warbler, the little red eyed bird hopping about in the branches of an olive tree and then to a Redstart on the ground in front.

'Time to go home,' Nathalie said bringing the wheelchair round so they were facing back in the direction of the house. Just then, the sound of a car coming along the road caught her attention. She turned and saw a little blue Seat pull up by the gate and a girl in sunglasses, a beautiful girl with long black hair and her face made up like the face of a model in a magazine, wind down the window and call over to her.

'Señorita, can you tell me if this the way to Los Tidos?'

'Yes,' Nathalie replied in the language that was not her own. 'Straight on. It is no more than two kilometres.' The girl held up her hand to show her appreciation then, with a toss of her long black hair, she was off again, disappearing down the road and changing up through the gears.

Back at the house Maman was waiting for them, sitting on the front patio looking anxious.

'You have been a long time,' she said watching Nathalie pull the wheelchair backwards up the short flight of steps. 'And I wish you wouldn't do that on your own. Why can't you get Juan to help?'

'I can manage,' said Nathalie positioning the wheelchair so Christine was in the shade and where she could see the doves strutting about on the dove house.

'There is some fresh orange juice in the fridge,' said Maman going back to her mending. 'Maria pressed it this morning. I'm sure Christine would like a glass to drink.' Christine laughed and beat her fists on the armrests of the wheelchair to show her approval.

The tradition in the Theroux household was not to speak Spanish except when addressing the servants. When he was alive, Nathalie's father, Pierre Theroux, had insisted that they always talk to one another in their mother tongue. French, in his view was the noblest of languages and, even though France herself had fallen prey to socialists and traitors, people who had treated them shabbily, he was convinced the day would come when it would return to its former glory and greatness. Then they, the Theroux family, would go back and take up residence in Auxerre again. But for Pierre Theroux that day had never dawned. He had died of a heart attack six months ago when he was just fifty-three. Though it was something he had never wanted, it proved to be his destiny for his bones to be laid to rest in a foreign land.

'Did you go far?' Madame Theroux was watching Nathalie

as she helped Christine with her drink, wiping up the juice that had dribbled down the younger girl's chin.

'As far as the gate, Maman.'

'Tcha, you know I don't like you going near the road. It is so quiet, so lonely. You never know who is going to be about.'

'No Maman.'

'Did you see anyone?'

'Only a girl in a car, Maman. She stopped to ask for directions.'

Madame Theroux looked up sharply. 'A girl, you say. What girl was this?'

'I have no idea Maman. I have never seen her before. I took her to be a stranger. Why else would she want to know the way?'

'Strangers are what the police tell us to watch out for. There are gangs of thieves from the big cities who have started to roam along the carretera looking for big houses like these to steal from.'

'This girl was on her own.'

'She could be working for a gang, Nathalie. You have lived so long in this little backwater, you are innocent of the ways of the world. You need to be less trusting of people you meet. Do you understand?'

'Yes Maman.'

Lola carried on along the road just like the girl in the black dress had told her to do. Pretty soon she came to a crossroads with a couple of dirt tracks going off on either side then a little further on, a rise in the ground from the top of which there was a fine view of Los Tidos with its blue domed church sitting on the top of a hill. She glanced at her wristwatch. It was just after nine. She had already breakfasted in a roadside cafeteria then combed her hair, and fixed her make-up in the backroom that passed for the ladies' lavatory. The journey had taken her far longer than she expected and, several times as she drove along twisting back roads and saw the sun come up, she regretted not having taken the carretera. All the same, she told herself, she'd achieved what she wanted to achieve. She had got to this place without anyone scrutinising her too closely or wanting to see her papers. With Franco coming, there might be road blocks on the carretera, and that was a chance Lola did not want to take. Besides she now knew the quiet way in and out of town and, in the opinion of Lola Martinez, it always paid to know the quiet way in and out of places.

For now however, she was quite happy to put Franco and his kidnapping out of her mind. All she wanted was to get out of the clothes she'd been in for nearly two days and soak in a nice hot bath before curling up between the sheets for eight hours. A hotel commended itself but a hotel wasn't going to be suitable for what Lola had in mind during her stay. What she needed was a quiet apartment or a villa – and in a seaside place at this time of year, she guessed there should be plenty of empty apartments and villas for the taking.

Soon the road she was on met another road, this time a busy road, where after following the signs to the town centre, she crossed over an old bridge, (the Puente de San Marco though she did not know it) before finally coming to the Avenida with its magnificent palms. There, among the offices of lawyers and various public functionaries, she saw what she was looking for: letting agents and a number of them. Swinging the steering wheel sharply into a side street she parked the Seat as inconspicuously as possible in a line of cars.

From the glove compartment she removed the various documents that Enrico the Avis man at Valencia Airport had given to her and wiped off the steering wheel, gear stick and handbrake with a Kleenex she took from a packet in her shoulder bag. After she'd retrieved her suitcase and her fur coat from the back seat and made sure no-one was watching, she repeated this process with the door handles. 'Adios,' she whispered softly as she dropped the car keys into a drain.

She chose one of the letting agents on the Avenida by the simple method of going into the first she came to. The disappointment, however, was that there was a girl behind the counter. A man would have been far easier to deal with. With a man Lola Martinez knew she could always end up getting exactly what she wanted.

'I am looking for somewhere to stay,' she said to the girl.

The girl looked at her 'You have a reservation?' There was no 'Señora' and the girl used the familiar 'tu' instead of the formal 'usted' which Lola took as a sign of insolence and bad upbringing.

'You have a sign in your window saying you let properties. If that is not the case then tell me and I will go somewhere else.' The tone Lola used was high handed and the two 'usteds' in her first sentence were given extra emphasis. The girl shrugged and came round the counter in a slovenly fashion. Lola noticed that not only did she have bad skin but she wore trousers and her backside was like that of a pregnant cow

'This is our portfolio,' said the girl bringing across a loose-leaf binder containing colour photographs of various properties mounted on laminated card and much thumbed. 'Have a look through if you want to and see if there is anywhere you like.'

'Where are these places?' Lola snapped as she flicked through the photographs noticing the girl's further use of 'Tu'.

The girl shrugged again. 'All over,' she said. 'Most of our properties are on the coast. None of them are too far out of town.'

'How far?'

The girl shrugged again. 'Two or three kilometres, perhaps. Ten at the most.'

'I am looking for a place in town.'

'Here in Los Tidos?'

'Yes, here in Los Tidos. I do not want to have to walk ten kilometres every time I need to go to the shops.'

'We have no lettings in the town.'

'What is this place then?' Lola was pointing with one of her long red fingernails at a poster on the wall advertising luxury suites in an apartment block called the Edificio Los Angeles. The Edificio Los Angeles, according to the poster, overlooked the sea and was just two minutes from the centre of the town.

'These apartment are for sale. They are not for letting.'

'But some of them are empty?'

'That is possible; I cannot say.'

'Then who can say?'

Another shrug. 'The Conserja would be the best person. You would have to ask her.'

Lola considered asking for directions but because she was fed up with the girl and her bad manners she took herself back onto the Avenida to see if she could find the Edificio Los Angeles without her assistance. The sea, she could see, was just a few blocks away at the bottom of the wide street with its tall palm trees and that was the direction she took carrying her suitcase in one hand, her bag over her shoulder and the sable coat draped over her free arm because she had already noticed that the weather was too warm to wear it in comfort.

She had tottered no more than six metres in her high heels when three cars pulled up and the drivers started an argument among themselves over who was going to give her a lift. They finally settled matters by tossing a coin and the winner, a young man named Oswaldo in a Simca Elysee, spent the ensuing journey experiencing great difficulty in keeping his eyes on the road. Oswaldo, it turned out, was well acquainted with the Edificio Los Angeles and he dropped Lola at the entrance making a great show of helping her out of the car and at the same time taking in an eyeful of her cleavage. Assured by Lola that she needed no more assistance, Oswaldo pressed a card into her hand with his telephone number written on it.

'Call me anytime night or day,' he grinned before doing a U turn and shooting off back towards the Avenida.

Lola took in her surroundings. What met her eye she immediately found pleasing. The Edificio Los Angeles was on a tranquil part of the seafront set in its own gardens and at the end of a small easily observed service road. On the other side it backed onto a narrow spit of land that separated the town beach from the new yacht marina. In either direction along the shore she saw there were lots of possibilities for quick getaways – footpaths leading here and there over rough land dotted with cabinas and wild tamarisk bushes all of which provided plenty of cover. The marina was only a little way off and consisted of a network of interconnecting boardwalks and jetties, a perfect place to lose any pursuer. Then the Edificio itself, ten storeys high, with what she guessed to be excellent fields of vision from the upper floors. The only drawback she could see was the absence of an outside fire escape, a drawback the residents of the Edificio Los Angeles would find themselves deeply regretting twenty years later when the place caught fire and burned to the ground.

Lola had already spotted the doorway round the side with 'Conserja' stencilled on it in white letters. The feminine form of the noun bothered her immediately – she realised she was going to have to deal with yet another woman.

Sighing to herself she went over and pressed on the bell push. There was silence for a while.

'Who is it?' came a man's gruff voice.

'I wish to speak to the Conserja.' Lola had already noticed the fisheye in the door and the other eye behind it which blinked a number of times as she reached down to fasten a suspender. There followed a crashing back of bolts and the door opened to reveal a man in a vest with his face unshaven and his braces hanging down over his trousers. On his feet, Lola noticed, he wore carpet slippers and the slippers had holes in them through which his dirty yellow toenails peeped. From inside came a waft of stale food and babies' nappies.

'The Conserja is not in,' the man said his eyeballs turning in concentric circles as he looked her up and down.

'That is a pity,' said Lola putting on one of her well-practised damsel in distress pouts. 'I need to speak to her on an urgent matter.'

'I am the Conserja's husband,' the man put in quickly. 'It is possible I may be able to help?'

'Do you think so?' said Lola fluttering her eyelashes in a manner she had copied from various Hollywood actresses. 'You see I am here for a short holiday and I have no place to stay.'

'It is always advisable to make a reservation, Señora, even at this time of year.'

'I know Señor; but a girl on her own is so helpless.'

'You are looking to stay here? Is that the matter you wish to speak to my wife about?'

'There is a problem Señor? You are going to tell me all your apartments are full, is that it?

'No Señora – the problem is that these apartments are not available for letting. They belong to families, rich people from places like Madrid and Valencia, who come here for weekends and holidays. If you have been sent here, someone has given you the wrong information. I am sorry Señora – truly I am.'

Lola's pout turned into a pout of dejection. Her bottom lip started to quiver and tears welled up in her eyes. 'It is not your fault Señor. It is just that I am so weary from walking the streets.' At that she leant forward to pick up her suitcase, exaggerating the movement so that the front of her blouse fell forward before the Conserja's husband's rapidly telescoping eyes.

'Wait,' he said as she turned away, 'I think I have an idea.'

CHAPTER FOUR

A China Doll

In his cold attic office high above the streets of Madrid, Suarez put his elbows on the desk and held his head in his hands. The phone call he had just taken was from Eduardo whose job it was to listen to the whispers from the high passes over the Pyrenees east of Irun. The news Eduardo had brought was bad news, news that had put Suarez off all thoughts of his lunch. It had been reported to Eduardo that El Serpiente, the one they feared most, had left his lair in the mountains and had last been seen heading south. Was Eduardo sure? Yes, Eduardo confirmed he was absolutely sure. His sources were at this moment in the cells pleading for mercy with splints down their finger nails.

Suarez smoothed down the hair at the back of his neck. It was unthinkable but was it possible that El Serpiente had got wind of the Caudillo's trip? If so the finger of suspicion pointed at someone in the Caudillo's circle, someone with a loose tongue or someone with other, more sinister, motives. Yet, El Serpiente or not, Suarez knew the reception he would get if he suggested despatching a regiment of soldiers to go after the Caudillo and bring him back. It would be Señor Suarez putting out frightening stories and not for the first time. It would Señor Suarez who was losing his grip and the excuse for some to start asking questions about how long he should be allowed to remain in his post. On the other hand, if El Serpiente was at large, he could not sit back and do nothing. Then Suarez's thoughts turned to the Capitan from Cordoba and his assistant. Where, he wondered, were the two of them at this moment? He had asked them to check with him as soon as they arrived in Los Tidos but he had heard nothing. It was not a good start.

★ ★ ★

Without the car they had to abandon with a broken front axle and still down a ditch, Capitan Luis Garcia and Ramon Ramon had completed their journey to Los Tidos by the ferrocarril, the little narrow gauge train that ambled slowly through the orange groves and stopped at every station. They spent the time in the company of local farmers on their way to market, many of whom, carried their produce with them including in some cases, geese and chickens. So it was they alighted from the train at the little estacion that marked their destination with feathers still clinging to their clothes.

'So here we are at last,' Garcia announced striking a match on the hat band of Ramon Ramon's fedora and lighting a cigar. 'Hey you,' he then called out as his eyes fell on a consumptive looking character in a railway company uniform sidling off down the platform as the train pulled out. 'We need someone to carry our baggages. See to it pronto.'

The consumptive looking character stared back at him and shrugged. 'There is only me Señor.'

Garcia looked him up and down. 'Then you will have to do. Be quick, hombre, we don't have all day.'

'But it is not my job to carry suitcases Señor,' the consumptive looking man whined.

'It is now,' Garcia snapped back at him, at the same time exhaling a great cloud of black cigar smoke in his face. 'We need to be taken to the Comisaria. Show us the way, and be quick about it.'

'The Comisaria, Señor, that is a kilometre at least and all uphill.'

'The walk will do you good hombre. You look like you need exercise. As you are, you look too weak to pick up your own prick.'

Ten minutes later, as they walked along the steep dusty road between back gardens, the consumptive looking man from the estacion carrying their suitcases was struggling harder and harder to keep up.

'Señores, can we not rest for a few moments please?' he wailed.

'Keep going,' Garcia barked back at him. 'Think of the muscles you are growing.'

★ ★ ★

Lola Martinez hiked up her hemline a few centimetres. This was not just because the staircase in the Edificio Los Angeles was steep and difficult to climb in her tight fitting skirt but also because the Conserja's husband was not far behind struggling with her suitcase and not able to take his eyes off her stocking seams.

'I am sorry that the lift is out of order, Señora.' The Conserja's husband was saying, his breathing becoming more and more laboured – not entirely, she guessed, because of the exertion of carrying her suitcase up ten flights of stairs. The suggestion that Lola could stay in the penthouse suite on the top floor had been entirely his. 'It belongs to this big shot from Lerida,' he explained. 'He only comes here now and then, usually when he's got some new floozy he want show his place off to. We won't see him again this side of Christmas so there is nothing to worry about.'

'You are very kind,' said Lola giving him the kind of look film people describe as smouldering.

'Only my wife must not find out about this Señora,' the man in his vest and with his braces still hanging down over his trousers warned. 'It would get me into trouble with her if she knew I was letting someone stay here.'

'I can be very discreet, Señor. You have no reason to worry.'

The top floor landing was bare of furnishings but Lola noticed an iron ladder set in the wall going up to a trap door in the ceiling. The trap door, she saw, was padlocked.

'Where does that go to?' she asked.

'Only to the roof Señora,' the Conserja's husband replied getting his breath back. 'The water tanks are up there and the winding house for the lift. I am the only one who has a key.'

Opening the door to the penthouse suite, the Conserja's husband stepped aside to let her go in first. Inside she saw it was exactly the kind place a playboy would keep for entertaining his mistresses. Large and richly decorated with lots of gilt and drapes: she had been in many such places and found them as tasteless as the people who owned them.

'What do you think?' said the Conserja's husband putting her suitcase down and handing her the key.

'It will suit me perfectly,' she smouldered on cue. 'I am very grateful and I must think of some way in which I can repay you.' The Conserja's husband blinked. At this point Lola noticed that he blinked with one eye at a time, which gave the impression he was winking. She put it down to some nervous affliction but at the same time she found it amusing.

'I must ask you to excuse me now Señor. I am very tired and I need to get out of these clothes. We will talk again tomorrow and perhaps you can spare the time for us to have a little drink together. Would you like to do that?'

'I would like that very much, Señora.'

'Until tomorrow then.'

'Until tomorrow Señora.'

The Conserja's husband withdrew. Lola waited a few seconds then, choosing a chair that was in full view of the door, she sat down and slowly peeled off her stockings one by one in a manner that would have done credit to the top billing artiste in a striptease show. She heard the shufflings from outside and smiled to herself. She imagined the Conserja's husband out there on the landing crouched down with his eye to the keyhole and his hand down the front of his pants. That was enough for now, she decided and gathering up the stockings she went into the bathroom and closed the door.

★ ★ ★

The desk sergeant in the Comisaria looked up as the two men in fedoras, the big one and the little one, walked in. They looked like something out of a forties' gangster movie, he thought to himself with some amusement, and he wondered why they both had feathers on their clothes. Stranger still, the local station master followed them carrying two suitcases and looking all in. The desk sergeant and the station master were of course acquainted so they briefly exchanged greetings.

'Are you in charge here?' the bigger of the two men demanded abruptly.

The desk sergeant looked round to make sure that it was he who was being addressed. 'Me?' he said pointing a thumb to his chest.

'I am Capitan Luis Garcia from the Guardia Civil in Cordoba. I am here to carry out special orders and I am placing you under my direct command. Do you understand?'

The desk sergeant's jaw dropped. Either this man was a lunatic escaped from the lunatic asylum or it was the boys from trafico getting their own back for the hoax they played on them last April Fool's Day but before he had too long to reflect on this, the big man was talking again. It was the station master he was addressing this time. 'What are you waiting for hombre? 'Do you not have work to be getting back to?'

The station master looked confused. Finally he stammered. 'It is customary, is it not, to give a tip to someone who has carried your baggages such a long way?'

'Tip? You are paid a wage by the railway company, are you not? Be off with you, you scoundrel, or the only tip you will be getting off me is the tip of my boot in the seat of your trousers.'

The station master left as quickly as his thin legs would carry him. The big man who had called himself Capitan Garcia then turned his attention back to the desk sergeant.

'Your first order is to find accommodation for me and my assistant here. Do you think you can do that?'

Joke or not, the desk sergeant was getting tired of Capitan Garcia and his high-handed manners. 'Sure,' he said 'We will find you accommodation. We've got just the place for two people like you.'

The clock outside the Relojeria said twenty to five as Jaime Campello walked by after locking up his workshop. It gave him plenty of time to get to Paco's Rincon to keep the appointment with Pepe Gomez and he ambled along slowly, stopping here and there to look in shop windows. He saw Old Roberto with Emilia coming back from their smallholding and wished them both 'Buenos Tardes'. The shadows were lengthening as he left the houses behind and went across the fields in the opposite direction to the sea so the sun was shining in his eyes as it sank lower and lower in the sky over the mountains.

Paco's Rincon was on the busy road linking the port with the carretera and Campello was taking a short cut across the terraces of almond trees that would be a mass of bloom in early February. Here it was that he came across Felipe the town shepherd drawing water from a stone-walled well while his two dogs kept his small flock of sheep and goats together.

'Buenos Tardes Jaime,' Felipe called out as he filled his stone drinking jug.

'Buenes Tardes Felipe,' Campello replied.

Felipe's eyes followed Campello as he made his way across the terraces. It struck him as odd that the carpenter should be walking in this direction at this particular hour but, like many things Felipe found odd, he kept it to himself.

The corner that gave Paco's Rincon its name was the corner between the Port Road and a little used road that went up the hill towards the Cemetario. It was a large modern flat-roofed building that stood on its own among the almond groves with, on one side, a patch of rough ground where truck drivers could pull off the road. The fact that Paco's Rincon catered for truck drivers was made obvious by the large number of trucks and trailers drawn up outside both day and night, (Paco's Rincon was open twenty-four hours). The eponymous Paco was, like Zamora, an outsider but, unlike Pepe Gomez's neighbour, he had made a huge success of his business and now resided in one of the big haciendas out on the Old Valencia Highway not far from where the Theroux family lived. The work in Paco's Rincon was done by shifts of cooks and waiters who came and went round the clock.

The first thing that struck any visitor to Paco's Rincon was the sheer volume of noise: not just from trucks stopping and starting outside but from the television set that hung off the wall and that was always turned up as loud as it would go, from the shouts of customers and waiters alike and from the clattering of zinc tables and chairs against the tiled terrazzo floor and, put together, all of these echoed a hundred times over off the bare plaster walls. Campello ordered a beer as he walked in and stood at the bar waiting for Pepe Gomez to arrive. By the clock behind the bar he noticed it was five to five. Most of the truckers who came and went were strangers to Campello and similarly with the staff of Paco's Rincon who were, in many cases, men bussed in from small villages out in the country for rumour had it they worked for less money than men from the town. Those among them who did know Campello knew him only as the local carpenter who came out there to do jobs when required but even they had no time to stop and talk for Paco's Rincon was always busy and the pace of work never slackened.

Campello had not seen Pepe Gomez since the afternoon of his humiliation in the street at the hands of the fearful

Conchita and he was struck right away by the change in the little man's appearance. Gone was the spring in his stride and, in its place, there was a leaden dejection so that he shuffled through the door of Paco's Rincon with his shoulders sagged forwards and his chest sunken in. Campello noticed too the red rings round his friend's eyes, a tell tale sign of sleeplessness, and the beaten expression on his face. Gomez ordered two coñacs then drew Campello across to a table in the corner well out of earshot of anyone coming in and standing at the bar.

'Jaime I am sorry to have to ask you to come here but the matter I wish to speak to you about is very confidential.'

Campello nodded to say he understood and Gomez proceeded to pour out his troubles while all the time, he twirled the stem of the coñac glass round in his fat little fingers. Campello listened, mostly in silence, though occasionally he said something to show he was following the gist of what his friend was saying.

The reason why Pepe Gomez had asked for Conchita's hand in marriage in the first place was lost in the murky depths of the past but many in Los Tidos would have said it had a lot to do with the Bar Madrid belonging to Conchita's family and the Bar Madrid also being a place where Pepe Gomez spent much of his time. It was true Conchita and Pepe had been blessed with twelve children, proving that they had not permanently been at odds yet those who knew the Gomez couple well knew that Pepe's habitual laziness had always rankled with Conchita and her tolerance of him had grown less with the years. 'Still, it is not right for a man to be humiliated in front of the street,' Gomez was saying with feeling. 'If there is something to be discussed between husband and wife then it should be said in private.'

Campello nodded again. Campello had no experience of dealing with domestic arguments but what Gomez was saying seemed reasonable enough.

'This has brought me to a decision,' said the little fat man with an air of gravity that didn't seem to go with him. 'I have had enough and I am going to do away with her. I can put up with the woman no more.'

The suddenness with which Gomez made this announcement took Campello completely by surprise. At first, he thought he had not heard correctly then when the full force of what Gomez had said sunk in – he swallowed a whole mouthful of coñac and succumbed to a violent choking fit.

'Do away with her, Pepe?' he said when he had finally composed himself. 'Are you serious? Do you mean what I think you mean?'

'Goodbye Conchita, farewell, my lovely, see you next at Judgement Day.' And to make the point further he drew his finger in a line slowly across his throat.

'You mean to slit her throat?' said Campello who had a tendency to take things literally.

'I am going to poison her,' hissed Gomez thrusting his face forward so his bulging eyeballs were not more than half a metre away from Campello's nose. 'I will see to it that something is put into her food so that she will die writhing in agony. That will teach her to disgrace me. She will pay for the misery she has caused me.'

Campello looked round to check that no-one was looking at them. 'This is madness, Pepe. Have you not thought of the consequences? They will garrotte you, for sure.'

'That is where you are wrong. I have worked out a clever plan and that, my friend, is where you come in.'

★ ★ ★

A hundred kilometres inland from Los Tidos on a pass high up in the mountains a man in motorcycling leathers crouched down beside a boulder with a big knife in his hand that he was using to whittle away at a stick. The man's face was rugged and would have been called handsome by some but for the fact that an ugly scar twisted and turned like a snake from the corner of his eye down to a point just beneath his chin. It was this scar that had given the man the name by which he was known by all and feared by some: El Serpiente – the snake. To Generalisimo Francisco Franco and his followers, he was the most dangerous man in all of Spain. He had eluded all attempts to capture him and he had been at large since he first appeared on the scene as the champion of the poor and oppressed over twenty years before.

Waiting as he was doing now was no problem for El Serpiente; he had been waiting for most of his life dodging from one safe place in the mountains to the next, always keeping one step ahead of the Guardia always coming out of hiding only to despatch one of the despised olive-greens or when it was necessary to put the ambitions of one of Franco's acolytes to rest: Franco, who he would soon be meeting face to face the pity of it being that he was not going to be allowed to put a bullet in him. Yet El Serpiente was the first to see that the assassination of Franco would only result in terrible reprisals and the death of dozens of innocents. It would be a hollow gesture whereas Franco alive would be a powerful bargaining tool when it came to saving the lives of comrades held in Spain's prisons.

A haze over the valley, a trail of wood smoke from

someone's fire and a solitary eagle circling high up in the sky then down below in the pueblo where the lights were starting to come on he noticed a movement in the street. Raising his hand to his eyes to shield out the glare of the setting sun, he picked out the tell tale trail of dust then finally the big black limousine gathering speed as it emerged from between the white washed buildings and started the climb up into the pass. He threw the stick down and slid the knife back into the top of his high sided boot. His eyes were still on the pueblo. Five seconds, ten seconds; the information was correct: there was no flotilla of armed men at the back of the limousine. Franco was all on his own except for a chauffeur. An act of rashness? Or was it as some were saying – that the Old Butcher was losing his grip?

The limousine was changing down a gear to take the first of the hairpin bends and soon it was close enough to make out the profile of the driver and the passenger who sat in the back seat. The driver was an old man, in his sixties, even older maybe. He was taking the hairpin bends cautiously, bringing the steering wheel round by degrees. A glance back at the pueblo where El Serpiente saw there was still no sign of any followers, just a farmer leading a mule out to pasture and children kicking a football round in the street. He moved in closer to the boulder. His wish at this point was to observe and not to be seen. The car was only fifty metres away, picking up speed again as the gradient eased and he could see Franco clearly – a tiny figure sitting in the back seat, so small his pale face only just managed to show over the bottom of the window. Like a china doll, El Serpiente thought to himself: so fragile he could pick it up and crush it in his clenched fist.

The noise of the powerful six cylinder engine died away

as the limousine disappeared over the top of the pass and began its winding decent down the other side. El Serpiente stepped from behind the boulder and went across to where he had hidden his big American Harley-Davidson motorcycle behind some bushes, the metal studs on the bottoms of his boots crunching on the stones. From one of the panniers of the motorcycle he fetched out the rabbit he'd skinned earlier on and with his knife he cut some sprigs of rosemary from a nearby bush, which he used to make a fire. Later, as he watched the meat cooking over the herb-scented flames, his mind went back to Teruel and the brave battle they fought there. He and his father and his brothers, shoulder to shoulder in the freezing trenches until their ammunition ran out. Then Franco's Moros came and tore down their white flag of surrender with cries of laughter and derision before setting on their company and butchering them – first with the rifle then with the bayonet and the knife. The scar he now carried on his face was from one of those blades. For sure, they had left him for dead on the field of Teruel and his hate for Franco and all his works had grown deeper and deeper from that terrible day. Then after the battle he and his few surviving comrades made their way back to their own lines helped by the poor and desperate they met in every small village along the way who gave them food and shelter and urged them to fight on. Finally they became a unit again though some of them had no rifles. On they trudged, always retreating, always waiting for orders to stand fast that never came. Every day brought fresh horrors, not just the cold and rain but German Stuka bombers that came from the sky without warning leaving dead and wounded everywhere, and against which they had no defence. Here on the long march back to the French frontier El

Serpiente witnessed women in tears clutching onto dead babies and the wounded from the hospitals crawling along on their hands and knees. He tried to help some of them then gave up, using the justification it would be better to save himself so he could come back one day and exact revenge for all the bloodshed he had seen. But what he did not know back then was he would still be carrying on his one man fight against the fascist scourge almost a quarter of a century later.

El Serpiente took out his knife to cut off a piece of rabbit meat to see if it was cooked. One day Spain would wake up to better times, he told himself. He only hoped he would live to see it.

★ ★ ★

It was almost dark when Campello got back to the Villa Verde. The bats were out high above the alleyways and there was a fragrance in the air from the mimosas and the bougainvilleas still in bloom. Campello saw the house was empty as he let himself in. There was no sign anywhere of Uncle Pablo or of Waldorf and weary from the walk to Paco's Rincon and back and from all Pepe Gomez's talk, Campello flopped down in a soft chair with a bottle of beer from the fridge. It was almost seven o' clock he noticed and he supposed Uncle Pablo had gone out already. He had heard strange rumours about goings on involving Uncle Pablo in the bars down by the marina and he knew in his heart that no good would come of it. Waldorf he was less sure about for the dog had now been missing for a few days. This in itself was not unusual, for Waldorf being the wayward creature that he was, frequently went missing. The explanation, usually, was that he had detected some bitch on heat or a new source of scavenging had suddenly manifested itself – like Vilas putting out a tub of blood and guts at the back of his matadero or a hole appearing in one of the sheds in the fish market where they kept the rotten fish before sending them to the factory where they made them into fertiliser.

Waldorf had in fact visited the Villa Verde only quarter of an hour earlier and just as Uncle Pablo was leaving. Sadly, vagrancy was not proving as satisfactory an existence to Waldorf as he had hoped. The pickings round the Old Town proved to be abnormally lean and hunger was gnawing at his stomach, presenting him with a tricky dilemma: whether to go back to the Villa Verde where there was usually food put down for him at this hour and run the risk of being collared and put in a bath of soapy water again; or whether to steer clear of further such insults to his dignity and suffer the pains of starvation. In the end his craving for food won the day and so, slinking up narrow alleyways he made his way back to the place that was loosely his home.

Like all dogs Waldorf relied more on his senses of scent and hearing than on his eyesight hence the first indicator he had of someone standing outside the Villa Verde was the sound of a door slamming and a key turning in a lock. Waldorf froze. The thought immediately passed through his mind that this could be the younger Campello who, though his was the hand that put food down, he temporarily associated with soap and scrubbing brushes. Raising his gnarled snout, he sniffed the air. A familiar smell of mothballs and absenta reached his olfactory glands and, reassured that this was Uncle Pablo with whom he coexisted peacefully, Waldorf padded a few places forward.

Why Waldorf took it into his flea-bitten head to follow

Uncle Pablo again has no rational explanation. Food, if there was any, would have been put down for him in the back yard or, if it hadn't the second best hope was that something had been left out in the kitchen that he could steal. Yet Waldorf still chose to shadow the Old Man as he had done on the Night of the New Jumilla, the only explanation for which was that the wily dog's intention was simply to use Uncle Pablo to pilot him back to Zamora's cat with whom he still had a score to settle. On the other hand, Waldorf was a capricious creature and there was probably little more to his action than a momentary flight of fancy.

★ ★ ★

That night in the cells beneath the Comisaria a small voice piped up.

'Capitan Garcia, I think we may be in trouble over this. We can be of no help to the Caudillo while we are locked up in here.'

Shortly after, another voice replied. 'Shut up you idiot and let me get some sleep.'

CHAPTER FIVE

The Poisoning of the Paella

The plan to do away with Conchita that Pepe Gomez had thought up during his long sleepless nights, the plan he had told Jaime Campello about in Paco's Rincon, was this:

Every year on the occasion of their wedding anniversary, Conchita insisted on being taken to the best hotel in town, the Hotel Bahia, and treated to a plate of the finest paella prepared in the way that only Casares, the famous chef at the Hotel Bahia, knew how. At these annual events Pepe Gomez was required to wear his best suit, the one he normally reserved for weddings and funerals, and to polish his shoes and plaster his hair down with hair oil with a parting along the centre. Understandably the sight of the two of them setting off together in a taxi had become an occasion for great merriment and fun-poking in the Street of Two Eyes but Conchita stayed aloof from it all. On this night of all nights she was the grandest of ladies. She even took a trip to Valencia beforehand to buy herself a new frock and a new pair of shoes. Only Pepe saw that they were being ridiculed: yet this year, this celebration that he detested so much, presented him with the opportunity he was looking for. If poison happened to find its way into Conchita's paella how possibly could he be held to blame? It would be put down to contamination of the food at the Hotel Bahia and, after the fuss had died down, that would be that. He, Pepe Gomez, would be free to live his life as he pleased and, the more he thought about it, the more appealing the idea became.

The night of Conchita and Pepe Gomez's wedding anniversary was the night immediately after Pepe Gomez's meeting with Jaime Campello at Paco's Rincon so preparations for the poisoning of Conchita had to be made in a hurry, however, the problem of who was to sneak into the kitchens of the Hotel Bahia and put poison into the paella was one that Pepe Gomez had already resolved.

'You,' he said to Jaime Campello as they sat together in Paco's Rincon amidst all the clamour and comings and goings.

'Me?' Campello looked dumbfounded. 'Why me?'

'The answer is simple,' Gomez replied. 'You and I are the only ones who know about this and, since I will be sitting at the table with Conchita, that only leaves you to go round to the kitchens and do what is required.' Then with a crafty look in his eye he added. 'Think of my honour Jaime. If you let me down in this then the only course left open to me will be to take my own life.'

'I am thinking of the garrotte around my neck. Thank you very much.'

'But think how you would be tormented if my suicide was on your conscience for the rest of your life. Think what guilt you would feel.'

So it came to pass that on the morning of Pepe Gomez's wedding anniversary celebration the little man and Jaime Campello found themselves in a dingy part of town standing on the doorstep of Robles the Ratcatcher.

'I'm closed,' snarled Robles catching sight of the two of them out of the corner of one of his narrow reptilian eyes. Robles was sitting at a bench repairing a trap. All around him in his dungeon-like establishment were snares and devices of every shape and size; some were stacked high in corners, others were lining the dusty shelves. Traps even hung off hooks from the ceiling and, up one end of the vast cavernous workshop, Campello noticed a gibbet line strung out from which several huge dead and desiccated specimens of rat hung by their tails. He shuddered. He had heard the stories that went round Los Tidos of how Robles used the rats he caught in his estofadas.

Gomez came to the point of their visit straight away. 'I wish to purchase some poison from you,' he said.

Robles looked at him sternly. 'I'm closed, didn't you hear me? What do you want poison for anyway?'

'To poison rats of course.'

'Poison's no good,' said Robles going back to his work. 'Rats are clever creatures. They don't always take poison that's put down for them. Traps are best when it comes to rats. Take my word for it. I know my own trade.'

'This is a big rat,' said Gomez. 'A trap would be too small.'

Robles looked up. Campello could tell his professional interest had been aroused. 'Big, you say? How big is big?'

'This big at least,' said Gomez holding up his hands.

Robles whistled. 'Here in Los Tidos?'

'In my back yard.'

Robles raised his crusty eyebrows. 'I would like to see this rat,' he said.

'Can't you just sell me the poison?'

A sour look spread across the ratcatcher's tallow-coloured

face and Campello could tell he had taken offence. There was a danger, he feared, that he would now go and denounce them to the police but the moment seemed to pass and Robles got up from his work bench, took a key out of his waistcoat pocket and shuffled across to a cupboard at the far end of the workshop.

'Here,' he said unlocking the door of the cupboard and bringing out a little bottle with a skull and crossbones label on it and with a sinister iridescent greenish coloured liquid inside.

'This is poison?' Gomez enquired taking the bottle off him and examining it.

'The best,' said Robles with an unpleasant grin that showed off his blackened and rotting teeth. 'One lick of this and they run round in circles, screaming before biting off their own tails and dropping down dead on the floor. It's horrible to watch I can assure you.'

'I'll take it,' said Gomez without hesitation. 'How much?'

'One mil pesetas.'

'One mil pesetas! What's in this stuff, drops of gold?'

'Take it or leave it. I told you it's the best.'

'Ok, I'll take it', Gomez grumbled. 'Can you lend me five hundred pesetas Jaime?'

Campello brought out his wallet and between the two of them, they finally managed to make up the money. Campello noticed however the cunning look on Robles's face as he took the notes off them and stuffed them in his waistcoat pocket.

★ ★ ★

Downtown and far away from the premises of Robles the Ratcatcher, Lola Martinez woke up late in the luxurious penthouse suite of the Edificio Los Angeles where she had spent a restful night with only the gentle noise of the sea lapping on the shore outside. She ran a bath in the ostentatious bathroom with its gold plated taps and soaked in the bubbles for half an hour. After her bath, she breakfasted on black coffee and some rye crisp bread she found in a cupboard. She made a mental note to add milk and fresh fruit to the list of provisions she needed to get in.

Still in her bathrobe, she then wandered out onto the balcony to take in the view. Today was the day Franco was due to arrive in Los Tidos and today was the day of her first contact with the feared and mysterious El Serpiente. So far El Serpiente had acted in the way she'd been told to expect. A message with a telephone number and a time to ring had been left at the pension in Girona. Nothing else, just an instruction to make the call at five o'clock tonight.

From the balcony Lola could see the empty town beach over to her right and the long shoreline of the fabulous Bahia de Los Tidos going off into the distance. At that moment, however, a movement down in the gardens beneath caught her eye. A dumpy looking woman was leaving the apartment block and making her way along a path with empty shopping bags in both of her hands. The Conserja, she guessed, going to the market meaning the Conserja's husband would be all on his own. Time, she said to herself, to recruit a little unpaid help.

The penthouse suite had its own telephone and ten minutes later Lola Martinez was standing by it dressed in a long black negligee through which it was possible to see she wore nothing underneath. The two digit number for the Conserja's flat was written on the dial of the phone and she waited a few seconds for the line to ring out and the familiar voice to answer.

'Coffee time,' she said chirpily.

★ ★ ★

In his office in Madrid, Suarez was also standing by the telephone, staring at it and willing it to ring. The two men from Cordoba had still failed to make contact with him and the furrows in Suarez's brow were getting deeper by the minute. What was going on down there in Los Tidos? Had the Generalisimo arrived and, if so, was he safe? There was no news of El Serpiente either and this bothered Suarez even more. It was like a conspiracy of silence all around him and he didn't like it one bit. Finally his nerve broke. He picked up the handset and spoke sharply to the telefonista on the floor beneath. 'Get me the Chief of Police in Los Tidos and do it quick.'

★ ★ ★

It was quarter past ten when Campello got back to the Villa Verde with the bottle of rat poison stuffed inside his shirt. He had parted company with Pepe Gomez by the Church and he noticed that, as the little man walked away, the prospect of being rid of Conchita had already put some of the spring back in his stride.

Hurrying, so as not to run into Father Miguel and give himself away by a guilty look on his face, Campello had already made the decision not to go to work that day. Thanks to Pepe Gomez, he felt he had too much on his mind to give the new doors for the Ayuntamiento the attention they needed.

Checking first of all to see Uncle Pablo was still asleep, which he was, Campello went through to the white tiled bathroom to where the medicine chest was kept. The medicine chest, he'd already decided would be the best place to keep the bottle of poison until the time came for using it. It contained many other small bottles hence here it would not appear conspicuous. As he was making a space among the various ointments and cures, however his eyes fell on a another bottle: one containing a herbal emetic, which if he recalled correctly, had particularly devastating effects and it was this that gave him an idea. What if, instead of putting rat poison in Conchita's paella he substituted the emetic instead? True Conchita would be spending many hours in the bathroom but that had to be infinitely better than death preceded by the kind of cruel convulsions that Robles had described and, more importantly he, Campello, would not be responsible for her murder. Better still, Pepe Gomez would conclude that the poison Robles had given him was not strong enough and none of the blame for Conchita's survival would attach to him Jaime Campello. The more Campello thought about it, the more it seemed like a good way of getting off the hook. It was a deception, yes, but, of the choices facing the young carpenter at that moment, it seemed by far the most preferable. So feeling much happier about things Jaime Campello fastened up the medicine chest and slipped the bottle of emetic into his trouser pocket.

★ ★ ★

Down in the Comisaria at almost precisely the same moment, the Chief of Police put the phone down. The Chief of Police, a man named Flores, was in fact the Acting Chief of Police: the Chief of Police himself had been suspended from duty two months back following the denouncement of several senior officers over a matter of public morals in which four girls from

Fat Fatima's, champagne and fireworks had been involved.

Flores, being mindful of his temporary position, was wary of all telephone calls from higher authority but this call had not been from Valencia where most higher authority resided but Madrid, which was stratospheric as far as Flores was concerned.

Looking decidedly white round the gills, he picked up the phone again, this time to dial an internal number that connected him with the officer in charge of the cells.

'Does the name Capitan Luis Garcia ring any bells?' he asked.

★ ★ ★

The bell that was ringing on the top floor of the Edificio Los Angeles was not a bell in anyone's head but the bell to the penthouse suite. The person pushing it was none other than the Conserja's husband dressed, not as he had been the day before when he had first greeted Lola Martinez, but in a shirt of many colours, a pair of tight fitting trousers and zip sided boots with Cuban heels. To complete the effect his hair was slicked back like that of a pimp and his freshly shaven face was liberally splashed with a potent smelling aftershave lotion. One eye blinked like a camera shutter as Lola opened the door in her long black negligee.

'I must apologise for appearing before you in my lingerie,' she said as she stepped aside to make way for him. 'I washed some of my things this morning and it was not until I had invited you to come up that I realised I had nothing to put on.'

The Conserja's husband blinked. This time it was the other eye.

'You have been so kind to me Señor and yet I find I have another little favour to ask of you. I hope you are not going to think me too presumptuous.'

The Conserja's husband did not speak. His concentration was fixed on the folds of diaphanous black lace in front of him.

'I need to buy food – fruit, vegetables, groceries, fresh fish. There is nothing in this apartment for me to eat.'

'That is no problem Señora. There is a supermercado just across the road.'

'But you forget Señor I have no clothes to wear. I cannot go out onto the street looking like this.'

'You would like me to go to the supermercado for you? Is that it?'

'Your kindness knows no bounds Señor but I feel ashamed that I have to keep taking advantage of you.'

'It is no trouble to go to the supermercado. It will only take five minutes.'

'You are sure?'

'Yes, I am sure,' he said, still ogling. 'Just tell me what you want and I will bring it straightaway.'

'I have made a little list,' said Lola handing him a sheet of paper on which she had written the vast inventory of provisions she needed to keep herself, El Serpiente and their hostage for several days. She noticed the Conserja's husband's jaw drop as he saw the length of it. 'If it is too much for you then you must say.'

'No Señora, it is ok. I will manage. But it does seem rather a lot, if you don't mind me saying.'

'There, I am putting on you, please accept my apologies Señor. I will wait for my clothes to dry and go to the supermercado myself later on.'

'No, it is ok, I assure you. I am more than happy to do this for you.'

Her eyes filled with a look of admiration that was manufactured on film sets in Hollywood. 'You are so capable, Señor. I like a man who can take care of a woman. And now I am going to reward you by giving you what you came up here for.'

The Conserja's husband looked at her and both his eyes blinked together. 'What is that Señora?'

'A cup of coffee of course. I have kept you waiting so long I can see you had completely forgotten.'

★ ★ ★

The phone ringing in the Villa Verde woke Campello from the siesta he had decided to take in the shade of the fig tree out in the garden. He looked at the clock as he walked through into the house and saw that it was ten past three.

'Jaime.' It was Pepe Gomez's voice. 'I just rang you to wish you good luck tonight. Conchita is down at the hairdressers having her hair done. Think of her later, eh? Running round in circles, screaming her head off, chasing her own tail. Tomorrow, Amigo, I will be a free man celebrating the start of a new life. You and I will have a night on the town.'

★ ★ ★

Little celebrating however was going on down in the Comisaria where Capitan Garcia freshly released from the cells with his cheap chalk stripe suit crumpled up from a night spent sleeping on a hard wooden bench had put the entire local police force on parade. They stood rigidly to attention while he paced up and down in front of them, pausing in his chastisement only to fix one or other of them with a withering glare. Ramon Ramon for his part hung about in the background fidgeting with his fingers and shifting his weight from one foot to the other.

'So,' Garcia growled. 'You have not exactly made an auspicious start with the assistance and back up you were supposed to be providing me with. Now as a result of your collective stupidity each one of you faces an uphill struggle to redeem himself in my eyes. Is that understood?

There was a general sheepish mumbling of 'Si Capitan' all around the assembled company while Garcia bounced up and down on his heels.

'And if anyone steps out of line from here on, the very least he can expect is a twenty-five year posting to the filthiest fly infested shit hole in the Sahara. Is that understood too?'

'Si Capitan.'

'Right,' said Garcia flexing his gold teeth. 'Now we are all clear where we stand let's get down to business. You,' he said to Flores. 'Tell me where the Hotel Bahia is situated.'

'A little way out of town Capitan – a place in its own grounds not far from the carretera.'

'Excellent. Then we shall throw a cordon round it and stop anyone who tries to enter. What is it, hombre?'

Flores was indicating that he wished to speak. 'The Hotel Bahia is private property Capitan and the owner is a marquis who has many connections. We shall have to give a reason for stopping people from entering. Otherwise we shall never hear the last of it.'

'Reason did you say? Is not the life of the Caudillo himself reason enough?'

'The Caudillo, Capitan? I am sorry but what has the Caudillo got to do with the Hotel Bahia?'

'He is staying there tonight, that's what. He is travelling incognito and it is our job to protect him. And if he comes to any harm in your Marquis's hotel then I for one would not wish to be in his shoes. The only connections he will have will be the ones from the electric supply attached to his bollocks.'

There was a general gasp of astonishment around the room. 'Capitan Garcia,' Ramon Ramon piped up. 'I thought the Caudillo's presence here was meant to be a secret. You have let the cat out of the bag, so to speak.'

'Silence. I will ask for your opinions when I want them. I am the man in charge here. In the best traditions of the Guardia Civil I must make my own judgements and take responsibility. Never mind what people in Madrid think. Look at what fate has befallen President Kennedy. Do we want the same thing happening here in Los Tidos?'

'Of course not Capitan Garcia. I am sorry I interrupted.'

'Good.' Garcia straightened himself and transferred his glare back onto the line of policemen. 'Then we all know what we are doing hombres. Road blocks at strategic points in place by eighteen hundred hours; the Hotel Bahia cordoned off and isolated; any suspicious looking characters arrested on sight and thrown into the cells. Any questions?'

'Capitan.' It was Flores again. 'If the Hotel Bahia is to be isolated then how will the Caudillo be able to get in when he arrives?'

Garcia took a long deep breath. 'I would never insult an officer in front of his own men but believe me I am sorely tempted to do so by the stupidity of your question. How does the Caudillo get into the Hotel Bahia when he arrives?

Because your men will stand back and let him in, that is how. I hope that they will also remember to come to attention and salute him as they do.'

'But if the Caudillo is travelling incognito Capitan how will we know him?'

'That is a fair point Capitan Garcia,' Ramon Ramon agreed.

'Silence.'

Flores was still speaking however. 'If we turned the Caudillo away by mistake then in my opinion we really would be asking for trouble. I cannot see him being very pleased.'

There was a general muttering of agreement around the room.

'Silence. Silence. All of you. This is a matter of state security not some mothers' meeting down in the market place.'

Garcia paced up and down while the line of eyeballs followed him first one way then back the other. Finally he spoke.

'I am going to give you a lesson on how to recognise the Caudillo hombres. I hope everyone is listening carefully. The first thing you must do is put your hand in your pocket and take out a coin. If you then look at the head on the coin and compare it with the person you are looking at and if you see they are the same then the person you are looking at is the Caudillo. Is that simple enough for you? Surely I don't have to provide you with a set of his fingerprints? What more famous face is there than the face of the Generalisimo Franco?'

Garcia glared at them. No-one replied.

'Good. Now I have some special instructions concerning a most dangerous criminal who I have just been told about by the authorities in Madrid and who has designs on the Caudillo. It is likely he is heading in this direction and, if so hombres, it will be our job to intercept him. Fortunately he is easily recognisable because he has a scar on his face. If you see this man then you must arrest him immediately. If he attempts to resist then you have my personal authority to shoot him.'

'Capitan,' Flores again. 'There are many men with scars on their faces. How will we tell this criminal of yours from ordinary law abiding citizens going about their business?'

'The Chief is right,' another voice piped up 'I can think of ten men straight away who carry scars on their faces, old Pedro Vasquez for one. A boat hook, wasn't it? Back in fifty-six, if I remember correctly. It ripped his cheek open right to the bone.'

'And Carlos Lunes,' put in a third. 'It was Vilas's razor in his case.'

'Vilas the Butcher?'

'No his brother Vilas the Barber. With the number of throats he's slit perhaps he should be called Vilas the Butcher too.'

'Silence,' Garcia yelled in their faces. 'I don't believe my ears. Here we are facing a threat on the life of the Caudillo and all you people can do is gossip like a lot of old women standing in the queue outside the panaderia. Sharpen yourselves up hombres; otherwise I will be thinking that a stinking shit hole in the middle of the Sahara with only a camel for company is too good for you.'

'Capitan Garcia,' this time it was Ramon Ramon who spoke. 'If I was a dangerous criminal with an easily recognisable scar on my face I would grow a beard.'

'It is now sixteen hundred hours,' Garcia shook his head

in exasperation. 'There is a crisis going on here on the doorstep and all we have done so far is talk. Ok, if we have to, we will arrest every man who has a beard. Now tell me what's wrong with that.'

'It is the Feast of the Two Virgins soon,' Flores replied. 'In line with tradition those who are to take the parts of the Moors in the festivities are all growing beards. There must be around fifty of them in the town.'

'Then we will arrest them all!' Garcia screamed. 'All men with scars, all men with beards, all men pretending to be Moors, all of them will go to the cells.'

★ ★ ★

Back at the Edificio Los Angeles, the Conserja's husband staggered up the ten flights of steps carrying several plastic bags filled with shopping to where Lola Martinez was waiting for him on the top floor. He had had to make the trip to the supermarket and back twice, so large was the list that she had given to him, though little did he know that what he was bringing was provisions not just for the delectable lady herself but for the holding of none other than Generalisimo Francisco Franco as a hostage for several days. As far as the Conserja's husband was concerned the lady who had become the centre of his attentions simply had what appeared to be a very large appetite.

'Thank you,' Lola cooed as he finished his second trip, the multi-coloured shirt soaked in sweat and his legs bending at the knees inside the tightly fitting trousers. Lola was still in her filmy negligee, still looking cool and fresh and still smiling radiantly. 'I will get you a cold drink,' she said. 'Come and sit

out on the balcony with me and take the weight off your feet.'
The Conserja's husband made no reply. He was still gulping
down great lung-fulls of air.

'You are so willing and sweet,' Lola continued smoothly,
as she poured two glasses of the freshly pressed orange juice
that he had just fetched from the supermercado into which
she had added several cubes of ice. 'Perhaps now we know one
another better you will permit me a little intimacy.'

'Intimacy Señora?' The conserja's husband's eyelids went
into overdrive despite his state of exhaustion.

'Your name Señor?'

'My name Señora?'

'Yes, I wish to know your name, so I can use it instead of
addressing you as 'Señor' every time I speak to you. You must
tell me, however, if you feel I am being over-familiar.'

'My name is Ernesto.'

'Ernesto, I like Ernesto. If I call you Ernesto then you must
call me Beatriz. Ernesto, you notice there is one problem with
this balcony.'

'A problem, Señora?'

'Yes you see the sun goes off it in the afternoons and I am
unable to sunbathe.'

The conserja's husband looked bemused at the direction
the conversation seemed to be taking. 'It is the construction
of the building. Most people want to look at the sea so the
balconies face that way.'

'I know Ernesto but that does not help me if I want to
sunbathe.'

'There is the beach. You can sunbathe there. As you can
see it is only a short distance.'

'Ernesto, I am guilty of not explaining myself properly. You are a man of the world, I think. You are not hidebound by stupid narrow-minded views of what a woman can or cannot do with her body?' The blinks were coming rapidly again, staccato-fashion, one eye then the other. 'When I sunbathe Ernesto I like to take all my clothes off.'

'All?'

'That's right. I do not like to see white lines on my body. Speaking as a man of the world would you not agree that white lines on a woman's body spoils her appearance when she is naked?'

'Oh yes.'

'But if I went onto your beach out there and took off all my clothes then some ugly bitch of a woman would soon be along tut-tutting and calling for the police.'

'I can see that Señora … er … Beatriz.'

'You would not want me arrested Ernesto?'

'Of course not.'

'Then you can give me the key to the roof.'

'The roof!'

'Yes Ernesto, there are only the water tanks and the workings for the lift up there, you told me so yourself. The sun must shine all day on the roof. What is it Ernesto? I can see you look troubled. Tell me what is going through your poor little head.'

'Residents are not permitted on the roof. It is one of the rules. That is why I always have to keep it locked.'

'But I am not a resident, Ernesto. I have no official status here. As far as the world is concerned I do not exist.'

'But…'

'But Ernesto – your poor head is full of little buts. Don't fret so much. You would like to see my body the same colour all over would you not?'

The Conserja's husband did not answer. His mouth opened and shut but no words came out.

'There then that is settled. Give me the key and stop worrying. What we will have to do, is see if we can think up some little treats to help you to relax.'

★ ★ ★

Just at that time the Conserja's husband was not the only one beset with deep worries. In Madrid Suarez was pacing the floor of his office not reassured in the slightest by the telephone conversation he had just had with the Capitan from Cordoba who along with his assistant had spent the night in the cells for reasons that were not altogether clear. There was now more than an inkling of suspicion creeping into Suarez's mind that something was seriously amiss and he was feeling a compulsion to get to the bottom of it quickly.

Taking a key from a small bunch he kept in his pocket, he unlocked the top drawer of his desk. There, where it had been for the last fifteen years, was the revolver he had carried during the years in North Africa and all through the war of '36 to '39. He took it out and felt the weight in his hand, testing, at the same time the freedom of its moving parts. Never had he anticipated having to use it again or see it as anything except a souvenir of the past yet he judged the time had now come. Foremost in his thoughts was El Serpiente and where he might be. The worst fear of all – that he might be closing in on the Caudillo – was starting to move up on Suarez's scale of probabilities.

★ ★ ★

At that moment, however, the man who had spent the greater part of his life continuing the fight against Franco was pushing his big motorbike along a windswept mountain road with only the ravens and rock thrushes for company. He was cursing his fortune because of the puncture he had got from running his front wheel over a mule shoe and he was reflecting wryly on why such objects were supposed to be good luck.

After witnessing Franco's passage, he had spent the night wrapped up in a blanket on a cold mountainside although the cold itself did not bother him. He had spent many such nights on the highest ridges of the Pyrenees in the snows of winter, moving from one safe place to another. Comfort indeed had featured little in his life and, what he had never had, he did not miss.

Ahead of him the road stretched like a thin grey ribbon across the barren landscape. There were no trees up here on the plateau; just a few thorn bushes that grew no higher than a man's knee and overhead an enormous overcast sky that carried with it the threat of rain. El Serpiente pushed on then finally in the distance, he saw a few houses that marked a pueblo: a scattering of small buildings and tilled fields. He glanced at his watch – it was half past four in the afternoon – the chance was that if he could get the puncture mended here he might still make Los Tidos by nightfall. On he went but despite his great strength the bike seemed to grow heavier with every stride then, as he neared the pueblo, he pulled the bandana he wore round his neck up round his face. He was taking no chances. No-one in this one-street place would be getting a reward off the Guardia for recognising El Serpiente and turning him in.

Lola Martinez, now dressed in blue jeans and a matching denim shirt, had already sized up the roof top of the Edificio Los Angeles as ideal for her purposes. It offered fields of vision in every direction – a place from which she could see through her binoculars every face that came and went along the road, every man woman and child who walked up and down the Avenida and in and out of the yacht marina. Ernesto the Conserja's husband, had made a hasty retreat some time ago. The sight of his wife, the Conserja, returning from her sister's had sent him scuttling down the ten flights of steps to turn his attentions to watering the gardens, which was what he was supposed to be doing at this time of day instead of drooling over the delightful Señora Beatriz, the existence of whom, his wife was still ignorant.

The binoculars were a pair she had taken from their rightful owner many years ago. They were of East German make and excellent quality and, to prove the point, half way up the Avenida she could make out the face of Oswaldo the young man who had given her the lift the day before; then panning down a hundred metres or so, she spotted the girl with the fat behind from the letting agents, locking up the shop and sneaking off work early.

The Old Town up on the hill was directly in front of Lola as she stood on the roof top: the colours of the ancient red tiles, the purple bougainvilleas and blue dome of the Church on the summit were accentuated by the light of the late afternoon sun. She glanced at her watch – it was just before five; time she realised, to make an important telephone call.

Letting herself down the iron rung ladder, Lola took care to fasten the padlock holding the trapdoor in place. Back in the penthouse suite she closed the door and made sure that it too was securely locked. As an extra precaution she left the key in the key hole so Ernesto would get an eyeful of nothing if he should happen to venture upstairs on one of his peeping expeditions.

The number she had been given was prefixed with a San Sebastian dialling code. It rang out for a long time though she guessed it belonged to a public telephone out on a street somewhere. Finally a voice answered, deep and sounding disguised.

'Our mutual friend sends his apologies Señora.'

'For what reason?'

'He has been unavoidably delayed. He will now meet you at eight tomorrow evening. You are to suggest the place.'

Lola clicked her tongue. Delayed, she did not believe it. 'Very well,' she said. 'Tell our friend that the Avenida, which is the main street here, has a park in the middle with a fountain. I will meet him there. Tell him too the one we are interested in is only staying in this place for a few days so we cannot afford any more delays.'

After she put the phone down Lola went out onto the balcony and stood for a while gazing out at the sea. Delayed: the man who was to be her accomplice in this enterprise, the man who was feared the length and breadth of Spain, could not even manage to turn up on time. Delayed by some chica's pussy, she guessed. It again confirmed the lesson about men's weaknesses she learned a long time ago.

★ ★ ★

El Serpiente thanked the patron of the garage for letting him use the phone in his office to make the call to San Sebastian and the young man to whom Lola Martinez spoke a little while later. The puncture was mended but as he went to hand over the pesetas, the garage man waved him away.

'De nada, Señor, it is nothing – just a tyre plug, some rubber solution and two minutes of my time. What are such things between true lovers of the Harley Davidson motor cycle. No, on your way, Señor. Have a good journey and I hope to see you again on your return.'

El Serpiente thanked him again. 'We don't get many travellers through here,' the man continued to talk while wiping his hands on an oily rag. 'But there's a story going round the pueblo that General Franco himself came down the road last night in a big black shiny car. What do you make of that?'

'Some men say they have seen little green men in flying saucers,' El Serpiente replied getting on the big motorcycle and wrapping the bandana even more tightly around his face. 'Perhaps whoever started this story would be advised to drink a little less coñac.'

'That's just what I said,' the garage man roared with laughter. 'General Franco is never seen without a whole battalion of soldiers at his heels let alone drive through a rat hole like this.'

★ ✹ ⋏

As night began to fall on Los Tidos, Jaime Campello, his heart filled with trepidation, set off from the Villa Verde in the direction of the Hotel Bahia. Deciding against walking along the road he took the pathways he knew across terraced fields again except this time he went in the opposite direction to Paco's Rincon because the Hotel Bahia lay on the south side of town where the carretera cuts through wooded hillsides and comes down close to the coast. He was so lost in his own thoughts that he did not notice the grey shape slinking along in the shadows behind him.

★ ★ ★

Waldorf's excursion to the waterfront the previous night had left him in no doubt where the best pickings in Los Tidos were to be had. Trailing in Uncle Pablo's wake, he had come to a land of plenty where the garbage at the back of restaurants frequented by foreigners contained all manner of delicacies to tempt a dog's palate. The customers of these places, Waldorf quickly discovered, didn't chew every last bit of flesh and gristle off their bones the way the people in the Old Town did, nor did they put them in the stewpot for several days afterwards. On the contrary, they left whole chuletas and filetes on their plates and these chuletas and filetes found their away into the garbage where Waldorf in his state of semi-starvation had gorged himself on such delights for several hours – taking time out only to chase off other stray dogs that hung round and didn't seem to know their place. Soon, though, these dogs from the waterfront, began to develop a healthy respect for Waldorf and his bite and they learned to keep a safe distance until the dog who had come from the Old Town had had his fill.

Waldorf's mind, being firmly focused as it was on filling his stomach and extending his territory, soon made the connection between following the human inhabitants of the Villa Verde and being led to places that were to his liking. So it was that, with his tongue lolling out, his fetid breath putrefying the air and a gleam in his matted eyes, that Waldorf tagged onto Jaime Campello that fateful evening – a decision, innocent though it seemed, that was to have dreadful and far-reaching consequences, as we shall soon see.

Walking along the ancient stone walled terraces that kept to the contours of the hill on which Los Tidos stood, Campello with Waldorf trailing at his rear completed the half circle round the back of the town before he took a path that started to descend. Over to his right, flocks of goldfinches flew up from the seed heads of thistles and wild flowers while in the distance beyond the track of the ferrocaril he noticed that the traffic on the carretera had come to a standstill though why this should be he could not guess. He knew nothing, of course, of the secret visit of Generalisimo Franco or of Capitan Luis Garcia and his road blocks. At that moment Campello had in fact only one thing on his mind and that was the tiny bottle of emetic secreted in his trouser pocket.

The terrain he crossed was becoming more and more rugged and soon he left the terraces behind and followed a winding path across a secluded valley where any signs of cultivation had long since vanished and where only a few tumble-down buildings here and there offered any clue to what had gone on in the past. A hoopoe flew up in front of him, its black and white plumage showing up in the fading light like a giant moth, then came the sound of its strange echoing call. He crossed a dried up stream bed and then climbed the far side of the valley where he noticed the smell of thyme and lavender wafting up as his trousers caught against the bushes and then the smell of pine trees as he approached a wood at the top.

When he reached the trees, he paused to look back. Behind was the deserted valley and, beyond, the town where the sun still shone brilliantly on the blue-tiled dome of the Church. He saw Felipe with his flock in the distance and the lights of cars and lorries on the Port Road where there also seemed to be a hold up. But what he did not notice in the deep shadows a few metres away was the grey vulpine shape, skulking behind a strawberry tree. When Campello moved off again, the grey vulpine shape followed.

★ ★ ★

The fading of the light was beginning to bother El Serpiente as he turned the Harley Davidson along a dirt road that, if his guess was right, would take him in the direction he wished to go in. He was keen to reach Los Tidos by nightfall where there was still much work to be done. The chica from Barcelona was there already and, though she came with good credentials, it had troubled him from the start that kidnapping Franco might be out of her league. The thought was going through his head, as it had done several times, that he would have been better putting a bullet in Franco back at the pass. But the chica had got other ideas on what they could do with the Old Butcher once they got him in their hands and, since this was her show not his, he had decided to let her get on with it. In any case, if she did fuck up, he would be there to pick up the pieces. But for now, he decided, he would just carry out orders. If there was a time for improvisation it would be later.

The dirt road looked little used. There were no tyre tracks and deep ruts cut across the surface where rain had washed out the white clayey soil. The ruts became harder to see as the light became less and in the end he was forced to cut his speed down to a mule's pace to avoid running a wheel down a deep crack and doing damage. He was going downhill, he noticed, dropping into a dry valley, which twisted and turned between grey barren hillsides that looked pale and ghostly in this strange half light. Choking with the white dust thrown up from the front wheel, he drew the bandana even more tightly across his face. As he rode along his thoughts turned to those poor souls who had been arrested back in Pamplona, Santander and Logrono and where they were being held. One bonus to taking Franco alive was that the release of these patriots could be guaranteed – together with their safe passage to somewhere where they would be given political asylum. That much was good, El Serpiente conceded; if he'd done as his instincts told him and put the clip of bullets in Franco's head then their fate would already be sealed.

★ ★ ★

The Hotel Bahia dated from an era before the Civil War when the rich and the aristocracy from all over Europe drove down the coast of Spain to fashionable resorts further to the south and made it their overnight stopping place. In its own grounds and set in a forest of pine trees, it had the grace and elegance of a bygone age and, even though its glories had faded with the years, it could still count princes and dukes on its list of guests every year. With its reputation for cuisine and its internationally acclaimed candlelit dining room, the Hotel Bahia was therefore an obvious choice for Generalisimo Franco for his short stay in these parts, just as it was an obvious choice for Conchita Gomez from the Bar Madrid in the Street of Two Eyes to choose it for the celebration of her wedding anniversary. Little though, did either of these persons know of Jaime Campello's mission that night for, if they had, they would have acted differently.

The first thing that struck Campello as odd as he emerged from the path between the pine trees was the sight of two policemen standing beside the heavy ornamental wrought iron gates of the Hotel Bahia.

'Hola Jaime,' the first of these policemen said to Campello as he approached for he knew the carpenter well. Indeed the two of them had been to school together.

Campello returned the greeting and spoke to the other policeman too with whom he was also acquainted. 'So what's all this about?' he asked referring to their presence at the gate.

'Some flap', the policeman shrugged. 'We're not allowed to say what it is.'

Campello nodded. Police flaps were not unknown in Los Tidos. Usually they were to do with some foreigner up to no good and they died down again almost as quickly as they flared up. There was no reason, of course, for the two policeman to stop Campello from passing through their checkpoint. He was a local tradesman going about his business, a man with no known criminal connections; indeed and on the contrary, a church going man who led a harmless and, some would have said, colourless existence. Neither, for that matter, did he bear any kind of scar on his face or sport a beard.

About thirty seconds after Campello had passed by one policeman turned to the other and spoke.

'What was that?' he said referring to something that had brushed past his legs.

'Just a dog,' his companion replied.

★ ★ ★

El Serpiente pulled up on a bend in the dirt road at a point where a spectacular view had just opened up in front of him. The barren upland valley he had been following ended abruptly and the dirt road continued as a lane through terraced fields where it crossed a ferrocarril then joined a big wide carretera. Beyond in the amber and purple colours of gathering dusk he could just make out a lazy dark blue line. The sea, he said to himself.

The carretera, El Serpiente guessed correctly, was the main carretera from Valencia but what was puzzling him was why the traffic going south was at a standstill. Even more to the point he wondered whether the reason for the hold up had anything to do with Franco. Long strings of headlights stretched back to the north as far as his eye could make out and, even up here, the stench of diesel fumes from the traffic queue reached him. He shifted the Harley Davidson into low gear and crept forward to take a closer look. Coming to the crossing with the ferrocarril, he stopped again. This time he noticed a group of truck drivers hunkered down by the side of the highway. They were playing cards by the light of an oil lamp.

'Amigos; he called out to them. 'Que pasa?' Why is the traffic not moving? Has there been an accident or something?

'No Señor.' a grizzled looking man shouted back. 'The police are stopping everyone. Two kilometres down the road or so they say.'

Another voice spoke up angrily. 'The police don't have a load of pigs to get to market. They should be made to pay for our time.'

'Where are you going Señor?' the first man asked when the mutterings of agreement had died down.

'To Los Tidos,' El Serpiente replied

'If I had a fine motorcycle like yours I would not be hanging about here. There is a track that follows the ferrocaril. If you take it carefully you could be in Los Tidos in twenty minutes. Take my word for it; I come from these parts.'

El Serpiente thanked the man for his advice then turning the Harley Davidson round and, with the big powerful engine throbbing in the exhausts, he made his way back to the crossing and stopped again. Sure enough, it was just as the truck driver had said: there was a path running alongside the track ballast in both directions with enough room to take the width of his tyres. Keeping in low gear, he was soon travelling on a low embankment across the fields with the silhouette of the mountain escarpment he had just left to his right and the carretera with its traffic jam never very far away on the other side. The stars were coming out he noticed and it made him feel easier. He had spent most of his life travelling in mountains and the stars had always been his friends. Now they told him his direction – south, south east; south again, better than looking at any compass, he said to himself. A little further on, he came to a tiny country station – a low platform, a single shelter and all in darkness. Round here, he figured correctly, the trains didn't run at night.

★ ★ ★

Campello at that precise moment was looking furtively over his shoulder. Seeing no-one was watching him, he deviated suddenly from his path up the long drive to the Hotel Bahia where the magnificent avenue of palm trees was silhouetted against the sky and shot off into a dense dark shrubbery at the side. The shrubbery, it turned out, was a rose garden, a fact that Campello only discovered after sustaining several scratches to his hands and face and a rip down the sleeve of his coat. Not one to be discouraged easily Campello pressed on taking a circular course, which after several misadventures with low walls and ornamental pools, brought him out, as he had hoped, at the back of the hotel opposite the entrance to the kitchens.

He paused. Nervously now, he fingered the tiny bottle of emetic in his trouser pocket and, still under cover of the bushes, he checked to see if anyone was about. Campello's work as a carpenter had brought him at one time or another to most of the commercial establishments in and around Los Tidos and the layouts of nearly all of them were familiar to him. So it was with the Hotel Bahia where he had been working only three weeks before, replacing some old wood panelling in the famous candlelit dining room. The chef, Casares, was also known to Campello but as an ill-dispositioned and self-important individual who condescended to speak to artisans such as himself out of necessity if at all. Campello's answer to Casares was to steer clear of him as much as possible and certainly never – unless invited – to venture into the kitchens where Casares was King.

Even now from the safety of the bushes, the sight of Casares, busy at his stoves filled Campello with apprehension. He hesitated. There was no way he could see of dodging in the kitchen door without Casares, noticing him and without, as a consequence, incurring Casares's famous wrath. The chances of dumping the contents of his little bottle on

Casares's cooking seemed even more remote. Campello was indeed on the point of giving up his enterprise and going back to Pepe Gomez with the story that at least he had tried when Fate played a helpful hand. Casares disappeared and the kitchens, as far as Campello could see, were left unattended.

Quickly he covered the five metres from the bushes to the kitchen door. Quickly he checked round again to see that there was no-one about. He noticed straight away the huge paella pan simmering on the stove and equally quickly he darted in and emptied the bottle of emetic in to the saffron coloured rice. In a trice he was back in the bushes again with his heart pounding away furiously inside his chest. Time to make haste, he told himself, time to put as much distance as possible between himself and the Hotel Bahia and to do it well before Conchita and Pepe Gomez arrived. But as Jaime Campello left the back of the Hotel Bahia, what he did not notice was a grey shape skulking behind the garbage bins.

CHAPTER SIX

A Single Red Rose

The taxi bringing Conchita and Pepe Gomez to their wedding anniversary celebration at the Hotel Bahia was brought to a halt at the gate by two policemen holding up their hands. The dining room was closed to all but residents, the policemen explained, by special order of the Guardia Civil and no-one could go in. Conchita, sitting in the back of the taxi in her new frock and fresh from the hairdresser's, received the news with a face like flint. She turned to the figure of Pepe Gomez at her side. 'What are you going to do about this?' she demanded. Gomez had already gone through the ritual send off in the Street of Two Eyes with Conchita waving at the crowd like the Queen of England but now this news! His plan was in ruins thanks to some whim of the Guardia and he could hardly believe his ears. No paella in the candle-lit dining room meant life with Conchita was going to go on and the thought of it instantly filled him with misery. He thought also about Campello and wondered if he was out there somewhere in the darkness clutching Robles's bottle in his hand. Had Campello likewise been turned back when he arrived at the gate?

'Do,' he shrugged truculently. 'What can I do? If the dining room is closed then there is nothing further to be done.'

'Isn't that just like you?' Conchita accused. 'Why can't you tell these two policemen to step aside and let us through.'

'It would do no good,' one of the policeman offered in a conciliatory tone, 'Once you got up to the hotel they would refuse to let you in. Why not find some other place to go for your dinner?'

'Why?' hissed Conchita through the cab's open window. 'This is my wedding anniversary that is why. This is the one night of the year when I am not slaving behind a bar, serving ungrateful customers, washing up their glasses and keeping an eye on this lazy swine of a husband of mine. Do you not think I deserve to be taken to the best hotel in town?'

'Of course, Señora, but tonight it is not possible. That is all that I am saying.'

'Why don't *you* tell him?' she said turning on Pepe again. 'Why is it always me who has to end up fighting the arguments?'

'Tell him what?' Pepe Gomez groaned.

'Tell him to make way or fetch the management of the hotel down here to speak to us themselves.'

'The management of the hotel can do nothing,' the policeman explained. 'They have their orders like we do.' The taxi driver spoke next. 'If you ask me, we are doing no good here. Shall I drive you back home or is there some other place you would like to be taken to?'

Conchita eyed him coldly in the driving mirror. 'You are paid to drive your taxi,' she said. 'Not to offer your opinions.'

The taxi driver shrugged and picked up a newspaper from the seat at the side of him. It was going to be a long night, he could tell.

★ ★ ★

As he rode along the trackside path El Serpiente saw that the carretera was getting nearer. The long line of trucks and cars, some with their headlights switched off to conserve their batteries, were just a field's distance away now and up in front the single narrow gauge track bent sharply to the left then the skeletal silhouette shape of a girder bridge spanning the road appeared out of the darkness. He stopped. Down beneath in the stone walled fields he could make out the shadowy shapes of lemon trees with their incandescent fruit hanging down like the lights on a candelabra. An owl hooted from somewhere and he could smell the heavy scent of blossom. He checked the phosphorescent fingers of his watch. Half past eight: it reminded him he hadn't eaten since daybreak and even then, his food had consisted of the stale end of a loaf washed down with water from a nearby spring. Should he make camp here in the lemon groves? The idea appealed but in the end he decided to press on. For one thing it was too near the carretera and carreteras in his experience were where the police and the Guardia Civil were always to be found. He edged the Harley Davidson forward the last few metres till finally his front wheel was resting on the near parapet of the bridge. Peering down through the open ironwork, he saw the snaking line of traffic underneath. The drop was ten metres, no more, yet he hesitated. The way forward was along a narrow wooden plank fixed to the trestles: a plank little wider than the Harley Davidson's tyres and, though few people knew it, El Serpiente, who lived so much of his life in the mountains, did not have a head for heights.

Steeling himself he freed his face from the bandana, wiped the dust and sweat from his brow then brought up the revs of the motorcycle engine gently. Setting his sights on the far side of the bridge, he edged his way forward onto the plank. Metre by metre, never once casting his eyes downwards and shutting out all thoughts of falling, he made his way across – finally breathing a sigh of relief when he had reached the safety of the other side. Sixty seconds later and El Serpiente had left the carretera far behind.

Soon he was on a low embankment again, this time crossing a grey undulating plain lit wanly by an old moon where over to his left there were a few scattered lights of houses; lights as it happened belonging to big haciendas that included the one the Theroux family lived in. Further on he noticed for the first time, the crisp smell of sea air. The ferrocarril now went into a cutting with bare rock faces on either side and beneath a road bridge. Here he pulled over. The ferrocarril had become a double track and he had just passed a point with the hand lever for operating it set in an iron frame at the side of the ballast. A passing place for trains? Possibly – meaning, perhaps he was approaching a station. He turned off the motorcycle engine, appreciating for the first time the silence of the night broken only by the barking of dogs a long way off. Pushing the heavy bike, he took a few steps forward. Soon in the gloom among the rock faces he started to make out the shapes of buildings: it was a station; a bigger station than the country halt he had passed through earlier on.

Suddenly he stiffened. Instinctively he knew that someone was in front then he saw a shape standing on the low station platform watching him. Reaching down quickly he drew the big knife out of the top of his boot.

'Who is that?' a voice rang out in the darkness echoing against the rock faces.

111

Taking care to tighten the bandana again, El Serpiente waited for whoever it was to approach. Presently a torch came on though it became apparent that this was to help the bearer to pick his way across the ballast rather than to flash in his face.

'Identify yourself,' El Serpiente growled tightening his grip on the handle of the knife.

'I might be asking you the same question,' the voice came back. 'The station is closed. There are no trains till morning. What business have you here?'

El Serpiente let his muscles slacken. His questioner he saw was an elderly man, frail looking, wearing a railway worker's uniform and doing no more than he was paid to do. He slid the knife back into his boot quickly before the old man saw it.

'My apologies Amigo', El Serpiente said adjusting his voice 'I think I have taken a wrong turning and come this way by mistake.'

The old man muttered something. He was shaking his torch because the light had gone out.

'This is Los Tidos?' asked El Serpiente.

'This is the Estacion, Señor'; the old man corrected. 'The town of Los Tidos is a little way off. Is it the town you are making for?'

El Serpiente didn't answer though the old man hardly noticed because he was still busy trying to get his torch to work.

'The police are everywhere tonight,' he went on. 'Stopping people and searching cars. If you are going into Los Tidos, Amigo, you have chosen a bad time.'

'The police? What are they looking for?'

'I have no idea,' the old man shrugged finally giving up on the torch. 'Though if I had to put money on it I would say it

112

has something to do with the two men who arrived on yesterday morning's train. They are from some special section of the Guardia Civil, or so the rumour goes. They have been sent from Madrid on top secret business and the one in charge is a great brute of a fellow who forced me to carry his cases all the way up the hill: me, an old man who suffers with his chest, can you believe it? If I were you, Amigo, I would forget going into the town. Earlier on I heard someone say that they are arresting strangers and taking their papers away.'

★ ★ ★

Because Jaime Campello made his way back into Los Tidos from the Hotel Bahia using the same quiet paths that he had used on his outward journey he saw little of the activity the old station master was describing to the mysterious stranger on the motor cycle who had appeared out of the darkness along the ferrocarril. In fact, save for a few trips and stumbles in the dark, Campello's return to the Villa Verde was largely uneventful. Even the grey vulpine shape that had followed him earlier on was absent.

Exhausted by the day's events and determined to make up for his lost time at work by putting in an early start in the morning, Campello decided he would go to bed immediately. Cleaning his teeth in the bathroom, he saw in the mirror a big scratch that the rose bushes had left on his face. He wiped off the dried blood with a flannel then, knowing how scratches from thorns can go septic, he looked in the medicine chest for some antiseptic cream. Here his eyes fell once more on the bottle of rat poison with its skull and crossbones label and the sinister looking green liquid inside. He knew the sooner he was rid of it, the better and promised himself he would see to it first thing in the morning.

★ ★ ★

The identity of the guest who had arrived late the previous night in a black chauffeur driven limousine was made known to the manager of the Hotel Bahia by Acting Chief of Police, Flores. The manager, a man named Alvarez, who worried at the best of times about the responsibilities of his job, was thrown into a state of near panic by the news that the little gentleman with the hollow sunken eyes who was a friend of his boss the Marques and who had signed himself in as 'Señor Granjero'; was none other than the Caudillo himself on a private visit; a visit on which for some reason he wished to remain incognito.

'Not a word,' Flores warned tapping the side of his nose. 'There are dangerous terrorists about and our job is to make sure the Caudillo comes to no harm while he is here. All this we must do without him knowing. He will be angry if he thinks his privacy has been compromised.'

'Not a word' was all very well, Alvarez said to himself afterwards, but what if some bungling waiter not knowing any differently went and put his foot in it with Señor Granjero? What if one of these dangerous terrorists managed to foil the police and got in the hotel? Then who would be on the carpet?

Alvarez's gloom increased when, as one of his normal routines, he checked the list of reservations for the candlelit dining room with the Head Waiter, Herrero. With the exception of Señor Granjero the names on the list were all those of non-residents and non-residents, as Flores had been at pains to explain, were for security reasons going to be turned away by two of his officers standing on duty at the gates. Señor Granjero would be dining alone and somehow or other Alvarez had to think of a way of breaking this news to Casares the Chef.

Though Alvarez was a temperate man who made it a rule never to allow alcohol to pass his lips when on duty, he took out a bottle of the special Carlos V coñac he kept in the cabinet in his office for hospitality purposes and poured himself a large measure.

★ ★ ★

In contrast to the mood of Alvarez, out on the streets of Los Tidos Capitan Luis Garcia of the Guardia Civil now resplendent in his full uniform was having a fine time arresting men with beards. With the imminence of the Feast of the Two Virgins (of which more will be said later) a large number of men in the town were at that time growing beards because, in the processions and mock battles that formed part of the Fiesta, they had been given the parts of Moors to enact. In consequence the cells under the Comisaria were already full to overflowing.

'Capitan Garcia,' said Ramon Ramon trailing behind his revolver-brandishing superior. 'Can I have a word with you please?'

'Can't you see I'm busy hombre?' Garcia barked back at him, rounding up another four Moors from a bar and bundling them into the back of a police van.

'Capitan Garcia, this El Serpiente we are seeking is a clever and cunning man, yes?'

'He is the most dangerous and wanted criminal in the

whole of Spain. He has evaded the Guardia and the military for over twenty years. If we could detain him what a feather in our caps, eh?'

'Yes I realise Capitan but if this El Serpiente is so clever then surely he would not be walking the streets at night or drinking in bars. Surely he would be hiding himself up somewhere, waiting to pounce when the moment is right.'

Garcia stopped in his tracks and glared down at his little assistant. 'You are questioning my methods hombre?'

'No Capitan Garcia, I was just trying to suggest that we might do better by watching and waiting. All these arrests will only serve to put El Serpiente on his guard. The wise custodian stands in the shadows is what they say in the town I come from.'

'You think you could handle this assignment better than me?'

'No Capitan Garcia – but sometimes two minds are better than one, are they not?'

'And you put your mind on the same level as mine?'

'Not intentionally Capitan Garcia. I was merely using a figure of speech, that was all.'

'Figure of speech! Hombre, you talk like an intellectual. You know what I think of intellectuals don't you?'

'No Capitan Garcia.'

'Most of them are limp-wristed perverts; faggots who read too many books and who put their penises in other men's behinds.'

'I am not one of those Capitan Garcia.'

'But you will be if you carry on using these figures of speech. Some day, hombre, you will be grateful to me for keeping you on the straight and narrow path.'

'Yes Capitan Garcia.'

Four of the main characters in this story were already fast asleep when Generalisimo Francisco Franco descended the grand marble staircase of the Hotel Bahia in the guise of Señor Granjero and was ushered into the candlelit dining room by the Head Waiter, Herrero. First there was Jaime Campello who was having fitful dreams in which images of Conchita Gomez, Robles the Ratcatcher and a pretty young woman in a bridal veil with hearts and cupids around her head figured; then Lola Martınez with a big day ahead who slept as she always slept – naked, untroubled by dreams and with the king sized bed in the penthouse suite all to herself; next El Serpiente who lay stretched out on a hard wooden bench inside the Los Tidos station house courtesy of his new found friend the station master – a man with whom, earlier on he had shared a simple meal of *pan con tomate* done the Catalan way washed down with a bottle of the local rough red wine; then finally Nathalie Theroux who will come more into the story as it unfolds and whose cloistered life determined that she was normally in bed by this hour.

The fact the Generalisimo chose the paella for his evening meal was not as coincidental as it might seem. The dish was, after all, traditional to the Valencian region and a particular speciality of the Hotel Bahia. The fact that so much of the paella Casares the Chef had cooked that evening found its way into the garbage was not a coincidence either. The portion he put on a plate for little Señor Granjero hardly made a dent in the vast quantity he had prepared for the hundred or so guests who would normally have graced the candlelit dining room and, it was in a fit of pique and rage that Casares had ordered two of his kitchen hands to pick up the giant paella pan and empty its contents into the bins outside yet, as they performed this task, neither of them noticed the pair of gleaming yellow eyes that watched them from the shadows or the slavering jowls of the matted grey form to which they belonged.

In the early hours of the morning Generalisimo Francisco Franco alias Señor Granjero woke with strange pains in his stomach. The following day he was due to meet the Marques for breakfast then be taken to the private jetty where the Marques kept his yacht. The pains that the Generalisimo at first put down to indigestion however did not go away till finally at four o'clock he summoned his driver and gave orders to be taken back immediately to Madrid. Alvarez who was alerted by the night porter arrived on the scene in his dressing gown just in time to see the Generalisimo leaving. No words were spoken but Alvarez realised the abruptness with which the Generalisimo departed meant something somewhere must be amiss. Then the chilling thought struck him that the something in question could be something to do with the hotel, a thought which had him reaching again for the bottle of Carlos V coñac in the hope it would help him get back to sleep. There is no record of the Gernalisimo's journey back to the capital or of how many times he tapped his driver on the shoulder to tell him to stop so he could get out and stoop over a ditch.

As the limousine with its blinds pulled down swept out of the gates of the Hotel Bahia it was observed by the two policemen still on duty. They looked at one another. They had instructions to stop visitors entering the Hotel but not to prevent anyone leaving. They looked at one another again then, in the best traditions of the Los Tidos police service when faced with indecision, they decided to do nothing.

★ ★ ★

Unaware that the person he sought to capture was on his way back to Madrid, El Serpiente, in the station house of Los Tidos, woke early. When he opened his eyes the first thing he saw was the cold stone floor and the sun streaming in through a window with bars high up on the wall and, for a brief moment, he thought he was in prison. The moment and the panic passed and, rubbing himself to get the numbness out of his limbs from lying on a hard wooden bench all night, he got up and took a look round. Save for the bench and another like it set against the opposite wall the room contained no furnishings whatsoever and was, he guessed correctly, a place for people to wait for trains on cold or wet days. Still with a sense of relief he found that the big double doors were not bolted and the Harley Davidson was where he had left it last night, in the vestibule outside that led out onto the station platform. There he saw the station master already up and about, unlocking doors and checking the time on the big station clock.

'Buenos Dias Amigo,' he called across. 'I trust you slept well.'

El Serpiente raised his hand to acknowledge the greeting realising as he did, that he had forgotten to draw the bandana across his face so the scar by which he could immediately be recognised was clearly on display. The station master, however, had gone into a doorway further up the platform from which he reappeared a few seconds later carrying two tin mugs, a coffee pot and a basket filled with roughly cut and toasted hunks of bread.

'It is not much,' the old man commented indicating to El Serpiente to sit down with him on the edge of the platform.

'A station master's wages are poor. Were it not for the house I am provided with, the job would hardly be worth doing.'

'You must allow me to pay you for my lodgings,' El Serpiente began but the old man was already holding his hand up and shaking his head.

'I would not hear of it,' he said 'My house is your house. While you are here, I will share what I have with you. That is the way we treat our guests in these parts.'

El Serpiente thanked him for his kindness.

'I have some news,' the station master said shielding his eyes from the rising sun. 'There is a shepherd who passes by here every morning and I heard it from him. They are saying Franco is staying in town and that is why everyone is being asked to show their papers. Also many men have been arrested and put in prison.'

'Franco, you say?' El Serpiente was careful not to show anything other than a traveller's passing interest.

'He is staying at the Hotel Bahia and it is supposed to be a secret, but, believe me, nothing stays a secret for long round here. Are you planning to go far today, Amigo?'

'I am not sure.'

'It would be best if you kept well clear of the Hotel Bahia. If I were you I would go the other way.'

'Perhaps you are right. Where is this place?'

'It is on the other side of town, not far from the carretera. I am afraid I have little time for Franco and his lot. Back in '36 most of us in Los Tidos took up arms for the Republic and I do not see why he should show his face here.'

El Serpiente looked at him as he swilled the last dregs of strong tasting coffee round in his mouth. Something in his heavily scarred face softened but it was only for an instant. 'I

120

have no interest in politics,' he said to the station master.

★ ★ ★

The scene down at the Comisaria was one of chaos – the cells down below were full of bearded men who by now were all complaining vociferously and demanding to be fed.

'We cannot hold them much longer,' groaned Flores holding his head in his hands. The Capitan from Cordoba and his assistant were not present at that precise moment because they had both gone off for breakfast after spending the night in the Acting Chief of Police's private apartment from which the Acting Chief of Police had been summarily turned out.

'How long is this going to go on?' one of the officers standing in front of him asked.

Flores shrugged. 'For as long as the Caudillo is staying at the Hotel Bahia, I suppose. Let us hope he goes soon then we can be rid of Capitan Garcia and everything will go back to the way it was.'

★ ★ ★

Troubled by many strange dreams in the night, Jaime Campello did not wake early as he had intended; in fact, he overslept. In the end it was the sound of the telephone ringing that roused him from his slumbers.

'Campello,' he mumbled into the mouthpiece still rubbing the sleep out of his eyes while at the same time trying to hold up the bottom of his pyjamas from which the cord had mysteriously disappeared.

'Jaime, it is I.' It was Pepe Gomez again though whether it

was the fault of Campello still being half asleep or not, what he was saying didn't seem to make much sense. 'I cannot speak to you on the phone but it is urgent that we meet. Say in half an hour down in the Plaza de Los Reyes.' Then before Campello could say yes or no, the line went dead.

Campello frowned. Being a conscientious tradesman, the lack of progress on the new set of doors for the Ayuntamiento was beginning to bother him. Though Pepe Gomez was his friend, he felt that he was starting to be taken for granted and it was with a feeling of annoyance that Campello dressed and rushed his breakfast down before setting off at a race horse pace for the Plaza de Los Reyes. In any case, Campello presumed, Pepe Gomez only wanted to see him because Conchita had not run round in circles screaming her head off before falling dead on the floor but had suffered some minor upset of the stomach instead. He could not of course let on to Pepe Gomez that this was exactly the outcome he was expecting so he would have to go through with the pretence of being surprised.

Pepe Gomez was waiting for him when he arrived at the Plaza de Los Reyes.

'Thank God you have come,' said the little man with a anxious note in his voice. He took Campello by the elbow, and steered him towards a bar where the tables outside were empty.

When the waiter, a man they knew, had taken their orders for coffee and coñac, Gomez began by telling Campello about the night before. The news that he and Conchita had encountered two policemen at the gate of the Hotel Bahia came as no surprise to Campello because it tallied exactly with his own experience: The news that they had been turned away and that Conchita had emerged unscathed from her wedding anniversary celebrations, even from the effects of emetic, was received by Campello with some relief. It had troubled him from the beginning that one day Conchita would find out who had tampered with her food and, when that day dawned, Campello knew the sky would likely come down on his head.

'Perhaps it was for the best,' Campello mumbled hoping a few words of consolation would finally put the matter to rest and he could get off to his work.

'No Jaime, you do not understand.'

'What don't I understand?'

Pepe Gomez looked round before he spoke. 'The reason why the Hotel Bahia was closed; it's all over town. Franco is staying up there. That's why they wouldn't let us in.'

'Franco? Do you mean *the* Franco?'

'Is there any other Franco?'

'What are you trying to tell me Pepe?'

'Jaime, Franco ate the paella for his dinner last night. I heard it from Conchita's cousin Maria. Her son, Jose helps out in the gardens at the Hotel Bahia. Jaime, I don't know how to tell you this but I think you may have poisoned the Caudillo.'

It took a moment for this information to sink in. Before it did Pepe Gomez was speaking again. 'If they garrotte you Jaime I will say now that I would never forgive myself. If I had known this would happen I would never have involved you in the first place.'

Campello sat with a blank look on his face for several seconds. What Gomez did not know of course was that the bottle of rat poison was still sitting in the medicine chest at the Villa Verde and what was going through his thoughts was how someone who had put an emetic into the absolute ruler of the nation's food would be punished. Whatever method was chosen he had the feeling it would not be pleasant.

'Jaime?'

'What is it?'

'Why have you got a big scratch on your face?'

★ ★ ★

Realising he had a long journey ahead, Suarez left Madrid well before dawn. He had spent the afternoon before tidying his desk and briefing his deputy Gonzalez on what to do if some crisis should arise in his absence. It was raining steadily as he left the outskirts of the city behind and the windscreen wipers flicked backwards and forwards in front of his eyes. Despite the circumstances it felt good to be out of the office and he glanced over in the direction of the glove compartment where he had put his old service revolver along with a box full of bullets.

He had been going for about an hour when he heard the sound of a siren behind and caught sight of a policeman on a motor cycle coming up alongside. 'Señor Suarez,' the policeman said saluting smartly as Suarez wound down the window. I have orders to intercept you and ask you to contact your office in Madrid immediately. Some urgent matter of state requires your attention.'

★ ★ ★

Though she had nothing to do for several hours Lola Martinez was up well before eight. She breakfasted on coffee and the fresh fruit the Conserja's husband had brought from the supermercado the day before. Still naked after her shower and with her long black hair wrapped in a towel she went back into the bedroom where she emptied the contents of her shoulder bag onto the playboy's purple satin sheets. From among the assortment of lipsticks, powder compacts and keys she picked out the tiny silver pistol that went everywhere with her. She then spent several minutes cleaning it and examining it expertly. When she was satisfied, she put it back in her bag along with all her other belongings. The only item she left out was a pair of handcuffs and the key that went with them. Their previous owner had been a police officer from Gijon who had fallen under her spell. The handcuffs and their disappearance were still a mystery to him.

★ ★ ★

Parting company with Pepe Gomez in the Avenida, Jaime Campello made his way along a side street where, though it had no relevance to him at all, he passed a little blue Seat motorcar with its wheels pulled in neatly to the kerb. The walk back to the Villa Verde took him fifteen minutes during which time he crossed the path of only one policeman who made no attempt to arrest him and greeted him in the same friendly way that most policemen in Los Tidos greeted him. Turning a corner by the Church he almost ran straight into Father Miguel.

'Your face is all scratched,' said Father Miguel. 'What have you been doing?'

'An accident with a chisel,' Campello explained going bright red and realising what a poor liar he made.

'You need to be more careful,' Father Miguel said before bidding him goodbye and continuing on his way.

Campello had hardly got in the Villa Verde and locked and bolted the door from the inside when the phone started to ring.

'Is that you Señor Campello?' It was the business-like lady from the Diane Maitland Bureau of Friendship. 'Your voice sounded a little strange.'

Campello sighed. He could do without this just now. 'Yes, it is I,' he replied tersely still with his mind on what might happen to him if he was found guilty of high treason.

'We received your cheque Señor Campello and from your promptness I can see you wish to get on with finding the lady of your dreams. Are you still there Señor Campello?'

'Yes I am here.'

'We have carried out a search with our computer and we have identified the perfect lady for you – by a stroke of luck, a lady who also lives in Los Tidos. Would you not say that that is a happy coincidence Señor Campello?'

'I am sorry, something has cropped up that I was not expecting. Could we perhaps delay matters for a little while?'

'Delay, Señor Campello? In affairs of the heart, delay is never wise.'

'But…'

'You are nervous and it is perfectly understandable. We are arranging for you to meet the lady tonight.'

'Tonight!'

'The lady is also anxious for things to move swiftly and you would not wish to disappoint her would you? You are to meet her in the park in the Avenida at eight o'clock. You know this place I trust Señor Campello? There is a fountain nearby, I think.'

'Yes I know it.'

'Good. Now let me explain to you that the Diane Maitland Bureau of Friendship always leaves it to the happy couples to decide how much they tell each other about themselves so at this stage you will not even be told the lady's name and she will not know yours.'

'But how will we know one another?'

'I was coming to that. You will both carry a single red rose, a symbol of love, in your hand. In that way the lady will be able to recognise you and you will be able to recognise her. I would like to wish you a pleasant evening Señor Campello. Eternal happiness will soon be yours. Don't forget: eight o'clock; by the fountain in the park.'

CHAPTER SEVEN

A Night of Strange Encounters

The night before, after everything had gone quiet in the kitchens of the Hotel Bahia, Waldorf slunk out from his hiding place in the bushes and upended the giant garbage bins with his gnarled snout. For half an hour he had gorged himself on the mountain of paella that had been put there by Casares's assistants and, when he had had his fill, he had licked his chops and took himself off back into the bushes where he used his hind leg to scratch out a few of the fleas that had re-established themselves in his coat after Campello's scrubbing. Following this he curled up nose to tail and fell into a deep sleep.

The strange movements inside his stomach woke him in the early hours at almost exactly the same time that in the hotel's most palatial bedroom they woke Franco. At first the movements were a mystery and he responded in the way he always responded by turning out his stomach on the ground. Feeling better he went back to sleep and so missed the noise of the Generalisimo's limousine starting up. Then the strange symptoms started all over again and the process repeated itself so that before the night was out, Casares's kitchen garden was covered with the contents of Waldorf's stomach still just about recognisable as paella thank to its pale saffron colour. The next

128

problem Waldorf was to experience was a raging thirst. This he sought to slake by drinking huge quantities of water from the Hotel Bahia's ornamental fish pool and doubtless a large number of amoeba-like life forms as well. The intestinal churnings returned accompanied this time by a terrible liquid diarrhoea.

Panting and with his grey tongue hanging out Waldorf went back to the bushes to lie down. He was in trouble and he knew it. If the sickness and diarrhoea went on he would get weaker and weaker so something had to be done. A creature of instinct, his brain began to tick over till finally the answer came to him. Bones: not fresh bones with the marrow still soft inside them but old picked over and dried out bones. Bones of the kind they had up in the Old Town. Bones he could gnaw at and grind into a powder that would settle his stomach. And so it was that Waldorf decided to quit the high life and go back to his old haunts.

★ ★ ★

Lola Martinez spent most of the morning on the rooftop of the Edificio Los Angeles looking through her binoculars. She had seen the Conserja and her husband go out on some errand earlier on so she knew she would not be disturbed. Wearing a sweater because there was a freshness in the wind that hadn't been there the day before she scanned the faces on the street again, to see if she could spot a man with a scar like a snake on his cheek. The faces, however, were ordinary faces: the faces of men and women going about their ordinary business though she did notice the extra police activity. Something to do with Franco? She realised that she still had to find out where in town Franco was staying. Here she had been relying on El Serpiente but now El Serpiente had been delayed by some little distraction and she, Lola Martinez, was left kicking her heels. Eight o'clock tonight: the wait seemed interminable and patience had never been one of Lola Martinez's virtues.

Raising her binoculars again she looked further afield; first to the south and beyond the town beach to where the sands continued around the great empty crescent sweep of the Bahia – sands, incidentally, that would one day make Los Tidos famous throughout Europe. Seeing no signs of life in that direction she turned her binoculars northwards to the port and the masts of ships and cranes then further up the coast to what looked like the oblong shaped lakes of an old Salinas. Sweeping inland next she picked up the long straight intersecting lines of the carretera and a ferrocarril cutting through the vineyards and groves of oranges and olive trees. Close to the ferrocarril as it approached the town, she spotted the road she had used herself and the big haciendas she had passed. Focusing her binoculars even more she made out a tiny figure in black. A girl pushing someone in a wheelchair who, Lola realised immediately, was, the girl who had given her directions and whose accent was strange.

★ ★ ★

Christine gurgled excitedly. The great grey shrike they had been watching had gone up onto the pole carrying the telephone wires with the cicada it had just caught still writhing in its beak. Christine clapped her hands and the shrike flew off and Christine started to sulk.

They were nearing the gate, and, remembering Maman's words, Nathalie turned the wheelchair round and started to head back towards the house. Today though the highway was deserted. In both directions, as far as Nathalie could see, there was not a soul about.

Like Lola Martinez she had noticed the freshening of the wind and put a cardigan on before she came out while Maria wrapped a blanket round Christine to keep her warm. The wind had changed direction in the night. It was blowing from inland now, from the west, and a haziness that was filtering the strength from the sun, was starting to move across the sky. It served to remind Nathalie that winter was coming though winter in Los Tidos was never the same as winter in France. Yet the dark skies and the cold rooms with their cold tiled floors seemed to accentuate her plight. She would be twenty-nine in January, a foreigner in a foreign land where she had no friends and, where the loneliness had got worse since Papa died.

For no reason her thoughts turned to the girl she had spoken to at the gate the other day: a girl so self-assured, so chic in her sunglasses; her self-assuredness showing in the way she casually tossed her hair back. The girl would be about her own age, she judged, though the worldliness and style she exuded were things Nathalie Theroux could only dream about.

Christine was still sulking and Nathalie tried to interest her in the wheatears on the roof of Juan's shed. In front, across the valley with its trellises of bare vines was the ridge on which the Cemetario stood, the place she and Maman walked to on Sundays when the weather was fine to put fresh flowers on Papa's tomb. Further to the left and nearer the sea the land flattened out and Nathalie could make out the port, and beyond the new development around the yacht marina from which her father had been among those who profited. Beside the yacht marina she could see the tall unmistakable shape of the Edificio Los Angeles where, as she looked, the hazy sun briefly caught on something bright. That the something was a pair of binoculars trained on her would never have crossed Nathalie Theroux's mind.

Back at the house she saw that Maman and Maria were waiting for them on the terrace.

'Frio?' said Maria making the point by crossing her arms, rubbing her shoulders and looking up at the skies.

'I think Christine needs to go inside,' said Maman as they helped Nathalie get the wheelchair up the short flight of steps. Christine protested. Christine didn't want to go inside. Christine wanted to stay on the terrace where she could look at the birds.

'Mucho frio,' Maria explained to her as she took her off beating the arms of her wheelchair with her fists.

'Close the door after you please Maria,' Maman called after her. 'If we are not careful with this wind, we shall soon have the house full of dust.'

When they were alone she spoke to Nathalie.

'You don't look well my child. There are rings round your eyes and your face is so pale.'

'I thought my face was tanned. The summer has only just gone.'

'A suntan is only superficial Nathalie. Underneath your face looks like the face of a ghost. You need to eat more. I will ask Maria to get some beef from Vilas so that I can braise it for you. Beef will help to build you up.'

'Yes Maman.'

'Oh I almost forgot to say: there was a telephone call for you while you were out on your walk.'

'A telephone call?'

'A woman. She would not leave her name. I have written the number down on a piece of paper and put it on the little table.'

'It will be Señora Rey.'

'Señora Rey? Who is she?'

'She is the woman who wishes me to give her daughter piano lessons.'

'I hope these people are respectable.'

'She is the wife of Señor Rey, the manager of the Banco de Bilbao.'

'In my experience bank managers are the worst people in the world when it comes to paying. If I were you Nathalie I would get the money from this Señora Rey in advance.'

'Yes Maman – I will.'

★ ★ ★

Back in his cold office Suarez put the phone down. The caller was one of the simpering bureaucrats who the Caudillo in his wisdom surrounded himself with these days; a man with a high-pitched voice who Suarez had little time for. The Caudillo was back unexpectedly it seemed; his visit had been cut short and he was in hospital where his personal physician, Doctor Vicente Gil was attending to the mysterious stomach ailment he had picked up during his brief stay in Los Tidos.

'What we cannot rule out,' the bureaucrat went on dryly, 'is that someone down there has tried to poison him.'

Suarez kept quiet though he was sorely tempted to say 'I told you so' to this little creep who squeaked like a castrado. However, he had been round long enough in politics to realise that points were seldom scored by reminding people such as this that you had been right all along. 'I am instructed by the Caudillo,' the bureaucrat continued in his whining voice. 'To say that the matter needs to be thoroughly investigated. If there are elements in this town of Los Tidos who are hostile to the state then they must be brought to account.'

If! Suarez nearly scoffed into the phone. The question was not 'if' but 'how many?' Had the Caudillo and his cronies become so remote from reality that they imagined that he no longer had any enemies? The prisons the length and breadth of the country were stuffed with people who would do anything to get even with him – communists, separatists, monarchists, carlists, all sorts of -ists, all queuing up for the chance to make martyrs of themselves. And why was it these days the Caudillo never conveyed his instructions in person? Why did they always have to come through one of these boot-licking intermediaries? What was wrong with the men who'd fought with the Army of Africa and served the Caudillo for over thirty years?

'You will see to this matter?' the squeaking bureaucrat said as he drew the phone call to a close.

There was a brief silence while Suarez took a deep breath. 'Yes I will see to it,' he replied.

* * *

From his vantage point among a clump of pine trees on the top of a small knoll not too far from the Estacion, El Serpiente looked down on the Port Road to where a group of policemen were busy stopping the traffic. The road block, he noted with some amusement, consisted of two oil drums with a plank of

134

wood placed between them. The two oil drums had been hastily painted red and white and there were big drips of paint still running down the sides. As he watched he noticed too how the policemen's diligence appeared to be waning. They waved more and more vehicles through and, as a consequence, the long line of traffic that had trailed back onto the carretera the night before had almost disappeared.

El Serpiente was in no hurry. Thanks to the station master's gossip he knew where Franco was staying and, if she didn't know already, he would share this information with the chica later He looked at his watch. It was still only quarter to twelve, which, because he always avoided towns in daylight, meant he had over eight hours to wait. Taking the big knife from the side of his boot, he sat down on the ground with his back to the trunk of a tree and started to whittle a stick. In the distance, over the mountains, big dark cumulus clouds were starting to gather. If El Serpiente's guess was right a storm would be coming soon.

★ ★ ★

In the Chief of Police's office in the Comisaria, Flores was standing stiffly to attention though he was the only person in the room. The phone call he was taking was from the big noise up in Madrid again. This time the big noise sounded not too pleased. Was Capitan Garcia there? 'No Señor,' he replied. 'The Capitan is in town somewhere.'

'Then get him for me,' the big noise snapped – his voice made even more crackly by the crackly line.

Garcia was in fact only two blocks away, strutting along the street heading in the direction of the Comisaria with Ramon

Ramon tagging along close behind. Garcia was feeling pleased with himself. After a good night's sleep in Flores's comfortable bed, an excellent breakfast of ham and eggs charged to Flores's personal account, a morning spent chivvying up the local police and a coffee and coñac he had not paid for either, he was reflecting on what glories might await a hero of the nation who had saved the Caudillo from the attentions of numerous dangerous terrorists.

'There will be medals in this you see,' he said lighting a cigar he had lifted from the pockets of one of his bearded suspects. 'There could even be a promotion.'

'Most possibly Capitan Garcia.'

'I would decline a ministerial position of course. As a man of action I would always want command of men in the field. Something like the governor of colony commends itself – a place where there are native tribes to be put down.' He paused to flick the ash off the end of his cigar onto an old woman begging alms at the side of the street.

'Just imagine,' he went on. 'What would have happened if the fate of the Caudillo had been left in the hands of these dim-witted policemen? I have never witnessed such a lack of initiative. It was lucky for them that I was on the scene to sort them out. Look, there is one in front now, shouting and waving his arms in the air. Why is he doing that?'

'I think he is trying to attract our attention Capitan Garcia. It looks like trouble if you ask me.'

★ ★ ★

Nathalie waited for the hour to come when Maman went to her room for her afternoon rest and Maria took Christine out to watch Juan working in the kitchen garden. The piece of paper was by the telephone where Maman had put it down. The number was written in Maman's neat hand and the Albacete dialling code was one Nathalie immediately recognised.

★ ★ ★

Garcia did not do himself much good by assuring Suarez that the Caudillo was safe in his hotel with a police guard discreetly keeping watch outside. How strange, Suarez commented icily, since the Caudillo was also in Madrid with pains in his stomach. The Caudillo in two places at once! How did the Capitan explain this?

'Arrest him,' Garcia bawled to two policemen as he came out of Flores's office purple-faced and pointing at Flores himself. 'Take him to the cells on a charge of treason and don't let him out until I say so!'

'But I don't understand,' Flores protested looking dumbfounded. Flores had just vacated his office so Garcia could make his phone call in private and this reaction to his further hospitality was not what he was expecting.

'Your incompetent force of officers has allowed the Caudillo to be poisoned.'

'Poisoned?'

'That is what I said. As Acting Chief of Police you are responsible and you will pay the price. I will see to it myself that you get at least twenty-five years' hard labour in some pestilence-ridden place in the jungle. What is more your incompetent force of officers has failed to report that the Caudillo left the Hotel Bahia early this morning. As a consequence, I have been made to look a fool.'

★ ★ ★

Wardrobe was not a matter that troubled Jaime Campello habitually. He had the clothes he went to work in, clothes he changed into when he came back from work and the suit he wore to church on Sundays yet none of these seemed quite suitable for a meeting with a lady. He toyed with the idea of going down to Delgado's, the shop on the Avenida that sold a more fashionable line in men's attire but the Delgado in question knew Campello well and it would not be long before the news that the carpenter had been spending his money on a new shirt and a new pair of trousers reached the ears of Lopez and the others. That, Campello realised, was the last thing he wanted. It would not take long for them to be speculating on what he was up to.

Deciding to postpone his choice of clothes until last, he went into the bathroom to take a shower and shave his face even though he had shaved it once already that day. Then he remembered the rose; the businesslike lady at the Diane Maitland Bureau of Friendship had told him to carry a single red rose so that he could be recognised. The nearest florista was not far from the Church and it closed at six – but then he remembered that the florista was a cousin of Conchita Gomez and she would be inquisitive to say the least as to why Jaime Campello, the least likely of persons, was buying a single red rose. Again he wondered how long would it take for Lopez and the others to be sniggering and nudging themselves.

As he entered the bathroom, Campello saw his face in the mirror and the scratch, which had now turned an angry shade of purple. Shaving, he found, only served to make the inflammation worse as did the application of a strong aftershave lotion that belonged Uncle Pablo. To make matters worse his hair stood on end and refused to lie flat. He wondered about ringing the Diane Maitland Bureau of Friendship and calling the whole thing off by pleading he had broken a leg or gone down with a dreadful fever, but apart from tempting providence, which he never liked to do, he realised that it was now quarter to seven and the lady at the Diane Maitland Bureau of Friendship would have gone home long ago.

Returning to the question of what to wear he settled for his Sunday best suit. The red rose then came back to mind and, though Campello's experience in matters of courtship was practically none, he realised that the kind of red rose that he was expected to carry was the kind that had a long stem. Arming himself with a pair of secateurs he marched off into the garden where it was dark except for the lights from the house. There was a much-neglected rose tree by the wall that had been planted many years ago by his mother. The blooms were more orange than red and, partly due to the season and partly due to the lack of pruning, there were sadly few of them. Selecting the one he felt to be the best he used the secateurs to snip it off along with as much of the stem as possible. When he got it back into the house, however, he saw that the stem, apart from being gnarled and knotted, was, like the foliage itself, covered with some exotic form of aphis.

Deciding he had no more time to spend on the rose, he left it as it was. It would be dark in the park, he told himself, and the rose would hardly be noticed. Besides to avoid unwelcome attention, he had decided to take a circuitous route to the Avenida and to be on the safe side, he realised he needed to be leaving soon. Top priority on his journey was not to bump into anyone he knew, because they would be curious as to why he was wearing his Sunday best suit on a week day and carrying a rose in his hand. Some eventualities, however, he realised he had not catered for: like what to say to anyone who saw him standing in the park in the Avenida; what explanation to give for what he was doing in a place where courting couples traditionally met. Starting to cross his mind too was the problem of what he was supposed to do with this lady after he had met her. Maybe she would have some suggestion on where she would like to be taken or maybe it was up to him to do the suggesting. He realised that in this respect he would have to be careful. Suggesting they go to a bar, for example, might be taken by the lady as evidence that he was a drunkard and that would be unfortunate. Furthermore he was known by the proprietors of most bars in Los Tidos so if he walked in with a lady the cat would well and truly be out of the bag.

Slipping out of the door of the Villa Verde with these wildly random thoughts running through his head, he saw Uncle Pablo coming up the street. They spoke briefly as they passed though Campello was careful to keep the rose hidden behind his back. Not that he needed to have worried unduly because Uncle Pablo was too full of himself to have much thought for what his nephew might be doing going out dressed up like he was on his way to Church. Uncle Pablo in the guise of Pablo El Pescador was entertaining again that evening. This time, he told his nephew he was appearing at a night spot on the waterfront used by foreigners called the Club Gringo. He had become such a crowd puller that the management of Club Gringo had asked for him specially or so Uncle Pablo boasted. Many attractive ladies went to Club Gringo, he added with a twinkle in his eyes, and with any luck he might be invited back to spend the night with one of them.

★ ★ ★

Before getting dressed Lola Martinez had spent an hour in the bath sipping cold white Rueda from a tall stemmed glass and twiddling the gold plated taps with her toes. She had decided to put her hair up this evening and wear long earrings and had the tiny pistol tucked in the top of her stocking where not even a policeman would have the audacity to look. The skirt she chose to wear for her rendezvous with El Serpiente was a short one made from the finest Toledo leather that had been tailored for her specially and fitted like a glove. She checked her wristwatch – it was twenty to eight – time to go and find out whether the most dangerous man in Spain lived up to expectations.

Seeing the lift was still out of order, she set off down the stairs carrying her shoes in case her heels made too much noise on the marble steps. On the way down she met no-one suggesting to her again most of the apartments in the Edificio Los Angeles were unoccupied. Reaching the ground floor, she noticed a rear entrance – a door with a door closer situated at the back of the stairwell and it led, she was pleased to see, onto a quiet path that went through the gardens and from there straight out onto the street. A quick glance back at the apartment block where everything still seemed quiet – a few lights were on in some of the windows but for the most part the ten storey building was in darkness.

The walk to the Plaza de Los Reyes took just a few minutes. A chill wind cut through a gap in the buildings and Lola was glad of her sable coat. When she got to the Plaza she saw a group of policemen standing talking, as it happened about Acting Chief Flores being put in the cells. The only attention they paid to Lola was the usual attention men pay to a good looking woman. Besides if they were on the alert for anyone that night it was for a man with a scar like a snake down the side of his face not a classy looking chica in a fine fur coat.

★ ★ ★

Campello had already reached the meeting place by the fountain. His journey along the back alleys from the Villa Verde had been largely uneventful although at one point he had been chased by a goat that was loose on a piece of spare land and, as a result of this escapade and having to climb over a wall to escape, the petals on his rose had fallen off so he was left carrying just the bare stem.

He saw Lola Martinez in the light of the street lamps as she crossed over the Avenida, and came towards him. Even at a distance he could tell she had the looks of a woman who was out of his class. She came from Los Tidos or so he'd been told but he had certainly never set eyes on her before. Suddenly he felt an attack of panic. What was he supposed to say to her? How was he supposed to introduce himself and what conversation should he strike up. Then he remembered the rose and held it up in front of him like an altar boy holding up a crucifix.

Lola Martinez, who had spent her adolescent years in the big city of Barcelona, was used to men who hung around in public parks. Most of them, she found, wanted to expose themselves to her but this particular man she was approaching appeared to be brandishing a stick. On the other hand there was nothing about him to suggest that he was dangerous and the stick, on closer inspection, looked more like a twig. Taking this to be a manifestation of some strange sexual perversion peculiar to this individual Lola made to walk past him. As she did, however, she noticed the scar on his cheek.

'Is it you?' she whispered huskily taking in his height, his skinny frame and the trousers that ended ten centimetres above his ankles.

'Yes it is I,' Campello replied finding he was having problems with his tongue sticking to the roof of his mouth so it sounded like he had a lisp. The lady had forgotten to bring her rose he noticed. So much for all the trouble he had gone to.

'I do not like being kept waiting. I suppose the excuse for your delay is that the police are out looking for you.'

Campello swallowed. The police? Was it already common knowledge he was responsible for lacing Franco's food last night? Evidence sadly that Pepe Gomez had failed to hold his tongue? As for being kept waiting, he did not understand what she meant by this. It was only five to eight – from where he was standing he could see the clock tower over the Ayuntamiento plainly. Stunning though she was, it was beginning to enter Campello's head that there was something strange about this young lady and he felt it best to be wary.

'Enough of this chat,' she said abruptly. 'Can we get down to business?'

Campello's eyes nearly shot out of his head. Business? What could she possibly mean by business? The girls at Fat Fatima's did business.

'The Old Man,' she hissed rolling up her eyes in what

appeared to be exasperation. 'Do you know where he is or do I have to find out for myself?'

Old Man? This was a new slant and Campello was finding it hard to keep up. The only Old Man he could think of was Uncle Pablo but, with this thought, everything suddenly started to fit into place. This lady was seeking out Uncle Pablo not him. Doubtless she had heard of Uncle Pablo's sexual prowess and, though it still didn't make sense, it seemed to Campello there had been a mix up of names. After all they were both called Campello and the lady at the Diane Maitland Bureau of Friendship had taken it wrongly they were one and the same. Campello's heart began to sink. All he wanted now was to get away from this strange woman and go back home as quickly as he could.

'You will find him in the Club Gringo down by the waterfront,' he said. 'It is near the marina. You will not miss it.'

'What name is he going by?'

'Pablo El Pescador – so I understand.'

Lola opened her shoulder bag and took out a little notepad in a silver case with its own little silver propelling pencil. 'This is the telephone number where I am staying,' she said writing it down. 'Ring me here at ten o'clock tomorrow morning. Meanwhile it is best that we are not seen together. I will do what needs to be done tonight,' and with that she turned on her high spiked heels and was gone into the night.

★ ★ ★

Telling Maman a lie; that she needed the car to go into town to give Señora Rey's daughter a piano lesson, had not been easy for Nathalie.

'At eight o'clock in the evening?' Maman had said, her eyes filling with suspicion. 'That is no time for a child to start practising scales.'

Telling her the truth, however – that she was meeting a man in the park in the Avenida – would have started Maman asking all sorts of questions. Who was this man? What kind of family did he come from? And when Nathalie replied she did not know, Maman would want to know why she did not know till, bit by bit, it would come out that Nathalie had done the unthinkable and put her name down with a lonely hearts' bureau. Then all hell would be let loose. Maman would want to know what she was playing at and what about all those eligible young men they had introduced her to when she was eighteen? Señor Miro's son, Geraldo, who was going into the diplomatic service? Carlos Alberto Vasquez who had a career as a notario in front of him? Did she remember how she had treated them? With coldness and disdain, Maman would remind her – as if they were not good enough for her.

Turning right out of the big iron gates and onto the road into town, Nathalie glanced at the clock on the dashboard: it was ten to eight. The discussion with Maman had taken more time than she thought and now she feared, she was going to be late. As she approached the Port Road with its traffic she knew she had a choice: either to go straight up the hill, across the Puente de San Marco then through the narrow streets of the town or take the long way round by the port and the Plaza de Los Reyes. The narrow little streets, she knew, sometimes got choked with cars especially at this time of night when the shops were closing. For this reason she decided to take the Port Road. Soon after doing so, however, she realised she had made a mistake.

The traffic in front began to slow down till eventually it ground to a halt. She tapped her fingers on the steering wheel. Up ahead she could see the police were checking people's papers and, though she didn't know it, the barricade she could see across the road was the same barricade El Serpiente had witnessed earlier on from his vantage point on top of the little knoll. The little knoll in fact lay to Nathalie's left as she sat in the line of traffic with growing frustration. And what she did not know either, was that a new shift of policemen had just come on duty and that they were pursuing their task of checking papers with renewed diligence and rigour – partly because they were fresh and partly because they had just been given a fifteen minute roasting by one Capitan Luis Garcia of the Cordoba section of the Guardia Civil.

But when it came to Nathalie's turn to show her papers, the policeman simply waved her on. They were looking for a man with a big scar on his face of course, not a young woman with her hair tied up with a black ribbon to show she was in mourning.

It was two minutes to eight as she sped away from the road block. Miraculously the traffic in front thinned out and she was able to keep her foot down as she went along the deserted wharves and slipways of the port. Taking the shortcut via the yacht marina she saw the bright lights of Club Gringo on the waterfront though the sign outside advertising a performance tonight by Pablo El Pescador, the famous Valencian folk singer, meant nothing to her.

Still managing to keep her speed up, she went by the Edificio Los Angeles set back in its own grounds and largely in darkness, then entered the Plaza de los Reyes at just turned eight. There, though she did not notice her, she passed the self-assured girl who had driven the blue Seat and to whom she had spoken to at the gates of the hacienda the day before yesterday. The self-assured girl was in conversation with the driver of a taxi, asking him, as it happened, if he knew the Club Gringo and, if so, to take her there.

With relief, Nathalie saw there were few cars parked in the Avenida and she pulled up alongside the park with the fountain. It was five past eight she saw on the clock above the Ayuntamiento, hardly noticing the tall young man in the ill-fitting suit who had just crossed the street tearing up a piece of paper then putting it in a bin.

All her concentration so far had been on not being late for her meeting but now the reality of an encounter with a complete stranger was starting to dawn on her. The registration with the Diane Maitland Bureau of Friendship had been a chance thing, rather as it had been with Jaime Campello and like Jaime Campello, this was the first time an introduction had been arranged for her. Already she was starting to have second thoughts. What would this man think of her when he set eyes on her? Would he be expecting a girl ten years younger with fashionable clothes and large breasts? Would he be disappointed to see her thin body and pale face? Should she give him the chance to make his excuse and leave?

The wind was getting stronger as she entered the gardens with the rose in her hand: the rose in her case being one of the blooms Juan so carefully tended and to which she had helped herself hoping he would not notice. The light of the street lamp filtering through the moving palm fronds was making strange rippling patterns on the ground and there was a strangeness about her surroundings that Nathalie immediately found she did not like. Even though the street was not far away, she felt an urge to turn round. Then she saw the figure not ten metres in front – a tall man just like the bureau had said, but dressed from neck to foot in black leather and sitting astride a massive motor cycle – looking for all the world like the leader of a gang. His face, she saw, was puckered down one side with an ugly scar but, worse still, instead of the single red rose that the lady at the Diane Maitland Bureau of Friendship had told her to expect, this man was holding a huge and cruel looking knife in his hand.

'You have kept me waiting,' he said in what Nathalie took to be a threatening tone. 'You must learn that the Snake does not like to be kept waiting. See to it that it never happens again. Do you understand?'

★ ★ ★

Taking care to avoid the piece of spare land where earlier he had been chased by the goat Jaime Campello's return journey to the Villa Verde was largely without incident. The fact that the streets had gone quiet after dark was largely due to the police round-up the night before and the fear among the greater part of the population that, if they ventured out late, they might too end up in the cells. What all this fuss was about no-one knew for certain then, as the day wore on, the rumour started to go round that none other than Franco himself was staying up at the Hotel Bahia. It was typical, the more outspoken ones began to mutter. Everyone in town had to suffer just because the Old Butcher had decided to pay them a visit. Why could he not take himself off back to Madrid and stay there? After all, no-one had invited him. Then another rumour started doing the rounds – that Franco had left but something had happened to him during his stay at the Hotel Bahia explaining why the police were still making arrests.

Campello was just coming out of an alleyway by the Church when a movement in the deserted little square in front of him caused him to draw back into the shadows. It turned out to be Father Miguel with his long black cloak flapping at his heels except this time Father Miguel's iron grey head was bent forward like a man lost in his own deep thoughts, an impression further confirmed by the fact he was talking to himself. The priest approached but, although Campello strained his ears, he could not catch what he was saying. On the whole, Campello considered it best to stay where he was in case his sudden appearance should cause Father Miguel embarrassment. Soon the priest had passed and Campello continued his walk but it struck him that he had never seen Father Miguel act in this strange way before and he wondered what the cause might be. As he passed the front of the Church and the highest part of the hill on which the Old Town of Los Tidos stood, the view inland was before him – the lights of traffic moving on the carretera and nearer to, on the Port Road, the bright lights of Paco's Rincon. There were no stars out tonight, he noticed, then momentarily, over the distant mountains he saw an eerie pink flicker of lightning. He waited and listened but the storm was too far away for the roar of thunder to reach his ears.

CHAPTER EIGHT

A Storm in the Night and an Ancient Vow

Nathalie Theroux saw the flicker of lightning too as she sat in her mother's car on the deserted promenade looking back at the town. She had hurriedly left the park in the Avenida and the man with the big knife in his hand and made her way to the seafront because she felt it would be somewhere where, even though it was quiet and not well lit, she would be safe. It was still only twenty past eight by the clock on the dashboard; still far too early to go back home because, if she did, she knew she would have Maman asking all sorts of questions about Señor Rey's daughter's piano lesson and why it hadn't lasted very long.

It was not in Nathalie's nature to be frightened easily but the man with the knife was a warning that she had been foolish to agree to a meeting with a complete stranger. The suggestion of the park on the Avenida had been hers because it was known locally as a lovers' meeting place but the fact there were so few people on the streets that night surprised her. She must be more careful in future, she told herself.

From where Nathalie sat the lights of Plaza de Los Reyes were in front of her about a hundred metres away. Beyond and following the line of the shore marked out by a phosphorescent line of breaking surf, she could make out the

150

tall shape of the Edificio Los Angeles – a building she knew well because Papa had had a hand in its design. There were a few lights in the Edificio, as she had noted before, though none showed in the penthouse suite on the top floor. To the right of the Edificio she could make out the spit of land that struck out into the sea silhouetted by the bright lights of the marina further on. There were a few flat rocks at the end of the spit of land, a place where Papa used to take her swimming on hot summer days. Good times she reflected: Papa's eyes smiling at her through the mask of his snorkel and later on a dinner of fresh fish from the sea cooked in an old pan over a driftwood fire.

★ ★ ★

Getting out of the taxi and paying off the goggle-eyed driver who had spent most of the short trip from the Plaza de Los Reyes angling his mirror so he could see up her skirt. Lola Martinez was also looking at the little spit of land sticking out into the sea. The difference was that from where she stood the spit of land was closer to her and she was viewing it from the opposite side to Nathalie Theroux. Lola's observation was not, however, a piece of casual sight-seeing. The spit gave her a fix on the position of the Edificio Los Angeles because, from here, the Edificio Los Angeles was hidden from view by a large building containing a boat repair yard. The Edificio Los Angeles was, of course, where she had got to get Franco back to once she had kidnapped him and she was making a rough estimate of the distance.

Turning back to the waterfront, Lola was struck first of all by its tawdriness. Bright lights to Lola Martinez meant the bright lights of big cities like Barcelona and this, by comparison, was cheap and tacky. The fact that some of the signs outside the bars and restaurants were in German itself told a tale despite their Spanish nautical sounding names names such as Delfin Bar, Los Barcos, Club Faro. The clientele of these places were, as far as Lola could see, fat little men in sailor's caps and espadrilles in some cases accompanied by bloated looking women dressed in all their finery but red-faced and blotchy from spending too much time in the sun.

Club Gringo did not prove hard to find. It was one of the larger and more vulgar looking establishments on the waterfront with a red neon sign in the effigy of a gun toting cowboy that flashed on and off making the cowboy's hand appear to go up and down. What Franco was doing visiting a place like this Lola could hardly imagine. Still, this whole trip of his was shrouded in mystery.

Lola glanced at her wristwatch. It was quarter to nine. Time to move in she told herself touching her fingers lightly against her thigh and feeling the hard lump of the little silver pistol tucked in the top of her stocking under the soft leather.

Club Gringo was fronted by a garden of small palmetto bushes garishly lit with coloured bulbs and a man dressed in a white tuxedo stood at the door. He was busy adjusting the carnation in his lapel as Lola approached.

'Señora,' he said looking up. 'You are a member? If not it can be arranged. For ladies there is no charge.'

'I am looking for the one who goes by the name of Pablo El Pescador. Do you know this man?'

'Yes I know him,' the man replied, his smile beginning to fade.

'Can you tell me where he is?'

'He is right behind you, Señora. That is him lying in the bushes.'

★ ★ ★

Since his brief encounter with Jaime Campello just over an hour earlier, Uncle Pablo in expansive mood had finished off one bottle of absenta and fetched out another from the secret stock he kept under his bed. Thus fortified he set out for the waterfront and his appointment at Club Gringo. The fact that he got there in the first place was a small miracle but that his legs went from under him as he staggered up to the door was hardly surprising.

The man in the white tuxedo who was the long suffering manager of the Club Gringo witnessed the incident with his own eyes.

'There goes our entertainment,' he said dispassionately to one of his assistants. 'Put the old borracho in the bushes where he can sleep it off without anyone seeing him and in future remind me to stick to discos.'

The sign advertising the appearance of Pablo El Pescador that had been there when Nathalie Theroux drove past, was hurriedly taken down and, the famous Pescador himself was dragged by the heels into the palmettos. As a mark of respect to his age, however, the Manager of the Club Gringo retrieved his beret from the bushes and laid it on his chest in case he should miss it when he came round.

It was not, as it happened, the thought of his beret that first crossed Uncle Pablo's mind as he regained his senses. There had been a bottle of absenta in his hand, a bottle of absenta that had been only half empty and Uncle Pablo's initial urge was to discover where it had gone. The hand in question was his right hand but for some strange reason he discovered his right hand seemed incapable of movement.

Uncle Pablo shifted his position and opened his eyes. His right hand was still there alright at the end of his arm where it was usually to be found, but the mysterious paralysis seemed to persist and it puzzled him. He tried re-focusing his eyes then discovered the explanation. There was a spike sticking in his palm pinning it to the ground. Thinking momentarily that he had died and as a punishment for his misspent life he had been crucified to the doors of heaven as an example to others, Uncle Pablo started to mutter a prayer of repentance that came out as gibberish because he did not go to church and, as with all prayers, he did not know the words. But as his clouded vision started to clear he realised that the spike was not as he thought but the heel of a woman's shoe. The shoe, Uncle Pablo noticed with gathering interest, contained a foot and the foot was at the end of a leg – a long and shapely leg he saw when he studied it further – a leg in silk stockings of the finest quality. Whether this was Heaven or Hell or some limbo land in between, Uncle Pablo was suddenly past caring. Please God, he said to himself, don't summon me through the pearly gates just yet. Let me stay where I am.

Then a woman's voice spoke from above, a direction Uncle Pablo took to be generally consistent with the direction of Heaven. 'You must not resist,' said the voice.' You must come with me.'

Uncle Pablo nodded. The voice he now took to be that of an angel sent down to take care of him. No, he assured the voice, he had no intention of resisting. She could do with him as she pleased.

★ ★ ★

In his book-lined study with high clerestory windows set close to the ceiling, Father Miguel was alone at his desk drinking sherry.

'Don Antonio,' he said raising his glass.

One of the interesting customs Father Miguel discovered when he first came to Los Tidos was that the duty of keeping the priest's wine cellar stocked fell on certain local landowners. Hence it was a ritual of Father Miguel's that he always drank to the health of whichever gentleman had provided him with the particular bottle he was sampling. Father Miguel's mood was not as good though as it usually was at this time of day when evening prayers were said and the priest's tasks were done. Since Jaime Campello had seen him in the square by the church a little over an hour ago, he had become increasingly agitated and sombre and the sherry he was drinking was not out of an appreciation of its character or vintage but driven by a simple desire to get drunk. Father Miguel reflected that there had been few occasions in his life when he had resorted to the bottle to drown his troubles but this sadly was one of them.

The event that had prompted his bout of depression was a visitation earlier on by the Señoras Crespo, two sisters who had married two brothers, both now widows and both prominent members of his congregation. The Señoras Crespo had set themselves up long ago as arbiters of what was right and proper in the affairs of the Church and Father Miguel had learned from previous experiences to be wary when they appeared on his doorstep. Usually it was to deliver him with a rap on the knuckles for some ceremony he had overlooked or a laxity he had permitted or the words of a psalm he had got wrong. This time however it was worse.

155

'It is about the Feast of the Two Virgins,' the elder Señora Crespo began. 'We wondered how you were getting on with the preparations.'

'We have not heard yet who you have chosen to take the vows,' her younger sister took over eagerly. 'We trust you have the matter in hand.'

'Of course,' said Father Miguel glassy eyed and not having the faintest idea what either of them was talking about.

'Naturally everything needs to be done properly.'

'Naturally,' Father Miguel agreed.

After they had gone, he frantically searched the book shelves of his study. As far as he was concerned the Feast of the Two Virgins was one of those wretched mediaeval traditions he had so little time for – in this case, a ceremony peculiar to Los Tidos that came up every twenty-five years and which was due to be celebrated shortly – a ceremony that for him, meant extra work and time that would have been better spent visiting the sick.

Being a priest in the secular tradition Father Miguel had little inclination towards pomp and ritual but he realised that any sentiments expressed along those lines would only bring him into conflict with the Señoras Crespo and the Señoras Crespo were, as he found out on several occasions in the past, considerable forces in the Church of Los Tidos. To cross swords with them on any issue would only lead to trouble and Father Miguel was on the whole someone who preferred to take the easy route in life.

At last he found what he was looking for – a book of hand-written notes compiled by a painstaking if somewhat pedantic nineteenth century predecessor who had taken great joy in researching local religious customs and recording them in detail. The nineteenth century predecessor's notes had got Father Miguel out of tight corners before.

But as to vows? The old Father had scribed several pages of long hand on the subject of the Feast of the Two Virgins: the origins of the ceremony (the ancient legend from which the town took its name), the vault in the Cemetario supposedly containing the Two Virgins' relics, the blessing of the relics that took place every twenty-five years – all this Father Miguel had already taken steps to acquaint himself with but what he could not recall was seeing anything about vows until finally the explanation presented itself: two pages of the old Father's notes stuck together and which Father Miguel had to prise apart with a letter knife. Vows: it was all explained but as Father Miguel read more the complacent smile on his face started to fade.

★ ★ ★

The altogether puzzling co-operation of Generalisimo Francisco Franco continued long after Lola had got him back to the penthouse suite of the Edificio Los Angeles. The short walk from the marina by way of the rough land adjoining the shore had passed off without incident; Franco in front, Lola just a few steps behind and she telling him to go this way then that over the noise of the sea and the wind, as they picked their way across the broken path between the tamarisk bushes. All the time there were flickers of lightning in the background over the mountains, which cast a strange pink coloured light over the puckered ground in front of them and helped them see their way.

Reaching the Edificio Lola noticed with relief that the

place looked just as quiet as when she had left it over an hour before. She was relieved too to see that she had not broken one of her heels on the walk across the rough land.

Now, back in the penthouse apartment, she had her first chance to look at Franco in a good light. Yes, she decided, there was a definite resemblance with the familiar face she had seen on postage stamps and coins. The black coat gone shiny on the elbows and lapels and the peasant's beret he wore seemed out of place but she reasoned that these were all part of his disguise. He was after all posing as a fisherman.

'You must put all thoughts of escape out of your head,' she said reaching down to take the little silver pistol out of the top of her stocking.

Franco's eyes stayed riveted on the long expanse of silky smooth thigh. No, he reassured her, he was not thinking of escaping.

'Good, now you must take all your clothes off,' she ordered. 'And with those handcuffs you see on the table over there, you must handcuff yourself to the frame of the bed.'

To deprive Franco of his clothing was intended as a further deterrent to his escaping but the alacrity with which the Generalisimo complied with these instructions took Lola by surprise. Curious too were the grubby combinations he wore under his shirt and trousers, the holes in them looking suspiciously like the work of moths, though this, once again, she put down to being part of his disguise. But what was most amazing of all as he stood naked in front of her, apart from his emaciated form was that his penis was sticking upright and pointing straight at her and she saw too that his penis was a remarkable size.

'I want you to realise,' said Lola, not letting herself be put off by these observations, 'That you may be here with me for several days.'

Franco grinned. That was fine by him, he said, bouncing his bare bottom down on the bed and snapping the handcuffs onto his wrist.

★ ★ ★

Down in the cells beneath the Comisaria, Acting Chief of Police Flores stared eyeball to eyeball with a group of bearded men.

'Don't blame me,' he said glumly.

★ ★ ★

A shutter banging somewhere outside woke Jaime Campello from another sleep troubled by strange dreams. It was two in the morning, he saw from the alarm clock. Outside a storm was raging: rain lashed against the windows, echoes of thunder rolled round distant hillsides and, one after the other, flashes of lightning lit up his room. He got out of bed and holding up the bottoms of his pyjamas, still the ones with no cord, he went in search of the shutter that was making the noise. Another flash of lightning was followed almost immediately by a crash of thunder as he made his way along the hallway with tousled hair and red-rimmed eyes. He tried putting on the light but the electricity had gone off – a normal enough event in Los Tidos whenever there was a storm. The pocket torch he kept for such emergencies was in a drawer in the kitchen and so he shuffled through the house in his carpet slippers in search of it yawning and scratching his head at the same time. Another flash of lightning illuminated the carpets and furniture with its strange pink light followed by another even louder crash of thunder. The storm was almost overhead, he judged: there would be damage to be seen in the morning.

The loose shutter was at the kitchen window and Campello, with an oilcloth table cover over his head and shoulders to keep him dry, went outside and made quick work of fastening it back to its hook on the wall. Coming back through the house still with the torch in his hand, force of habit caused him to stop off and look in Uncle Pablo's room. The old man was not in his bed, he saw. The hour was late and he had visions of Uncle Pablo making his way home from Club Gringo soaked to the skin. Then the image of Uncle Pablo lying at the bottom of the barranco crossed his mind and the waters in the barranco swollen by heavy rain starting to rise. Alarm bells began to sound in his head but at that point Uncle Pablo's words from earlier on came back to him along with the lecherous leer on the old man's face. Uncle Pablo was hoping to pick up a woman to spend the night with, was he not? Campello's mind flitted automatically to the beautiful but strange woman he had met in the park, the woman who had expressed such an interest in meeting the old man. She would have gone to the Club Gringo in pursuit of him, would she not, and even now he could be sharing her bed. It was with this thought in his mind and with the storm still raging outside that Campello put his head back on the pillow.

★ ★ ★

For Father Miguel who, despite several glasses of Don Pedro's finest pale coñac, still lay awake at this hour, the coming of the great storm in the night was portentous. It was in a storm such as this that the legend of the Two Virgins had been born.

Many centuries ago, Los Tidos stood in the path of a great Moorish army. Under the standard of Islam, the Moors had already crossed over the narrow seas separating Spain from North Africa and spread their dark influence over much of the south. Next in their line of advance was the great city of Valencia and only Los Tidos, commanding the narrow plain between the sea and the mountains, stood in their way.

So it came to pass that the people of Los Tidos gathered together in their hill top fortress in their hour of darkness. The flocks were driven in from the fields and all eyes were turned to the south, the direction from which the crescent banners were soon expected to appear.

Then, at first light one morning, those who kept vigil in the towers called the alarm and pointed to the sea. There, on the horizon, a great armada of ships was gathering with their black sails already unfurling in the wind. Everyone rushed to the ramparts. Even at this distance, the cruel glint of steel could be seen on the ships' decks and the townspeople knew that what they saw was the coming of a great army. They saw too that their own plight was hopeless.

At that time there lived in the town a young man and a young woman who were betrothed to be married. The young man was a fisherman and she was the daughter of a goatherd. They were among those who stood on the ramparts that morning and watched the approach of the great Moorish armada.

It was in the first chill light of dawn that the men began to make their preparations for battle but the women wept because they saw how pitiful the numbers of their menfolk were. The armada of *Moros* seemed to get bigger as it got closer and, already, those blessed with long sight could make out the lines of dusky faces standing at the prows of the ships.

When the men were ready they went first to the Church to ask for God's help in the coming battle. There the priest kneeled down with them for he had a greater burden on his mind than any that morning. Like the other men he carried a sword but his sword was not for the throats of *Moros*. If all else failed, it would fall on him to save the women and children of the town from the wicked dark skinned invaders. He would use his sword to put them all to death before plunging the blade deep into his own heart because it was far better for them to die by his hand than in the hands of cruel savages.

So the men of Los Tidos looked up to the priest as he blessed them. They knew what he had to do and none of them would have wished to change places with him.

Just then the young fisherman stepped forward and all eyes fell on him as he knelt beside the priest in front of the altar. After he had finished praying he stood up and, taking the crucifix in his hand, he called to the goatherd's daughter to come and join him. Together, before the people of the town, they took a solemn vow of chastity. They promised that if God should spare them all from the *Moros* then in this way they would give Him their thanks.

In silence and with their eyes cast down everyone went back to the ramparts. The ships were so close now that the townspeople could hear the harsh voices of the sailors calling to each other across the waters. They could see too the wicked curved blades of the *Moros'* swords.

Gripping their own swords with white knuckles, the men with the young fisherman among them left the ramparts and made their way down to the shore to where they planned to engage the *Moros* as they waded in from the sea. There they stood shoulder to shoulder in a single thin line, brave yet knowing in their hearts that they were hopelessly outnumbered.

It was the women back on the ramparts who first noticed the freshening of the wind and the darkening of the sky. They saw too how the ships were beginning to pitch and roll in the shallow waters and soon cries of alarm could be heard. The heavens grew blacker; the wind stronger and the morning sun was blotted out by thick racing clouds. The men on the shore looked up as great jagged forks of lightning ripped across the sky and they saw how some of the closest ships had already capsized as great waves threw them up and brought them crashing down. The splitting of timbers and the screams of drowning men reached their ears as they stood waiting with their swords drawn.

Then the rain came. It rained as it had never rained before. The swirling black clouds seemed to open and a deluge swamped the decks of those ships still left afloat, so weighing them down with water that they too sank to the bottom of the Bahia.

The men of Los Tidos looked on with their hair and beards soaked by the rain and the spray of the raging sea. They marvelled at the violence of the storm and then at the suddenness of its passing. The rain stopped, the clouds dispersed and the sun came out again. And with the dropping of the wind, the sea became calm and the people of Los Tidos beheld an amazing sight. The waters of the Bahia were littered with the corpses of drowned men, the shattered spars of broken ships and the torn and tattered remnants of black sails.

Not a single one of the ships remained afloat and all who sailed with the great armada had been lost to the storm.

Led by the young fisherman, the men along the shore went down on their knees one by one and gave thanks to God for sparing them from the Moors. They were joined by the women and children up on the ramparts and, as the sun rose higher, the priest raised his sword above his head and cast it down onto the rocks below where it shattered into a thousand pieces, its blade untried.

That was a time for great rejoicing in Los Tidos, but not all rejoiced. The young man and the young woman spoke quietly to one another down by the shore. They spoke of their undying love and the vow they had taken and then joined hands and took the steep path of many steps that led up to the town pausing only to pick a handful of wild flowers from the wayside. Together they went to the top of one of the Church's tall towers and looked down at the people singing and dancing in the streets. Looking into each other's eyes, they smiled and briefly their lips touched before, still holding hands and still clutching onto their posies of wild flowers, they threw themselves from the tower to their deaths among the revellers beneath.

The names of the young man and the young woman were never recorded; some said because they would never have wanted to be made into saints. But ever since the day the great Moorish armada sunk in the Bahia de Los Tidos, each generation has given thanks to the young man and young woman whose selfless vow had saved the town – the fisherman and the goatherd's daughter whose love for each other was so deep they could no longer bear to live.

★ ★ ★

Father Miguel sighed. He could see that with the noise of the storm going on outside he would not be getting any sleep that night so he got out of bed and shuffled his feet into his slippers. Dressed in a long nightshirt and matching cap with a tassle on the top he made his way downstairs and back to his study. Finding, as Jaime Campello had done, that the electricity had failed he lit a candle but having no candlestick to hand, he ended up putting it in the empty bottle of Don Pedro's coñac.

Father Miguel had been priest in Los Tidos for more years than he cared to think and by his reckoning the last Feast of the Two Virgins must have been due to take place in 1938, five years before he arrived. The fact that it had not been celebrated was due to the Civil War that was raging at the time and tearing Spain apart. Indeed, he knew there were some in the town who blamed the victory of Franco and the butchery that followed on the failure to pay respect to the blessed Two Virgins in the proper form.

Sitting at his desk he got out the old Father's notes again. There by the flickering light of the candle he re-read the detailed description of the ceremony: how the relics of the Two Virgins were contained in an oak studded casket; how the oak studded casket was kept in a sealed vault in the Cemetario; how the seals were broken on the day of the fiesta; how the casket, supported on poles and carried on the shoulders of four unmarried men, was paraded through the streets of the town in a procession before being brought to the Church; how then the casket was put before the altar where it was given a blessing by the priest; how, for the occasion, the Church was decked with garlands of wild flowers – an acknowledgement, so the old Father opined, to the posies of wild flowers the Two

165

Virgins clutched in their hands as they jumped to their deaths.

But then Father Miguel came once more to the part of the ceremony that he had not been aware of previously and that was responsible for his present state of turmoil. The blessing of the casket over, two young people of the town had to come forward and, in the same way that the young fisherman and his betrothed had done all those centuries ago, they had to enter into a vow of chastity.

Father Miguel groaned. The Feast of the Two Virgins was not a week away and from somewhere he had to conjure up a young man and a young woman, prepared to take a vow of chastity. This was 1963, he said out loud, not the Middle Ages. Just where was he supposed to find volunteers to do such a thing?

In a wild moment earlier on he had wondered about giving this part of the ceremony a miss and hoping that, with the lapse of fifty years since the last Feast, no-one would notice. This, he quickly realised, was being stupidly naive. The Señoras Crespo would have their eyes on him and any glaring omissions such as this would have them down on him like a ton of bricks. More than likely it would end up with the Bishop.

The priest stroked back his iron grey hair and went over to the big chestnut wood dresser that filled one wall of his study. From there he took out an unopened bottle of coñac and poured a large measure into a balloon glass.

'Don Domingo,' he said studying the pale colour of the fine old brandy in the candlelight.

* * *

166

The next day dawned on a scene of devastation in Los Tidos. The storm in the night had fetched down trees and telephone wires and washed out soil and stones into the streets. The walls of terraces had collapsed and the barranco itself was a raging torrent of turgid mud – so spectacular that people came from all over the town to stand on the Puente de San Marco and stare in wonder and amazement at the sight beneath. On the shore a wrack of seaweed and driftwood had been cast high up the beach and, in the harbour, two fishing boats had broken loose from their moorings and run aground whilst the ferrocarril had been brought to a standstill because of a landslide in a cutting.

None of these events, however, deterred Capitan Luis Garcia of the Guardia Civil from making an early start. Fresh from yet another good night's sleep in Flores's comfortable bed from which the noise of the storm did not disturb him, Garcia, in the company of his assistant, Ramon Ramon, breakfasted on ham and eggs in an eating place just off the Avenida. The proprietor of this eating place had already heard about the Capitan from Cordoba who paid for nothing and didn't even bother presenting him with a bill. The word was round that anyone who crossed this officer in any way promptly got put into the cells and the proprietor was not keen to push his luck.

'So.' said Garcia, wiping the grease off his face and calling for more coffee. 'If our mission is to find a poisoner where is the best place to start?'

Ramon Ramon was looking out of the window.

'The answer is with the poison,' Garcia went on not waiting to hear his reply. 'Today we are going to track down all known purveyors of poisons in Los Tidos and interview them. Sooner or later one will crack under questioning and lead us to our man. In this case our man may be the notorious El Serpiente. What is it you are staring at hombre? You should be listening to what I am saying and not gazing out of the window like a simpleton.'

'There is a suspicious looking character over the street Capitan Garcia. He is getting on a motorcycle and wearing a bandana across his face in the way someone would do who is trying to conceal a scar.'

Garcia looked over his shoulder. 'Pah', he snorted. 'If you think that is El Serpiente then you are grievously mistaken. Someone as cunning as he would not present himself openly on the street. He will be hiding in a cave somewhere or holed up in a safe house. He has carried out his heinous crime now he is waiting for the coast to clear before he makes a run for it. To catch a terrorist, hombre, you must learn to think the way a terrorist thinks.'

★ ★ ★

El Serpiente's thoughts as he coasted down the Avenida on his Harley Davidson motorcycle were not on capture but on the chica from Barcelona who had made such a poor showing of things last night. After she had fled, El Serpiente spent the night in the park under the palm trees sheltering from the storm with a groundsheet draped over his head to keep the rain off him. The storm did not bother him for he had endured far worse storms on the knife-edge ridges of the Pyrenees. The scowl on his face was on account of the chica and the useless partner she had turned out to be. Her sudden flight El Serpiente put down to her inability to go through with the kidnapping of Franco. The chica had got cold feet and now it was left to him to finish the job off on his own.

El Serpiente had worked with women many times before but they, like himself, had been dedicated fighters for the cause not two bit opportunists who turned fickle for the slightest reason. Woman or man, he made a mental note never to get involved with opportunists again. But what of Franco? He was up in this Hotel Bahia, the place the station master had told him about, and, unless he acted quickly, the chance to take him would be gone. Then what would there be to bargain with for the lives of those held prisoner in the north?

Approaching the Plaza de Los Reyes, El Serpiente eased his speed. He could see several policemen in the Plaza standing in a group talking to one another but to his relief none of them took any notice of him and he made the right turn that took him along the promenade and past the place where Nathalie Theroux had parked her car the night before. Out to sea he could see the last of the storm: an opaque blackness blotting out the horizon and big rollers still pounding in up the beach. The storm had done its work. A good hundred metres of the promenade had now been completely washed away and El Serpiente had not gone far along its length before he was forced to come to a standstill. The sky overhead was grey, the wind still cold and fresh explaining why there was not a soul was to be seen on the beach. El Serpiente pulled down the bandana from around his face and tasted the salty wetness in the air. The noise of the waves drowned out everything, even the deep throaty roar of the Harley Davidson's exhausts as he took his bearings. To the south there was a low line of buff-coloured cliffs, hardly high enough to be called cliffs but convoluted and water-worn into strange shapes. The cliffs went on as far as the eye could see till they disappeared into the shifting mistiness that hid the far end of the Bahia where they became just another shade of grey. Then, just at the point where visibility ended, El Serpiente spotted something: a white zig-zag in the cliff face, a flight of lime washed steps such as might connect a big hotel with its own private beach beneath.

Giving the Harley Davidson the slightest touch of acceleration, El Serpiente picked his way forward through the wreckage of the promenade being careful not to puncture his tyres on one of the twisting pieces of reinforcing iron that stuck out in every direction from the rubble. Soon he was running on the smooth sand and picking up speed. There was a joyful feel to this, reminding him of the time just after the war when he had ridden a horse bareback on a beach such as this to escape from the camp prison where the French had put him with countless others and where so many of them died.

The haze on the beach made strange mirages. A flock of seagulls taking to the air took on the appearance of a twisting vortex then, in the distance, a stick shaped object came up out of the sand that, as he got closer to it, took on life. It turned out to be a dog, an emaciated specimen, padding along towards him in the spindrift with a sideways movement to compensate for the buffeting wind. They passed on a lonely stretch of the storm wracked beach – the man on the motorcycle and the grey emaciated dog though neither would ever know how their lives had touched.

CHAPTER NINE

The Wrong Generalisimo

Unlike Capitan Luis Garcia, Jaime Campello, jobbing carpenter of Los Tidos, had not enjoyed a peaceful night. The crashing and rumbling of thunder continued to keep him awake till finally he dropped off in the early hours into yet another sleep filled with strange dreams. This time the dreams were about Uncle Pablo taking part in unspeakable sexual acts with the lady in the fur coat who Campello had met under the palm trees, dreams in which for some reason, Uncle Pablo had horns on his head and a long tail.

Campello woke suddenly and in a cold sweat. It was broad daylight and the clock on his bedside table told him it was half past eight. The first anguished thought to enter his head was that the doors for the ayuntamiento were due to be finished that day. Hurriedly he got himself out of bed and into the bathroom where he shaved again his already scratched and over-shaved face. Memories of the night before came flooding back as he stood in front of the mirror and he vowed that he would have nothing more to do with the Diane Maitland Bureau of Friendship. He would write a letter to them that very evening, he promised himself, asking to be taken off their files and suggesting that he ought to have his money back!

A quick glance in Uncle Pablo's room on his way to the

kitchen confirmed that Uncle Pablo had not returned from his night at Club Gringo bringing the image in his dream back to him – that of Uncle Pablo with eyes like red hot coals coupled in a lewd sexual act with the lady in the fur coat. Campello shuddered. He wondered whether he ought to mention these strange images to Father Miguel at his next confession then decided that this was probably the least of his worries. What if Generalisimo Franco had swallowed a dose of the emetic in his paella as Pepe Gomez seemed to think? He could hardly believe that inadvertently he had purged the most important stomach in all of Spain, but, if it was so and if he was found out, then anything might happen to him. Still the best course of action, he decided, was to go about his business in the usual way and to act perfectly normally. Sooner or later all this would blow over or so he hoped.

The electricity was back on, Campello noticed, as he put a pan of water on the stove to boil. Oversleeping meant that he did not have time go down to Penedes's Panaderia for fresh bread so he made do with what was left of yesterday's loaf and toasted it lightly under the grill then coated it with fruit preserve to take away any taste of staleness. Followed by coffee and two boiled eggs this was Jaime Campello's breakfast on the morning after the big storm.

The big storm was much in evidence when later Campello stepped out of the front door of the Villa Verde to make the short journey to his workshop. Mud and bits off trees littered the streets and there was a cold damp smell in the air that made Campello glad of the pullover he had put on over his shirt and under his cardigan. The telephones were out of order, said someone he passed, and the wind in the night had fetched down a big bean tree onto a house near the Port Road. A little further on, Campello saw Old Roberto and his faithful mule Emilia making their way back up the steeply stepped street towards him. Emilia carried two panniers – one with Old Roberto's tools the other with a bunch of freshly pulled carrots from Old Roberto's small-holding.

'Hola Jaime,' Old Roberto greeted him, short of breath from the sharp pull up the hill. 'This is fine weather for snails but no good for my bones.'

Old Roberto was on his way home, he explained. The earth on his few hectares was soaked with water from the storm and it made for hard work. 'Best left for a day to dry out,' he said casting a doubtful eye up at the grey skies as if he half expected them to open again.

Listening to Old Roberto helped Campello to forget his troubles for a few moments as he turned his attention to what the small-holder had to say about this and that and how rain in November always brought swarms of mischievous insects that played havoc with his late tomatoes. The old man's nut-brown wrinkled face under his battered wide-brimmed straw hat and the gentle nuzzling of Emilia's nose against his arm put Campello's mind back to the way things had been before the fateful night at Paco's Rincon and the telephone calls from the business-like lady at the Diane Maitland Bureau. There was much to be said for the simple life, Campello said to himself, as he took his leave of Old Roberto and continued his walk to his workshop.

'Jaime,' Old Roberto called after him. 'Have you heard about what has happened to Robles?'

∗ ∗ ∗

An hour earlier, the irascible old ratcatcher had been sitting at his bench in his workshop setting a spring back in a trap when, without warning the door to the street burst open with a resounding crash. Being old and infested with worm the door responded to this treatment by coming off its hinges and disintegrating into a heap of splinters and sawdust on the floor. Once the dust settled, Robles saw the huge bulk of Capitan Luis Garcia profiled between the jambs and the lintel of the now doorless doorframe. Capitan Luis Garcia was back in plain clothes.

'You are Robles?' Garcia barked striding over the heap of rotten timber brandishing his revolver and with Ramon Ramon close behind with his fingers in his ears.

'My money is kept in the bank,' snarled Robles thinking this was some kind of stick-up. 'You will find nothing here.'

'You sell poisons,' said Garcia ignoring these remarks and looking round curiously at the array of traps and devices that had so impressed Campello. 'I will have you know that I am Capitan Garcia of the Guardia Civil and I am investigating a most serious crime. My advice to you therefore is to co-operate as fully as you can.'

Robles glared back. He said nothing but there was a look of sullen obstinacy on his face. It just so happened that at that moment the door to the poison cupboard was standing open and Garcia's eye fell on the rows of sinister looking bottles on the shelves.

'Aha!' he said with a triumphant smile, going over and picking up one of the bottles and inspecting its skull and cross bones label. 'Confirm that these bottles contain poisons Señor Robles.'

'Take a swig and see.'

'You are pushing your luck, hombre,' said Garcia coming across menacingly and standing over the ratcatcher, waving the revolver in his face. 'I have warned you about being co-operative and I will not warn you again. If you continue to impede my investigation then it will be the worse for you. Do you understand? Six months in leg irons breaking rocks might have to be the cure for your bad manners.'

Robles glared. It was a glare of dumb insolence.

'So,' Garcia continued. 'Are you an Anarchist or a Separatist or just someone who associates with such people? Which of these is it, Señor Robles?'

'I am a ratcatcher.'

'Correction. Ratcatching is your front. Your real business is overthrowing the government and bringing the curse of chaos and lawlessness down onto our nation once again. Take my advice, hombre, a confession would be far better for you in the long term.'

'I have nothing to confess.'

'We will see about that Señor Robles, if that is your real name. What is this object you are working on?'

'A trap. '

'A trap! We only have your word for that, hombre. Let me take a closer look at it. These springs and mechanisms have the appearance of a device for detonating a bomb. What do you say to that Señor Robles? How do you answer?'

'Capitan Garcia.' It was Ramon Ramon who piped up. 'If I were you I would not put my hand inside that thing. Think of what might happen to your fingers if it went off.'

★ ★ ★

In the Penthouse Suite of the Edificio Los Angeles Lola Martinez checked to see that the old man who she took to be Generalisimo Francisco Franco was still sleeping. He was, she was relieved to find still snoring loudly, still handcuffed to the playboy's bed, still with an ear-to-ear grin on his face and still with his huge penis sticking up in the air. More disgustingly still was the glass on the bedside table containing his heavily stained false teeth.

Still in her bathrobe, Lola decided to make her phone call before she took a shower. The number she wanted was written on a piece of paper inside her passport. It was an ex-directory number in Franco's private office – a number, according to Raul that would be answered by one of his private secretaries. Twice she dialled the digits; twice she got the unobtainable tone. Lola frowned. She decided to try the operator.

'I am trying to get a Madrid number,' she explained. 'For some reason I cannot get through.'

'I am sorry, Señora, but the lines to Madrid are out of order,' said the girl with her tone of voice giving away that she was repeating information she had given out many times that morning.

'But my call is urgent.' Lola protested. 'This is most unsatisfactory.'

'I am sorry Señora but the storm in the night brought down the telephone wires. The engineers are working on them now. I suggest you try again in two hours.'

Replacing the handset, Lola went back into the bedroom. Franco was still fast asleep, still snoring loudly, and she picked up the little silver pistol from where she had left it on a small chest of drawers and slipped it into her pocket. Passing through the lounge on her way back to the bathroom, she stopped suddenly. She thought she had just heard a faint scrabbling noise outside the door then, as she was about to put it down to a trick of her imagination, she heard it again.

Her hand felt for the pistol. Her thoughts went immediately to El Serpiente even though she had told him to ring her and it was not yet ten. Had he tried earlier? Had he had problems in getting through? Had he traced the telephone number she had given him to this address and was this him now presenting himself in person? The image of the skeletal young man in the ill fitting suit with the unruly mop of hair came back to her, the image that was so strangely at odds with the man's ruthless reputation.

Lola Martinez had met men before whose appearance belied their characters. Wolves in sheep's clothing she called them and in her estimation they were men who could never be trusted. So it might be with El Serpiente – a thief coming to steal Franco from her perhaps. Why else would he be hanging round outside and not ringing the bell?

On bare tip toes she went across to the door as silently and swiftly as an Apache brave. Realising she would need both hands free to turn the key and open the catch at the same time she reluctantly released her grip on the pistol. The door had no chain or a fish eye to see who was outside and this was a pity. To compensate for these shortcomings she balanced her weight on the balls of her feet as she had been trained to do and made ready to leap back if anyone should make an attempt to rush her.

Having the door opened to him so suddenly by Señora Beatriz came as quite a shock to Ernesto the Conserja's husband. He had been putting his eyeball to the keyhole before knocking the door on the off chance he might catch another glimpse of Señora Beatriz in her lacy black lingerie. Unfortunately though there was a key in the keyhole, blocking the view, so Ernesto was just on the point of giving his trousers a final adjustment when the door flew open and he found himself face to face with the lady of his fantasies sooner than he expected.

'Just what do you think you are doing here?' demanded Señora Beatriz in a curt voice he had never heard her use before. Neither had he seen Señora Beatriz without her make up or with her hair unbrushed.

'I can come back later,' he stammered, backing away towards the stairwell with his eyelids locked in a wide open position and looking every bit like a startled rabbit.

'You will do no such thing,' Lola snapped at him. 'If I see your face up here again I will let your wife know what a filthy little pervert you are and how you spy on women through keyholes with your prick in your hand.'

* * *

Up in Madrid, Suarez picked up the telephone for the umpteenth time.

'What has happened to my call?' he bellowed at the unfortunate telephonist when she came on the line.

'I am sorry Señor Suarez but all lines to Los Tidos are still out of order.'

Suarez took a deep breath. It was not the girl's fault after all he reminded himself. 'Alright,' he said. 'Keep trying.'

Allowing the more reasonable side of his nature to prevail a little longer, Suarez conceded that neither was Garcia to blame for the telephone lines to Los Tidos being brought down by a storm in the night. Yet the absence of any word from the Capitan from Cordoba was doing nothing to calm his increasing feeling of unease. Something was going badly wrong down there in Los Tidos, Suarez sensed it, and soon he would have the Caudillo's simpering bureaucrat on the phone again wanting to know what progress they were making.

His thoughts then turned to El Serpiente. There had been no word of him either. He was not back in his old haunts in the north so what mischief was he brewing up? But to link El Serpiente with an attempt at poisoning the Caudillo was giving Suarez a problem. Poisoning had never been El Serpiente's style. To kill with the knife or the gun or even with his bare hands, yes, but by putting poison in someone's food, never. Poisoning, in Suarez's book was woman's work but, the more he thought about it, the less sense it all made.

★ ★ ★

At the moment Suarez was thinking about El Serpiente and what he might be up to, El Serpiente was at the foot of the zig-zag flight of steps that had attracted his attention from the promenade. The steps and the retaining walls on either side of them were constructed out of concrete and finished with lime wash so that they stood out starkly against the colour of the the cliff. The storm in the night, however, had brought down a fall of rocks and in one place the steps were completely blocked ruling out any ideas El Serpiente might have been having for taking the Harley Davidson up that way.

The loneliness and emptiness of the beach struck El Serpiente again as he reached for the flask of coñac he kept in one of his panniers. Back the way he had come he could see, for so far, the tracks his tyres had left in the wet sand and in the distance the faint grey outline of Los Tidos and the narrow pencil shape of the Edificio Los Angeles elongated by the mirage effect.

In the opposite direction, going south, the cliffs became higher till they finally curved into a headland that marked the end of the beach. The big breakers were still pounding in and as El Serpiente sat on the Harley Davidson and swilled the rough fiery coñac round in his mouth, he contemplated the solitude. It never entered his head that in fifteen years this scene would be changed beyond all recognition and the line of low cliffs would be bulldozed back to make way for two kilometres of sky scraper hotels and swimming pools served by a six lane highway.

But, though his affection for lonely places was great and the imminence of the destruction of what he saw would have caused him much sadness if he had known about it, El Serpiente's only concern at that moment was how to get the Harley Davidson off the beach where it might be seen.

Returning the flask to the pannier and wiping his unshaven face on the sleeve of his leather jacket, he brought the motorcycle handle bars back round and set off again along the beach retracing the tracks of his tyres. He had only gone a short distance when he stopped again. This was the place he remembered. A narrow channel of water hardly noticeable at first, a trickle crossing the beach that had cut a narrow cleft in the cliff face into which he managed to squeeze even though it was choked with canes and reeds.

Using the bike to force a way through, El Serpiente found himself in a small secluded valley, the same valley coincidentally that Jaime Campello had crossed at a higher point on his way to Hotel Bahia. With the sound of the breakers now muffled El Serpiente stopped. It might be best to carry out a reconnoitre on foot he decided. Though he had seen no-one on his ride along the beach apart from the dog and no faces had peered down at him from the tops of the cliffs, he could not take it for granted that his approach had not been observed. Franco was without his protectors, perhaps, but the police activity he had witnessed back in Los Tidos made him wary.

The canes made a good hiding place for the Harley Davidson though El Serpiente took the extra precaution of covering his most prized possession with the olive green ground sheet. This, he judged, would remove the chance of someone catching sight of the shiny chrome work from up on the cliff.

The water in the stream bed was little more than a trickle leading El Serpiente to suspect that this was the result of the rain in the night and that the valley was normally dry. The noise of a car closer than he expected caused him to freeze. Round the next corner he had the explanation – a road crossing the stream and a bridge. Cautiously he back tracked then scrambled up the left hand side of the valley to make higher ground. There he discovered a flat rock that he could lay out on with the road and the bridge fully in view. He waited patiently. Five minutes – nothing. Ten minutes – the count consisted of a small van and a motorised pedal cycle. The road, he judged, was the road connecting the Hotel Bahia with Los Tidos: a road, if he had the lie of the land right, that eventually wound its way back onto the carretera and was clearly little used except by locals. He watched for another five minutes – one more car came past, an old blue Mercedes this time with Murcia number plates.

Feeling it safe to move on he continued his ascent up the side of the valley, using his pointed steel toe caps to give him extra purchase on the slope. Soon he was entering a stand of pine trees then just beyond he came face to face with the big gate that marked the Hotel Bahia's splendid entrance and no longer with two policemen on duty.

Back at the Harley Davidson El Serpiente took a big hunk of cheese and an onion out of the pannier satchel and proceeded to carve off slices with his knife. He washed this made-do meal down with coñac from his flask and brackish tasting water from the stream. After finishing eating and with his head resting against the frame of the motorcycle he put himself into a deep and dreamless sleep.

★ ★ ★

The memory of the rough looking man with the scar on his face was still fresh in Nathalie's mind as she gazed out of the window of her room across the tops of the apricots to where she could just make out the old windmill by the Salinas de San Vicente and beyond that, the sea. The sea was not her usual friend today – deep blue and sparkling like a jewel. Today it was dull and flat-looking like a sheet of grey lead; cold and lifeless too.

Maman had gone into town to take some curtains to the cleaners and Christine was with Maria somewhere. Their morning walk to look for birds and count how many kinds they could see had been cancelled because Maman thought it might rain again and, if Christine got wet, it would be bad for her chest.

Nathalie sighed. For some reason, she had been thinking about the afternoons when Papa was alive and when Doctor

Pascal would come and play chess with him; how she, Nathalie, would watch them appraising every move and Papa would tease her for putting him off his game and make it his excuse for losing. Some people called Papa a profiteer and said that all those who had their fingers in land speculation and property development had no interest in anything except making themselves rich. Whether it was true or not Nathalie did not know because Papa never talked about these things. For Nathalie, Papa was simply Papa. When he stepped into the house, the place came alive and, now he was gone, it was like a morgue.

So lost in these thoughts was Nathalie that the noise from downstairs at first failed to register with her. It was only after a few seconds that she realised the telephone was ringing.

★ ★ ★

Suarez, in contrast, snatched up his telephone straight away. To his disappointment it was not Capitan Garcia on the other end of the line as he hoped but the simpering bureaucrat with the high pitched voice again.

'Señor Suarez, we have just received a most strange telephone call.'

'Strange? What do you call strange?'

'A woman's voice, claiming she has kidnapped the Caudillo, no less, and that she is holding him to ransom.'

'It sounds like the work of a crank. The Caudillo is safe with Doctor Gil as we all know.'

'There are two things to mention to you Señor Suarez. Firstly the call came through on one of the green phones and secondly we have traced where it originated.'

The green phones Suarez knew were ex-directory

numbers only for the use of government ministers, top officials and leading figures in the military. Even he did not have access to a green phone. Still it was not inconceivable a crank could have got hold of one of the numbers. Such things had been known. But a woman? This was intriguing. A woman and the link with poisoning, a theory that Suarez instinctively felt best to keep to himself.

'I thought you would be interested to know that the call came from Los Tidos, Señor Suarez. We have traced it to public telephone.'

'That is impossible. The telephone lines to Los Tidos are out of order. I know because I have been trying to contact my people down there all day.'

'The telephone lines *were* out of order,' the bureaucrat whined smoothly, the smug tone in his voice giving away just how much he enjoyed putting one over on the security chief, particularly on a point of information. 'Perhaps you should try telephoning your people now. You will probably find you are able to get through.'

For five minutes Suarez's mood was volcanic. To be put right by some mincing little pen pusher was one thing; to be patronised at the same time was quite another. He seethed. He simmered. Finally with Carlita's words about not getting worked up ringing in his ears, he managed to wrestle his temper back under control. He picked up the phone again. 'Can you try Capitan Garcia once more,' he said to the telefonista.

* * *

Garcia was, at that moment, sitting in Doctor Pascal's surgery having his fingers set in splints.

'I would be more careful in future,' Doctor Pascal advised, not knowing what to make of this officer of the Guardia Civil who was causing such upset in the town.

'It is my left hand, fortunately,' Garcia remarked to Ramon Ramon as they left the Doctor's surgery and made their way along the street. 'My revolver hand is still functioning excellently so this will do nothing to impair my ability to continue with the investigation.'

Apart from the mishap with the rat trap, Garcia was feeling pretty pleased with himself. The suspect Robles, was now languishing in the cells having given him the name of someone called Gomez – a man who had purchased rat poison from him recently or so he said. Whether this was a ploy on the part of Robles to take the heat off himself, or whether Gomez was indeed the next link in the chain that would lead to the perpetrator of the crime against the Generalisimo, Garcia had yet to determine.

'We will arrest this fellow Gomez immediately and see what he has to say for himself.'

'Yes Capitan Garcia.'

'It is possible of course that Gomez and El Serpiente are the same person. From what we know of the man he has several identities and Gomez could be one of these.'

'Where are we going Capitan Garcia?'

'For lunch of course. We cannot arrest terrorists on an empty stomach.'

★ ★ ★

Just as the two Guardia Civil officers from Cordoba were entering the elegant portals of La Robinia, an exclusive restaurant used by businessmen just off the Avenida, Jaime Campello was a block away negotiating the narrow streets and parked cars behind the wheel of his old Citroen van. Thanks to two hours concerted effort, the new doors for the Ayuntamiento were at last finished and Campello was on his way back from delivering them in person to the foreman of works at the Ayuntamiento, a crotchety individual named Moliero.

'Cutting it fine as usual I see,' Moliero grumped, not offering to help with the offloading.

Campello made no reply because his thoughts were elsewhere. The news of Robles's arrest, as conveyed to him by Old Roberto was still going round in his head like a hornet loose in the kitchen, and he had made a resolution earlier on that, as soon as the doors were disposed of, he would pay Pepe Gomez a visit and find out what was going on. The Citroen van Campello was driving was one of the long-standing assets of Campello y Hico. It had been purchased by Campello Senior second hand from a fishmonger and, for some reason, it had never quite managed to rid itself of the smell of fish. Its other unfortunate characteristic was the frequency with which it broke down and, since Campello Senior and Campello Junior were both completely lacking in mechanical skills, the van spent long periods in enforced idleness parked up on a vacant lot at the back of the Campello y Hico workshop usually with one or other of the tyres flat.

Deciding it would be best to approach the Bar Madrid on foot and thus enhance his chances of not bumping into Conchita, Campello left the van parked in a side street. He did not lock the doors for the simple reason that the van did not have any. 'Who would want to steal it anyway?' was the way

Campello's father saw it and most of those who knew the Citroen and its smell had to admit he had a point.

By now it was two o'clock in the afternoon and, being a time when many people were eating their lunch, the Street of Two Eyes was quiet. Keeping as close as possible to the line of buildings, Campello approached the Bar Madrid from the direction that made it necessary for him to cross in front of the Bar Zamora.

Zamora was inside sweeping and dusting as usual and dreaming up new schemes for attracting the custom of film stars and presidents. Zamora still had the big plaster on his bulbous nose from the Night of the New Jumilla when it had been broken by an irate customer and all because of the intrusion of a wretched dog. The wretched dog in question, Zamora had since found out, belonged to none other than his neighbour Gomez's tall thin friend Campello and Campello, Zamora was incensed to see, had just gone past his door with little regard for the area of pavement that formed part of his property. Campello was even now standing on the Bar Zamora side of the invisible line among the Bar Zamora tables and chairs and using the Bar Zamora canvas awning for what looked like concealment.

Campello was in fact trying to attract the attention of Lopez without Conchita seeing him. As usual at this hour, Lopez and the others, were playing cards just inside the open doorway of the Bar Madrid and eating tapas.

'Psst,' called Campello.

At first Lopez didn't see the carpenter's face outside peering round Zamora's awning. He put down the noise he'd just heard to the wax in his ears and went back to his game of cards.

'Psst,' Campello hissed again. This time Lopez spotted

him as he looked up though why Campello should be standing round the corner instead of coming in was a complete mystery to him. Still, Campello could be a strange young man at times.

'I want to speak to Pepe,' Campello said in a hoarse whisper. 'Can you ask him to come outside and see me?'

'Why not ask him yourself?'

'I do not want to come in. I have my reasons.'

Lopez looked at the others and exchanged smirks. The reasons they didn't need to guess at. Campello was still smarting from the ticking off he got from Conchita out in the street hence he was hoping not to attract her attention. Now here was a chance for a bit of sport.

'Pepe', Lopez called out at the top of his voice 'Jaime Campello is here saying he wants a word with you.'

'Not so loud,' Campello hissed turning ashen and putting his finger to his lips. Fortunately for him though Pepe Gomez came out of the back just at that precise moment with his shirt sleeves rolled up and soap suds dripping from his arms. Taking no notice of Lopez and the others or their nudging and winking at one another, he went outside quickly to where Campello was waiting for him.

'I need to speak to you urgently and privately,' Campello explained. 'Perhaps it would be better if we met somewhere else.'

Gomez shook his head. 'It would be more than my life's worth, Jaime. This afternoon Conchita has got me marked down for sweeping up the mess in the yard after last night's rain. Then afterwards she will be finding me more glasses to wash and more crates to fetch and carry. I can tell you Jaime, my life is back to being worse than that of a dog. She watches my every move like a hawk.'

'Robles was arrested this morning.'

'Robles!'

'You know nothing about it?'

'Not a word, I swear. I have spent all morning in the kitchens. I have not spoken to anyone.

Zamora, looking on, was now feeling quite beside himself. Campello, the owner of the filthy dog, that had wrought such havoc on what was to have been his glittering night of the year, now had the cheek to be standing on his property holding a conversation with Gomez from next door – the same Gomez whose awful wife and screaming children and stinking septic tank were the bane of his life. Furious and still with the broom in his hand, Zamora advanced on the pair of them. What he did not notice, however, was Conchita approaching from the opposite direction, hidden from his view, by the canvas side sheeting of his awning. When he became aware of her looming presence it was already too late to beat a retreat.

'What do you think you are doing?' yelled Conchita, the 'you' in question being her hapless husband Pepe. 'I leave you to do a job and the minute I turn my back I find you out here wasting your time.'

Lopez and the others stopped their game of cards. There was a fair chance this was going to end with Pepe Gomez having his ears boxed or some other damage inflicted on his person and if that happened, no-one wanted to miss it.

'Señor Campello here wished to speak to me.' Gomez offered lamely, doing his best to keep Campello between him and Conchita.

'Speak about what? If Señor Campello wishes to speak to you why does he not come to the bar counter like anyone else would do?' Conchita's cold glare then transferred itself from Campello to Zamora.

'Señor Zamora, I did not see you standing there. Are you also a participant in this conversation with my husband? Otherwise you have the appearance of one who is eavesdropping.'

'This person is standing on my property,' Zamora blustered jabbing a finger in the direction of Campello. 'He is not one of my customers and I was just on the point of asking him to remove himself.'

Unfortunately what Zamora had failed to notice was that, during the course of these words, Campello had shifted his position slightly so that he was now standing on the Bar Madrid's side of the invisible line.

'I am not on your property,' said Campello as a simple statement of fact; the reason for Zamora's hostility still a mystery to him.

'Yes you are,' blazed Zamora. 'After what has happened how you even have the nerve to show your face round here, I shall never know.'

'Señor Campello is not on your property.' These words were from Conchita, her arms folded across her bosom and the look in her eye, like that of a viper about to strike. 'If you look closely you will see Señor Campello is standing on my property, Señor Zamora. So would you not say it is up to me to decide whether he stays or not?'

Zamora looked perplexed. The most sensible course of action by far would have been to disengage from this conversation – apologise, eat humble pie or simply admit he was mistaken but Zamora being Zamora felt he had a point to make so he continued to mince words with Conchita, which, as anyone in Los Tidos would have told him, was never a wise thing to do.

'He *was* standing on my property, Señora Gomez. I am exercising my right to chastise him for a previous act.'

'You are intruding on a private conversation Señor Zamora. I am speaking to my idle pig of a husband here and you are poking your nose into something that is none of your concern.'

'Who comes onto my property *is* my concern Señora Gomez.'

'And he who sticks his big nose in where it is not wanted is my concern Señor Zamora. Speaking of noses, it is no wonder you had yours broken for you. In future perhaps you should learn to mind your own business. In that way you would come to less harm.'

Zamora hesitated. To any impartial observer, he was clearly already on the losing end of this war of words. Besides Conchita's arms were now unfolded and she was rounding on him with her hands planted on her hips. At this point his nerve failed.

'You have not heard the last of this,' he muttered, turning away broom in hand and disappearing through his beaded curtain while Lopez and the others standing in the open doorway of the Bar Madrid chuckled to themselves. The detested Zamora had been faced down and humiliated by Conchita. This would make a fine tale to spread round the town later on.

'Now for you,' said Conchita turning to where her husband Pepe had been standing with Jaime Campello but where neither of them were standing any more. Seizing their opportunity while Conchita was engaged with Zamora and not seen by her, the pair of them had slunk off and made themselves scarce.

'Come here you idle pig,' bawled Conchita so that the Street of Two Eyes reverberated with her voice and people two hundred metres away turned and stared before taking to their doors. But the summons was to no avail. The Aubergine and the Beanstick had vanished into thin air.

★ ★ ★

In the cells below the Comissaria, Robles the Ratcatcher, Acting Chief of Police Flores and a large number of bearded men sat in silence all staring at one another.

★ ★ ★

Several things were troubling Lola Martinez as she stood on the balcony twirling the little silver pistol round her finger and staring out to sea. The first was El Serpiente and the absence of any phone call from him. Then there was the strange behaviour of Generalisimo Francisco Franco who she had left just a few minutes before still handcuffed to the bed and grinning a toothless grin at her. But as if El Serpiente's desertion and Franco's strange behaviour were not enough to worry about, Lola was also at a loss to understand why the Generalisimo's office in Madrid seemed to attach so little importance to his kidnapping. Remembering this time to go to a public cabina and not use the phone in the apartment she had got through to the number in Madrid just after midday then been kept waiting for a full five minutes while Señor So-and-So finished another call. All this time she was feeding coins in the slot and realising that they could be keeping her hanging on like this to put a trace on the line and find out where the strange woman who wouldn't give her name was calling from. Had she not told them she had important information to give about the Generalisimo and his whereabouts and would this not alert them? She was just on the point of disengaging when a smooth high pitched voice came on the line.

'Generalisimo who?' enquired the voice.

'Franco,' snapped Lola irritably. 'Are you a complete and utter fool?'

There was a silence for a while. Lola imagined Señor So-and-So at the other end had been taken aback by her chastisement and was now struggling to regain his composure. That would teach him for trying to be cool with her.

'Señora, you say that you are holding Generalisimo Franco and that you will only release him subject to certain conditions?'

'That is correct.'

'May I enquire as to the nature of these conditions?'

'Ten million American dollars paid in a manner I will specify later.'

'You represent some group or organisation Señora?'

'That is none of your business. Are you in a position to negotiate with me on these matters or do I have to speak to someone in higher authority?'

'I will have to get back to you Señora. How do I make contact?'

'You don't. I will ring you again in exactly one hour. Any funny business in the meantime and you will find your precious Generalisimo in a ditch with a bullet in his head. Just bear that in mind.'

But in all, Lola had now made three fruitless journeys to

the cabina in the Plaza de Los Reyes. Each time she had run the risk of bumping into the Conserja or some other busy body; each time she had had to leave Generalisimo Franco on his own; each time Señor So-and-So had pleaded for longer. What was this, she began to wonder. A stalling operation? The prelude to a trap? And if everything was about to go wrong who was to blame other than El Serpiente? It was he who should have been with her now taking turns at standing guard over Franco and doing his share of the to-ing and fro-ing.

But the question now was how much longer could she hold out like this? Even allowing El Serpiente the benefit of the doubt, who was to say he had not been arrested and was not at this very moment giving her away to the Guardia? Who was to say how long Franco would remain compliant either?

★ ★ ★

After feasting on a meal of the choicest filete and knocking back two bottles of La Robinia's most expensive Gran Reserva, Capitan Luis Garcia and his assistant Ramon Ramon, emerged back on to the Avenida. Garcia was still smoking the large Havana cigar he had ordered to go with his coñac and roaring with laughter because the head waiter, one of the few head waiters left in Los Tidos who had not heard of the Capitan or his penchant for free meals, had tried to present him with a bill.

'What's this?' snapped Garcia eyeing the slip of paper that had been brought in on a plate and placed in front of him.

'Your bill Señor,' said the head waiter matter-of-factly.

Garcia seemed to reflect on his splintered fingers for a few moments before speaking again. 'You are familiar, I take it, with what is known as the what if question?'

'I think so Señor…'

'That is good because I want to ask you some what if questions starting with what you would do if I refused to pay your bill.'

The head waiter looked puzzled. 'Your meal was not satisfactory Señor?'

'The meal was perfectly satisfactory.'

'Then I suppose I would have to report you to the police or the Guardia Civil. Not that I would want to do such a thing of course.'

'But then what if I were to inform you that we are the Guardia Civil?'

'Señores?'

'Which leads me to my last what if question. What if we had to close your fine restaurant here for six months on grounds of national security? Your boss would not be too pleased, I take it?'

The head waiter shifted his eyes from side to side nervously. 'I think I follow the drift of what you are saying Señor.'

Garcia smiled showing his row of perfectly capped gold teeth. 'You are very sharp,' he said tearing up the bill and putting the shreds one by one into the top pocket of the head waiter's black coat. 'And we are so impressed with the service at your fine establishment that we shall make a point of eating here again.'

★ ★ ★

Zamora was up a ladder fixing his canvas awning when the Capitan from Cordoba and his slightly bewildered looking assistant rounded the corner of the Street of Two Eyes. By now it was half past four in the afternoon, a sleepy time when the back streets of Los Tidos were quiet.

Zamora was still smarting from the dressing down he had received from Conchita that was still ringing in his ears. Thankfully the dreadful woman had now gone inside somewhere and her equally dreadful husband had not reappeared. Zamora would get his own back, he vowed. For a start he would get out a pen and paper when he had fixed the awning and write an anonymous letter to the Ayuntamiento about the disgrace of the Bar Madrid's leaky septic tank and the threat it posed to public health. That would teach Gomez and his wife to meddle with him.

The Bar Zamora's awning had parted from its fixings in the gale in the night and Zamora standing at the highest point of the ladder was concentrating on drilling out two new holes in the wall with a powerful electric drill that he had recently bought. In many ways it was understandable that Garcia mistook the Bar Madrid and the Bar Zamora as part of the same concern. The two establishments stood next to one another and only a more discerning eye than that of the Capitan from Cordoba would have picked out the smarter decor of the Bar Zamora and its shinier tables and chairs. It was also understandable that he took the figure up the ladder to be Gomez the proprietor, – the same Gomez who the ratcatcher rogue had pointed to as having recently purchased a particularly potent type of poison from him. But what clinched the issue of recognition as far as Garcia was concerned was the big plaster anchored to the man up the ladder's cheeks and bridging his nose.

'See, he wears some kind of mask over his face,' Garcia

hissed in Ramon Ramon's ear. 'That mask conceals his scar, I would put my money on it. That man, my friend, is El Serpiente, in one of his many guises. We have him now and he shall not escape.'

Garcia advanced swiftly and purposefully to the foot of the ladder. 'Gomez!' he shouted at the man who was busily drilling holes but the man ignored him and still ignored him when he shouted again.

There were two possible and perfectly logical explanations to why Zamora took no notice of Garcia. The first was that the big electric drill made a lot of noise over which he may not have heard the Capitan from Cordoba calling up to him and, the second that his name was Zamora not Gomez and, in any case, he was used to people yelling Gomez in the street – either at the odious little man himself or at one of his equally odious children.

'Capitan Garcia, perhaps this man is deaf,' Ramon Ramon suggested doing his best to be helpful.

'He will be deaf when I have finished with him,' snarled Garcia. 'He will have no ears left on his head.'

Just across the street from the Bar Zamora and the Bar Madrid was a fereteria or ironmonger's store owned by a man name Sanchez. Sanchez was one of Lopez's cronies and, true to form at this time of day, he was in the Bar Madrid playing cards and swapping yarns. This meant that the ferreteria was left in the hands of his son Esteban and it was Esteban Sanchez who greeted Capitan Garcia when he walked through the door.

Esteban Sanchez, it has to be explained was a young man of seventeen years of age who was taking a correspondence course in retail salesmanship. The school in Madrid, to which he had already subscribed several hundred pesetas, laid great emphasis on the use of a number of new American sales techniques which, when applied correctly, or so the school claimed, brought students success on a lavish scale. To illustrate how lavish its prospectus had a colour picture on the front cover, a picture of a dashing young man at the wheel of a sports car with a crowd of admiring onlookers many of whom happened to be pretty young girls. The young man in question had particularly perfect white teeth and bright blue eyes. Esteban Sanchez, for the record, had eyes that were of no particular colour, a brace round his teeth and he rode a bike – and, sadly the effect of his newly acquired salesmanship techniques had so far been to put most of the customers of the Ferreteria Sanchez off, a fact which was still puzzling to his father because young Esteban only put the lessons into practice behind the old man's back.

Still Esteban Sanchez was nothing if not keen and he greeted Garcia as he came in with an over stretched smile that would have sent most people scuttling for the door.

'Buenos Dias Señor. How can I help you?'

'Give me a ladder,' snapped Garcia pointing to several lying on the floor.

'A ladder Señor? Right away. We have wooden ladders, we have aluminium ladders we have short ladders and we have long ladders. Which type would the Señor prefer?

'Just give me any ladder and make it quick,' said Garcia showing the first signs of irritability.

'A standard length wooden ladder coming up Señor. It is made in Cartegena from the finest timber from Sweden. Is the Señor doing a job? If so, is there anything else the Señor needs to purchase? We carry the best range of paints and varnishes in Los Tidos…' At this point Esteban Sanchez's voice trailed away. He had stopped speaking because the big man in the ill-fitting chalk stripe suit with splints on his fingers wasn't listening to him any more. In fact the big man was picking up the wooden ladder, hoisting it on his shoulder and walking out of the door.

'How would the Señor like to pay?' Esteban called after him.

Waldorf, still plagued by the effects of the emetic, was at that moment slinking up the narrow alleyway separating the Ferreteria Sanchez from the house next door. Waldorf was making his way from the beach, where El Serpiente had seen him earlier on, back to familiar territory in the Old Town. So far the bones that his instincts told him would cure the churnings in his stomach had eluded him. The oily dead fish he had found washed up on the beach and eaten had only served to make matters worse.

As Esteban Sanchez sighed and reached for his manuals on retail salesmanship techniques to find out where he had gone wrong, a gnarled snout poked out from the shadows in the alleyway and sniffed the air. Like all dogs, Waldorf relied greatly on his sense of scent and as his eyesight had declined with the years, his nostrils had grown accustomed to compensating. What Waldorf picked out first was the smell of paraffin and camphor that wafted from Sanchez's ferreteria and mixed with the smell of fried churro from the Churreria up the street. But then a far more interesting smell begin to register – a more interesting smell to Waldorf – the quite definite and unmistakable smell of a tom-cat and somewhere not too far off too.

Waldorf pulled back into the shadows. He had just seen

the figure of a man crossing the street carrying what looked like a ladder. Waldorf had little faith in men carrying ladders. Usually they were workmen who instantly recognised his mange-encrusted form as belonging to the cur who made off with their bocadillos and they usually forestalled any such action by aiming a brick in his direction (or whatever else happened to come into their hands). No, Waldorf decided it would be best to bide his time for the moment and stay out of sight till the coast was clear.

The tom-cat smell that Waldorf had noticed was of course the smell of Zamora's cat Theobald. With the curiosity that consumes all cats, Theobald had roused himself from the cushion that his master had placed so lovingly for him to lie on and ventured sedately out in the street to see what the noise was about. The noise at first was simply the noise of his master using an electric drill but then there had been another and more objectionable noise: the noise of a man yelling Gomez over and over again and so loud it made the bottles and glasses on the shelves inside the Bar Zamora rattle and shake.

As Theobald emerged through the beaded curtain, blinking his big round eyes in the strong light and with his tail held high in the air, he was just in time to see the shouting man re-crossing the street from Sanchez's ferreteria carrying a ladder on his shoulder. Theobald looked on impassively as the man propped this ladder alongside the ladder his master was standing on.

Zamora, who all this time had been busy drilling out holes and ignoring the clamour down below, turned in surprise when he saw another ladder appear beside his own. Even more surprising there was a man already climbing the ladder and down beneath a second man standing on the terrace kicking

200

his heels. Seeing this as yet another intrusion on his private property by people who had no business, Zamora's first inclination was to feel furious. 'What do you want?' he demanded aggressively as Garcia came up level with him.

'I want you off this ladder,' Garcia barked back at him.

'You are trespassing and just who do you think you are putting a ladder up against my wall? Do you have no respect?'

'I am Capitan Luis Garcia of the Guardia Civil and you, hombre, are under arrest.'

Zamora's reaction to this information is not recorded for the simple reason that, at the same time, that this exchange with Garcia was going on, there had been another, more catastrophic development down at street level. The gnarled snout poked out of the shadows again. The stench of tom-cat had become overpowering and, there across the street, Waldorf could now make out the round marmalade coloured shape that brought back memories of the night he followed Uncle Pablo to the waterfront. His eyes narrowed and his hackles rose. It was without a doubt the same sleek overfed creature that had strutted so arrogantly in front of him and stared him out. On that occasion, retribution and restoration of the proper order of things had been thwarted by a man with a broom in his hand but now there was no man with a broom that Waldorf could see; only a second chance to show this cocky orange coloured fat cat with his tail in the air who was the real boss in Los Tidos.

Despite his weakened state, Waldorf shot out of the alleyway like a torpedo. One second the scene outside the Bar Zamora was that of two men at the top of two ladders arguing and a third man and a cat looking on from beneath; the next, tables and chairs were being capsized as they were hit by the hurricane force of Waldorf's form. Theobald quickly appraised the situation. It was the wild eyed dog coming after him again and he took refuge in the only place that offered immediate sanctuary from the snapping teeth and slavering jaws: behind the two ladders standing parallel to one another.

The shock waves that struck the ladders as Waldorf charged into them were felt simultaneously by both Garcia and Zamora. For a moment they stared at one another in disbelief, each man rendered speechless and thinking that somehow the other was to blame, as the ladders began to topple over gathering momentum till finally Garcia and Zamora lost their balance and plunged towards the terrazo.

The awning Zamora was working on was mostly to thank for breaking their fall though the outstretched canvas was not capable of bearing their combined weights for long and soon a ripping sound announced the final two metres of their descent.

When the dust had settled and the last of the aluminium poles supporting the awning had clattered to the ground Ramon Ramon surveyed the wreckage of overturned tables, the shards of ashtrays and plant pots and the two groaning bodies in a heap at his feet.

'Capitan Garcia,' he said slowly. 'This man's drill appears to have gone through one of your toes.'

Raising himself after he had fallen from the ladder, Zamora had just been in time to see Waldorf in hot pursuit of his beloved Theobald and the two of them disappearing up the alleyway at the side of Sanchez's ferreteria. The damage to his awning and to his geraniums pots and tables and chairs was the next thing to strike him.

'Campello,' he screamed in a fit of rage. 'Campello is

responsible for this,' and he took the dazed Garcia by the lapels and shook him.

'Get this lunatic off me,' Garcia yelled to Ramon Ramon whose attention was still riveted on the drill bit sticking out of the Capitan's toe.

Zamora had continued to rave about Campello all the way to the Comisaria until even the two policemen escorting him and who knew him began to think that he had seriously taken leave of his senses.

CHAPTER TEN

The Haunted Lagoon

Pepe Gomez's break for freedom in the company of Jaime Campello had turned into a despondent affair. Away from the watchful eye of Conchita the fat little man had quickly fallen prey to the bottle and while Campello, on the pretext of having to return to work, kept to mineral water, Gomez downed glass after glass of coñac.

The refuge the two of them had found was a seaman's bar called Rudi's in the port. There they sat among a throng of noisy matelots discussing what they should do now Robles had been arrested. The ratcatcher, they agreed, could not be trusted but there the discussion petered out and Gomez slid back into his former state of gloom. When finally they parted by the Puente de San Marco, Campello watched him go off with his shoulders slumped forward and wondered what reception he might get when he returned home. A more Christian act by far would have been to go with him and help him face the fearful Conchita but as Campello reminded himself, doing Pepe Gomez favours was what had got him into this mess in the beginning.

Making a mental note to collect the van later, Campello made his way back up the hill to the Old Town just as darkness was beginning to fall. The walk was uneventful except for a police ambulance pulling up outside Doctor Pascal's surgery and a man in a striped suit being carried in on a stretcher with something sticking in his toe.

Uncle Pablo was still missing he noticed when he arrived back at the Villa Verde and it entered his head not for the first time that some dreadful scandal was about to erupt involving Uncle Pablo and the lady in the fur coat. This thought would have gone on troubling him had it not been for the fact the phone started ringing.

'Señor Campello?' It was the businesslike lady from the Diane Maitland Bureau. 'Señor Campello, I have been trying to contact you all day. The lady is distraught: whatever happened to you last night? Señor Campello, are you still there?'

'Yes I am still here.'

'The lady says you stood her up Señor Campello. Is this true?'

Stood her up! This was a fine line. 'No I did not stand her up,' said Campello with the indignation ringing in his voice. 'If anyone has a right to be distraught then it is I.'

'I am sorry Señor Campello; I do not understand.'

'She tricked me and she has tricked you by the sounds of it too. She is only interested in the attentions of another and she wanted to use me as a go between. It is even possible that she is a woman of the streets.'

'Forgive me Señor Campello but I have difficulty in following what you are saying. The lady who came to meet you last night comes from a very respectable family. Her version of events is that there was no-one in the park by the fountain at eight o'clock except some ruffian on a motorcycle who brandished a knife at her.'

'That was not me, I assure you!'

'I was not suggesting that it was you Señor Campello but it appears there has been a terrible mix up.' The businesslike lady paused for a few seconds. 'Señor Campello in hindsight a park may not have been a good choice for a first meeting. When two people do not know one another and where there are all sorts of strange characters hanging about anything can go wrong. It seems to me, Señor Campello that both the lady and you have been the victim of circumstances.'

'Yes it is possible, I suppose.'

'I have already made this point to the lady, Señor Campello and I have agreed with her that it would be better by far if you met her somewhere a little more discreet – somewhere where the presence of others could not cause confusion.'

'Such as where?'

'The lady has suggested the Salinas de San Vicente. Do you know this place?'

Campello hesitated. The Salinas de San Vicente was a very quiet place indeed but it had a bad reputation. It certainly seemed an odd choice for a romantic assignation.

'Señor Campello, I asked you if you knew this place.'

'Yes I know it.'

'Good. Then it is eight o'clock tonight, Señor Campello, by the Salinas de San Vicente and don't forget the single red rose.'

'Tonight!'

'Is that a problem for you Señor Campello?'

'Only that it seems a bit soon.'

'After what has happened you would not want to keep the lady waiting any longer would you Señor Campello? Besides in affairs of the heart delay is never a good tactic. Oh, and finally Señor Campello I must ask you to let us have a cheque for another five hundred pesetas to cover our fee for arranging a second meeting.'

★ ★ ★

It was nearly four o'clock when El Serpiente woke up though the uniformly grey sky gave no clues to the position of the sun. Working his elbow to get the use back into the arm he had been lying on, he made his way to the edge of the thicket of canes to a point where he could see out over the beach. The tide was in, he noticed, though it made little difference in the Mediterranean where tides don't go in and out very far but otherwise the scene was still the same as it had been in the morning. The beach was deserted in both directions; and the only sign of life was a pair of ravens about a hundred metres away picking among the storm wrack. Satisfied, he went back to the Harley Davidson and got the flask of cheap coñac out of the pannier.

Darkness would be here soon, he reflected, and with darkness would come his chance to make a move against Franco up at the hotel. But the question remained as to what to do when he got face to face with the Old Butcher – whether to gun him down or whether to do as the chica had planned and take him hostage? There were still the comrades in prison up north to consider. With Franco dead, their lives would not be worth a single dinero and martyrdom of so many seemed a high price to pay for what he had to concede would be little more than a symbolic gesture. He unfastened the Harley Davidson's other pannier, the one he had not opened before. From this he took out what to the inexperienced eye appeared to be a length of precision machined stainless steel tube and a welded alloy frame. When expertly assembled by El Serpiente however, it became a perfect sniper's rifle.

★ ★ ★

Suarez tapped the end of yet another cigarette on his silver cigarette case while cradling the telephone under his chin. He had been chain smoking for most of the afternoon and now he was aware that the irritability he was feeling was starting to show in his voice.

'Then where is Capitan Garcia?' he barked at the unfortunate Los Tidos policeman who had picked up his call.

'As far as I know Señor he is out on the streets somewhere rounding up suspects.'

'Suspects?'

'Yes Señor, the cells are full of them. We have scarcely room to move downstairs.' Suarez closed his eyes. He allowed a few seconds before he spoke again.

'In which case can I speak to Acting Chief of Police Flores please?'

'I am sorry Señor but he is also in the cells.'

'Do you mean he is busy?'

'No Señor I mean he is under lock and key; on the instructions of Capitan Garcia.'

When Suarez had finished on the phone he sat and reflected for a few moments. From the beginning he had had a premonition that the Capitan from Cordoba meant trouble but now he was being presented with the proof. The irony of it was, however, that it was he, Suarez, who would be taking the rap for Garcia's bungling and in the twilight of his career when he was at his most vulnerable. The whining little bureaucrat and those like him would be arching their eyebrows when they got to hear about the officer of the Guardia, the agent of the security services, who was charging round Los Tidos like a bull in a china shop. The tale of how Garcia had arrested the Acting Chief of Police would go down particularly well with them. They would also be making much of the fact that the Caudillo's presence in the town was meant to be kept a secret – and what better way to alert the attentions of a poisoner or a terrorist than by carrying on in the way that this officer was being allowed to carry on? But who was responsible at the end of the day for allowing this officer of the Guardia Civil to carry on in the way he had done? Why none other than the irascible Señor Suarez and perhaps now was the time for Señor Suarez to be put forward as a candidate for early retirement with his pension reduced accordingly.

Suarez gritted his teeth. The whining bureaucrat was one of the bootlickers who had failed to talk the Caudillo out of his trip in the first place. Then he bowed and scraped like the rest of them and, if someone really had tried to poison the Caudillo, then, properly speaking, he and his clique were the ones to blame.

But Suarez was enough of a realist to appreciate that the axe of justice when it descends does not always fall in the right place. The operation in Los Tidos had gone wrong so now it had to be brought to a swift conclusion. Whether or not there had been an attempt to poison the Caudillo was assuming secondary importance.

His old service revolver was back in the bottom drawer to where he had returned it after his first aborted journey to Los Tidos. This time, he vowed to himself as he took it out, he would see to it that he got to his destination.

After ringing Carlita to tell her to pack his overnight bag, Suarez left the office on foot.

Three blocks from the ugly grey building he stood in a queue for a telephone cabina and when it was his turn the numbers he pressed were numbers that appeared in no directory and that had only ever been recorded in his head.

'The eagle is circling over the mountain,' he whispered hoarsely as a voice answered. 'Tell Diego that Mateo wishes to speak to him and that it is urgent.'

* * *

In the last dwindling light of day El Serpiente made his way back up the beach with the grey outline of Los Tidos in front of him. The tide was now at its fullest height but it still left a good twenty or thirty metres of soft sand to ride on. In front of him small wading birds dashed backwards and forwards with each incoming and outgoing of the surf before taking to the wing when they heard the roar of the Harley Davidson's exhausts. The wind had died down since the morning but a fine drizzle had set in.

When he reached it El Serpiente found the promenade as lifeless and deserted as it had been earlier. The telephone was where he remembered it: half way along the promenade mounted on a metal post with an acoustic hood. He picked up the handset then tapped in the numbers and waited for the line to connect.

* * *

Ten minutes later, El Serpiente was sitting on the sea wall

smoking a cigarette with the lit end cupped in the palm of his hand, an old soldier's trick for avoiding a bullet in the dark. The news he had just heard made little sense. Suarez of all people was asking for a parley with him: no witnesses, just the two of them man to man. It was a matter of great mutual concern or so Suarez had told the people up in San Sebastian but what could this mean, El Serpiente wondered? Suarez seemed to know he was in Los Tidos but was this just smart guesswork on his part or had someone talked? Now the old fox was waiting for his answer – a time, a place, a reminder that they might be digging shallow graves in Logrono and Pamplona in the morning if nothing was heard.

Stubbing out the cigarette on the seawall he went back to the telephone.

'Tell Mateo I will meet him at noon tomorrow. In Los Tidos there is a bridge over a stream bed on the road from the town to the Hotel Bahia. Tell him I will see him there and you had better tell him also that I have got back-up if I need it – just in case he has got any funny tricks up his sleeve.'

★ ★ ★

It took Doctor Pascal fifteen minutes to remove the masonry drill from Capitan Garcia's toe but the bandages he used on the wound made it impossible for the Capitan to put his shoe back on so the doctor kindly lent him one of his carpet slippers.

Back at the Comisaria, Garcia was greeted by the policeman who had taken the call from Suarez.

'Capitan, there was a message from Madrid earlier on.'

'Do not bother me with messages from Madrid now.'

Garcia snarled as he hobbled past. 'I am on my way to apprehend another suspect and I do not want my mind cluttered with messages.'

★ ★ ★

'So,' said Garcia lining up six officers who were on duty. 'We have followed the trail of the poison from the ratcatcher to Gomez who may or may not be the wanted terrorist El Serpiente. Now Gomez in turn is implicating someone named Campello. Does anyone know this person?'

The six officers remained silent. They felt it best not to tell the Capitan from Cordoba that the man who had been taken to the cells and put in a straight jacket was not Gomez as he thought but Zamora, his neighbour and neither Gomez nor Zamora were wanted terrorists of any sort. It was hard enough not to stare at the Capitan's splintered fingers and bandaged toe let alone ask for trouble by crossing him.

'Campello,' snarled Garcia. 'I am asking you people for local knowledge and I am not getting any.' His eyes fell on the officer standing at the end of the line who happened to be the officer who had mistaken him for a hoaxer from the boys in Trafico on the day that he arrived. 'You,' he said watching the sweat starting to come out over the man's eyebrows. 'Have you lived long in this town?'

'All my life, Capitan.'

'Then you should know this Campello.'

'Yes Capitan.'

'And...'

'There are two Campellos, Capitan. One is Jaime Campello, the carpenter and the other is his Uncle Pablo.'

'Good now we are getting somewhere. Are these Campellos men of good character?'

'The young one, yes; the old man is drunk a lot of the time and he has a long record of convictions for minor offences against public morals.'

'I see. And which one of these Campellos would you associate with Gomez?'

'Jaime, the young one Capitan. He and Gomez are the best of friends.'

'Aha, now we are getting somewhere. They are friends no more it seems – the honour between these two rogues has broken down and Gomez is trying to shift the blame for his crimes onto Campello but they are both in it together from what I can see. What is it? Are you trying to say something, hombre? If so, speak up.'

'It is just that Jaime Campello is not the sort to get involved in anything political or criminal, Capitan. I have known him since he was a boy and he has always been a quiet and well behaved person.'

'Not a paragon of virtue,' scoffed Garcia. 'Has it not occurred to you that any terrorist worth his salt would go to great pains to put up a front of respectability? No, hombres, in the hunt we are conducting, a spotless character is the clearest indication of guilt.'

★ ★ ★

The travel clock in the little folding case that Nathalie kept at the side of her bed told her that it was just after seven. She had had to tell Maman another lie – that Señora Rey's daughter wanted a further piano lesson and could she borrow the car

213

again? Nathalie hated lies and it passed through her head that it might be better to make a clean breast of it with Maman and tell her that she was going out to meet a boy. She was over twenty-one after all and what could Maman say except perhaps that it was too soon after Papa's death and disrespectful to his memory? But the problem with Maman was that she would want to know all about the boy – who was he and what about his family? There Nathalie would be stumped – she knew nothing about the boy; she didn't even know his name.

The choice of the Salinas de San Vicente for the rendezvous was something Nathalie was starting to have second thoughts about. The lady at the Diane Maitland Bureau had asked her to think of somewhere quiet and away from the kind of places where undesirables hung out and the Salinas simply came to her mind because she had been looking out that way from the window of her room earlier on. Only now did it occur to her that she had never been to the Salinas on her own or at night. The enchanted loneliness of the place where she went for picnics with Christine on calm autumn afternoons might take on a sinister and frightening appearance after dark. The memory of the man with the knife still haunted her and who was to say that this boy could be trusted? She had only the bureau's word that he was not some philandering husband or a lecherous rake on the look out for a good time.

But it was silly to start having such thoughts she scolded herself, as she went over to the dressing table mirror. If she didn't take chances with men she would end up an old maid: a *soliterona,* the Spanish people would call her – the old French lady who gives everyone's children music lessons and who, poor thing, had never married and had children of her own.

214

Twenty past seven – she brushed out her hair for what seemed like the twentieth time and tied it back with a piece of black ribbon. Black ribbon: it went with the black cardigan, black skirt, black stockings and black shoes – the image of a girl in mourning with no jewellery except for the little silver studs in her ears. A dab of perfume? There was the bottle of Chanel Papa bought her for her last birthday and the long white chiffon scarf that added a touch of sophistication. Perhaps she ought to have gone to the hairdressers to have her hair cut in a more fashionable style – a bob like Audrey Hepburn or left long but with a fringe like Juliette Greco? Still, no new hairstyle would ever take away the plainness of her face or the thinness of her arms.

She went over to the window. By the light over the patio she saw that the rain had started again.

★ ★ ★

In the penthouse suite of the Edificio Los Angeles Lola Martinez also noticed the rain as she drew the curtain over the door to the balcony and switched on the light in the lounge. She had now made no less than six trips to the telephone cabina in the Plaza de Los Reyes and each time she had been met with the same wall of prevarication.

'I am sorry Señora but I have still not been able to contact the right people. Everyone appears to be out of town.'

This was a trap, she decided. Someone up in Madrid was being clever and trying to put a trace on her calls. The cabina in the Plaza de Los Reyes was no longer safe. Soon she would be forced to find another cabina and already she was starting to regret parting company with the little blue Seat and the mobility that it would have given her. Her plan for holding Franco, she began to see; was not as well thought out as she had believed. For a start she had not allowed for this lack of urgency among Franco's officials. It was almost as if they did not care what happened to him.

And to add to her problems there was still the mystery of El Serpiente and his whereabouts. Was he in custody? Were they torturing him? If so how long would it be before he talked and gave her away? Then what chance would she have of leaving town without someone stopping her?

Lola bit her lip. Perhaps the sensible course of action was to get out now while the going was good. If her phone calls had been traced to the cabina in the Plaza de Los Reyes then it would not be long before a regiment of special soldiers would be despatched to surround the area. Yet somehow there had to be a way for her to come out of this other than completely empty handed. Even if she had to kiss goodbye to the ten million dollars that would secure her future for ever someone, somewhere had to be willing to pay a good price for Generalisimo Franco dead or alive. The question was who?

★ ★ ★

The Salinas de San Vicente were in fact the three oblong-shaped lagoons that Lola Martinez had observed through her binoculars from the roof top of the Edificio Los Angeles shortly after her arrival. Three kilometres north of Los Tidos, they stood at the end of a little used dirt road that began at the cross roads on the Old Valencia Highway not far from the Theroux hacienda.

The technique of extracting salt from sea water by using the power of the sun has been used by people since Roman times and possibly for much longer. First the sea is let into shallow lagoons like those at San Vicente through narrow channels controlled by sluices. The sluices are then closed and nature is allowed to do the rest. The sea water evaporates in the hot sun leaving a thick crust of white salt at the bottom of the dried out lagoon which is then raked up.

There was a sinister legend surrounding the Salinas de San Vicente that had given it its bad reputation and it was this. There had once been a village at the end of the dirt road just beyond the lagoons or so the story went. It was a poor village whose people eked out a living from raking the salt and from the fish they caught from the sea. A time came when the fish grew scarce and the price of salt fell, so the village became poorer and its people starved. At that time many families left to look for other places to live and according to the tale, those who stayed grew so thin their bones stuck out.

One day a rich merchant came to the village. He was travelling to Valencia and lost his way, taking the dirt road past the Salinas by mistake. Some said that this merchant was a Moor, others that he was a Jew from Sevilla, for he wore rich clothes and many rings on the fingers of both hands. The day was hot, the road dusty and, seeing the lagoons, the merchant mistook them for pools of fresh water and got down off his horse to take a drink. Quickly realising his mistake he took a pinch of salt from the edge of the lagoon and let it trickle slowly into the palm of his hand. By then several of the villagers who had been working on the Salinas had gathered round to see who this stranger was in his fine clothes. The merchant looked up and spoke to them. What price were they getting for their salt, he asked and when they told him he offered to double it and promised to return within a month. The merchant, it turned out, was as good as his word. He came back with a cart pulled by four strong horses, which the villagers loaded with salt till it was full to the top then the merchant paid them with gold coins from a purse that hung from his belt.

The merchant returned to the village many times; always with his cart pulled by four strong horses, always paying for the salt he took with gold coins from his purse. Soon the village grew rich and prosperous and many of those who had left came back. Even the fish returned to the sea and the villagers thanked God for sending the merchant their way; But there were those among the village folk who were less well disposed to the merchant and who eyed his purse filled with gold coins with greed and envy.

Late one night after loading the cart with salt the merchant set off down the track and into the darkness. He had planned to stay at an inn in Los Tidos but he never arrived. Some of those who had cast avaricious eyes on his purse lay in wait for him by the Salinas and, as he passed, they jumped out and pulled him from his cart. There, beside the track, they beat him mercilessly then cut the purse from his belt and ran off into the night. The merchant called out for help but no-one heard him and in the morning the villagers found him dead with his eyes pecked out by the ravens.

Though they tried for many years, the villagers never did find where the merchant sold their salt for such a good price and things went back to the way they had been before. The fish became scarce again and what few crops the villagers grew were stricken with a strange blight. Then one night there was a terrible storm when the wind blew with a violent force and thunder and lightning split the heavens and there out on the track a ghastly figure appeared – a cart pulled by four horses, and standing at the reins, the merchant with his eyes pecked out and his finger pointing to the sea. The villagers turned to look and, in a flash of lightning, they saw an awesome and terrifying sight – a gigantic wave, a dark wall of water, ten times higher than the highest house in the village and heading towards them. Some of them fled; some of them went down onto their knees to pray but the wave kept coming till it crashed upon the shore with a noise so tremendous it dwarfed even the noise of the thunder. On it came, over the houses, over the lagoons, over the people, drowning every single one of them – so that for many, the last sight they ever saw was the spectre of the merchant on his cart, with black holes where his eyes should have been, laughing at them as the waters engulfed them.

No sign of the village of San Vicente remained though those who believed in the old legend said that it was still there under the sea and that on dark winter nights the snort of a horse, the soft chink of harness and the creaking of a cart can sometimes be heard out on the old dirt road. But those who claimed to have seen the figure with black holes for eye sockets standing up on his cart, and pointing his finger out to the sea, were generally laughed at in Los Tidos and told to take more water with their anis. Yet it was amazing how few ventured out to San Vicente after the sun went down.

Jaime Campello was not a superstitious person but it was with a feeling of some apprehension that he left the Villa Verde at ten past seven with his best Sunday suit on again. It was not just the sinister reputation of the Salinas that was bothering him but the fear also that he might be in for another strange encounter like the one he had suffered the night before. He was still not sure about the Diane Maitland Bureau and its integrity though he had dutifully posted off the cheque for five hundred pesetas just as the businesslike lady had asked him to do. At the last moment he remembered the single red rose and he rushed out into the darkness in the back garden with his scissors in his hand only to come back with an even more blown and blighted specimen than the one he had picked twenty-four hours before.

Uncle Pablo had still not returned and this was continuing to play on Campello's mind along now with the equally mysterious disappearance of Waldorf. Never before had the grey matted shape and the unmistakable smell been missing from the Villa Verde for so long and Campello was beginning to think that the vanishing of the old man and the dog might somehow be linked. Had it not been for his assignation with the lady, he would have been spending the evening visiting Club Gringo to see if anyone there had information on Uncle Pablo's whereabouts.

To get to the Salinas de San Vicente Campello would need the van and the van was still in the side street not far from the Street of Two Eyes where he had left it earlier on. No longer caring who saw him, he took the direct route down the steeply stepped street, but, as it turned out few people were out on such a wet night. Yet what he did not notice, as he left the Villa Verde were the three figures bunched in the shadows of the alleyway on the opposite side of the street.

'Capitan Garcia…'

'Shush, what is it?'

'Your elbow is in my ear.'

In company with Garcia and his assistant (now both back in uniform) was the Los Tidos policeman who had earlier on given the Capitan from Cordoba his information about Campello and who had been brought along to make the necessary identification. The three of them had been standing in the rain in the alleyway opposite the Villa Verde for nearly an hour and they were now all soaked to the skin.

'Are you going to arrest him?' asked the policeman still dubious about the whole business but well past the end of his shift and anxious to be on his way home.

'We shall wait and see where he is going,' said Garcia tapping the side of his nose. 'He is carrying something in his hand and it does not look like a carpenter's tool.'

'I think it is a flower Capitan.'

'A carpenter with a flower hombres – you do not think that is strange?'

'Perhaps he is an effeminate carpenter Capitan.'

'A symbol of his allegiance to some political group, more likely. He is probably on his way to a meeting now. We shall follow him and with a bit of luck we will have a whole bunch of them in the bag. Think of that, hombres. We will be toasted the length and breadth of Spain if we manage to round up everyone in El Serpiente's gang.'

Campello had now reached the Citroen. Climbing inside he tried to start the engine.

'Look he is stealing that van.'

'It is his Capitan.'

Just then the van's engine came to life and once Campello had managed to force it into first gear it lurched off down the street in a series of jumps and stops.

'Quick, he is getting away.'

'We cannot run after a van Capitan. We will never keep up.'

'Fool, we are going to appropriate a vehicle. We are the law in this town, are we not?'

At that Garcia took his revolver out of its holster and stepped out into the road just as Oswaldo, the young man who had given Lola Martinez a lift to the Edificio Los Angeles on her first day in Los Tidos, came along in his Simca Elysee. Oswaldo wasn't taking too much notice of what was in front at that precise moment because a young lady named Elvira was cuddled up close to him on the front seat. Oswaldo's hand had just gone on Elvira's knee as the big man appeared in front brandishing a revolver. Too late, he put his foot on the brake. Too late, he saw the big man's face turn from ashen grey to sepia and back to ashen grey.

'Capitan Garcia, this car has just gone over your foot. It was your good foot Capitan. Now you have no good feet.'
'Silence, shut up. And you, get out of that car and the putilla with you. Pronto or you will find yourself in worse trouble than you are in already.'

The grin Oswaldo habitually wore on his face had been completely wiped away. Oswaldo had never had a gun pointed at him before and was convinced that he had become the victim of a street hold-up. The big man pointing the gun had a mean look to him too and Oswaldo noticed how the fingers of his left hand were stiffened with splints – a pugilistic device, Oswaldo assumed, worn by men who carried out street hold-ups. To make matters worse, he had just accidentally driven his car over this desperado's foot and Oswaldo now had a feeling that, if he didn't do as he was told, he would be finding out how the pugilistic device was used. Elvira for her part was

222

in a sullen and less deferential frame of mind. The man with the gun had called her a putilla and, though she wasn't sure exactly what it meant, she was certain it wasn't nice. She wasn't too pleased either about being forced out of the car and made to stand in the rain.

'What are you going to do about this?' she demanded of Oswaldo with the make-up already starting to run down her face. But Oswaldo's thoughts were elsewhere. He had seen that one of the three men hi-jacking his car was wearing a policeman's uniform and the other two were dressed as officers of the Guardia Civil. This, he thought, was very strange indeed.

★ ★ ★

With the single windscreen wiper flicking only occasionally and the headlights going dim every time he changed gear, Campello drove the van with all his attention focused on not crashing into objects such as traffic signs and lamp posts. Apart from the Avenida and the Plaza de Los Reyes, the streets of Los Tidos had never been particularly well lit and, passing over the Puente de San Marco, Campello shuddered at the thought of what might happen to him if he drove over the edge and plunged into the swirling mud down in the barranco beneath. Campello was in truth not a very confident driver and used the van only when he had to. Driving at night he found particularly daunting – coupled with the fact that the van's open sides left him exposed to the elements so that, on top of being wet from the walk from the Villa Verde, he was now also cold and miserable. Crossing over the Port Road and starting to leave the lights of the town behind, he took the Old Valencia

Highway and engaged fourth gear for the first time. Soon, however, the van began to labour on the long hill and he had to change down again. Just as he did, he saw the triangle sign ahead warning him that the crossroads and the turn to San Vicente was approaching.

The crossroads were familiar territory to Jaime Campello. On Sunday afternoons he would often take a walk across the almond terraces, passing Paco's Rincon on the Port Road on the way, then up the hill to the Cemetario where his parents' grave was to be found. More times than not he would take a bunch of flowers, carnations usually for they were his mother's favourite, then after he had visited the Cemetario he would continue his walk along the high ridge with an enormous sky over his head to where a view of the sea opened up to him. The lane from the Cemetario ended at the crossroads and on his walks Campello would turn right onto the Old Valencia Highway and head back into town. Seldom in his life had he gone down the dirt road in front that led to the Salinas.

On this night, however, as he made the turn onto the dirt road he noticed a strange thing. A solitary pair of headlights that had been behind him all the way from Los Tidos also turned. Someone else was paying a visit to the Salinas it seemed but at this time of night, who could it be? At first the thought of the lady crossed his mind: was it she on her way to meet him? Then, as the windscreen wiper continued to beat its slow rhythmic pattern and the engine whined in low gear, the thought entered his head that others apart from those involved in romantic trysts might have a use for the deserted lagoons to which no-one ever went. Smugglers had been associated with Los Tidos since ancient times. Smugglers today, Campello reasoned, might be smugglers of things like drugs and guns and such men he imagined were not men to be tampered with. He glanced in the rear view mirror – the headlights were still back at the crossroads. Whoever it was had stopped – a wrong turn, perhaps: someone looking for one of the big haciendas up along the Old Valencia Highway had mistaken the dirt road for a driveway to a big house. Campello concentrated on the ruts and pot holes. By the luminous dial on his watch he saw it was ten to eight. The van's headlights would not adjust onto full beam for some reason so his vision of what was ahead was restricted to ten metres. The stone-walled vineyards that had been on the either side at the beginning had now petered out and the dirt road twisted between hummocks in the ground and became hard to make out. From the crossroads to the Salinas was about two kilometres as far as Campello could recollect and he calculated he had now covered about half that distance. Just then in the rear view mirror he saw something that made him start. The solitary pair of headlights was following him again – he briefly caught a glimpse of them as he went over a rise.

★ ★ ★

On Garcia's orders, the Simca was being driven by the Los Tidos policeman because he knew the lie of the land. The Citroen van with no doors on the side did not, however, prove hard to follow for it only went slowly with the brake lights coming on every time it approached a bend. Ramon Ramon sat beside the policeman and Garcia was in the back seat learning forward with the revolver still in his hand. Every time he made a point or issued an order, he jabbed the barrel in the policeman's shoulder and this, in turn, made the policeman nervous.

'Where is he going?' hissed Garcia as they followed the Citroen through a part of Los Tidos he had not visited before.

'This is the area at the back of the port Capitan. There are many warehouses here containing shipments of raisins and bottles of muscatel wine for export. Los Tidos is well known for these things.'

'Hombre, I am not a tourist. I do not give a damn about what you get up to in this place so long as it does not threaten national security.'

'I am sorry Capitan.'

'See, what is he up to now?'

'He is waiting for the traffic on the Port Road Capitan. He is going straight across I think.'

'Where does that lead to?'

'It is the Old Valencia Highway Capitan. Before they built the carretera, it used to be the main road to the north.'

'Valencia you say?'

'It is a long way to Valencia, Capitan.'

'I know it is a long way to Valencia, idiot. What do you take me for? A simpleton?'

'I am sorry Capitan.'

'Look you are driving too close to him. Have you never tailed anyone before? The idea is not to alert the suspect to the fact that he is being followed.'

'I am sorry Capitan but he has slowed down. I think his old van is having problems getting up the hill.'

'What is that?'

'It is his indicator Capitan.'

'I can see it is his indicator but why is it flashing?'

'I think he is indicating that he is turning right. If so, it would be strange.'

'Strange? Why do you say strange?'

'The road to the right is just a dirt road that goes down to the old Salinas and nowhere else. I cannot see what business Jaime Campello could possibly have down at the old Salinas at this time of night.'

'See,' said Garcia triumphantly jabbing the revolver in the policeman's shoulder blade. 'What did I tell you about this man? He leads a double life. He is not this simple carpenter that you make him out to be. He is someone who creeps out at night when he thinks no-one is watching him and goes to meet up with the rest of his criminal gang. This time, however, hombres, we shall have a surprise in store for Señor Campello and his friends. Pull up here. There is something I have seen that I want to take a closer look at.'

'Yes Capitan.'

Relieved not to have the gun pressing in his neck for a few seconds the policeman stopped the Simca a few metres past the turn off onto the dirt track. Garcia got out and hobbled round to the pool of light in front of the car. 'Look,' he said when the others gathered round to see what he was peering at. 'There are two fresh sets of tyre tracks in the mud. Here are our friend's but another vehicle has passed this way recently. Where do you say this road goes to?'

'Only to the Old Salinas Capitan. No-one lives there and the Salinas have not been used for many years. Many local people think they are haunted. I can assure you few would go there after dark.'

'Very convenient,' mused Garcia. 'If a terrorist gang wished to organise a clandestine meeting then what better place to choose than a place where no-one goes. Hombres, these second tracks are further proof that we are about to interrupt proceedings of a very dangerous band of people – without a doubt the same people who are responsible for making an attempt on the life of the Caudillo.'

'Capitan Garcia.' It was Ramon Ramon who spoke. 'There are only three of us. Would it not be safer to call in some reinforcements?'

Garcia drew himself to his full height and pumped out his chest so that momentarily he looked like a strutting cock pigeon. 'An officer of the Guardia Civil does not acknowledge the word fear. Outnumbered or outgunned, he will continue to do his duty irrespective of the odds. Besides, hombres, waiting for reinforcements will take time. By then this Campello fellow and his associates may well have given us the slip.'

The second set of tracks that Garcia was so pleased with himself for noticing did not however belong to a vehicle in the hands of a dangerous band of political assassins but instead to a rather ordinary Peugeot saloon, the property of Madame Florence Theroux – the lights of whose hacienda were just out of sight behind the ridge. The Peugeot had been driven that way five minutes earlier by Madame Theroux's eldest daughter, Nathalie, en route to the rendezvous that had been arranged for her by the Diane Maitland Bureau of Friendship. Nathalie had set out at twenty to eight realising that the short journey to the Salinas would only take her ten minutes at the most but that to leave it any later would not be consistent with the story she had given her mother; that she was going to give the bank manager's daughter a piano lesson at eight.

With the wipers raking the windscreen it took Nathalie only a couple of minutes to reach the crossroads. At this point it crossed her mind to go up and down the highway a few times just to kill time but, as she left the house with Maman throwing suspicious glances at her, Nathalie hit on what seemed like sensible idea after the previous night's experiences. She would go down to the Salinas early and hide herself up in one of the places she knew from her outings with Christine. She would then wait and see who turned up and, if it happened to be someone she didn't like the look of, she would have the option of staying in hiding.

Nathalie was familiar with the dirt road and its twists and turns because she had been along it many times. It struck her though how very different it seemed in the dark. As a child, Maria and Juan had told her scary stores about the curse of San Vicente and the ghostly cart with its driver, a man with no eyes, but she had laughed at them knowing that they were only trying to frighten her from straying too far from the house when she was playing. Yet the scary stores came back to her now she was out here on her own, trying to pick out landmarks in the headlights. The rain and the storm the night before had left the road surface greasy and treacherous and several times she felt the tyres slip. A bird flew up in front, a dark raked back shape that she knew straight away was a nightjar. Finally she made out the silhouette of the tower of the old windmill that she could see from her bedroom, a dark outline against the sky and she knew that the Salinas were only a few metres further on. A last twist round a hummocky knoll and there they were, glassy and still in front of her.

How long it had been since anyone last worked the Salinas, Nathalie had no idea. The little channel through which they had once let in the sea water with its sluices was still there though it was now choked with weeds and stones. The shallow lagoons themselves were filled with brackish water, part rain, part spray from the sea and in the hot summer months they dried out completely into flat pans of hard baked silt

Further on and beyond the lagoons the road petered out on a low shelf of rocks overlooking the sea but Nathalie did not intend to go that far. Instead she pulled up behind one of the low hummocks where the car could not be seen by anyone coming down the track.

It was ten to eight according to the clock on the dashboard and, slipping on an old black oil skin and a fisherman's sou'wester that had once belonged to Papa and that she had managed to smuggle out of the house, Nathalie opened the door of the car and got out. The first thing she noticed was the mud underfoot. Maman kept a pair of old rubber boots in the back of the car and, retrieving these, she quickly changed out of her best patent leather shoes. As she was doing this she saw the red rose she had picked from the garden when Juan's back was turned. Gathering it up she locked the car door and set out.

The sea she noticed was calm after last night's storm, its luminous surface rose with the swell like a supple skin and she could hear the waves lapping gently on the rocky shore somewhere beneath. She retraced her tracks back to the lagoons noticing at once the smell of wet earth. She stopped. The sound of the rain pitter pattering on the brim of her sou'wester and the waves coming in against the shore – then the sound she thought she had heard the first time but hadn't been certain. Nearer and clearer this time, it was quite definitely the sound of a car being driven in low gear.

★ ★ ★

Campello was also having problems with the greasy surface of the track, not helped, in his case, by the fact that Citroen's tyres were bald. What was occupying his attention most, however, was not the constant skidding and slipping of the van but the two headlights which now looked to be no more than two hundred metres back and seemed to be closing up. He did not like the way these headlights had followed him all the way from town and, in his own mind, he was now certain that Lopez and some of the others were tailing him. Sensing something was going on between him and Pepe Gomez they had decided to find out for themselves and seeing him take the turning onto the road down to the Salinas must have really whetted their appetites. What could Campello possibly be up to, he could hear them saying. Why was he coming this way on a dark wet night?

Now it was on the cards that, unless he did something, Lopez and his cronies would be there to witness his meeting with the mysterious lady and in the morning it would be all round the town that Jaime Campello had a secret woman. Soon it would come out that he had been using the services of a marriage bureau and he would be made into an object of fun. His life then would not be worth living, Campello reflected gloomily. The only path left to him would be to pack his bags and leave Los Tidos for good. Again he cursed the day that he had set eyes on the advertisement for the Diane Maitland Bureau.

One of the hummocky knolls that dotted the area around San Vicente loomed up in the darkness to his left, and with the fatalism of a desperate man Campello swung the wheel of the van over, taking no account of the possibility of hidden holes or ditches that might be in his path. He extinguished the headlights quickly then sat and waited.

The car behind was up on him soon enough. Inside he could make out three shadowy figures, two in the front, one in the back – Lopez, Sanchez the ironmonger and who else, Campello wondered. The car was a Simca, not a car he could immediately recognise, but his ruse seemed to have worked. The car went by and continued along the road in the direction of the Salinas. They had not noticed him parked up beside the knoll.

★ ★ ★

'I can no longer see his lights Capitan Garcia. Do you think he has given us the slip?'

'That is impossible,' said the policeman sweating nervously once more because Garcia had the gun barrel poking in his jugular vein. 'There is no way out of this place except back along the road.'

'I smell a trap,' Garcia growled from the back seat. 'How far would you say it is to where these Salinas are situated?'

'Quarter of a kilometre at the most Capitan. We are almost there.'

'Then stop the car. We will proceed for the rest of the way on foot. If an ambush is being prepared for us then we will take them by surprise.'

'But Capitan Garcia, how can you proceed on foot when you have no good feet left?'

'Because I am an officer of the Guardia Civil: that is how. Pain is part of my job. Pain is inscribed on my heart.'

Getting out of the Simca, Garcia, Ramon Ramon and the policeman fanned out in a line.

'Who is that man standing on the hill?'

'It is a windmill, Capitan.'

★ ★ ★

Nathalie was mystified. The noise of the car had come and gone and at one point and quite distinctly she had thought she heard the sound of two cars. Now, save for the sea and the gentle hiss of the rain, all was silent again.

Her eyes had become used to the dark and she could follow the pale line of the dirt road all the way back as far as the windmill. Nothing had moved that way. No car headlights appeared over the top of the brow; no figure came walking along the road carrying a rose in his hand – the symbol by which she would identify the man who had come to meet her.

Nathalie was now standing at the edge of the nearest of the three lagoons holding her own rose and knowing she must look a strange sight in the oil skin and the sou'wester and wearing Maman's old boots. The glassy stillness of the water struck her again; the surface pocked-marked only by the steady downpour of the rain. The man had stood her up once more, she began to think. Or had he changed his mind at the last minute and driven off back to town explaining the sound of the car she had heard?

She stiffened. She thought she heard a voice from somewhere on the far side of the lagoon. A trick of the night? A sound from the sea that had reverberated back off the land? The scary stories started to flood back to her. She felt unsafe. If she ran it would only take her a few seconds to get back to the car; but she stayed rooted to the spot and why she never knew. A few minutes later it would be something that she would deeply regret.

★ ★ ★

'Where are these confounded lagoons?'

'I think you are standing in one Capitan.'

'Capitan Garcia, from where I am I can see someone on the other side of the water. A figure in black, can you make it out?'

'Is it Campello?'

'I think not Capitan. The carpenter is tall and this figure is only medium height.'

'An accomplice no doubt. How do we get across this lake?'

'Capitan Garcia there is a boat over by me.'

'Why didn't you say so?'

'I just did.'

Garcia joined his diminutive assistant at the water's edge. The boat Ramon Ramon had discovered was a small one and it looked like it had been in the reed beds for many years.

'There is only room for one of us.' Garcia pronounced. 'As senior officer present I nominate that I will be the person to have the honour of capturing Campello's accomplice. I will do this single handed and that it is how I wish it to appear in my citation.'

The policeman joined them. 'Capitan the boat has got no oars. You will not be able to row it.'

'All the better. Oars splash and make a noise. No, hombres, I will get into the boat then you two will push it so I will glide soundlessly across the water and when I reach the other side I will leap out and take this terrorist person by surprise. Do you understand?'

'Si Capitan.'

'Si Capitan.'

'Ok you can push me now.' Garcia's embarkation in the little boat was followed by a silence.

'Are you alright out there Capitan?'

'This is strange hombres, the boat seems to be getting lower in the water.'

'Capitan Garcia, I think you are sinking.'

★ ★ ★

Nathalie had now heard a number of strange noises from the far side of the lagoon followed by a series of plops and a strange cry not like the cry of any bird she had ever heard. Her eyes were now focused on a disturbance in the water about twenty metres from the further shore but then, as she watched, a huge dark shape rose up out of the lagoon like a giant slug encrusted in silt and slime. It seemed to wallow in its own filth at first then she saw to her horror that it had a great clawing hand with tentacle like fingers sticking out reminding her of the tale of the old merchant's pointing finger. She saw too how water spewed out of its orifice like the bilge pours out of the bottom of a ship and she recoiled. It was without doubt the most horrible looking creature that she had ever seen in her life. A monstrous life form from the bottom of the lagoon or some ghostly apparition? She neither knew nor cared for she had seen that the thing was coming towards her – unbelievable, though it seemed, half swimming, half wading, it was thrashing its way across to her side of the water.

At last she managed to tear herself away from the hypnotic spell with which this loathsome leech-like creature seemed to be holding her. She fled, stumbling in the rubber boots, so she felt like someone fleeing in a nightmare. The world – the sea, the sky, the few stars that were out – everything seemed to spin round in her head. At last she was back at the car, her pulse jumping in the back of her throat then the slow trickle of relief as she got the key out of her pocket and unlocked the door.

Her night vision went as soon as the courtesy light came on. Was the thing still out there in the darkness, still following her? She fired the engine and it started first time: a gear, any gear, a brief awareness she was biting her lip then, foot flat down on the accelerator and tyres screaming and skidding in the mud, she took off down the dirt road with the only thought in her mind to put as much distance as possible between herself and what she had just seen.

It took only a few minutes to arrive back at the crossroads. She did not notice the abandoned-looking Simca near the windmill or the grey van with no doors parked up by one of the hummocky little knolls. What did come back to her later though was that the thing that crawled out of the lagoon had a strange crest-like protuberance on its head; a protuberance that to her mind resembled one of the funny little hats that officers of the Guardia Civil wear.

CHAPTER ELEVEN

Two Men on a Bridge

The Peugeot that had just driven past him at high speed was a complete mystery to Campello. His attention, however, was now on the three figures he took to be Lopez and a couple of his cronies and who were now coming back from the direction of the lagoon. This time he could hear their voices: one voice in particular shouting angrily over the others. Was it Lopez? The more Campello listened, the less he was convinced. The words he could not catch but the intonations were not those a speaker of the local dialect would use.

All this was deeply puzzling to Campello. Had these men followed him from the town and, if so, who were they? Then there was the riddle of the lady: was it she who had just taken off past him in the Peugeot or was she still waiting for him down at the Salinas? The thought crossed Campello's mind randomly that the three men in the Simca might somehow be connected with her. A jealous boyfriend perhaps, or even a husband – someone who had become suspicious about the lady going out at night and had gone after her taking a couple of friends to back him up.

For this reason Campello decided it would be best if he stayed in hiding. By now the three men had got back in the Simca and the engine was being started up. Campello watched as it shot forwards and backwards a few times to reverse direction then set off in the direction of the crossroads. After a few seconds the noise of its engine was gone and the night was quiet again.

Campello shivered. His suit was wet, the thick woollen material seemed to hold in the damp. The air coming through the open side of the van made him feel cold and even more miserable still. He would go back home soon, he consoled himself, sit in front of the fire with a hot drink and a glass of coñac and never again in his life agree to meetings with strange ladies in places such as this.

He glanced at the luminous dial on his wrist watch. It was ten past eight. The landscape around San Vicente had an eerie quality; the old windmill tower and the hummocky hills taking on strange shapes in the dark and Campello tried to keep his mind off the tales of its haunting and the phantasmal figures that were reputed to appear on the old dirt road at night. Should he wait any longer? There didn't seem to be much point. He got out of the van and mindless of the mud on his shoes he ambled a little away along the track.

The rain was stopping, and there was a freshening in the wind that made his wet clothes cling to him and feel even worse. The Salinas were in front of him as he came over the rise by the windmill. Their flat surface was stirred by the wind and a waning moon appeared through the clouds casting a grey shadowy light over the lunar-like landscape. Finally he stopped by the water's edge, not far from the place where Nathalie had stood a little earlier, and he reflected on these latest experiences. He would meet a nice girl some day, he told himself, not a girl picked out for him by a computer, but an ordinary girl who he would come across in the ordinary course of his life. Besides the more he thought about these assignations, the more it occurred to him that the sort of woman who would put herself on the files of a marriage bureau would be like the one he had met in the park last night. A woman of the night or as it seemed now, a married woman looking for diversions and cheating on her husband. The list was endless: old women, fat women, ugly women, women like Conchita Gomez, women no-one wanted. No, Campello declared, this kind of business was not for him. He had made a mistake twice but he would not make it again.

As he turned to go he noticed something, floating on the waters of the Salinas. It was, he saw by the light of the moon, a single red rose.

★ ★ ★

A plaintive cry echoed outside the Bar Zamora, which was all locked up because its proprietor had been taken off to the Comisaria and put in a straight jacket. The plaintive cry was the cry of Zamora's tom-cat, Theobald and Theobald was making this noise because he was hungry. It had been a bad day for Theobald. He had been chased along the alley next to Sanchez's ferreteria then over a wall and onto the roof of an outhouse pursued all the time by the wild-eyed dog. Like many others in Los Tidos that night, Theobald pined for the day when things would get back to the way they had always been.

★ ★ ★

The wild-eyed dog in question was at that moment slinking

round the back of Vilas's Matadero where it was usually a safe bet that a few old bones would be lying round. Vilas, however, had been having a tidy up. The Feast of the Two Virgins was due to be celebrated shortly and, Vilas being a religious man, didn't want the casket of the blessed couple paraded past his premises in full sight of all the discarded bits of animal carcasses that normally littered the place. Waldorf slunk off back into the night. He would have to look for old bones somewhere else.

* * *

Doctor Pascal sighed as he looked out of the window into the street and saw that the banging on the door was the Capitan from Cordoba yet again with his little assistant in tow. From the light of the street lamp he could see that the Capitan's uniform was filthied with a grey coloured slime and he looked wet through. It was nine o'clock he saw and fleetingly it crossed the mind of Los Tidos's long suffering doctor to ignore the banging and go back to the good book he was reading and the glass of red wine he was enjoying while Señora Pascal was out visiting her cousin. Sadly, however, the Capitan from Cordoba had seen his face at the window and was calling up to him to open the door. Peace abandoned, Doctor Pascal sighed to himself. What had this buffoon gone and done to himself this time?

* * *

The rest of the night passed off peacefully in Los Tidos: Pepe Gomez alone in the back kitchen of the Bar Madrid slumped over a bottle of anis with the mewling of Theobald out in the street; Jaime Campello in front of the electric fire in his pyjamas, drinking hot chocolate and feeling the start of a cold coming on; Nathalie Theroux saying her prayers and vowing never to go out on dark nights on her own again; Uncle Pablo naked on purple satin sheets wondering what the the delectable lady might have in mind for him next. El Serpiente asleep in the thicket of canes with his head resting against the saddle of the Harley Davidson; Suarez behind the wheel of his car somewhere on the Madrid to Valencia road; Flores, Robles and the company of bearded men, down beneath the Comisaria listening to Zamora ranting and raving in his padded cell; Capitan Garcia limping along the street with his assistant, Ramon Ramon; now with both of Doctor Pascal's slippers on his feet; Waldorf standing on the hillside under the moon, looking down on Paco's Rincon and wondering where next to go in search of old bones and finally Father Miguel in his study, gloomily toasting the local gentry and trying to fathom out where to recruit two virgins on the quick.

★ ★ ★

Next morning and after yet another excellent night's sleep in the Acting Chief of Police's vacant apartment Garcia and Ramon Ramon ate a hearty breakfast in one of the cafeterias on the Avenida.

'It's on the house,' said the proprietor with more than a hint of sarcasm, eyeing the two men up and down and seeing how the Capitan's uniform was stained with mud and how the Capitan himself was wearing carpet slippers on his feet.

★ ★ ★

Lola Martinez used the phone in the apartment to put her call through to Kovacs in Barcelona. Kovacs had come out of Budapest during the rising in fifty-six and rewarded the nation that had so kindly given him political asylum by making it the base for his criminal operations. Lola and Kovacs went back a long way.

'Lola darling,' came the smooth crooning voice at the other end of the line. 'What an unexpected surprise and so early in the morning. I can picture you in your little peignoir propped up among the pillows. To what does Kovacs owe this pleasure?'

'I want to talk business.'

'Business with you little lark? Kovacs is all ears.'

'What would you say if I told you I was holding Franco prisoner?'

'I would say that you were pulling my leg sweetness.'

'I am giving you the first option to buy him from me. Think of the ransom money Emil. It could be yours.'

'Lola, if what you are telling Kovacs is true – and in this case the if is a big if – then why are you not putting in for his ransom yourself? Delightful creature though you may be, you would have to admit to yourself that you are not one to let a chance to line your own pocket slip through your fingers.'

'There are some complications at this end. It would not be wise to try to explain over the phone.'

'Complications? Now I see it, you are offloading are you not? Could it be you have bitten off a little more than you can chew? Are you trying to wriggle off a hook you have got yourself on?'

'Go to hell Emil: seven million.'

'Pesetas?'

'Dollars.'

'You forget the rules of the game. Offloading incurs a discount. Even hypothetically if Kovacs was interested in what you have to offer – even if he believed that what you are saying is true – the most he would go to is two.'

'Five; and don't play with me you grubby little bastard. You know you could name your own price for the head of someone like Franco.'

'You forget the risks Lola. Two and a half and only as a special favour to you.

'Payable how?'

'Fifty percent on delivery of the said gentleman to a place of our choosing; the rest when we get the ransom money. Lola, is this really Franco, you are holding? Please don't think badly of Kovacs for finding it difficult to believe.'

'Yes it is he. I took him when everyone else's back was turned.'

Kovacs whistled. 'Look Lola,' he said after a pause. 'The two of us may be old partners in deceit but there are others at this end who may need more convincing that what you are saying is the truth.'

'What are you suggesting Emil?'

'That I need to make some checks. I need corroboration from another source to say that Franco is missing. Do you see my point?'

'And how do you propose to do that?'

'Contacts Lola – have you not heard that half the government is on Kovacs' payroll?'

'How long will this take?'

'Two hours; maybe three: it depends on who is available. Is there a number I can call you back on?'

'I will ring you at midday. That gives you just over two hours. Hasta luego, Emil.'

Back in the bedroom, Lola looked at the sparse naked figure on the sheets and the glass on the table containing his teeth. To think that for most of her life this man had held Spain in his iron grip and that many quaked at the mere mention of his name.

★ ★ ★

'Señor Campello.' It was the businesslike lady who had called him before he had chance to call her. He was late for work again sniffing and sneezing and just finishing his breakfast of boiled eggs and fresh bread from Penedes's Panaderia when the phone rang. 'Señor Campello, I have been speaking to the lady just a few moments ago and she has told me that your meeting with her last night went wrong yet again. She did not say a lot but hopefully I have managed to smooth things over by giving her your apologies!'

Apologies! Campello did not believe his ears. What did he have to apologise for? The businesslike lady was still speaking however: 'I have made an arrangement for you to meet her at lunch time today Señor Campello. There would seem to be less chance for mishaps occurring in daylight. The Hotel Bahia will be known to you of course. I have suggested you meet the lady for aperitifs at one o'clock. Can I confirm that you will be there?'

Campello didn't believe he was hearing this correctly. 'I am sorry but I have to be at work today, he replied icily, 'Also

I think it would be better if we decided not to pursue this any further…'

'Work, Señor Campello? Do you think a day's work should come before a lifetime's happiness?'

Campello fidgeted. There was a right answer to this but he could not bring it to mind quickly enough and before he could, the lady was speaking again. 'Señor Campello what can you be thinking of? You must remember the advice I gave you before: in affairs of the heart it is fatal to procrastinate. Do you recall those words Señor Campello?'

'Yes I do.'

'Good. At one o'clock it is then, in the Cocktail Bar of the Hotel Bahia. And don't forget the red rose so the lady will be able to recognise you. We don't want any more of our ships to pass in the night, do we?'

★ ★ ★

As it so often did, the change in the weather that brought the storm was followed by several days of grey skies and rain. It also brought a minor epidemic of coughs and colds to Los Tidos and, apart from Jaime Campello, one of those who went down was Conchita's youngest sister, Isabella. It was off to see Isabella that Conchita went shortly after breakfast.

Left to his own devices, Pepe Gomez could hardly believe his good fortune. Leaving the washing up in the sink and taking a bottle of beer from the ice bin he settled down at one of the empty tables and lit a cigar. It would be an hour before Lopez and the others came shuffling in; another hour before the lunchtime trade descended: he would pass the time with his feet up doing exactly as he pleased. No Conchita to nag away at him. Even Zamora's place was all shut up hence there was no prospect of a disturbance of the peace from that direction either. Much to Gomez's delight Zamora had been arrested by the Guardia yesterday afternoon while he was down at Rudi's with Jaime Campello. Zamora was up to no good, it was rumoured, a fact Pepe Gomez found easy to believe. Any man who spent his days dusting shelves and sweeping floors without being forced to had to be suspect. Suddenly Pepe Gomez's smile froze.

Out of the corner of one eye he noticed someone looking at him as he sat with his feet up. It was one of his sons, Ricardo or Tomas, he couldn't think which. The child was watching him, taking it in every time he raised the beer bottle to his lips and every time he puffed at the cigar. Conchita had posted her spies it seemed and Pepe Gomez wondered how much it was going to cost him to buy silence.

★ ★ ★

Nathalie was quieter than usual as she drank her coffee. 'The car is in a filthy state,' Maman was saying, 'Wherever did you go in it last night?' Nathalie looked up. From where they were sitting on the patio she could see Christine in the rose garden with Maria and, a little further off, Juan busy mending the trellises that had been blown down by the storm. 'Nathalie, are you listening to me?'

'The roads are covered in mud Maman. The rain has washed some of the soil off the fields.'

'And where is it you are going later on?'

Nathalie felt her flesh prickle. It was soon after her conversation with the lady at the Diane Maitland Bureau that

246

she had asked Maman if she could borrow the car again.

'Nowhere in particular Maman. Into town to look at the shops then perhaps lunch and a walk along the beach.'

'You should be careful walking along the beach. There are many strange characters about in the town and I hear the police are looking for a gang of terrorists.'

'I have heard these stories too Maman. I will keep my eyes open for anyone who looks suspicious.'

It had already crossed Nathalie's mind that the tales going round of people being arrested might be linked to the man with the knife. If so, how close had she come to bumping into a real desperado? At this point in time, the rumour that Franco was staying at the Hotel Bahia had not reached the Theroux household for, if it had, Nathalie would never have suggested it as a meeting place with the young man whose acquaintance had so far eluded her.

★ ★ ★

In complete contrast, the choice of the Hotel Bahia for cocktails was the cause of a great anxiety to the young man concerned. The Hotel Bahia was where Franco was supposed to have been be staying and where, on his last visit, Jaime Campello had dumped the emetic into the paella. Showing his face there again and so soon seemed to him like asking for trouble. There again showing he had no qualms about going to the Hotel Bahia seemed a good way of saying he had nothing to fear.

Having come to the conclusion that there was little point in attempting to do half a day's work from which he would have to deduct a further two hours for the purpose of having a shower and washing the sawdust out of his hair, Campello decided to fill in time by paying a visit to the Street of Two Eyes. The purpose was to see if Pepe Gomez had any further news of Robles but the thought of Robles reminded him that the incriminating bottle of poison was still in the medicine chest so as he left the Villa Verde (not in his Sunday best suit because his Sunday best suit was still drying) the small bottle containing the sinister green fluid was making a bulge in his trouser pocket. He would dispose of it somewhere, he told himself, as he set off in the direction of his workshop where he had parked the van last night.

As he stepped out into the street he noticed that the rain had stopped and, even though the sky was still overcast, the sun was trying to come out. Despite his cold, it felt warm enough to go out in a pair of light cotton slacks and a short-sleeved shirt with just a sweater over the top. The cold, however was concerning him. What would the lady think of his sniffing and sneezing and his blocked up nose? Would she feel it inconsiderate of him to expose her to the risk of catching it? It was with these thoughts going through his head that Jaime Campello made his way down the steeply stepped streets of the Old Town where, overhead, the serins were singing once more on the telephone wires and the water dripped from the freshly watered geranium pots up on the wrought iron balconies. As usual he spoke to the people he met: the postman, Penedes from the Panaderia and Old Roberto sitting in his doorway. Indeed, it was almost like old times, he reflected: the way things had been before Pepe Gomez took it into his head to do away with Conchita; before he got involved with the Diane Maitland Bureau, and before Uncle Pablo and Waldorf went missing. As far as the Diane

Maitland Bureau was concerned, Campello had already made up his mind up that if this next meeting with the young lady went wrong then that would be the end. In future he would leave his love life in the hands of the fates and, if it was written in the stars that he was destined to remain a bachelor, then he would accept that it was so. Never again would he be lulled into going off on one of these blind dates. Campello paused by the piece of spare land, the spot from where he had observed the flamingos, though this time he did not stop to look at the view. Among the discarded bricks and tiles and seed heads of camomiles he slipped the tiny bottle of poison into a crack in the ground where he thought it would be hidden. What he did not notice, however, as he walked away was that two pairs of eyes were watching him.

★ ★ ★

As soon as Campello had disappeared down the street Garcia with Ramon Ramon in his shadow emerged from their place of concealment in a doorway and went across to the place where they had seen the young carpenter foraging in the rubble.

'So,' cried Garcia triumphantly bringing out the little bottle with its tell-tale skull and crossbones label. 'This is the person who everyone tells me is innocent – the person who was cute enough to give us the slip last night when we tailed him. Now, hombre, we have the proof that he is the person who attempted take the life of the Caudillo. Thanks to our persistence we have caught him red handed in the act of trying to dispose of the evidence.'

★ ★ ★

The time on Lola's wristwatch was twelve noon precisely. 'I am sorry to say I have some bad news for you.' Kovacs had dropped the soft croon from his voice. 'Generalisimo Franco is safe in Madrid and I have this on good authority. He has been in hospital with a stomach ailment but he has made a complete recovery. He is due to chair a meeting of his cabinet this very afternoon so, Lola, I have no idea who this man is that you are holding but he is certainly not Franco. Whatever your plans, I would advise you to abort them quickly.'

For a while after putting the phone down on Kovacs, Lola sat on the long black leather sofa still in her bathrobe and still fingering the trigger of the tiny silver pistol. The more she thought about it the more she realised the suspicion had been there from the start. The peasant's beret; the gruff Valencian dialect; the old man's lecherous looks: she had allowed herself to be blinded to these facts that stared her in the face by the prospect of fast and easy money.

She went through to the bedroom where the old man was still sleeping, still with his false teeth in the glass, still with his huge penis sticking up in the air and as she looked down into his face, a sudden and violent anger filled her heart.

★ ★ ★

Suarez had learned of the Caudillo's return to health from his deputy. He telephoned Madrid from the garage where he had his car refuelled, and the oil and tyres checked. Did Señor Suarez still intend to continue with his journey? His deputy asked. Suarez fingered the cord on the telephone before replying that he did although he offered no explanation. Only Suarez knew of the meeting with El Serpiente at noon and he had his own reasons for wishing to keep it quiet.

As he neared Los Tidos, Suarez chose to ignore the signs directing him to the town from the carretera. Like Lola Martinez, he subscribed to the view that it paid to know the quiet way in and out of places so instead he went a further two kilometres to where the main road began to twist and turn through hillsides wooded with Mediterranean scrub and pines. Finally he came to the turn he had noticed on the map: a road to the left and a discreet sign confirming that this was indeed the way to the Hotel Bahia then a glimpse of the iron grey sea shrouded in mist through the trees.

Once past the gates to the hotel Suarez pulled over in the trees at the side of the road and took the old service revolver from where he had put it inside the glove compartment of the Mercedes. He then got out of the car and set off on foot along the road. If his map reading was correct, the bridge on which he had arranged to meet El Serpiente was somewhere just a little further on along the road but the thought striking Suarez as he moved forward stealthily was just how close this most dangerous of men had got to the Caudillo's hotel. The fact that he had found out about the Caudillo's trip and where he was staying was bad enough but to be within shooting distance of the only road in and out was worrying. So much for crying wolf, Suarez thought to himself. Equally worrying was that someone in the Caudillo's circle had a loose tongue.

★ ★ ★

El Serpiente had left his hiding place in the thicket of canes just ten minutes before. Like Suarez he was also being cautious. He distrusted all servants of Franco and Suarez, the wiliest one of all, had been responsible for the deaths of many patriots and comrades. Therefore across his chest as he jumped from rock to rock El Serpiente carried the assassin's rifle and, if he needed it, the big knife was still tucked inside his boot. He had tied his bandana around his head to keep the hair off his face so the terrible scar was fully on view to strike fear into the heart of anyone who beheld him.

Gaining higher ground and coming to the flat rock from which he had carried out his first reconnaissance of the bridge, El Serpiente stretched out face down with the rifle at the ready. It was ten to twelve he saw on his wristwatch and his mind flicked over again what the old fox could possibly want with him. El Serpiente was hungry. His food had run out and he had rationed himself to a frugal breakfast of a single piece of ham and the last of the onion washed down with gritty water from the stream.

It was from the direction of Los Tidos that El Serpiente was expecting Suarez to approach so it took him by surprise when the tall stooped figure in a charcoal grey overcoat appeared out of the trees on his side of the valley. From his vantage point up on the rock, El Serpiente saw how the tall figure, still with his back to him, moved methodically from one piece of cover to the next, a tree trunk then an oleander bush, a stone wall then a rise in the ground, till he came finally to the bridge's nearest parapet and peered over the edge to check out the bed of the stream beneath. He carried a revolver in his hand, El Serpiente noticed, an old fashioned army type and this reminded him of the tales he had heard of Suarez the soldier who had fought for Franco in the campaigns in Morocco long before the Civil War.

The tall stooped figure was now crossing the bridge still with his back to the man on the rock. He stopped when he reached the far side and turned round so for the first time in his life El Serpiente saw the face that went with the reputation: a pale, drawn and curiously fragile face, an old man's face with hollowed out cheeks and tired-looking eyes.

'Arriba!' he cried across the valley and Suarez showing no sign of being startled slowly raised the hand holding the revolver into the air.

El Serpiente came down quickly off the rock observing the usual conventions by holding the tubular framework of the assassin's rifle at arm's length till he gained the roadway and stood facing Suarez across the bridge.

The exchange of code words seemed unnecessary and by unspoken agreement they disposed with it. Simultaneously they laid their weapons on the end parapets then approached one another, stopping only when they stood five metres apart. Two men who had been adversaries for quarter of a century now face-to-face for the first time ever and El Serpiente's terrible disfigurement struck Suarez immediately. He had heard the stories of how some mercenaries had done this to him and killed his father and his brothers at the same time. Small wonder, Suarez thought to himself, that this man carried such hatred in his heart. Yet when Suarez spoke his voice betrayed no feelings of compassion.

'Franco is no longer here.' he said without any preliminary. 'You are wasting your time in this place and exposing yourself to danger.'

El Serpiente held the sunken tired-looking eyes in his gaze. To his right he heard the call of a bird in the bushes and further off the sound of the sea. This was the man on whose orders the thumbscrews were put on two of his comrades before they were put in front of a firing squad when they refused to give names. Why should this man suddenly be so interested in his welfare?

'I can tell you are puzzled as to my motives,' said Suarez reading the other man's thoughts. 'I am here to make a deal with you if that is what you want to know. My end of the bargain is your free and unmolested passage back to the north.'

'A deal has two sides to it,' growled El Serpiente, speaking for the first time. 'What is expected from me in return for this offer of yours?'

Suarez looked away. For a while his eyes seemed to focus on a distant point. 'I have ten months to go to my retirement,' he said finally. 'I want your absolute assurance that you will stay quiet till a date in September next year, a date that I will give to you. After that you can do as you please.'

El Serpiente reflected on these words. He drew the back of his hand across the roughness of his chin then spat out on the ground. 'There are those you are holding prisoner in Pamplona and Santander, yet more in Logrono.'

'They will be released, I will see to it. There are no charges against them yet and my word will be sufficient.'

'Release is not enough. They will need safe passage to countries where they will be granted political asylum. What do you say to that?'

'I will agree to it.'

El Serpiente smiled. 'You give a lot my friend and ask so little in return. Ten months is hardly any time to someone such as I who has waged a war for the greater part of his life. I am still looking for the catch.'

'There is no catch. Do you find that so hard to believe?'

'Convince me. You are not the kind to seek a quiet life for its own sake. There must be some bigger reason why you want to serve out the rest of your time in peace.'

Suarez fixed his sight on the distant point again. For a moment El Serpiente thought that tears were about to well in those deep sunken eyes. Then the tall stooped figure began to speak. As an old soldier to an old soldier, he explained, to pass off why he should be telling his greatest enemy the secret he had told to no others: of how Carlita had been told by the doctors that she had no more than three years left to live; of the cost of her treatment that would take every peseta of his pension; of the lump sum he needed on his retirement to buy the little finca in La Mancha that Carlita had set her heart on; of those in Madrid who would seek to deny it to him, of how another terrorist atrocity would be their excuse for putting him out to grass with only a pittance to live on.

As they made to part a few minutes later there was a brief moment as each felt the compulsion to shake hands. In the end, however, they turned away without touching flesh and walked back to their respective ends of the bridge and their weapons. When Suarez looked again the figure in motorcycle leathers with a bandana tied round his head was gone.

* * *

Partly because he had gorged himself on such huge quantities of Casares's paella; partly because of the many litres of bacteria-infested water he had since drunk, the effects of the emetic were lingering much longer in Waldorf's stomach than they had done in the stomach of Generalisimo Francisco Franco. Still the bouts of retching and diarrhoea plagued him, still he was arching his back every fifteen minutes and heaving out everything he had eaten, still the craving for old bones drove him on. After a night spent rooting at the back of Paco's Rincon, Waldorf, from the cover of a ditch, was eyeing up the heavy traffic on the Port Road. The garbage containers at the back of Paco's Rincon had proved a disappointment. They were modern contraptions with lids that clamped down with handles – coupled with the fact that there was a steady procession of kitchen staff backwards and forwards all night – men who chased him off with harsh shouts.

Waldorf raised his gnarled snout. From behind in the direction of the town he had picked up the scent of Felipe's flock of sheep and goats and of the two sheepdogs that kept the shepherd company everywhere he went. Waldorf was especially wary of Felipe's sheepdogs. They were trained to work as a team and they had managed to out manoeuvre him on several occasions in the past. As Waldorf pinned down one of them, the other would come up at the back and nip him in the haunches. No, Waldorf decided. In his weakened state it would be best to steer clear of Felipe's sheepdogs. He would wait for a gap in the traffic then take his chance on the other side of the road – territory into which Waldorf had never strayed before.

* * *

The sudden change in the delectable lady's manner took Uncle Pablo by surprise. Though he was used to the capriciousness of women, the fury with which she had taken the handcuffs off him and ejected him from her apartment was quite beyond belief. Waving that tiny silver pistol of hers in his face, she had bundled him out onto the landing and shut the door in his face. Worse still, apart from the beret on his head, she didn't give him chance to pick up his clothes so it was in a state of nakedness that Uncle Pablo found himself having to make his way down the ten flights of stairs. Fortunately for him though he passed no-one as he left the Edificio Los Angeles although two objects from the skies narrowly missed hitting him on the head as he made for the cover of a tamarisk bush, two objects that he recovered and which turned out to be his false teeth.

On the whole and being the kind of person he was, Uncle Pablo viewed these experiences phlegmatically. Yes, it was inconvenient being turned out on the street naked and, if he got caught, it would undoubtedly land him in trouble with the police, but to compensate for these setbacks he had enjoyed several days of ogling at the delectable lady in various states of undress and drinking dry the contents of the playboy's cocktail cabinet. How many days, Uncle Pablo was not exactly sure, for the recent past seemed to merge into one single and delightful event in which time had stood still and the passage of day and night had been irrelevant.

Uncle Pablo screwed up his eyes as he peered out from behind the tamarisk. The question now was how was he going to get back to the Villa Verde without being seen. He could wait for nightfall, of course, but the position of the sun in the hazy sky told him that nightfall was still a long way off. Sooner or later someone would come along this way and see him; some woman on her way to the town beach who would raise the alarm that there was a pervert in the bushes and call for the police.

No, Uncle Pablo decided, it would be best to keep moving

and avoid, if possible, any places where there might be people. This, he realised was going to be difficult. In between where he stood and the Old Town was the back of the port quarter – an area that was heavily built up and full of the comings and goings of people who worked in the warehouses and wharves. Going that way seemed to be inviting trouble, even if he tried to make his way through back yards and along alleyways. Then an idea came to him.

* * *

When Jaime Campello walked into the Bar Madrid the scene was one of chaos. It was twenty past twelve and the place was already full of irate customers demanding service and banging their fists on the bar. There was no sign of Conchita and two of the Gomez children, Tomas and little Joaquin, were struggling gamely to keep the flow of tapas going and the glasses topped up. There was no sign of Lopez and the others either. Unknown to Campello the card players had left ten minutes before fed up with all the clamour and gone in search of somewhere quieter to sit.

Campello's eye then fell on Pepe Gomez at a table by himself with a half-empty glass of anis in front of him and a big cigar in his hand. From the big glassy-eyed smile on his face, Campello knew that Gomez had been drinking for some time.

'Jaime,' Gomez called across beckoning to the young carpenter to come and join him and to little Joaquin to go and fetch another glass. 'You need not look so anxious. Conchita is at her sister's and I have been left to run the place by myself.'

Passing no comment except to sneeze into his

handkerchief, Campello sat down at the table. On his way past the Bar Zamora, he had noticed the torn awning and the place all shut up. His first question to Gomez therefore was to ask what had become of his neighbour.

'The Guardia have arrested him,' said Gomez with a smug smile topping up the freshly arrived glass with anis. 'There is a rumour that he is a terrorist living here under an assumed identity. Knowing the man, I can hardly say that I am surprised.'

'Pepe, I came to see if you had heard anything of Robles.'

'Robles? What about Robles?'

'I hear he is still in police custody. Surely it is only going to be a matter of time before he denounces us.'

'You worry too much Jaime. Drink your anis.'

'I cannot stay long Pepe, I have an appointment.'

'An appointment? Where?'

Whether Campello should have answered this question truthfully or not was a matter for conjecture on his part later on. The fact that he did was partly due to an unguarded moment, partly to his basically truthful nature and partly to a weariness with trying to conduct his life in secret. Immediately, however, he saw his mistake.

'A lady Jaime! You did not tell me you had a lady. Do I know her? Is she shapely?' Gomez was on his feet now with the cigar between his teeth and a hand resting on Campello's shoulder. 'And the Hotel Bahia too. What better place to take a lady? She will be impressed, my friend, you have my word on it. The place is open again I hear after the business when Franco was staying up there. What is her name? You are a dark horse, Jaime, keeping this from me.'

Bit by bit and because Campello saw no other way, the

story came out: everything except the Diane Maitland Bureau which Campello could not bring himself to say anything about in case it leaked from Gomez to Lopez and the others and from there to the rest of the town. The arrangements to meet the lady he said, had been made by a third party, using the term because it was vaguely the truth and hopefully important enough sounding to put Pepe Gomez off asking further questions. The next development, however, was not one Campello was expecting.

'Jaime,' Gomez announced, tightening the grip on Campello's shoulder, 'I will come with you to the Hotel Bahia and make sure that everything goes right for you this time. It is the least I can do after the danger you put yourself in to help me. I will stand by you, my friend, just as you stood by me.'

As they left the Bar Madrid, however, what Campello and Gomez did not notice was the blue Simca Elysee parked behind Campello's old grey Citroen van or the two officers of the Guardia Civil sitting inside it.

★ ★ ★

Uncle Pablo's route took him across the stretch of wasteland between the Edificio Los Angeles and the Marina, dashing from one tamarisk to the next with his beret on his head and, for reasons of modesty, one hand clasped over his private parts. Fortunately for him at this late point in the season, there were relatively few people about and no-one saw his strange figure as it flitted from bush to bush. The plan he had devised was next to use the cover provided by the line of parked cars and yachts drawn up on the foreshore then the clutter of the boatyard beyond to get him to the wall separating the marina from the fishing harbour and from there to make his way through the wharves and jetties of the port to the mouth of the barranco. By following the course of the latter he knew he would come to one of the quiet sheep paths that would take him back to the Old Town.

It was in the boatyard where Uncle Pablo came across a pot of tar used for caulking the planks of boats complete with a tar brush left standing in it. This gave him the idea of daubing his loins with tar so, from a distance at least, it would give the appearance that he was wearing a pair of swimming trunks thus helping him to avoid too much attention. This experiment, as it turned out, was a total failure. The tar would not adhere to his skin with any consistency so that he ended up with black hands and looking rather like a spotted hyena. Abandoning the tar brush, he pressed on.

★ ★ ★

Waiting for Juan to turn his back so she could snip a bloom from one of the rose bushes without being seen took far longer than Nathalie anticipated. It was quarter to one, she saw on the clock on the dashboard as she slid behind the steering wheel of the Peugeot. She realised it would be cutting it fine to get to the Hotel Bahia in fifteen minutes, especially if there was traffic in the town. Using the driving mirror to check the little bit of make up she had put on her face, she slipped the car into first gear and set off down the drive. The sun was starting to come out as she turned onto the Old Valencia Highway and the wet patches on the ground were already starting to dry. Passing the crossroads, she couldn't help glancing to the left towards the Salinas though all she saw in that direction was the winding dirt road and in the distance the old broken down windmill. Coming down the hill towards the Port Road she had to brake suddenly to avoid a collar-less and emaciated looking stray dog that crossed in front of her and that looked up at her as she passed. An omen? A harbinger of further bad luck? She shuddered at the thought. Could it be that this third meeting with the young man the computers at the Diane Maitland Bureau had matched her with would end up with yet another frightening experience?

Judging, as she had two nights before, that the narrow streets in the town might be busy and seeing that she had only ten minutes left, Nathalie took the Port Road again. The police road block was now gone she noticed but as she passed the boatyard in the marina a curious sight met her eyes – an old man, completely naked except for a beret on his head and daubing his private parts, or so it seemed, with some kind of black paste. Taking this to be a further manifestation of the strange people that were reputed to be infiltrating the town, Nathalie put her foot on the accelerator. The way to the Hotel Bahia next took her past the Edificio Los Angeles where Lola Martinez was inside busy packing her suitcase then through the Plaza de Los Reyes and up the Avenida where she passed the little park with the fountain and the palm trees. Five to one she noticed on the clock above the Ayuntamiento; five to one it also said on the clock on the dashboard. She was now leaving the town behind, taking a quiet road with terraces of almond trees over to her right and occasional glimpses of the sea to the left. She engaged a lower gear to take the sharp twisting corners and passed a black Mercedes going the other way with a man behind the wheel whose face she clearly saw: a man in his sixties with sunken cheeks and an angular face, a man who seemed lost in his thoughts.

Soon she was crossing the bridge where a little earlier this same man had struck an old soldier's deal with a rough looking type in motorcycle leathers who Nathalie Theroux would have immediately recognised.

CHAPTER TWELVE

A Sad Bouquet of Rue

Navarro the Alcalde or Town Mayor of Los Tidos chose a bad moment for his return. Navarro and his mistress had been availing themselves of a free holiday in Gran Canaria courtesy of the company that provided the municipal rubbish removal service, the employers of the notorious basureros and, as he walked into the Ayuntamiento he was confronted by a throng of people all demanding his immediate attention. Navarro blanched. Being by nature an indolent man, the prospect of having so many problems hurled at him all at once, especially on his first day back, did not appeal one bit. Yet he was at heart a politician and he realised that his continuing incumbency in the position of Alcalde and the enjoyment of the perks that went with it depended entirely on the votes of these people. To court unpopularity on any issue was not a good idea.

'Amigos,' he said greeting the crowd with his arms out wide and a smile that showed off the teeth that had been crowned by a dentist in Alicante entirely at the expense of one Señor Llorca, a millionaire property developer from Oviedo who had recently sought to iron out any objections the Alcalde might have to his appropriation of several hectares of unspoiled seashore for the purpose of building a twenty-five storey hotel. 'Amigos, if you speak one at a time I will listen to everything you have to tell me.' But as the outpourings began, the smile on Navarro's face rapidly started to evaporate.

★ ★ ★

Conchita was furious. Returning from her sister's sickbed, she found her husband missing and the Bar Madrid in the middle of the lunchtime rush left in the charge of her children. And it was from her children that she found out that her husband had gone off with the carpenter Campello again – this time in his best shirt and trousers and with a big fat cigar in his mouth. 'To where?' she enquired, and those in the bar who sensed that it might be worse for them if they kept quiet replied: 'To the Hotel Bahia.'

The words stung. The memories of the night of their disastrous wedding anniversary celebration flooded back to her and the ignominy of ending up in a cheap cafeteria used by truck drivers and being made to eat off tin plates. Now what was her husband up to going off to the Hotel Bahia with Jaime Campello – and behind her back at that?

Picking up the telephone she summoned her brother-in-law Federico to come immediately to look after the bar. Still wearing her apron, she set off. and those who walked in the Street of Two Eyes at that time stood aside to let her pass because they saw the look on her face and the savage glare in her eye. Someone was in trouble, they all knew, and it didn't take much racking of the brains to guess who it might be.

★ ★ ★

At that exact moment the who in question was preening

himself before a gilt framed mirror in the reception hall of the Hotel Bahia. To his own eye he was no longer a bar keeper from a dusty back street in the port quarter but a big shot with a big cigar between his teeth who was there to look after his old friend Jaime Campello and generally organise things. Had he known that Conchita was no longer with her sister and already on his trail an alarm bell would have been sounding in his anis-pickled brain – an alarm bell that would have been telling him to seek sanctuary in some dark corner of the gardens instead of standing on full view to anyone who chanced to walk through the door.

Pepe Gomez had cast himself in this role of master of ceremonies unasked. In part, he saw himself as the older man; on hand, if required, to put words of fatherly advice in young Campello's ear whereas, in part, he also saw himself as the fixer: the man of the world who knew how to deal with head waiters, how to get the best table, how to press pesetas in the right hands and how to pick the best food and wine.

Herrero, the head waiter at the Hotel Bahia was one of a dying breed. He was now an old man but his back was still as straight as the day he first set foot in the Hotel Bahia forty years ago. In that time he had seen many comings and goings: many managers, many chefs, many young waiters. He had served under two owners, the Old Marquis and now his son and, little went on in the famous candlelit dining room without Herrero knowing and approving. He had been told that the Señor Granjero on whose table he had waited was none other than Generalisimo Franco travelling incognito but he took the information in his stride. Over the years Herrero had waited on many kings and presidents.

Over the years a hostility had developed between Herrero

and the chef, Casares and this hostility centred round who was the more senior in the hotel's hierarchy. Herrero felt that this was he, simply on account of his long service, whereas Casares considered that in the natural order of things the position of chef was superior to that of head waiter. And in any case what reason did people have for coming to Herrero's candlelit dining room? Was it not to taste the wonderful estofadas and paellas that Casares cooked? As a consequence of the hostility between these two a tradition had grown up where messages from the kitchen to the dining room and back to the kitchen were taken by intermediaries, unfortunate messengers who carried the stinging words backwards and forwards usually prefaced by 'Señor Casares says this…' or 'Señor Herroro is not satisfied with that…' Frequently these exchanges became heated and abusive. Herrero would order one of his young waiters to 'Tell Señor Casares that his filete is like the sole of my boot,' and Casares would send the waiter back to inform Señor Herrero that he would gladly put his boot on the plancha to make it more tender preferably with Señor Herrero's foot still inside it.

Alvarez the manager presided nervously over these vicarious bickerings fearing that one day they would turn into fisticuffs but he need not have worried because, when the two men met face to face, their conversation was always the stuff of sweetness and light. The man who had just sent one of his kitchen staff along to the dining room to tell the head waiter where to put the Lenguado Gallego if he didn't like the look of it, would bump into Herrero in the washroom and wish him good-day and enquire into the health of his wife and his newly-arrived grandson Ignatio. In return Herrero would ask about Señora Casares and how little Margarita was getting on with her lessons at school and, when they parted, they would do so with smiles and polite inclinations of the head. 'After you, Señor Casares,' Herrero would say as they stood before the washroom door. 'No, after you,' Casares would reply.

It was Herrero who now had his eye fixed firmly on the swaying figure of Pepe Gomez standing before the mirror. This man who the head waiter knew faintly as the proprietor of a grubby bar somewhere in the town, had just had the temerity to stroll into the candlelit dining room, with no jacket and tie and drop ash from the end of his cigar onto the fine Moroccan carpet. Even worse, this man had just thrust five grubby coins into his hand and asked for the best table to be put aside for his friend and a lady. Now, unbelievably, this man was helping himself to a red rose from the display of flowers on the Reception Desk and calling for the carta and wine list so he could order for his friend.

★ ★ ★

The friend in question was at that moment in the gentleman's cloakroom blowing his nose and putting the final touches to his appearance. His appearance, also in a shirt and trousers, fell well short of the standards of the fabulous candlelit dining room and Campello had been the first to realise this. In fact he had spent most of the journey to the Hotel Bahia in the old Citroen van trying to explain to Pepe Gomez that he was meeting the lady for a drink in the cocktail bar and not for luncheon – but Gomez, whose brain was swollen by the several bottles of beer and quarter litre of anis he had drunk, would have none of it. On the contrary, the fat little man was insistent that he knew all about how to sweep a young lady off her feet. 'You won't do it with a glass of martini,' he expounded. 'You will need to wine her and dine her properly – and where better to do it than in the candlelit dining room. After that, my friend, you have no difficulty in getting her into bed. A word in the right ear and you shall have the bridal suite set aside for your use.'

The red rose and the fact he had forgotten to bring one came to Campello as he and Pepe Gomez walked in through the Hotel Bahia's magnificent portico.

'No problem,' said Gomez, his eye falling on the arrangement on the reception desk, and it was at this point that Jaime Campello decided to make himself scarce. He already had the premonition something was going to go wrong and Pepe Gomez's drunken presence and general behaviour now seemed to guarantee it.

★ ★ ★

Conchita Gomez made the journey to the Hotel Bahia by taxi, coincidentally the same taxi that had transported her and her husband to the Hotel Bahia on the night of their wedding anniversary. But when the taxi driver chose to reminisce on the way that evening had ended, he caught the cold steely eye glaring at him in the driving mirror and decided it would be best for him to say no more.

'Wait for me here,' snapped Conchita as they drove up the gravel driveway between the magnificent avenue of palms and pulled up by the portico.

★ ★ ★

Capitan Luis Garcia in Oswaldo's blue Simca Elysee with Ramon Ramon behind the steering wheel because of the injuries to the Capitan's feet experienced a rather more troublesome journey. Tailing Campello's van with Campello and Gomez (the real Gomez) inside, the direction they were heading in suddenly became apparent. 'This is the way to the Hotel Bahia!' exclaimed Garcia bringing his fist down on the dashboard. 'The criminals are returning to the scene of their crime!'

The effect of these sudden noises, Garcia's exclamation and the noise of his fist crashing down on the plastic dashboard, caused the ever-nervous Ramon Ramon to brake and swerve. At that moment they happened to be passing a wall that the little Simca went into thus flattening it to the ground.

After the noise and dust had died away, it was Ramon Ramon who spoke first. 'Capitan there are pieces of glass in your face. I think it is because your head has gone through the windscreen.'

The wall belonged to a man called Ruiz and right now Ruiz was not very happy, not just because his wall had been demolished by these two officers of the Guardia Civil but because he happened to be standing behind it at the time.

'Look what you have done,' he shouted as he crawled out from under the heap of rubble. 'Who is going to pay for all this damage?'

These remarks were directed at Garcia who was busy picking broken glass from his nose as he got out of the wreckage of Oswaldo's car. 'Silence,' he snapped at Ruiz fixing him with a glare through his cracked sunglasses. 'Do you not see that you are addressing a high-ranking officer of the

Guardia Civil? It would pay you to show a little more respect when speaking to me, hombre.'

'What respect have you shown to my wall? Let me see the colour of your money then I will decide whether to give you any respect or not.'

'You clearly need teaching some manners,' growled Garcia drawing himself up to his full height.

A small crowd had started to gather and an urchin was passing among them taking bets on how this might turn out. Ruiz had distinguished himself in his younger days in the art of boxing and it was known that he still packed a good punch. The Capitan from Cordoba on the other hand was big and talked tough but he was still an unknown quantity.

'You have just reduced my wall to ruins,' Ruiz continued. 'Now you have the nerve to be lecturing me on my manners. Am I hearing you correctly Señor?'

Two men in the crowd decided to change their bets.

'I warn you, hombre, you are obstructing two officers of the Guardia Civil in the execution of their duty. Any more from you and you will find you end your days tied to a stake in the middle of the Sahara with only the flies to watch you die from thirst.'

The crowd got bigger. More pesetas were pressed into the urchin's hand.

'Capitan Garcia,' Ramon Ramon had just managed to crawl out from behind the crumpled up steering wheel. 'I am sure that all this can be sorted out amicably.'

'Shut up. Silence.'

The urchin called fresh odds. More coins were showered onto the pavement.

'Well,' said Ruiz belligerently. 'What is it to be? Do I get a cheque from you now and an apology or do I have to take you down to my notario's office in the Avenida? In which case you will have to pay my notario's bill too.'

'You are courting disaster, hombre. Step out of my way immediately or I will have no alternative except to arrest you.'

'Arrest me! Let me see you try it.' The urchin closed his book.

'Capitan Garcia, I think it would be a mistake to push this man any further.' But Ramon Ramon's words had come too late. Garcia had already prodded Ruiz in the chest and Ruiz had already responded by punching Garcia in the eye. The crowd cheered. The Capitan from Cordoba reeled, then fell back over the heap of rubble that had once been Ruiz's wall and cracked his head on the bent remains of Oswaldo's fender. The urchin paid out and pocketed the two hundred pesetas he had just made.

'What is this?' Ramon Ramon asked the boy as he pressed a coin into his hand.

'Ten pesetas commission,' the urchin replied. 'Give it to your Capitan when he comes round and tell him he has earned it.'

* * *

The first sight that met Conchita's eyes as she walked into the Reception Hall of the Hotel Bahia still wearing her apron was that of her husband at the far end in his best shirt and trousers with a big cigar in his mouth and a red rose in his hand. There was no sign of Jaime Campello among the flow of guests arriving for lunch and immediately dark clouds of suspicion flooded into her mind. What was going on here? With that,

272

the scarcely believable thought started to dawn on her that her fat idle anis-swilling husband was meeting a woman. What other reason could there be for the red rose he was carrying? He had never been known to have any interest in flowers. Not that the Bar Madrid had a garden but Conchita had always had to nag him even to water the few geraniums that lived in pots on the window sills. Her eyes narrowed. So this was what he was up to when he disappeared for hours on end in the company of Jaime Campello. And what was this she was witnessing other than some kind of foursome. Not that it mattered for Jaime Campello because he was a single man; but her husband, a cheat, a Lothario and here, of all places, in the Hotel Bahia where she herself so loved to come and where he only brought her once a year and, even then, grudgingly. Her fists tightened. The muscles in her biceps and forearms bulged like ships' hawsers. She was already half way across the elegant hallway when Pepe Gomez saw her coming but by then it was far too late for him to make an escape.

The sound when it came echoed through the tiled corridors of the Hotel Bahia, made the vases and the chandeliers shake and even rattled the cutlery in the candlelit dining room. Jaime Campello even heard it in the men's room though at the time he did not realise that the sound that made ripples in the water in the wash hand basin was the sound of his friend Pepe Gomez having his skull cracked against the wall.

There was one final incident before Conchita got back in her taxi and ordered the driver to take her back to the Street of Two Eyes. A Peugeot drew up outside the Hotel Bahia undistinguished except for the splatters of mud on its sides. A thin girl got out, a girl in her twenties dressed in black like someone in mourning, except all that Conchita noticed about her was that she too was carrying a red rose in her hand.

'Jezebel!' she cried going over to the girl and shaking her fist. 'The man you are here to meet is my husband and the father of my twelve children. What kind of woman does that make you? Huh? You have lost your tongue now, I see. Shall I tell you about my husband? He is a fat idle coňac-swilling pig and now to add to his list of weaknesses I discover that he is also a philanderer. Now ask yourself what you are doing with someone such as him.'

★ ★ ★

Despite the buckled front end and twisted steering column, Oswaldo's Simca was still driveable once it was reversed out of the ruins of Ruiz's wall. The crowd that had gathered to watch the stand-off between Ruiz and the Capitan from Cordoba had all disappeared and so had Ruiz himself meaning Garcia on recovering consciousness, had to be content with marking him down for arrest and punishment later.

Heads turned as the Simca with its silencer box split and its fender dragging on the road continued its journey through the outskirts of town towards the Hotel Bahia and soon Garcia and Ramon Ramon passed the place where the road they were on joined with the top end of the Avenida – the only significance to this fact being that Suarez in his Mercedes had just gone in the opposite direction so they narrowly missed catching sight of one another. Garcia for his part was not a pretty spectacle to behold. To add to his injured feet and the splinted fingers of his left hand, his face was now a mass of cuts and the eye that Ruiz had punched was already starting to discolour and close.

Leaving the town behind and crossing the deserted valley with its little bridge where Suarez and El Serpiente had held their secret meeting neither of the Guardia Civil men realised that the notorious terrorist they sought was only two hundred and fifty metres away retrieving his Harley Davidson from the thicket of canes at the mouth of the little stream that ran beneath them.

Pulling up outside the Hotel Bahia, Garcia and Ramon Ramon arrived just in time to see Nathalie Theroux white-faced and shaken getting back into her Peugeot and, in the background, Campello's grey van parked in a line of cars.

'See,' Garcia hissed. 'That girl over there carries a red rose in her hand – the same flower that the carpenter carried last night. I said to you, did I not, that it was the emblem of some clandestine political organisation – a means by which the members of the group are able to recognise one another. What's more she is a woman.'

'Half the population are women Capitan. I do not think that it is unusual.'

'Fool. What I meant was that we are looking for a woman. Poisoning is a woman's crime, did I not say this to you? Was it not my idea that we should be looking for a woman?'

'I thought the idea came from Señor Suarez, Capitan.'

'That is not important: pay attention to what you are doing and get on with it.'

'What am I doing Capitan?'

'You are following that woman, before she gets away. If my guess is correct she is the professional poisoner in this town and her presence here shows that she is acquainted with the very hotel where the Caudillo stayed. Put these two facts together and the final piece of the jigsaw is in place: Gomez

275

alias El Serpiente is the ring-leader, Campello is the message-carrier and this girl, whoever she is, is the assassin, a femme fatale nonetheless. It is clever when you think about it: getting a woman to do the dirty work. Most important though, hombre, by my patient observation and gathering of intelligence we have scooped up the whole gang of these desperados. Thanks to me these extremists will never be able to threaten the security of the state again. One decoration will surely not cover the service I have rendered to the nation over these last few days. A whole row of medals would be more appropriate, do you not think?'

* * *

Under the watchful eye of Herrero, Campello helped Pepe Gomez to get to his feet. A combination of the large quantity of alcohol he had consumed and the banging of his head against the wall by the fearful Conchita, had rendered him temporarily senseless and so it was with Pepe Gomez almost like a dead weight that Campello struggled to get him back to the van. The van being without doors caused a further problem. If Pepe Gomez was sitting in the passenger seat and if Campello happened to turn a left hand corner, centrifugal forces would serve to throw him out. Campello finally resolved this difficulty by loading Gomez in the back where at least he would be safe except for the fishy smell.

But as he drove back towards Los Tidos, Campello's thoughts went to the mysterious lady and her non-appearance again. That would be the end of his dealings with the Diane Maitland Bureau, he decided emphatically and nothing, not even the businesslike lady, would ever persuade him otherwise. Never again would he be found creeping out of the house carrying a rose in his hand; no more would he be wasting his time on girls who repeatedly stood him up. He was destined to remain a bachelor and, judging by the experience of his friend Pepe Gomez who now lay on the steel floor in the back of the van groaning with every bump and lurch, remaining a bachelor did not seem such a bad thing.

★ ★ ★

Climbing over the wall of the marina and catching sight of the gun toting cowboy sign on top of Club Gringo (not switched on of course in the middle of the day), Uncle Pablo reflected for a moment on his brief career as El Pescador, the singing fisherman, and wondered whether he would ever be able to pick up the pieces again. The next obstacle that stood in his path as he made his way back to the Old Town without his clothes was the commercial harbour which included the jetties where the fishing boats tied up. Here fortune continued to smile on him. Being still as yet early afternoon, the fishing boats were out at sea and activity was minimal. A few retired fishermen were sitting cross-legged on the ground mending nets but they were too engrossed in what they were doing to pay any attention to the strange naked figure with black hands and black spots who dodged at the back of them. A little further on Uncle Pablo had a lucky find: an old sack that he managed to tie round his waist like an apron so except from behind – from which angle his bare fleshless buttocks were on display – he resembled one of the men who worked gutting fish in the fish market.

When he reached it Uncle Pablo saw the barranco had

been turned into a swirling river of orange mud by the great storm but the mud was already starting to dry and it had just reached the stage where it had taken on the glutinous consistency of wet cement hence as he made his way up the barranco's narrow valley it wasn't long before he acquired the appearance of a Polynesian tribesman who adorns himself with mud as part of a ritual. Uncle Pablo's luck continued to hold, however, and no-one chanced to look down from the parapets of the Puente de San Marco at the strange sight of the mudman down beneath and no children were playing along the winding sheep paths as they sometimes did. Children, fortunately for Uncle Pablo, were still at school.

Because Uncle Pablo's front door key was in his trouser pocket and because his trousers were still in the penthouse suite of the Edificio Los Angeles, he had to gain access to the Villa Verde by scaling the back wall. This he accomplished with great agility for a man of his age and, discarding the sack in the yard, he entered the house through a window that his nephew had forgotten to close.

Home at last, Uncle Pablo's first thought was to retrieve one of the bottles of absenta from the emergency stock he kept under his bed. Just as he had done this and just as he was gearing himself up for the first tonsil biting swig the phone started to ring.

'Hold on,' said Uncle Pablo into the mouthpiece of the telephone whilst pulling the cork out of the bottle of absenta with his teeth and taking such a deep draught that when he took his dribbling mouth away from the bottle nearly a quarter of the liquor had gone.

'Señor Campello?' It was the businesslike lady from the Diane Maitland Bureau, not that her voice meant anything to

Uncle Pablo because he had never spoken to her before. 'Señor Campello, is that you?'

'Yes this is Señor Campello,' said Uncle Pablo as he took yet another large swig from the bottle.

'I am sorry Señor Campello, I did not recognise your voice. It is about the young lady as you probably guessed.' Slowly Uncle Pablo's brain started to focus. Young lady – did this mean the delectable young lady who had just evicted him from her apartment and who had entertained him with such relish over the last few days? 'Señor Campello, this seems a strange question to ask at this point in time but before we go any further could you please confirm that you are unmarried and not the father of twelve children?' It was indeed a strange question to ask but Uncle Pablo had no qualms about answering. He was not married and never had been. As to twelve children, he had sown many seeds in his time but he was not aware that any of his couplings had given rise to children. Twelve was most certainly out of the question. 'Thank you for those assurances Señor Campello and on this basis I am pleased to say the young lady is happy to set up another meeting with you.'

Being a firm believer in tasting the fruit rather than asking too many questions about where it comes from Uncle Pablo had gathered from the conversation so far that the young lady under discussion was a different young lady to the one who had just thrown him out naked onto the street. How this came about he hardly cared yet it was beginning to enter his alcohol befuddled head that, through his exploits as Pablo El Pescador, he had found his way onto the network of a circle of nymphomaniacs. This new woman through her intermediary was propositioning him for sex and this, to someone like Uncle Pablo, sounded perfectly acceptable.

'You are sure you are willing to proceed Señor Campello?' Yes, Uncle Pablo, reassured the lady with the businesslike voice, swallowing another mouthful of absenta, he was more than willing to proceed. 'Good, then to avoid any more mix ups the bureau suggests that you call at her house. What do you think Señor Campello?' Uncle Pablo agreed. Calling at the lady's house seemed a very good idea. What better place to play whatever games she wanted to play than in her cosy boudoir. 'The young lady's name is Nathalie Theroux, Señor Campello, I will tell you this now. She is French and she lives in a hacienda called Los Arcos on the Old Valencia Highway. It is about two kilometres out of Los Tidos. I understand. Will you be able to find this place from these directions Señor Campello or do you need some more details?' Uncle Pablo assured the lady acting as the intermediary for the nymphomaniac circle that he would have no problem at all in finding Los Arcos or any other place she wanted to send him. The fact that this young lady was French had also registered with him. French women had the reputation of being the best of all when it came to the art of lovemaking. Uncle Pablo licked his lips. Up to now it had never been his privilege to have a dalliance with a French woman and the prospect was already whetting his appetite. 'I will tell Mademoiselle Theroux to expect you at four o'clock. And be sure to take a rose with you. In that way we will be certain that she will know who you are.'

★ ★ ★

Suarez had lunch at La Robinia: though he did not know it, the scene of one of Capitan Garcia's many free meals. He declined alcohol because he was already weary after driving all through the night and he knew the effect of wine would dull his senses when he still had important work to do. It was three o'clock when he left the restaurant and drove the remaining few hundred metres to the Comisaria where he hoped he would be able to pick up news of the two Guardia Civil officers whose operation he was here to terminate. He had heard enough already about Capitan Garcia's methods and the tales of arrests, including the arrest of the Assistant Chief of Police, but nothing prepared him for the situation that greeted him when he arrived at the Comisaria. Outside, there was a line of angry people that continued through the door till at its head Suarez saw a man with a toothbrush moustache and expensive looking mohair suit confronting the harassed looking sergeant who stood behind the duty desk.

'I demand the release of all prisoners you are holding here who have not been charged with crimes,' the man with the toothbrush moustache was saying. 'I demand also that this Capitan from Cordoba be brought here in person to explain his behaviour for himself.'

It was obvious to Suarez that this well-tailored individual was playing to the crowd and the crowd, on cue, was cheering his every word.

'The Feast of the Two Virgins is due to be celebrated in a few days and those who are to play the parts of Moors are all locked up in your cells.'

'My Primero,' yelled someone.

'And my Cristóbel,' yelled someone else.

'Don't forget my car!' called a young man from the back.

'And my compensation for being called bad names,' said the young woman standing next to him.

'And the compensation for knocking my wall down. In a blue Simca Elysee would you believe it, not more than three hours ago.'

'A blue Simca Elysee? That car is my car, Señor Ruiz.'

'In which case I am sorry to say your car is a write-off, my young friend.'

The desk sergeant raked his fingers through his hair and looked from side to side for means of escape. At that very moment Suarez stepped forward.

'What is going on here?' he snapped putting his credentials on the desk for the sergeant to see.

'Señor,' said the sergeant, coming to attention with his eyes growing round in his head for before him stood one of Spain's most powerful and respected men.

'Who are you?' Navarro demanded curtly, slightly irritated at this newcomer who had taken the limelight off him. Navarro had been warming to the role of espouser of populist causes, a role that he saw as a sure vote winner in next year's municipal elections. The left wing, the working class flank of public opinion, would be impressed by his stand against authority whereas the catholic conservative element would rally to his championing of the Feast of the Two Virgins.

'Señor Navarro is the Alcalde,' the desk sergeant explained to Suarez, not knowing yet what the great man from Madrid was doing here. 'The town has been the centre of a security operation recently and the Alcalde is expressing his concerns.'

Suarez's eyes narrowed. He had already taken a dislike to the shifty looking individual in the twenty mil peseta suit with the hand sewn lapels. Hearing that he was a jumped-up local politician served only to downgrade the man even further in Suarez's opinion. Yet he held his tongue. He had not heard yet the full extent of what Capitan Garcia and his assistant had been up to and, till he did, his inbuilt sense of caution told him it was wise not to say too much.

'Señor Navarro, I am here from Madrid to take charge of matters personally,' he said smoothly and with nothing in the tone of his voice to give away any of his deeper feelings. 'You may rest assured that any man who is not guilty of a crime will be released within the hour.

'What about my wall?'

'And my car?'

'And my reputation? He called me a putilla: I have witnesses.'

'And these bills for meals in my restaurant that your Capitan from Cordoba did not pay?'

'He ate in my restaurant too.'

'And mine.'

Suarez held up his hand. 'Anyone who wishes to make a claim for compensation should set out the details in writing and present them here at the Comisaria within seven days. Any genuine loss will be repaid. I will make sure that the funds are available.'

Ruiz spoke. 'Señor, your words are welcome, but how long will all this take?'

'The sooner things are cleared up, the better. Trust me to act expediently, Señor, even though I can make no guarantees.'

There was a general muttering that this seemed to be fair enough and the crowd started to drift away.

'Wait a minute,' interjected Navarro who saw that all the credit for putting matters right was being taken by the man in the grey overcoat who had not even said his name. 'How are we to know that you have the authority to make these promises?'

Suarez fixed his stare on the Alcalde with his toothbrush moustache and scented smell who reminded him of a pimp. The stare conveyed all the contempt and hatred he felt for those who aspired in the field of politics; men who would freely change sides and ideologies if they saw that it could profit them; men who would never put their lives on the line on the field of battle if it ever came to war again.

'As I said, you will have to trust me,' he said flatly.

Navarro turned round but seeing most of his audience was gone, he too decided to take his leave. He had done some good to his reputation, he comforted himself as he walked back to the Ayuntamiento, though these tales that were going round that Franco had been in town while he was away in Gran Canaria still puzzled him. Franco, it seemed, had been the reason for the Capitan from Cordoba's coming though none of it made much sense. Navarro shook his head. His thoughts then turned to more pleasant things: like the prospect of spending the rest of the afternoon in bed with his mistress and in the future negotiating the contract for rebuilding the promenade over many splendid meals at the Hotel Bahia. As he entered the Ayuntamiento, he noticed the new doors. Someone, he reflected, had put a lot of effort into making them.

★ ★ ★

Capitan Garcia, the officer on whom Suarez's attentions were now being turned, sat in the battered remains of Oswaldo's Simca with the window wound down listening to the plaintive cry of a lark outside and the droning screech of a lone cicada up on the telephone wire. In the driving seat, sat Ramon Ramon and together they were staring at the big iron gates that

284

stood open and the sign on the pillar that said 'Los Arcos'. This was the place on the Old Valencia Highway to which they had followed the girl in the Peugeot and the fact that it was the entrance to a substantial property was now occupying Garcia's attention as he bit the end off a fresh cigar and spat it out into the road.

'Our little lady assassin is from a well-off family so it seems. Hombre, it never fails to amaze me, why these children of the rich should take sides against the Caudillo. They and their parents are those who have profited most from the stability he has brought to our country yet they are there, in universities and places of learning, joining hands with strikers and other troublemakers who make mischief in the streets. If you ask me they are dreamers, the lot of them. Before the Caudillo came we saw for ourselves what a shambles dreamers reduced the country into. The saints preserve us if we go back to government by idealists such as these.'

'Capitan Garcia, do you want me to drive up to this house in the car?'

Garcia studied the driveway that went up over a rise in the ground with trellises of vines on one side and fruit trees on the other. 'No, hombre, we will proceed on foot and with stealth. Who knows what reception might be awaiting us?'

★ ★ ★

Noticing when she got back to the house that Maman was out in the garden with Juan inspecting some fresh blight that had infested the acacias and discussing what kind of pesticide they needed to purchase, Nathalie used the opportunity to phone the businesslike lady at the Diane Maitland Bureau to tell her about her further dreadful experience. The businesslike lady was speechless for a moment. That the young man who she had arranged for Señorita Theroux to meet was in real life some lecher, a married man with twelve children no less who was playing around behind his wife's back, she found hard to believe. 'He is not yet thirty,' she protested. 'To have fathered so many children by such an age is scarcely possible. I will phone him immediately and see if I can get an explanation. Do not despair Señorita Theroux, I will get to the bottom of this and come back to you.' Nathalie did not have a chance to say that it no longer mattered to her whether the businesslike lady got to the bottom of this or not. Like Jaime Campello, she was beginning to see that these secret meetings had been doomed from the beginning. Whatever the explanation for the irate woman who had intercepted her outside the Hotel Bahia, the fates had determined that she and this young man would never meet. It had been decided already that she would end up a lonely old spinster: unloved, unwanted, a stranger in a strange land with only the wild birds for her friends.

Nathalie went up to her room but no sooner had she taken off her dress to lay down on her bed and rest than a commotion started up outside.

* * *

Seeing Nathalie return in the car a little more than three quarters of an hour after she had gone out prompted Madame Theroux to curtail her conversation with Juan and make her way back to the house to see what had gone wrong. Still in the wide-brimmed straw hat that she always wore when she went out into the garden, she came round the corner of the building to be confronted by an unexpected sight. A sinister looking man was creeping out of the trees in the front of the patio followed by another much smaller man and both of them wearing the uniforms of officers of the Guardia Civil.

Over the last few years Madame Theroux had formed the view that the world was becoming a strange place. Fashions were changing, girls thought it smart to wear trousers and all over Europe people were doing a grotesque dance called the Twist. Even in a backwater like Los Tidos there had been rumours of hashish from Morocco being smuggled in through the port and peculiar outlandish people coming and going. Now before her very eyes was this sinister man and his dwarf-like companion who, judging by the fidgeting he was doing, seemed to be badly afflicted by his nerves. Immediately her mind flew to a conclusion formed by her reading of articles in popular French newspapers that she took on subscription – a conclusion that this little man's behaviour was a symptom of drug use. Drug use, furthermore, was what had probably stunted his growth.

The other, the sinister looking man had now seen her and was coming over. Why he was wearing the uniform of an officer of the Guardia Civil was at first a mystery to Madame Theroux till it occurred to her that it must be the perfect disguise for someone in the business of smuggling drugs. Who would think to search an officer of the Guardia's pockets for hashish? Who would dare? Yet the level of the man's intelligence was betrayed by the fact that he had not thought to complete his disguise by putting proper shoes on his feet. His feet, rather stupidly, were in a pair of old carpet slippers and Madame Theroux remembered a piece in one of the Paris newspapers she read that said how the taking of drugs over long periods of time eventually impaired the user's mental processes to such an extent that clear thought became impossible. The strange contraption she noticed on his left hand, the function of which seemed to be to hold his fingers in place, she took as a device for smoking reefers but, what gave this man away definitely as the drug addict that he undoubtedly was, were the large number of puncture wounds all over his face. Plain evidence, Madame Theroux noted with distaste, of where this undesirable man injected his needles. The black eye he was sporting simply confirmed he was a ruffian who mixed with low company and got into brawls. This, she concluded, was the way of life in the opium dens he doubtless hung out in. Yet the brazen audacity of the man's words when he spoke to Madame Theroux took her back.

'I have followed a girl in a Peugeot to this address. I wish to speak to her immediately.'

Nathalie did he mean? What could this uncouth specimen possibly want with Nathalie? The fact that he and his dwarfish companion had trailed the girl was bad enough but to be so bold as to come to the house and demand to see her was little short of brazen.

'Get off my property,' she said without hesitation, 'You are filth of the worst kind and people like you should be put in prison.'

Garcia laughed out loud. 'Woman you talk with the air of someone who is blameless. If anyone needs to be fearful of prison then it is you.'

Madame Theroux could not believe her ears. Not only had this man failed to heed her instruction to leave, he had now had the cheek to address her as 'woman'. She had read that these drug pushers were forceful types but manners such as these were inexcusable. His business with Nathalie was presumably to lure her into taking his drugs then, once addicted, he would put his prices up till finally he would drain the poor girl of every last centime she had. How many others had he waylaid in this shameless way? Again Madame Theroux marvelled at his audacity; a further manifestation perhaps of the power over the mind of the drugs he used.

'I give you one last warning, Señor. Your behaviour is insulting and if you do not leave immediately you will give me no alternative other than to have you removed forcefully.'

Garcia, for his part, was finding this woman's behaviour as equally brazen as she was finding his. The fact that she had a foreign accent had registered with him from her very first words. In his mind he was now entertaining the possibility that the terrorist organisation with which he was dealing had international connections – indeed the hornet's nest he had stirred up was bigger than anyone up to now had presumed to think. Could it even be that he had stumbled across the same gang that had planned the assassination of President Kennedy? If so, which other world leaders were they plotting to kill? So it was to Garcia that he was already taking on the mantle of saviour of the western world and that was the thought he was preening himself with when he felt Ramon Ramon tugging at his sleeve.

'Capitan Garcia…'

'In the name of the Mother of Jesus, hombre, why is it you always start bothering me when I am in the middle of dealing with dangerous criminals?'

'Capitan Garcia, I thought I ought to warn you that there is a man approaching from your rear.'

'Then deal with him why don't you? Can't you see that if

I take my eyes off this woman, I will be giving her the chance to pull a gun on me?'

'He is a big man Capitan Garcia.'

'Very well, I will deal with him myself.'

'He is bigger than you Capitan Garcia.'

★ ★ ★

As she left the Edificio Los Angeles with the sable coat around her shoulders and her suitcase in her hand, Lola Martinez noticed the figure of Ernesto, the Conserja's husband, crouched behind a bush peering at two girls who were baring their legs on the beach. The fact that the little man with the twitching eyeballs didn't see the erstwhile Señora Beatriz who had delighted him with her charms up to the point she suddenly turned on him suited Lola down to the ground. She wanted no witnesses to her departure and no conversations with anyone. She wished to leave this town as quickly as she could and put the business of Franco and his botched up kidnapping behind her. A holiday somewhere nice was already figuring in her thoughts: she would draw out some of the money she had salted away in a savings account and go off to the kind of a place where gullible millionaires hung out for the winter – Nice or Monte Carlo possibly. Her first problem, however, was getting back to her apartment in Barcelona and she regretted once more that she had acted rashly in disposing of the little Seat 600. The only choice open to her, apart from going by bus or on the ferrocarril, was hiring a car from another car hire firm but there was a worry for her here and the worry was that the Avis company had circulated a description of the mysterious Señora Rosa Ramirez around the trade with a warning that she was the woman who was wanted for illegally appropriating one of their vehicles. Lola sighed. Being one who was not drawn towards the use of public transport, there was, as she saw it, only one thing to do. As she stood at the end of the little service road up to the Edifico Los Angeles watching the traffic go by between the marina and the Plaza de Los Reyes, she hiked up her skirt a few centimetres and extended one of her shapely silk-stockinged legs towards the edge of the kerb.

★ ★ ★

Garcia picked himself out of the ditch from where Juan had just dropped him. The Capitan from Cordoba could still see the gardener's muscular shoulders and straw sombrero as they disappeared up the gravel drive between the vines and the fruit trees.

'Well?' he snapped at Ramon Ramon who was standing in the middle of the road kicking his heels.

'I did not say anything Capitan Garcia.'

'It is incredible. Why is it that when there is some crisis afoot you are incapable of holding your tongue yet when your assistance is needed you are as silent as a Trappist monk? God knows why I selected you to come on this mission with me.'

'You wanted me to say something Capitan Garcia?'

'I wanted you to tell that oaf to take his hands off me.'

Ramon Ramon frowned. 'But that is precisely what you were saying to him Capitan Garcia and, as you have seen, for yourself it did no good at all.'

'I can see we need reinforcements,' growled Garcia as they got back to the car. 'Not these small town policemen but some real professional firepower.'

'Who did you have in mind, Capitan?'

'The military: a battalion of trained storm troops with automatic weapons. In my opinion this hacienda is the headquarters of an international gang of assassins and it would not surprise me to find that they are on the payroll of the Kremlin. If this is the case then they will be heavily armed, I assure you.'

As they drove back into town in Oswaldo's Simca with the silencer box trailing on the road making sparks Garcia and Ramon Ramon passed the strange figure of an old man coming towards them. The old man was swigging from a bottle and grinning from ear to ear.

'Do you want me to stop Capitan Garcia?'

'No, drive on. He is just some old borracho.'

★ ★ ★

Realising that the walk to the French lady's house would take him at least three quarters of an hour, Uncle Pablo made do with a quick wash in the kitchen sink meaning that he missed some of the orange coloured mud from the barranco still adhering to him especially at the back of his neck and behind his ears. He overlooked entirely the blobs of tar still clinging to his private parts and, selecting a suit that had been greatly fashionable when it was made for him in 1932 and ignoring the moth-holes in the waist coat, he set out from the Villa Verde at a jaunty pace. The decision to take along the half-empty bottle of absenta was one he made at the last minute. Though it had been many years since he last set foot on the Old Valencia Highway he recalled the steep climb up the hill to the crossroads where the road to the left led to the

Cemetario and the one to the right went down to the old Salinas. After such a climb, he told himself, he would need fortification and what better way to do it than a few slugs of absenta? After all there was no point in arriving at the French lady's house in a state of exhaustion when he would be expected immediately to perform in the bedroom.

Crossing the Puente de San Marco, it did not particularly register with Uncle Pablo that only a few hours earlier he had passed beneath in a state of nakedness. The past held little interest for Uncle Pablo at that moment. A whole new future was opening up for him – a future in which he, Uncle Pablo, would be called upon to service wealthy women of a nymphomaniac disposition on a regular basis and the thought had already gone through his head that as his reputation spread he might be able to exact a fee for these services: a gigolo indeed, although he conceded that, if any quibble presented itself on this front, the question of payment would be something he would be prepared to waive. Narrowly missing death under the wheels of a twenty tonne truck as he staggered across the Port Road, Uncle Pablo next focused his eyes on the long rise in front. The hill up which the Old Valencia Highway went looked formidable from the bottom and he was glad that it was not the height of summer so he would not have the hot sun on the back of his neck to contend with. Still, he needed to keep his spirits up and, with this in mind, he took a long pull from the bottle of absenta before setting off on the climb.

The traffic on the road was light as usual and, apart from a battered Simca with two officers of the Guardia Civil sitting inside, nothing passed Uncle Pablo in either direction. Soon, despite the effort of the climb, the joys of the open road and the prospect of the French lady's boudoir brought on the urge to break into song and. with just the rock thrushes, the larks and the geckos for an audience, Uncle Pablo launched off into one of his famous ditties with words he made up as he went along. This one concerned a wandering minstrel who went from town to town strumming his guitar and singing to ladies who threw down coins from their balconies. There was a novelty to this wandering minstrel's repertoire however and it was that he then went on to entertain the ladies in an interesting range of ways. So taken was Uncle Pablo with this new composition and its endless possibilities for improvised verses that he began to re-invent himself in a new role: that of Pablo El Trovador (the troubadour) and it was in this state of flamboyant swagger that he finally came to the gates of Los Arcos. There, he paused. The lady on the telephone had said something about a flower, had she not? Uncle Pablo did not have a flower, quite simply he had forgotten all about it, and, figuring that the flower might have some psychological impact as far as nymphomaniacs were concerned he searched round at the roadside for anything that might pass off as floral.

Had this been spring time, the roadside verges would have been filled with wild flowers but, as it was now November, all that was left was the dried-off heads of where their seeds had once been. He searched further until finally he came across a plant of rue. This he decided would have to do, not noticing in his alcohol befuddled state the quite appalling tom-cat smell that the leaves of this plant gave off when they were squeezed in his horny hands.

★ ★ ★

Nathalie sighed. Nathalie had been sighing ever since she put the phone down to the lady at the Diane Maitland Bureau and that was twenty minutes ago. The lady had come back to her, as she had promised and reassured her that as far as the young man was concerned he had never been married and neither was he the father of twelve children. Scarcely believable though it seemed, the only explanation was that there must have been another dreadful mix up: a consequence yet again of arranging a meeting in a place where other people would be present – and with this thought in mind the businesslike lady had decided to take the bull by the horns and suggest to the young man that he call on Mademoiselle Theroux in person at four o'clock that very afternoon. The lady realised of course that she had not sought Mademoiselle Theroux's permission to take this step to advance her love life at least to the starting line – but she could foresee a situation where if nothing was done, Mademoiselle Theroux and the young man with whom the computer had matched her so exactly would continue to pass like ships in the night.

Nathalie was speechless for a while. 'His name?' she finally asked because it was all she could think to say.

'Señor Campello – his first name is Jaime and he is a carpenter.'

Señor Campello, Nathalie was thinking to herself now. Whatever would Maman say when this poor young man presented himself at the door? What icy unwelcoming stares would she be giving him? It was her own fault that she had not explained to the lady at the bureau about Maman. Maman, she saw, was back inspecting the acacias with Juan and casting glances up at Nathalie as she stood at the window of her room. It was already five to four, Nathalie noticed as she turned away and looked across at the little travelling clock by her bedside.

Zamora narrowed his eyes. He had just been released from the padded cell beneath the Comisaria where the strait jacket had been removed from his arms by a man in a charcoal grey overcoat who had the bearing of someone important. There were even words of apology from this man and an assurance that if he cared to present the Comisaria with an itemised bill for the business he had lost due to his false imprisonment then full compensation would be paid.

Slightly mollified by this treatment, Zamora made his way back to the Street of Two Eyes where he found his bar had been shuttered and padlocked by the two Guardia Civil officers who, for no sane reason he could think of, had mistaken him for the drunken little worm Gomez – the drunken little worm who along with his friend Campello, Zamora now had even more scores to settle with. Indeed it was the drunken little worm Gomez on who Zamora's eyes had now fallen and this was what had caused them to narrow.

Gomez was skulking behind the remains of Zamora's canopy, behaving furtively and, without any doubt, on the wrong side of the notorious invisible line. But what Zamora did not know was why Gomez was acting in this way. Gomez with his consciousness restored and full of woe had been dropped off by Jaime Campello ten minutes earlier and what he was trying to do now was sneak back in the Bar Madrid without running into Conchita. The plan of action he had worked out was to lie low in the bottle store in the yard and wait till Conchita had calmed down before attempting to reason with her. He would then explain that it was Jaime Campello who was meeting a woman at the Hotel Bahia and that he had simply gone along as a chaperone. Yes, perhaps, he had done wrong by leaving the children to look after the bar but, surely, that was no great crime. But just as Gomez was stepping forward on tip toe to make a dash for the bottle store he caught sight of Zamora approaching out of the corner of his eye. 'You impudent scoundrel!' yelled Zamora waving his fist, still with the big plaster across his nose. 'I have just been put in prison and treated like a madman on your account. Now when I am let out I find you trespassing on my property. Have you no sense of what is right and wrong, Señor Gomez?'

Gomez attempted a weak conciliatory smile while all the time his eyes kept flicking backwards and forwards – from Zamora to the front entrance of the Bar Madrid (the direction Conchita might suddenly appear from) then back to Zamora and so on.

Zamora meanwhile had noticed the smell of fish that hung round Gomez's person after riding in the back of Jaime Campello's van and beneath the big plaster his bulbous nose wrinkled in disgust.

'What is this commotion about?'

Gomez groaned. The inevitable had happened and the sound of Zamora's raised voice had attracted Conchita's attention. Conchita had been busy behind the bar when she heard the shouting in the street.

'Your husband is on my property,' hissed Zamora forgetting who he was talking to. 'What is more he has quite obviously had too much to drink.'

Pepe Gomez edged back nervously. The silly grin on his face was meant to be an expression of sheepish innocence yet neither Conchita nor Zamora noticed it because they were already embarked on an exchange of caustic words.

'Are you calling my husband a drunkard Señor Zamora?' The forms of Lopez and the others emerged at the back of Conchita. Word had already got round about what had happened up at the Hotel Bahia.

'Yes I am, Señora Gomez. Are you attempting to deny it? He is a fat idle anis-swilling pig and you have said so yourself many times. I want him off my property immediately and I never want to see his face again.'

'You have no right to be calling my husband names, Señor Zamora. He may be a fat idle anis-swilling pig but he is *my* fat idle anis-swilling pig, and I won't have you forget it.'

'He is a fat idle anis-swilling pig but he is her fat idle anis-swilling pig,' Lopez and the others chanted in agreement.

'If your husband invites himself on to my property in a drunken stupor then I have the right to deal with him as I see fit.' Zamora snapped back.

'And if you continue to interfere in the affairs of husband and wife, Señor Zamora, I also have the right to deal with you as I feel fit.'

'She has the right, she has the right.' crowed Lopez and the others, anticipating exactly what was coming.

'You are threatening me Señora Gomez?'

'Yes I am threatening you Señor Zamora. An insult against my husband is an insult against me. You should bear that in mind before you say any more.'

The bad judgement that Zamora had exercised when he purchased the property in the Street of Two Eyes as a venue for the rich and famous in the first place was to manifest itself again on this occasion. 'I do not respond to threats,' he said to Conchita in a high handed manner and that, as anyone knew, was asking for trouble.

★ ★ ★

As Madame Theroux turned her attention to pruning the bougainvillea that hung down over the arched patio that gave the hacienda its name, she noticed an old man with a beret on his head staggering up the gravel driveway towards her carrying what looked like a bunch of weeds in one hand and clutching a bottle of liquor in the other. The fact that he was extremely drunk was plain for anyone to see and, whether it was because of his condition or some defect in his eyesight, it was also plain to see that he had not noticed her for he proceeded to relieve himself against the wall of the house.

Madame Theroux gasped in horror and only then did the old man notice her standing on the small set of steps with the pruning secateurs in her hand. Shaking his penis, he turned towards her, raised his beret and leered showing off a grimy set of false teeth. For some reason this disgusting character's ears and his neck seemed to be daubed with an orange substance and more of the orange substance was visible on the back of his hands whilst his penis – though she did her best to avert her eyes – was for some reason blackened at the end.

That this old man belonged to the same circle of drug addicts as the sinister character and the dwarf, who Juan had just seen off briefly crossed Madame Theroux's mind – but whoever he was, he was clearly a degenerate and, as he approached squinting with his eyes because he seemed unable to focus, she caught a waft of absenta on his breath. Faugh! Madame Theroux reeled back.

'Mademoiselle...' he began then trailed off because it seemed to require all his attention to stand upright. 'Mademoiselle Theroux?' he finally managed to say though, apart from being slurred, his pronunciation of her name was terrible. The old man had the appearance of a vagrant but because he addressed her by name and though it was scarcely believable it seemed he had been sent on an errand.

'*Madame* Theroux,' she corrected him coldly wondering what possible business he could have with her.

The old man leered again. Though Nathalie's mother did not know it, the old man had recently been an entertainer of sorts in the bars along the Los Tidos waterfront and he was aware from his dealings with the cosmopolitan yachting set of the distinction between 'mademoiselle' and 'madame'. She would have been quite alarmed, however, to know that by emphasising that she was a married woman she was confirming to Uncle Pablo what he most wished to hear. Here was a woman, a nymphomaniac, who found the attentions given to her by her husband not enough.

'Please state what you want and be quick about it,' she said continuing in her cold tone of voice.

The old man leered yet again and then proceeded to tell her in graphic terms exactly what he wanted, sparing no detail as he did, and Madame Theroux's jaw dropped in absolute disbelief at what she was hearing. Here she was, only recently widowed and still in mourning and this degenerate, with his black penis still in his hand, describing the lewd acts in which he wished her to participate. Worse still he did not stop. The depths to his depravity seemed bottomless and, as one suggestion followed the next, he accompanied each with a sly wink. Finally he thrust the bunch of weeds under her nose. Faugh! The weeds stank of cat pee and Madame Theroux recoiled again almost toppling off the steps as she did.

Fortunately just then Juan appeared on the scene. Seeing

300

his mistress in a state of obvious distress, he came across quickly and took the old man who was exposing himself firmly by the scruff of his skinny neck and marched him off. Juan knew the old man faintly. He was a drunkard and a scrounger and, when he got him back to the highway, he had no compunction about throwing him into the same ditch where he had earlier deposited Capitan Luis Garcia of the Cordoba section of the Guardia Civil.

★ ★ ★

The shapely leg of Lola Martinez did not have to spend too much time at the kerb side. A large white cadillac screeched to a halt with a man with a bald head who looked to be well into his seventies behind the wheel.

'The car I hired has not arrived,' she explained bending over to speak to him through the open window and letting the front of her blouse fall open so that an eyeful of cleavage and black lace came on full display. 'I am travelling north and I would be very grateful for a lift if you happen to be going that way.'

As she sank into the cadillac's luxurious beige hide upholstery and with her suitcase safely in the trunk, Lola took her last look at Los Tidos. The bald-headed man said his name was Eric and that he was an American though Lola had gathered that much already. Eric had been visiting the town to inspect what berthing the marina could offer for a large yacht he owned. Eric, it turned out, was a multimillionaire who had made his fortune from an engineering business in Michigan City that he had sold out to his competitors. Sadly, said Eric, he had never married because he had never found the time and, now he was freed from his work, the doctors had told him that he had a bad heart and could die at any time.

'It seems such a pity,' he said as they sped out along the Old Valencia Highway, following Lola's directions and keeping to her principle of always taking the quiet way in and out of places. 'No woman would want me now I am a sick man and all that money I made over all those years will end up in the pockets of my brothers' and sisters' children: a miserable bunch who never even invited me once for Thanksgiving dinner. I am sorry, young lady I did not quite catch your name.

'My name is Lola.'

'You must forgive me Lola for talking too much – it's an old man's habit. I think it comes of spending a lot of time on my own.'

'I like to listen. Besides it is not right that an attractive man such as yourself should have no-one to talk to.

'Attractive? Me? Hey, you're pulling my leg. There's no way a beautiful sophisticated young woman like you would find an old timer like me attractive. I bet all the boys in town are chasing after you. Isn't that so Lola?'

'Boys don't interest me. I prefer the company of older men. They know how to treat a woman.'

'Well I give you that. Gee whizz, Lola, we've only just met one another and here we are getting on like a house on fire. It's amazing, don't you think?'

'Yes, it is amazing.' Lola's eyes drifted from contemplating the bulging vein in Eric's temples to where the sun was already starting to set over the mountains in the west and to where the new carretera and the ferrocarril ran on a parallel course. It was there along the ferrocarril that Lola fancied she saw a man riding a big motor cycle, a man with a bandana tied round his head, but the glimpse was only fleeting and the ferrocarril soon disappeared from view.

'Lola my destination is Zurich in Switzerland: I have not asked you yet how far you plan to go with me.'

Lola stretched back in her soft seat allowing her skirt to ride up several centimetres above her knees. 'Eric,' she said. 'With you I think I will be going all the way.'

★ ★ ★

Uncle Pablo narrowly missed going under the wheels of the white cadillac as he crawled out of the ditch. Briefly, he caught sight of the delectable lady's profile as the big American car sped by and, for several seconds, he tried to get his alcohol befuddled mind round the various strange things that had been happening to him recently. In the end, however, his alcohol befuddled mind proved incapable of coping with anything so complicated and he gave up. At heart, Uncle Pablo was a philosophical man who asked few questions and for the most part, accepted what life handed out to him, both the good and the bad. On balance, he had come out on top over the last few days or so he thought. The episode with the French lady had been a disappointment yes, but he put this down not to any failing on his part but to the unexpected arrival on the scene of the big man in the straw sombrero who, judging from his aggressive reaction, was her husband or a jealous fancy man. The bottle of absenta was still clasped in his hand unbroken and he braced himself with a gigantic slug before making the attempt to get back onto his feet. Steadying himself before he set off and with the setting sun shining on his face, Uncle Pablo consoled himself with the fact that the nymphomaniac circle still had his telephone number and the career of Pablo El Trovador was about to begin. With these thoughts in his head he made his way back to town along the deserted highway singing to the larks, the rock thrushes and the geckos as he went, singing all about the wandering minstrel and what he got up to on the balconies of the fair ladies who threw coins down to him.

★ ★ ★

The last of the oil in Oswaldo's Simca seeped from the cracked sump as the little blue car carrying Capitan Luis Garcia and Ramon Ramon was crossing the Puente de San Marco and there it seized up. This meant the two of them had to continue their journey to the Comisaria on foot but as they approached their destination they began to see groups of bearded men dispersing into the side streets.

'Quick, after them,' hissed Garcia. 'They are the suspects we put under arrest and they are getting away.'

Ramon Ramon frowned. 'They don't look like men breaking out of prison, Capitan Garcia. They are behaving quite openly. Perhaps we should see what is going on at the Comisaria before we do anything.'

Entering the austere grey building with the orange and gold national flag hanging limply from its flagpole over the door, the two Guardia Civil men came face to face, however, with someone they did not expect to see.

'Señor Suarez…'

'Capitan Garcia.'

Suarez was sitting on the front desk alone swinging his legs and eating salted almonds from the palm of his hand. The sheaf of papers he was reading were in fact the first of the compensation claims from people in the town and these gave graphic details of the Capitan from Cordoba's escapades, often described in the most colourful terms. The flesh between Suarez's cheekbones and jaw had already begun to tauten. The Capitan from Cordoba had indeed been busy and it was lucky no-one in Madrid had got to hear of these goings-on.

'Señor Suarez, I am glad you are here. My investigation into the poisoning attempt on the Caudillo has just been brought a successful conclusion. I have unearthed a nest of terrorists who are holed up in a hacienda not far from here…'

Suarez listened to the Capitan from Cordoba as he ranted on about a ratcatcher then someone called Gomez then another called Campello and finally a woman. As he listened Suarez continued to pop salted almonds into his mouth pausing only to wince at some of the Capitan's more preposterous allegations but, all the time, taking in the man's alarming appearance: the black eye, the puncture wounds in his face, the splinted fingers, the carpet slippers on his feet and the traces of silt from the Salinas still on his uniform. But nothing in the blank expression on the old security chief's face betrayed his real thoughts or intentions.

★ ★ ★

Few witnessed the bulky figure in a strait jacket being loaded into the back of a special ambulance and not too gently by two policemen who had been at the receiving end of several of the Capitan from Cordoba's tongue lashings. Few indeed heard his protestations through the restraints placed across his mouth and few were saddened by the news that the destination of the special ambulance was the asylum in Murcia where the most dangerous lunatics were kept in chains in deep dungeons and often for years on end.

Doctor Pascal at his upstairs window saw the ambulance as it passed by but it never crossed his mind that inside was the person whose account he was now busy preparing. 'To the treatment of facial contusions,' he wrote on the last line in his finest hand writing then totalled up the amounts. He had heard the Capitan from Cordoba didn't pay his bills and hadn't bothered pressing his claim for payment up to now. But some big noise had arrived from Madrid and he was settling all the bills the Guardia Civil man had run up. Doctor Pascal therefore was keen to join the queue before the money ran out or the big noise from Madrid changed his mind.

As the special ambulance disappeared from sight, something triggered in the doctor's memory. 'To one pair of carpet slippers not returned,' he wrote down.

CHAPTER THIRTEEN

A Few Old Bones

G radually things got back to normal in Los Tidos. It
was, in any event, a quiet time of year when few
visitors came and went and when many of the bars
and restaurants along the waterfront put up their shutters and
closed for the winter. The storms and rains eventually passed
and the sun came out again though there was a chill in the wind
that hadn't been there before and which caused the townspeople
to fetch out their woollens and go round complaining.

No-one could say for certain when the man with the
drawn face left town in his big black Mercedes: the man who,
rumour had it, was one of Franco's top men and who had been
responsible for despatching the Capitan from Cordoba with
such alacrity. Some said he stayed for a few days at the Hotel
Bahia while others said he drove off up the carretera towards
Valencia as soon as the Capitan from Cordoba was out of the
way. No-one had heard any more about the Guardia Civil
officer either or what had become of him since his departure
and few particularly cared.

After many furtive visits to the top floor of the Edificio Los
Angeles to put his twitching eyeball to the keyhole of the door
to the penthouse suite, the Conserja's husband Ernesto had to
conclude that the delectable if unpredictable Señora Beatriz

had vanished. Letting himself in with the master key, he inspected the place only to find a pair of handcuffs and a heap of men's clothes the only items that were not part of the normal fixtures and fittings. The men's clothes were worn and shabby and included a moth-eaten pair of combinations. What connection these objects could have with the delectable Señora Beatriz was something that puzzled Ernesto for many years.

★ ★ ★

An uneasy silence reigned over the Street of Two Eyes where it was almost as if a curfew had been declared. Zamora had stayed indoors since the day the fearful Conchita had cracked him over the head with his own broom handle and there he commiserated with his tom-cat, Theobald and drafted anonymous letters to Navarro the Alcalde about the Bar Madrid's leaky septic tank and the danger it presented to public health. Even for Pepe Gomez who would normally have drawn great satisfaction from Zamora's discomfiture there was little joy. Day in, day out and far into the night he stood at the kitchen sink washing glasses and cups and saucers and, when he wasn't doing this, he was fetching bottles, cleaning out the spittoons or going round the lavatories with a mop and bucket. A dog's life had turned into something worse: now it was that of galley slave in shackles. 'Womaniser!' Conchita would hiss at him every time she passed. 'Let me see those glasses sparkle and don't let me catch you ever again with the smell of liquor on your breath.' Even in the bar itself, Lopez and the others were subdued. The excitement of the last few days had died down and an atmosphere of anti-climax prevailed. The Feast of the Two Virgins was coming up but no-one seemed to have any interest in it. That, however, was set to change.

★ ★ ★

Florence Theroux had been watching her daughter Nathalie very closely ever since the day she had gone off into town on her own. It wasn't the fact that Nathalie's return had been closely followed first by the visit of the sinister character with the dwarf in tow and then by the despicable old man that troubled her so much as Nathalie's general behaviour. Quiet though the girl was normally, she had become even quieter giving the impression that she was going through some inner turmoil. The thought of drugs had crossed Madame Theroux's mind more than once: that Nathalie had got in with a bad crowd and that this withdrawal into herself was a manifestation of some narcotic that they had introduced her to. Indeed these suspicions had prompted Madame Theroux to make discreet enquiries into the daughter of Señora Rey and her piano lessons – whereupon she had discovered that Señora Rey's daughter was a fiction: the manager of the Banco de Bilbao and his wife had only sons.

Outwardly Nathalie still kept to her routines. Still she took Christine out every morning and chatted to the poor child about the birds they had seen. Still, she spent the afternoons reading or with her board and easel painting the view from her room or some scene from her imagination. In the past Pierre would have been there to share the unease with her and it struck Madame Theroux how the girl was like her father in her closeness. But something was boding, she told herself, and in this reading of things, events were to prove that Madame Theroux was right.

* * *

Nathalie noticed her mother's watchfulness. Everywhere she went she felt Maman's eyes on her though she went no further than the garden and always kept within sight of the house. She had told the lady at the Diane Maitland Bureau that the gentleman whose praises she had sung so highly had turned out to be a drunken old man who had behaved insultingly to her mother and that she wanted no further meetings arranged for her. The lady had said that she regretted anything that had happened but that she could still not understand what had gone wrong. The mysterious Señor Campello had in any case telephoned that very morning also to take his name off the bureau's files, though he had declined to offer a reason why. In parting the lady said she regretted too that she could not reimburse any of the fees that Nathalie had paid and hoped that she would understand.

Fees, however, were not of any concern to Nathalie. Going to the Diane Maitland Bureau had been an act of desperation as far as she was concerned: a final hope that somewhere out there was a young man sensitive enough to see her as person of wit and intelligence not just a Plain Jane with thin arms and a flat chest. But the experiment had failed. The files of the Diane Maitland Bureau, as she had feared, turned out to be a repository of misfits and perverts: men like the man in motor cycle leathers with his big knife or the old man who had come staggering to the door. Even worse, it attracted married men on the look out for a good time behind their wives' backs and the man she had been sent to meet at the Hotel Bahia bore witness to this fact. As to Señor Campello, Nathalie had come to the conclusion that he did not exist. The name was a cover used by the bureau to help men who did not want their identities to be known. In short, she, Nathalie, had been cunningly tricked. It was a lesson in life, she said to herself, something she would put down to experience and something she would never be foolish enough to do again.

The day of the Feast of the Two Virgins dawned bright and sunny. In the Old Town, flags were draped from every balcony and the buntings and the streamers that hung across the narrow streets were stirred by a gentle breeze. The basureros had come and gone in the early hours by special order of Navarro the Alcalde and everywhere was spotless.

Up in the square by the Church the Town Band was already practising. The players in the town band, it has to be explained, were not very accomplished musicians though they always strove to compensate for any lack of skill by seeing who could play the loudest and the fastest. Their conductor was a man named Araya, the function of whose baton was simply to signal the off whereupon the individual instrumentalists would compete ferociously to beat, bang, hoot, honk and whistle their way as quickly and as stridently as they could to the finish. The result was a dreadful cacophony – a cacophony that was, to everyone except Araya who smiled and waved his baton throughout every performance as if he heard some sound other than the monstrous din that reached everyone else's ears.

The other peculiarity of the Town Band was its repertoire. Although Araya called out different names at the start of every piece, every tune sounded exactly the same and this was the way it had always been. Distressingly, and for reasons no-one understood, the Town Band found it necessary to warm up well before any event and this was bad news for mothers of small babies and hung-over late sleepers who dreaded these days.

By nine o'clock crowds had begun to gather in the streets. Mainly these were local people though some had come in from surrounding villages to witness an event that only took place twice in most people's lifetimes. Some, it has to be said, came out of curiosity to see who was going to take the famous vow of chastity, indeed in the bars of the Old Town the talk had been of nothing else for the last forty eight hours giving rise to a whole new school of low wit and ribaldry, chief architects of which were Lopez and the others.

By tradition finding four strong men to carry the oak studded casket on their shoulders was decided by the drawing of lots, a task performed by the priest. One of the stipulations for this job was that the casket-bearers had to be unmarried so it was only the names of the town's bachelors that went into the hat.

First out was Ruiz, the man whose wall had been demolished by the Capitan from Cordoba and whose name was greeted with applause because Ruiz was not only strong but a God-fearing man who attended mass regularly. In contrast the next name was greeted with stony silence. It was that of Zamora the cantankerous bar-keeper who nobody liked and who, besides, was not a native of the town. Thirdly came Esteban Sanchez, the ironmonger's ambitious son who hardly qualified on the grounds of being strong but who nobody wished to offend so his name was left to stand. But it was the fourth lot drawn that wiped the smile off Father Miguel's face.

It was the name of Pablo Campello and everyone said afterwards that the priest made a mistake by not putting it back in the hat immediately.

★ ★ ★

The Town Band who, having assembled and warmed up in the square outside the Church, now made their way down the hill, past Paco's Rincon, and on to the Cemetario where the procession carrying the relics of the Two Virgins was due to start. The Cemetario being on top of a ridge, they had had to struggle the last three hundred metres grumbling all the way at the weight of their instruments and shouting to Araya that he should have laid on transport. Finally assembled on a piece of dusty ground outside the tiled topped walls of the Cemetario and at the signal from Araya's baton they launched into a spirited if tuneless rendition of suitably dignified selections from well-known composers. Trumpeting and banging their way through the various pieces, they paid scant regard to most of the lesser notes and all of the composers' instructions on passages that required less resonant treatment. They played at an alarming pace, as was usual, ignoring bars, spaces and all other forms of musical punctuation so that at times the more elderly members of the band found themselves lagging far behind. In the midst of all this Araya continued as usual to beam ecstatically waving his baton in the air to a different beat to that acknowledged by the two thirds of the percussion section. At one point, a bassoonist was playing a completely different tune to everyone else: not that he realised because the bassoonist was stone deaf, a symptom perhaps of playing in the Town Band for too long.

By the time Uncle Pablo arrived at the Cemetario he had consumed five glasses of absenta not counting the two he had had at the Villa Verde before setting out. A crowd had followed the Town Band up the hill and they clapped and cheered when the last of the four strong casket bearers appeared. Uncle Pablo was pleased at this reception and with stage manners befitting El Trovador he acknowledged the greeting of the crowd with a flourish of his hand and a bow.

The Shrine of the Two Virgins was at the furthest end of the Cemetario and Father Miguel, as required by tradition, carried the key to the sealed vault. The vault was built out of closely cut blocks of local limestone into which was let a narrow and heavily lintelled doorway with the door itself made out of beaten bronze tarnished green with age. First was the job of removing the seals that had been put there, so Father Miguel guessed, when the vault was last opened fifty years ago. This task was given to Ruiz who coincidentally earned his living as a metalworker and hence had no difficulty at all in removing the small rivets holding the seals with a specially tempered chisel.

With the Town Band straining to reach some new crescendo in the background, Father Miguel then stepped forward to put his key in the lock. The door was stiff but opened with a little pressure from Ruiz's shoulder. Inside, the vault was a simple cell-like room, dry smelling the priest noticed and with a single oblong block of stone in the centre of which stood the ancient casket made out of oak, heavily studded and clasped with iron. By the light from the entrance Father Miguel's eyes next fell on the two long poles for supporting the casket, which had been stood in one corner of the vault. The priest raised his hand to make a blessing and Ruiz nudged Uncle Pablo in the back to remind him to remove his beret.

Assisted by Zamora and Esteban Sanchez, Father Miguel next attached the poles to the casket, which he did by sliding them through iron hoops riveted to the sides. the priest then draped the casket with a cloth of gold – an artefact that by tradition was kept in the Church and which had been embroidered centuries ago with a simple depiction of the ancient legend. The four casket bearers then positioned themselves one at each end of the poles and with an 'uno, dos, tres,' from Ruiz they heaved the casket onto their shoulders, straining under the enormous weight of ancient oak – all except Uncle Pablo who did nothing because he had just fallen to the floor. Seeing poor Esteban Sanchez on his own with the front end of the casket and his legs already starting to buckle, Father Miguel ordered it to be put back down on the block of stone.

Zamora had by this time gathered that the old borracho who seemed destined to cause trouble bore the name Campello, and a few discreet enquiries into the ear of young Sanchez from the ferreteria across the road as they made their way up to the Cemetario together, revealed that this was indeed the uncle of Gomez's friend, Campello the Carpenter. Zamora's eyes narrowed. His bulbous nose, now out of plaster and slightly bent, wrinkled in disgust. That someone like this should be given a part in a religious festival was bad enough. That the part brought him into such close proximity with Zamora was unthinkable.

Uncle Pablo was brought to his feet by Ruiz and, assuring

everyone that he had merely slipped, the casket bearers tried again. Thus the relics of the Two Virgins left the vault to make their long journey to the Church. Father Miguel followed them keeping a careful eye on Uncle Pablo for he had guessed correctly that the old man was drunk. Indeed anyone standing behind Father Miguel at that moment would have seen that the priest had his fingers crossed behind his back.

Waldorf, it will be remembered, had last been seen by Nathalie Theroux as she drove along the Old Valencia Highway on her way to the Hotel Bahia. Since then no-one had set eyes on him fuelling a theory that he had been run down by a truck on the carretera or shot by a farmer. Waldorf had in fact been continuing his search for old bones of the kind that would settle his stomach, a search that had taken him all over Los Tidos and one that had so far yielded no result. Waldorf by coincidence was not far from the Cemetario as the procession with the casket of the Two Virgins emerged from its gates. However what caused Waldorf to follow the procession was a mystery. It could have been that his gnarled snout picked up the scent of stale absenta wafting in his direction from somewhere and that his flea-bitten brain made the connection with Uncle Pablo. Or it could have simply been curiosity but, whatever the reason, Waldorf tagged along behind the procession as it made its way down hill from the Cemetario keeping always out of sight and at a discreet distance.

★ ★ ★

Father Miguel breathed a sigh of relief when the casket of the Two Virgins arrived outside the Church without further incident though admittedly Uncle Pablo seemed to be using the pole to hang onto rather than to give support to the weight. The chance would perhaps present itself later to find a substitute for the return trip to the Cemetario, Father Miguel consoled himself, but in the meantime he thanked God that things had gone smoothly so far.

Father Miguel, it has to be said, was finding the Town Band a bit of a strain and he wondered if he could gently persuade Araya to go and play somewhere else. In a black moment he wondered if the Two Virgins whose relics were in the casket had really thrown themselves off the Church tower not because of the Moors but because some ancestors of Araya and his crew had been about in their time also.

Pepe Gomez was in the flower-decked Church with his twelve children and behind him the fearsome Conchita. The little man could feel her eyes in his back and, from time to time and in a rather more literal sense, the tip of her finger poking him and telling him to sit up straight. For once Pepe Gomez had not been forced into coming to Church. Like many others that morning he came to see what everyone wanted to see and what had so far been kept a secret. Who was going to take the vow of chastity? Now he and the rest of Los Tidos had the answer for standing before the altar done up in a surplice and staring up at the ceiling so as to avoid eye contact with anyone was none other than his old friend Jaime Campello. What had got into Campello, Gomez had no idea for he had not spoken to the young man since the afternoon after the fiasco at the Hotel Bahia. That it might have something to do with him and his plan to do away with Conchita was already starting to trouble Gomez's normally trouble free conscience. Then deciding it would be better not to dwell too long on the failed attempt to poison his wife while sitting in the house of the Almighty Pepe Gomez turned his attention to the other side of the altar where Nathalie Theroux stood in a pretty white dress with wild flowers woven into her hair and a posy of wild flowers clasped in her hand to represent the posy of flowers that the original two virgins had clasped as they plunged to their deaths. What he did not notice though was the proud woman in black, her face covered in a veil, in the front row of seats behind Nathalie or the girl in a wheelchair at her side.

The procession had now entered the nave of the Church; the Town Band playing the dirge they usually played at funerals followed by Father Miguel whose face did not betray that he was cringing at every note; then the casket bearers carrying the casket beneath its cloth of gold on their shoulders and the wobbling form of Uncle Pablo who had now been put at the back with the stout arm of Ruiz to support him.

All eyes were turned to the altar as Father Miguel went forward to take his place beside Nathalie and Jaime. In his hand was the card on which the words of the ancient vow of chastity were written and which Nathalie and Jaime would soon be asked to read out loud. What no-one had noticed at the precise point, however, was the gnarled snout that poked round the door of the church or the grey shape to which it belonged.

★ ★ ★

Much has been written about what happened next, and even more spoken, though the blame that was put on Zamora was to a large part due to the fact that he was so disliked in the town. Yet it has to be said that it was Zamora who kicked out at Waldorf as he slunk past because he recognised the creature that had caused such havoc in his bar on the night of the New Jumilla, the same creature that had also fetched him down off the ladder along with the Capitan from Cordoba and landed him in the cells. The fact that Waldorf turned on him could hardly be described as surprising for it was Waldorf's way to retaliate when attacked though it was perhaps unfortunate for Zamora that Waldorf chose to sink his fangs in the man with the big nose's private parts. Given the circumstances, the howl of pain that Zamora let out was hardly surprising either or the fact that he took no further interest in the casket of the Two Virgins, which, without his support promptly lurched to one side and threw Uncle Pablo to the floor where he remained. Meanwhile Esteban Sanchez's knees started to buckle under the great weight of ancient oak and iron now divided awkwardly between Ruiz and himself. That these two struggled valiantly was without a doubt though criticism could be directed at those able bodied men who stood nearby and who, in typical Los Tidos fashion, did nothing to help. The rest was as day follows night: the heavy casket started to go over, gathering momentum as it went, the cloth of gold fell away, the poles whipped round catching Zamora in the face and inflicting him with further pain then came the terrible sound of the casket as it hit the Church's solid stone floor.

Oak split, iron snapped and the relics of the blessed Two Virgins spilled out. Yet worse was to come for Waldorf, releasing his vice-like grip on Zamora's testicles, saw the ancient bones and fell on them with glee. Those nearest drew back in horror while some crossed themselves and the Señoras Crespo were seen to faint simultaneously. Femurs cracked in

Waldorf's jaws though, rallied by Ruiz, some of the braver souls present tried to pull him off. Everywhere there seemed to be grunting, wailing, cursing, kicking men and, in their midst, Waldorf snapping and snarling and jealously guarding his nearly acquired prize of bones. The band stopped playing – the musicians stood and stared with their instruments in their hands and their mouths wide open although Araya carried on conducting adding fuel to the rumour that he heard other music in his head.

Up by the altar Father Miguel watched the commotion with an increasing feeling of resignation. Behind one of the vases of flowers he had noticed a bottle of communion wine and while everyone's eyes were distracted he helped himself to a deep draught.

A few paces away, Jaime Campello in his white surplice had been trying to ignore the screamings and wailings, the shouts and curses, the snappings and snarlings and instead to keep his eyes focused on the ceiling and the direction of Heaven. Finally the barrage of noise defeated him and he turned round to see beyond the frozen face of Pepe Gomez, a scene of devastation with pews overturned and fists flying in anger and bodies rolling on the floor. In the middle of it all he saw Waldorf like an apparition that had returned from the dead with his jowls slavering and surrounded, for reasons Campello could not immediately identify, by a huge pile of bones. Turning back to the altar he saw first of all the close-cropped iron grey head of Father Miguel before his eyes fell on a girl in a white dress with flowers in her hair and a posy of flowers in her hand. At that moment she too looked at him and in that split second the shouting and stamping and swearing faded away and the world stopped turning and for both of them they knew that everything in their lives had changed.

It was Father Miguel whose attention was first drawn to them. Putting the bottle of communion wine down, he sighed and shrugged his shoulders then tore up the card in his hand. He knew no-one would have any use for a vow of chastity that day.